About

Mark Durman is a former British Army brigadier who served on operations in several parts of the world — West and Central Africa, Borneo, Cyprus, The Oman, Northern Ireland. He had NATO appointments in Belgium and Holland. After taking early retirement from the military, he was Director of Security for Europe, the Middle East and Africa for a US international security company. He is a graduate of politics and economics and of the British Army staff college, Camberley, and the NATO Defence College, Rome. He currently divides his time between Alicante, Spain and Paris.

ADSUM

MISSION AND PASSION

Based on a true story

Mark Durman

ADSUM

MISSION AND PASSION

Based on a true story

Vanguard Press

VANGUARD PAPERBACK

© Copyright 2020
Mark Durman

A CIP catalogue record for this title is
available from the British Library.

ISBN 978 1 784658 91 5

Vanguard Press is an imprint of
Pegasus Elliot MacKenzie Publishers Ltd.
www.pegasuspublishers.com

First Published in 2020

Vanguard Press
Sheraton House Castle Park
Cambridge England

Printed & Bound in Great Britain

Dedication

For Anthony and William.

Acknowledgements

In writing this book, I had to delve deep back into the records of some sixty years ago. I'm very grateful to the many ex-soldiers I consulted to ensure the geographical and military/political events are as accurate as possible. In particular, I want to single out both Stan Barnes (ex-Devizes recruit!) for his assistance and advice and Thomas Forster for his computer expertise in producing the photos and maps. I also wish to thank Madame Lucette Hanocq for her patient assistance and first-hand knowledge regarding the section dealing with the Congo. She was also there.

Preamble

A few words of introduction. My original intention was to write this book as an autobiography — a two-year period of my life. These events occurred a long time ago so to avoid any possible misrepresentation, I decided instead to describe the book as a "novel based on a true story". I've called the central character Peter Chambers and have changed some of the names of the other players. Despite this, the events described are as accurate as I can recall.

When I reread the book's draft, and took the views of my proof readers, to whom I'm greatly indebted, I debated whether to include so much minutiae about British national service conscript training in the late 1950s. Despite much research, I can find no comprehensive record elsewhere of this conscription programme. I therefore decided to leave this detail in as I believe it was an important, and now lost, part of the maturing process of British young men at that time. It's a story that, in my opinion, needs to be told.

Mark Durman

Chapter One

I see the envelope as soon as I open our front door. It's a buff brown colour with the formal "On Her Majesty's Service" official heading. Under the heading is printed: "Mr Peter James Chambers, 23 Beech Road, Saltford, Near Bath, England." The date stamp is: 12 March 1959.

Peter Chambers — that's me. I'm eighteen years old and it's the first time I've ever received an official letter and the first time anyone has addressed me as "Mr". I suppose my mother collected our post earlier today and propped the envelope up on our hall table to be sure I would see it when I came home. My first thought is that the police have followed up on the "little accident" I had on my Lambretta motor scooter last month. Perhaps it's a court summons on a charge of dangerous driving. With some trepidation, I open the envelope and take out the letter. I'm wrong about the Lambretta business. The letter informs me that I'm required to serve two years' national military service. It instructs me to report to a clearing centre at an address in Bristol in two weeks' time where I "will be processed" — or words to that effect!

Two years of national military service! It takes a while for it to sink in. I suppose I'd realised I was liable to be "called up" but I knew that the government had announced that compulsory national service would end in 1962 or 63 and I vaguely thought or hoped I wouldn't be picked. When I left school last summer, most of my class mates went off to university in September and were therefore exempt from national service for the duration of their degree courses. But me — due to my misplaced sense of I don't know what — teenage snobbery perhaps — I declined a perfectly decent place at Bristol University as I hadn't achieved high enough "A" level grades to get into Cambridge. I was also fed up with being permanently broke so I'd taken a job at a retail department store in Bristol. Not a great job but it has its pluses and at least I'm earning enough to maintain my Lambretta (now crashed!), and to afford to take out my (now ex!) girlfriend and buy a few beers at weekends. Now the system has caught up with me.

I give the letter a second read and see there's a bit at the end about deferments and how to apply. Perhaps I can find a good excuse to wriggle out of this national service thing. I remember Johnny Fisher, one of my mates in our village, telling me he got his deferment by signing up for an apprenticeship. It's evening now and he should be home so I give him a call. He's there. I tell him about my letter and ask about his deferment.

"It's no big deal, Peter," he tells me. "I got exactly the same letter as you. When I read about the deferment option, I applied through the local City & Guilds people and they fixed for me to sign up for a formal two-year apprenticeship in electrical engineering. It's not a full degree course but it gives a qualification and that was enough to get me out of square bashing in the army. By the time the two years are up, the national service commitment should have been phased out, so that should let me off the hook completely. You could do the same. It doesn't have to be engineering, anything on the approved list will do."

I thank Johnny and sign off. I'm still puzzling over how to react to the letter when my mother appears. She must have heard me talking on the phone. She comes straight to the point:

"I see you've opened that letter, Peter. Is it to tell you you've been called up?" My mother is as perceptive as ever. We hadn't discussed it before, but I suppose she's realised I'm likely to be on the conscription list and has suspected this was the letter. I haven't told her about the Lambretta business so that couldn't cloud her thinking.

So far in my life, I haven't had many big issues to deal with but whatever there have been, my mother has always been there for me in a consistent, supportive way. I've always accepted her advice and encouragement.

"You're right," I tell her. "And I have to check in to a centre in Bristol in a couple of weeks. I've just talked to Johnny Fisher and he tells me he got a deferment because of his apprenticeship. S'pose I could try the same. I'm not sure. What do you think?"

"Yes, I've talked to Johnny's mother about that. But is that really what you want to do? I also remember Mr Potter, your school headmaster, saying that if you were to apply yourself and retake your "A" levels you should get a place at Cambridge for next year. That could achieve what you wanted a year ago and avoid you having to do national service."

I know my mother is right, as she always is. But I don't fancy the idea of returning to the school environment and swotting for those bloody exams again. Nor is an apprenticeship appealing. And most of all, I'm eighteen now and can't stand the idea of being permanently broke again. I tell my mother I need to get my head around this new development and try to work out what's the best thing to do.

I would like my father to be more involved but he never has been. He's an artist, a good one, who lives in a world of artists and arty people — I suppose that's partly why we're living near Bath. My father spends much of his time painting in the Bath area, usually in the company of his many long-haired, open-toe-sandaled, under washed arty friends. He's away painting at present somewhere in the Isle of Skye. I think he loves me in a detached sort of way and I like him well enough, too, but more as a friendly uncle than as a father. It's my mother who is and always has been the one who has guided me up until now.

About the Lambretta accident. I bought that motor scooter from the earnings I made by working on building sites during my school holidays. It was second hand, of course. It cost me £85 with another fiver for a helmet and other bits and pieces. It was my first material possession and I treasured it as if it was made of gold. Although I'll never be a good mechanic, I learnt to take it to bits and put it back together again. I cleaned and polished it regularly. It was so precious to me because for the first time in my short life it gave me a freedom of movement I had not previously experienced. Until my Lambretta, I had always been restricted either to walking or cycling everywhere or by our local bus service timetable. This was limiting as, for example, the last bus from Bath to my home village leaves at ten-fifteen pm. But with my Lambretta, I could make my own timetable and come and go as it suited me. What's more, and this was a really big deal, I found I could pull the girls — at least those who were brave enough or foolhardy enough to ride pillion behind me.

During the last few months, I have been dating a girl named Jilly who works at the same department store in Bristol as I do. She's a really nice girl, pretty, outgoing and fun to be with. We've so far not got beyond the "cuddling up" stage but I'm ever hopeful. I like (or liked) her parents well enough and they seemed to take to me OK, at least as far as allowing me to take Jilly every Saturday evening on my Lambretta from her home in Bristol to my favourite jazz club in Bath. Their stipulation was that I must get her home by eleven p.m. This arrangement worked well, that is until a couple of weeks ago. That Saturday, on a cold, wet, blustery evening in early March, I had picked up Jilly as usual and we were en route towards Bath on the back road via Kelston. I was just negotiating a bend when disaster struck. Perhaps it was the wet surface, or the new gravel that had been laid or perhaps, if I'm honest, I may have been going too fast around that bend. Perhaps it was a mixture of all these. Anyway, my Lambretta jolted away from under me, hit a curb and I remember seeing it flying up over my head as I was thrown into a ditch at the side of the road.

I picked myself up and, apart from being completely soaked and covered in mud, I felt OK. Problem was that I couldn't see poor Jilly anywhere in the pitch-black darkness. I called her name. There was no reply. I called out again, louder this time. "Jilly, where are you?" Again, this time shouting. "Jilly, where are you?" Still nothing. I started to panic. "My God, what the bloody hell have I done?"

I shouted out again, and this time, to my relief, I heard a faint reply. "I'm over here!" And there she was, stuck in a field on the other side of a hedge. She must have been flung upwards when the Lambretta overturned and catapulted her up over the top of the bloody hedge. "Are you OK?" I stupidly asked. "I think so," was all she could manage to reply. I located her position and tried to get to her but the hedge was made of prickly hawthorn grown to keep straying sheep from getting onto the road. In our case, it was blocking me from getting to help Jilly. I took off my sodden anorak and, by laying it across the hedge, I managed to cross over it and extract my poor girlfriend. She was conscious but shaking violently. I could also tell she was bleeding but, because it was so dark, I couldn't see where or how badly.

The next issue was to recover my beloved Lambretta. I found it a short distance away. It was on its side, partly on the verge of the road and partly in the ditch that I had fallen into. I pulled it out of the ditch, stood it upright and kicked the starter pedal. Bless it, the engine started first go. I took stock. We had taken a tumble but no one else was involved. I was

OK, the Lambretta seemed to be serviceable, but my girlfriend was in some sort of shock and needed a medical check. I reckoned we were only about three miles from Bath, which meant nine or so from Bristol. So better to get on to Bath than to try to return back to Bristol — and face Jilly's parents just yet!

I had always got on well with my geography teacher at my Bath school, and also with his lovely wife, Bridget, who I knew was or had been a nurse. I remembered they had an apartment near to my old school in the centre of Bath. So, I decided to head there, hoping that they would be home and Bridget could take care of Jilly. It seemed like a good plan. The next problem was the Lambretta. Although its engine had readily sprung into life, when I got on it I found the steering bar was badly bent out of shape. In order to keep the wheels pointing straight I had to hold the steering bar at a full right angle to the wheels. I couldn't straighten it out.

With Jilly clutching on behind, we gingerly limped into Bath and, much to my relief, found my ex-geography teacher at home. I explained our predicament and Bridget immediately took charge of Jilly, who by this stage was in a pretty bad shape. It was only when we were inside the apartment that I could see that Jilly had been bleeding profusely from cuts to her hands, face and shoulder.

The conclusion of this story was that Bridget did a great job of patching up and comforting poor Jilly. At one point, I actually thought we might be able to continue on to the jazz club but I reckoned that would have been selfish as my main responsibility was to make sure that I got Jilly home safely to her parents. In any case, the incident had taken up the whole evening and I realised I would not make the eleven o'clock deadline. When Jilly was bandaged up, bless her, she even managed a wan smile, although by now she'd come out in a bad skin rash caused, according to Bridget, by the stress of her ordeal. We rode back to Bristol at a snail's pace, due to the wonky steering, with Jilly sort of hanging on around my waist. It was after midnight when eventually we got back to Jilly's parents' house. Their reaction was, I suppose, inevitable. I was banned from ever seeing Jilly again and Jilly's father said he would report me to the police.

Not the best evening of my life so far. I lost a sweet girlfriend and was threatened with a police summons. Later, I found my Lambretta had a twisted frame and would cost more to repair than I had paid for it. That was the end of that! After the Lambretta saga, I was back to catching the bus and walking, though I did get out my old bike, which I hadn't used for some time and needed a new inner tyre and a good clean up. It took me from A to B but after the Lambretta — well!

So now I'm back to thinking about two years of national service. What about a deferment? Should I apply for a City & Guilds apprenticeship? Should I get my school books out again and study to retake my "A" levels to try to get good enough grades for Cambridge? I talk it all through again with my mother. She's as patient as ever but won't make a firm recommendation, one way or the other. She tells me it's time I made up my own mind. This makes me quite resentful but I suppose she's right. In fact, I know she's right.

I can't say I fancy being tied down for two long years in the military, especially as most of my friends have managed to escape being called up. On the other hand, I'm getting bored with my life, as it is now, but I don't feel like studying again or learning a new trade. I don't have a girlfriend any more and, most of all, I'm broke again. I still don't know what to do for the best.

Chapter Two

It's now early April and I'm at the national service clearing centre in Bristol. I've decided against applying for a deferment, at least until I learn more about what will be involved. I'm not the only one here. I arrive a good ten minutes before my ten-thirty appointment but already there are several guys waiting — all about my age and, of course, all male. I don't recognise anyone I know and feel rather nervous about what's going to happen.

The centre is in a red brick building in a nondescript road in central Bristol. Inside, the floor is covered with brown linoleum and filled with canteen-type wooden chairs. The room has a smell of mixed polish and disinfectant, which reminds me of a hospital. The walls are painted a cream colour, which age is turning brown like the floor linoleum. They are brightened by a few posters showing military equipment, guns, tanks, ships and aircraft and pictures of keen-looking soldiers, sailors and airmen. I suppose they're there to make us feel patriotic or motivated or something. I give my name to a clerk behind a desk. He's probably only in his thirties but he looks quite old compared to all of us eighteen-year-olds. He checks my name against an official-looking list and tells me to sit down with the others and wait to be called.

The session starts at about ten-forty-five when the clerk begins calling out names in, I presume, alphabetic order. There's an "Archer", then next a "Brown", then my turn when I hear the name "Chambers". I'm told to go to a door marked "Med". Inside is a man in a white overall with a stethoscope hanging around his neck. He tells me to strip off completely. I do so with some apprehension. I stand there, bollock naked in front of him feeling a bit of a wally. Then the doctor says:

"OK, Chambers. I need to check your medical condition. Have you had any major illnesses or been in hospital during your life?"

I don't need much time to think about this as I've been in hospital only once in my life. I reply: "Yes, about four years ago I had stomach pains and had my appendix removed in St Saviour's Hospital in Bath.

That's all"

"Fine, I already have a record of that. Anything else?"

"No, nothing."

He looks me up and down, then says: "Right. You look a healthy young fellow. I'll just do a quick check"

The doctor does his thing, prodding and tapping away at my body. He checks my feet to see if I have fallen arches or flat feet. I have not. He makes me sit then taps my knees with a little rubber hammer to see if there's any nerve reaction. There is. He listens to my heartbeat through his stethoscope. He nods indicating that it's hammering away evenly. He makes me cough while he holds my testicles, I've no idea why, then he tells me to say "Ahh" while he looks into my mouth. He sticks an implement into my ears then, while covering each eye alternately, I have to read out letters from a wall chart. No problem with that. The doctor even checks my hair for lice. At last, he seems satisfied.

"Right, Chambers," he concludes. "You're an A1. Now you need to get dressed and take this medical report to the room marked 'Registration 1' along this corridor."

I don't know whether I should be pleased or sorry that I have been passed fully fit. Pleased, I think, as I know a chum who was downgraded because of his flat feet but still had to do his two-year stint. He was put in the Army Pay Corps and sent to Ashton-under-Lyne for the whole two years. He told me he was bored to distraction there as all he had to do was handle pay slips and records. At least if I have to do my time, I hope I might be sent somewhere interesting.

I wonder whether I should have told the doctor about my stammer. Since I can remember, my stammer has been a problem that crops up in various situations. Normally, with my school and village friends, it's barely noticeable. But I get really stuck in some situations such as having to read out loud at school or when I'm tired or stressed. Then, I get seriously stuck when I'm faced with words starting with "hard" syllables such as d, t, l, and p. It can be really embarrassing at times. A recent example was when I faced Jill's irate father after the Lambretta accident. I just couldn't get a word out and just had to mime my apology as I backed away and left on my fucked-up scooter. In general though, I've found I can control the stammer quite well in most circumstances by finding an alternative phrase that doesn't entail using the "hard" first syllables. I didn't tell the army doctor any of this and I suppose it's now too late as I've been despatched to the next Registration room clutching my medical report saying that I'm A1.

Inside the room marked "Registration 1" is an older man, in civilian clothes. He introduces himself as Harris. He has quite an avuncular manner and I wonder whether he had been a schoolmaster in an earlier life. He has a file with my name on it and tells me to check the details. It lists my parents' names, my address, my date of birth, blood group, school, exams passed, etc. I confirm that all the details have been correctly collated.

Mr Harris riffles back through the file, purses his lips then looks directly at me.

"Right Chambers, I see from your file you are an active young man and the doctor's report here confirms you're fit and healthy. I propose to post you to the army rather than the air force and we are not taking conscripts into the Royal Navy at this time. Any comments?"

I didn't know what was expected so I just said: "No sir!"

"Do you have any particular trade aptitudes, for example in electronics or engineering, which might fit you for one of our specialist regiments such as our Royal Engineers or Royal Signals. They can always use good tradesmen."

I don't have any such skills so again all I reply is: "No sir!"

"Right Chambers, infantry it is. Here in the West Country, our infantry is grouped in what we call the 'Wessex Brigade'. At the moment this comprises: the Glosters, the Devon and Dorsets, the Hampshire, Berkshire and Wiltshire regiments. It's the Hampshires who have the recruiting priority this month, so you will be posted to that regiment and will carry out basic recruit training with the next intake." Mr Harris consulted a chart and continued, "The intake forms up on 30 April, that's a Thursday. Any questions?"

I don't know what to say. I thought I would have been given a chance to talk about possible deferment but Mr Harris doesn't mention that. Perhaps I've already left it too late! In any case, in some strange way I feel some sort of elation that a positive decision has at last been made for me. I decide to drop the idea of deferment.

I reply to Mr Harris, "No sir. Only where must I report and where are the Hampshires based?"

"You'll be getting a letter in the next few days telling you where to report and, any other details you will need. I can tell you though that basic training for both the Hampshires and the Wilts and Berks (who are shortly to amalgamate) is carried out at Le Marchant Barracks in Devizes, Wiltshire. The training takes twelve weeks then you will join the regiment. Here's the good news, Chambers. The regiment is based in Lemgo, Germany, at present but later this year will redeploy to the Caribbean, with its headquarters stationed in Jamaica, and detachments in British Guyana, Honduras and the Bahamas. You will be posted to one of these. You know, Chambers, you could be in for an exciting two years. Any further questions?"

As Mr Harris is speaking, there's a knock at his door and another young guy is waiting his turn. Mr Harris looks at his watch and I can tell he's anxious to get on and to assess his next potential conscript. I realise I don't care anymore about deferment. The dye has now been cast. I'm going to have to do my conscript National Service. I'm going to be posted to the Royal Hampshire Regiment and sent to what sounds a pretty exotic part of the world. So far, I've never been out of the UK so the idea of going anywhere abroad and, bloody hell, to the Caribbean, does indeed sound exciting.

I tell Mr Harris I have no further questions and leave the Bristol clearing centre with mixed feelings of nervousness, anticipation and excitement wondering how the next two years of my life will pan out.

Chapter Three

The day finally arrives: Thursday 30 April 1959. I haven't done much in the few weeks since I was at the Bristol clearing centre. I told my parents I am not being deferred, I collected my last pay packet from the department store, had a couple of nights at the pub with my chums — lots of commiserations as an excuse to have another round! I phoned Jilly at her parents' house. Fortunately, she picked up and told me her father was out. I was relieved to learn she was pretty much recovered from the Lambretta epic. She also told me she didn't think her father had reported me to the police. We had a good warm chat ending up wishing each other all the best for our future. I told her I'll send her a card from Jamaica or wherever. It was sad to have to leave it like that as I have a genuine affection for Jilly. But in a way, I'm glad to be leaving with no ties left behind.

The letter confirming details of my posting to the Royal Hampshires arrived a few days after my briefing by Mr Harris. It instructed me to report to the "Reception Sergeant" at Devizes Railway Station at 14.00 hours, 30 April 1959. It said I was not to bring anything else with me — no spare clothes, or pyjamas, not even a toothbrush. Seemed a bit odd!

I kiss my mother goodbye and give a little self-conscious hug to my father (he is surprisingly at home for once!), and catch the number thirty-three bus into Bath. I'd heard that the army always gives its recruit soldiers a severe "short back and sides" haircut so I arrive in Bath early and go to my usual barber. I ask him to give me a short haircut, hoping this will be sufficient to pass army regulations. When he's finished up, I look in the mirror and think I look as if I've been scalped. I've already checked that the train takes just over an hour from Bath Spa to Devizes and there's one leaving at 12.45, arriving at 13.52. That's the one I take.

The train arrives on time and I'm on the platform at Devizes just before 14.00 hours as per the letter. I see a line of young lads up ahead reporting in to a tall burly guy wearing a smart army uniform with the three stripes of sergeant on each arm. Other lads arrive and form up behind me. My turn comes and the sergeant barks out to me: "Name?" I answer: "Peter Chambers, sir."

"It's sergeant to you lad, not sir. You'll soon learn!" He snaps at me as he ticks my name off on the list clipped to his millboard. Then he says: "Now go outside and you'll see a couple of trucks lined up outside the station entrance. Get up in one of those and wait."

I find the trucks and see there are several other guys already on board one of them. I climb up and join them. I realise these are to be my squad mates during our training. Nervously, we start to exchange names. No one seems to know what the initial procedure will be. We'll just have to wait and see.

Gradually, more and more guys emerge from the station and climb up into our truck. I look around the rest of the guys and I think it might be difficult to get on with some of them. A lot have strong regional accents from, I think, the Portsmouth area, though I'm guessing as I've never actually been there. My lighter Somerset brogue probably sounds very different to their ears. There are a couple of guys who stand out straight away. Both have come dressed as if they were going to a night club — real Teddy Boy kit; "brothel creeper" suede shoes, drainpipe trousers, long jackets with wide shoulders and covered in sequins. Then the hair! — heavily Brylcreemed and scooped up in the front in a sort of Elvis style and at the back curled into what my generation calls a "duck's ass" shape. I wonder what the sergeant will make of these two! I realise this is just the beginning of a new experience for us all. The one common factor among us seems to be our age — eighteen or so but there are a few who seem rather older — perhaps they got deferrals due to a trade course or university but after that still got lumbered with the two-year stint.

After waiting in our trucks for some time, the sergeant emerges from Devizes station. He seems satisfied that he has accounted for everyone on his list. He shouts out to the truck drivers to raise up the tailgates. These are held in place by metal retaining pins on each side of the tailgate. Once secured, we're off. There are wooden benches along the sides of the truck. Some sit down on these, the rest of us keep standing and hang on to overhead rails to keep our balance. Some of the guys are cracking jokes and waving at passers-by as we drive through the streets of Devizes town. I think this jocularity is probably brought on by nervous tension rather than confidence.

We're told it's only a short trip from the station to Le Marchant Barracks. For us in the back of the truck, we can only see the road behind us so our first view of our new home is watching the security barrier lowered behind us as we're driven into the barracks. The trucks lumber on past what I guess is the barrack square then both grind to a halt. The drivers come around to the back of the truck, the retaining pins are removed and the tailgates are lowered. Someone shouts to us to jump down so we all do.

In front of us is a hangar-type building with a large sign saying. "Quartermaster's Store". We are met by four or five soldiers, all looking very smart and business-like in their sharply pressed uniforms and highly polished boots. From my school cadet days, I recognise the ranks of three corporals, one sergeant and one sergeant-major. It is the sergeant-major who is very much in charge. The corporals get us to line up in three rows and the sergeant-major orders us to stand up straight and pay attention. He is not tall but has a commanding presence. Even the two "Teddy Boy" types seem impressed enough to shut up and do as they are told.

The sergeant-major carries a wooden cane that, I think, is called a pace-stick. He holds this with his left hand holding the forward tip and the stick tucked under his left armpit at an angle precisely parallel to the ground. When he is sure he has our full attention, he walks slowly along the front row making eye contact with each of us as he passes. He then walks back to the centre of our group, turns and pauses.

Then he says: "I am Company Sergeant-Major Willis. You may not have heard my name before but you will never forget it after today! I'm looking right now at a bunch of scruffy young immature boys."

He pauses again, looking along the front row of our motley group. He then continues: "My task during the next twelve weeks is to turn you lot into a squad of smart disciplined soldiers, ready to join the ranks of one of most distinguished regiments in the British Army. Be in no doubt, I will succeed in that task. On my right, here is Sergeant Beck who will be your platoon sergeant during your recruit training. You are to follow his instructions precisely and immediately. He is assisted by Corporals Warburton, Andrews and Pitcher — all fully trained soldiers, hand-picked to assist in your training. You will get to know all these gentlemen very well indeed while you are here. That is all for now. Carry on Sergeant Beck!"

Sergeant Beck snaps to attention and shouts out "Sir!" as Company Sergeant-Major Willis turns to leave. Then Beck faces us and gives us our first instruction. He has a strong gruff voice, which allows no room for misinterpretation or challenge. He puts an extra stress on each executive word. He tells us: "Right, let's get MOVING! You are to FILE into the QM Stores here. You will each be issued with a full set of coveralls, underwear and boots. You are to CHANGE into these. BUNDLE all your personal clothes and personal belongings ready to post back to your mother. And I do mean ALL. We'll then deal with the rest of your induction when you've changed. Now MOVE!"

We do as we are told, get into a single file and shuffle into the hangar-type building marked Quartermaster's Stores. The QM hangar is huge. For our reception today, I see a set of wooden trestle tables has been lined up with clothing and other stores piled in neat rows on the racking behind. There are four soldiers behind the tables whose job is to issue out the clothing and stores to each of us new recruits. I'm somewhere in the middle of the line queuing up here and I feel I'm drifting into a sort of zombie-like world. On Day One of my conscription, I realise I'm now into a system over which I have absolutely no control. I just have to go along with whatever happens, to follow the instructions I'm given. I can't question the rationale of what I am being told to do or take any individual action. My school had strong discipline but in an entirely different way and now there's no going home to Mother at the end of the day!

My turn comes to get to the front of the line. I'm facing a young soldier whose job it is to handle this stage of the induction process. He's not much older than me. I suspect he did his own recruit training some months ago and for whatever reason has now been allocated this task. Despite only being a simple private grade soldier himself, he has the air of an old hand and looks condescendingly down at us raw recruits. He takes my name and gives me a checklist of clothing and other items. He pulls out a pre-prepared set and I'm required to confirm that I am correctly receiving: denims, vests, sweater, underpants, socks, woollen shirts, tie, webbing belt and gaiters, small pack, groundsheet (all khaki coloured), blue beret, two pairs of black boots, PT shoes, spare laces, towel, sets of washing/shaving kit, mess tins with knife, fork and spoon, pack of needles and thread, pack with dusters, boot polish, "Brasso" and khaki "Blanco" and, finally, a sausage-shape kit bag.

The QM soldier then says: "That's it, mate. Clothes sizes are either small, medium or large. I've given you large. Should fit OK. Too bad if not. And I've given you size 9 boots and PT shoes. That OK? Now sign here! You'll get fitted out for your battledress and other kit later."

I look around and see my fellow recruits are in the same situation. The QM soldier holds a copy of the checklist towards me with a biro pen. I sign. He then says: "Right mate, you're done here. Now go through there and strip off as the sergeant told you. You'll see there's a pile of brown paper, some string, scissors and some pens. Put your stuff together, parcel it up, tie with the string provided and write your mother's name and address. It'll find its way back to her. If you're married, post it to your wife — that's if she's prepared to wash out all your smellies! Don't forget to put in everything personal including your watch, cash, any rings etc. If you don't, they'll be confiscated and you'll never see them again. You won't be needing any of your own stuff for the next twelve weeks so get used to it."

I do as the QM soldier tells me. Putting on this new kit seems strange and alien. The army vest is OK but the shirt is made of some sort of rough material that feels like horse hair and immediately itches. The boots are stiff but are the right size, thank goodness! I imagine that's the most important item as I'm sure we'll be spending a lot of our time on our feet. I find the brown paper, pack up my own kit and hand the parcel addressed to my mother to another QM soldier.

We are not done yet. I'm told to get in line for a compulsory haircut with the military barber. I think about protesting as I've just been scalped in Bath earlier today but I realize it won't make any difference; I'm going to have to have another one anyway. Some compensation is the sight of one of the "Teddy Boys" who's just up ahead of me. When his turn comes, the barber takes a malicious delight in sheering off the poor guy's tenderly groomed coiffure. Now he looks like a baldy, just the same as everyone else. I can imagine the immediate impact it must have on his sense of status and morale.

At last, we come to the end of the QM process. The three corporals we were earlier introduced to are sitting behind a table, near an exit door to the QM hangar. We are again required to form up in a line and wait until our names are called out. When it's my turn, I'm called to stand in front of one of the corporals. His manner is firm but not aggressive.

He tells me: "Chambers, my name is Corporal Andrews and you are allocated to my section and my barrack room — that's room number twelve in block D. You will be sharing with fifteen other recruits."

Corporal Andrews then hands me two disks with chords hanging from them. He says: "Right, Chambers, listen in. We call these disks 'dog tags'. You are to wear these around your neck at all times, day and night. You will see they have your name embossed on them. Also, they show your blood group, in your case 'O' pos. Correct? And your eight-digit regimental number. Yours is: 23636241. This number is your military identification. It is very important you learn it off by heart. Is that clear?"

"Yes corporal," is all I can say.

I take the dog tags and hang them around my neck as instructed. I now realise, in this short time, the army has now taken away my individuality. I own nothing. I am only a number.

Photo: Le Marchant Barracks, Devizes, Wiltshire 1959

Photo: Le Marchant Barracks. Recruits accommodation and parade ground.

Chapter Four

It's nearly three weeks since our incarceration in Le Marchant Barracks. We're not yet allowed to leave the barracks but at least we're provided with notepaper, envelopes and a couple of biros. Postage is free so we can send and receive personal mail. I've already written a couple of times to my parents and got sympathetic replies. I've also written once to Jilly but so far there's been nothing back from her.

Now I'm lying on my bed in our barrack room. It's about 23.00 hours, and, as far as I can tell from the volume of snuffling and snoring, my fifteen fellow recruits in our barrack room are all asleep already. But I can't sleep yet. Today has been as active and wearing as every other day of our seven days a week routine and at last we are allowed to go to bed and lights have been turned off. My metal frame bed is third up on the right-hand side from the entrance door. My bed is two foot four inches wide and just six feet long — the same as all the rest. The paillasse mattress is thin but adequate and I'm covered by my single grey blanket. It's late May and quite mild. My feet overhang the end by a couple of inches but I've managed to adjust my sleeping position to cope.

Between our bed-spaces are metal lockers, in which we keep most of our kit, each item lined up precisely as directed by Corporal Andrews. The locker contents, like everything else we have been issued with, are inspected every morning. At the bottom section of the locker are two pairs of boots, one for every day, the other for "best". The everyday boots are always kept clean and polished but the "best" ones are now "highly bulled". We give them an extra half hour's spit and polish every evening to try to achieve a perfect shine on the toecaps. Next to the boots are our gym shoes, used for indoor exercising. Above the footwear section, we hang our denims, shirts, PT vests and the parade battledress we have recently been issued. This has to be kept neatly pressed at all times. Next up are two cubicles: in one we keep our blue beret and next to this our webbing belt and gaiters, which have to be freshly "blancoed" every day and all brasses immaculately polished. In the top locker cubicle, we line up all our cleaning/feeding kit — washing/shaving set, mess tins with knife, fork and spoon, polishing cloths, Brasso, Blanco, "Cherry Blossom" boot polish, sewing set appropriately called a "housewife"! All items have their set places and are neatly folded. On the top of our locker we store our "small" pack, which has to be squared off and, like our belt and gaiters, has to be "Blancoed" and "Brassoed" afresh every day. Finally, placed on the small pack is our helmet with its scrim net attached. That's it — neatly arranged in that precise order.

We've already come a long way from the totally disparate group of individuals who turned up at Devizes station last month. Our days are quite similar. At 06.30 hours, Cpl Andrews bursts open the door and shouts: "Right you lot, hands off your cocks, feet on the floor!" So begins our day. We file into the washroom and carry out our ablutions, then dress and prepare for the "Stand by your beds!" order while we wait for the dreaded kit and bed inspection. This is usually carried out by the gruff Sergeant Beck but on occasion by Company Sergeant-Major Willis himself, not a pleasant experience.

At this first parade every morning, we are inspected to ensure everything is present and always impeccable. We have to line up standing to attention in front of our bed-spaces. Never a day goes by when faults are not found and the erring recruits are admonished and told to redo, re-clean and/or re-polish the offending items of kit and produce them for further inspection at a later parade.

Like all new army recruits, we have to begin at the beginning. First lesson: how to form up as a squad, and learn drill and marching. We are taught to form up in three ranks, and perform such elementary drills as turns, inclines, taking dressing in line with the right marker, et cetera. Everything is to "One—p a u se—Two Three—p a u s e—-One!" commands. Not exactly rocket science but when it comes to marching, one guy, Oldfield I think his name is, proves to be totally "march dyslectic". For most people, it's natural to put one leg forward and at the same time to swing the opposite arm. Poor Oldfield can't do this. When he leads with his left leg, he instinctively also swings his left arm forward making a comic crab-like movement. Sergeant Beck barks out at Oldfield to march with left leg and right arm then right leg and left arm. It's no good, no matter how hard Oldfield tries, he still continues his disjointed movements. The more Sergeant Beck yells at him, the more nervous and flustered Oldfield becomes. In the end, the poor guy is removed from the squad and we later hear that one of our training corporals marched him continuously round the barracks practising "left leg, right arm, then right leg, left arm" movements until he eventually got it. He's now re-joined our squad and marches the same as the rest of us.

My two nearest bed-space neighbours are, on my left, Jim White (known as Chalky) and, on my right, Keith Hignett. Both come from Portsmouth as do the majority of the rest of our platoon. We three get along OK together, as we must, but we're never likely to become close friends. I don't know why no one else here comes from the Bath area and only one or two from the wider Somerset or Wiltshire counties. By now, I've just about learnt the names of the rest of the other fifteen guys in our barrack room and most of the other sixteen from our intake platoon who are billeted in the next room to ours. But more than just names, despite our present total uniformity of dress and routine, I'm slowly learning more about each person as an individual — some are cocky and brash, others cheery and bright, some are natural optimists and comics, others are always moaning, some are naturally neat and smart, others struggle with their kit and are always last on parade. Whatever, we're all thrown in together and it's no matter whether you like or dislike the next guy, we all have to coexist in what started out as an alien world for us all. Everyone seems to be getting along pretty well together as we are all in exactly the same boat. From our reveille at 06.30 till lights out at 22.30, we are pushed, chased and harried by our instructors. We have almost zero free time. After final parade, we are occupied with bulling our boots, pressing our uniform, polishing our brasses and blancoing our webbing. Some complain and suffer from our instructors as a result. Most of us decide it's best to shut up, do what's required of us and get on.

I'm still trying to get used to the, sometimes, overpowering smell we generate in our barrack-room. For a start, there's the pungent odour of the orange coloured polish we're given for the lino floor. We have to spread it on quite thickly leaving a dull cloudy surface. We leave it for a few minutes to harden then it's an on our knees job to rub like mad to give the lino a shiny surface. This aroma blends with the strong whiff of "Brasso" polish and the Cherry Blossom we use to bull our boots. Added to this cocktail are the personal body odours of the sixteen occupants of the room. Quite a heady mix!

There is one problem with our group. I've noticed that the (ex?) Teddy Boy-type who had his locks shaved off on Day One seems to have recovered his cocky confidence after the blow to his self-perceived social status by being shorn of his Elvis/Tony Curtis-style hair. I've learnt his name is Darrell Roberts. He has a chum called Rik Parfitt who somehow has acquired the next bed-space to Darrell's. The two of them are very close and it turns out they have known each other for some years and belong to the same group/gang in Portsmouth. Rik is not tall but very muscular and likes everyone else to know it. Yesterday, the two of them picked on a guy called Steve Jenkins for some reason — possibly accusing him of jumping the canteen queue — or perhaps that was just an excuse. Anyway, the two of them cornered Steve and threatened him. I don't know whether they actually hit him but they certainly gave him a load of grief. Steve is just an ordinary guy trying to mind his own business and get through our basic army training here like the rest of us. He was pretty gutted by the experience. In hindsight, I think it was probably just a demonstration to the rest of us, I don't know what about exactly, probably for us to accept their control of who does what? I'm still wondering if I, or others who saw their viciousness, should have tried to intervene. I think Rik suspected I was going to react because he shouted out to me:

"Back off, Chambers, this has nothing to do with a posh boy like you!"

Posh boy! Me! I'd never been called that in my life before and I was stung by his stupid remark. Why would this guy think of me as "posh"? My parents are very poor; we live in a small, unprepossessing house. I've always thought myself to be just an average, ordinary guy. It's true I managed to pass my eleven plus exam and got a free scholarship to a good school but that had nothing to do with money or social status. I'm really pissed off about being called "posh".

I still can't sleep as I keep thinking about my confrontation with Darrell earlier today. After the incident with Steve Jenkins, I had a feeling I was the next on Darrell and Rik's hit list. I knew I had to be prepared. After our evening meal, it happened; but not in the way I had feared. I was taking a leak in the urinal outside our canteen when Darrell appeared and also started to have a pee. There was no one else in the urinal stall at the time. There was room there for Darrell to stand well away from me but he chose to come right up close. I wondered what he planned and I braced myself for what might come next. If they wanted to scrap, OK, I decided I would do all I could to defend myself. I didn't intend to back off as that would only encourage him. I suspected his sidekick, Rik, would appear and I would be surrounded by these two. To my surprise, and to be honest, my relief, that didn't happen. As we came to the natural end of our pee, Darrel said quietly:

"I need a word with you outside, mate?" That was all.

We left the urinal together and Darrell asked me to walk with him away from the canteen to an area where there was no chance of being overheard. His chum Rik did not appear. I could see that Darrell was nervous. He took his time to build himself up. Then from inside his coverall jacket he pulled out a letter. He held this out to me and said:

"Look, mate. I've been given this letter by Corporal Andrews today. Thing is — I'm not too good at reading. Could you — er — tell me what it says?"

I looked straight at Darrell and could see he was hesitant and embarrassed. The penny dropped and I realised he was illiterate. This guy, who hid behind a veneer of macho toughness, was secretly ashamed that he couldn't even read a simple letter. I could spot an opportunity here. I replied:

"Sure, Darrell, no problem. Let's have a look. OK, well for a start the writer's got very pretty handwriting! It says: "My dearest Darrell. I keep thinking about the night before you left to go to the Army. You gave me such a good time — you know what I mean!!! Can't wait to see you again. When are they going to let you out? Please let me know. Love and kisses. Tracey." That's it, Darrell. Look, you can see she's put a string of exclamation marks after she writes "you know what I mean" and she ends with lots of Xs, meaning kisses. Looks like you've scored heavily there!"

Darrell has been concentrating as I read the letter to him. He hesitates again, then says:

"Thanks mate. Do you think you could write her a reply?"

"Well of course I can, what do you want me to say?"

"You know — the usual stuff you have to tell girls"

"OK, but I need to know a bit about your Tracey. For starters, do you want to see her again? Did you have it away with her last time? Is she your regular or just a bit on the side?"

Again, the hesitation, then Darrel launched into a description of his relationship with Tracey. No, she's not a regular, but yes, they did have sex after spending the evening in the pub. Yes, he wants to see her again and wants his letter to be quite amorous. I tell him that's no problem; I will write something suitable. I explain to Darrell that her address is on her letter so I can get it all prepared, read it out to him to see if it suits then it'll just need posting.

I could tell that Darrell seemed heavily relieved. Then he looked at me hard and said earnestly:

"Look, mate. You mustn't breath a word about this to no one. Not even to Rik. Promise?"

I was beginning to learn a little about life's realities. I told him:

"Sure Darrell, but how about you do something for me in return? I saw what you and Rik did to that guy Jenkins yesterday. He didn't do you any harm. So you and Rik must lay off the tough stuff. We've enough to put up with here in this sodding camp without you two giving the rest of us a hard time. So, the deal is — I write your letter and keep my mouth shut about it, you and Rik cool it and watch my back for me. Agreed?"

I don't know what Darrell had expected. He paused for a while, pursed his lips then looked at me with a half-smile.

"OK mate, deal agreed."

I suppose it's reflecting about this incident with Darrell that's keeping me awake. I had no idea before that there were guys like him who act tough but have no brains to back it up. I'm thinking that's his problem and my good luck to be able to take advantage of his inability to read or write. Why not? I think I've learnt a lesson today. Nothing is for nothing! If I play my cards right, perhaps I can even get him to polish my boots.

Chapter Five

We're now into the sixth week of our basic recruit training and are beginning to look and act like soldiers. We're still given very little free time, which is probably just as well as we're still confined to barracks, except when participating in authorised squad activity. We're told there's no chance of a week-end pass for at least another week or more. We're now into June and the weather is dry and fine. Most of our time is spent out of doors and we march everywhere as a squad even between the barrack block and the mess canteen. Our marching is getting smarter and more coordinated. Our steps are snappier and, on our drill corporal's command, we come to a sharp halt in pretty good unison.

We're all getting fitter as we're required to do a lot of physical activity. This includes route marches around the roads and tracks of Wiltshire. We've been taught to march at a constant 120 paces to the minute, alternating with the odd burst of running as a squad. The command for this is called "double time". A couple of times we've done these marches at night, with our corporal instructors wearing fluorescent jackets with inbuilt torches to ensure we don't get mown down by passing traffic. So far so good. A few guys have struggled physically on these marches — not a good idea as they then have to undergo additional PT to toughen them up. It seems to be working. We've all had blisters as we wear in our new boots but that seems to go with the territory and now our feet have hardened up and, through constant wear, our boots have moulded to the shape of our feet.

We also spend a lot of time on the obstacle course, this being designed to test our balance and upper body strength and to further develop squad cohesion. The course includes: running along a series of logs positioned several feet above ground, scrambling on our bellies under a screen of barbed wire, pulling ourselves hand over hand along an overhead metal trapeze, taking a running jump at an eight-foot high wall then pulling ourselves up and over it; flinging ourselves over a water obstacle and carrying one of our colleagues in a "fireman's lift" for fifty yards. We started our training on this course just wearing our denim uniforms but now we have to tackle the same obstacles wearing full webbing kit, small pack, helmet and carrying our rifles.

Our training is not all physical. We have been given instruction about army ranks and the difference between non-commissioned officers, such as Sergeant Beck and Company Sergeant-Major Willis, and commissioned officers whose ranks start with second lieutenant. We've been taught to recognise commissioned officers as they wear their badges of rank on each shoulder, rather than on the sleeve and they usually wear flat hats rather than berries. We're also taught about military rank abbreviations and how they're usually written. The term "non-commissioned officer" is normally written as NCO, corporal is Cpl, sergeant is Sgt, company sergeant-major is CSM, and the top rank of regimental sergeant-major is RSM. With the commissioned officers, lieutenant is Lt, captain is Capt, major remains major, but lieutenant colonel is abbreviated to Lt Col. We're told that Lt Col is the highest rank we're likely to encounter as a Lt Col is the rank of our commanding officer, known as the CO. We're asked if this is clear. We all nod our heads but I'm not sure it has really sunk in!

We've been taught how to salute correctly, by bringing the right arm up from the side to a position one inch above the right eye. The right arm and hand must be held in a straight line and not be bent. We hold the salute for three seconds then whip our arm straight back down to our side. As Sergeant Beck succinctly puts it: "UP the long way, DOWN the short!" We practise this movement many times and are told we must salute all commissioned officers whenever we pass them — this being a recognition not of the individual but that these officers are holders of the Queen's Commission. Everyone nods at these explanations but I'm not sure all of us really follow the logic. We just need to accept what we are told about this and realise it's all part of the mystique of the British Army.

We have now been introduced to our platoon commander, a young officer called Lieutenant (or Lt as we've now learnt) Fleming who gave us a lecture about the history of our future regiment, the Royal Hampshires. We will be joining the 1st Battalion of this regiment. We realise this is a unit with a long and distinguished history.

After over five weeks of living, working and eating in our communal world of sixteen guys per barrack room and all facing the same challenges of our new environment and tough discipline, we're now beginning to gel and work well together. On the whole, our morale is OK and most of us help each other out and muck in together with all the communal chores we are required to carry out. There's still a problem with Darrell and Rik. Darrell seems to be less of a prat and has kept off my back since our letter reading/writing episode. Rik still likes to push his weight around. He is a naturally tough guy with a broad barrel chest. He tends to threaten those who are not as physically robust as he is. One of his latest victims is Chalky White, one of my bed-space neighbours. Chalky is a good cheerful little guy who I've come to like and respect. He is physically quite short and lacks muscle. He is only now beginning to have gained enough strength to pull himself up onto the eight-foot wall on the obstacle course. He can do without the hassle from Rik. If this goes on, I suppose I shall have to get involved. We'll see.

The subject of girls is, not surprisingly, one of the favourite topics of conversation in the barrack room. A couple of our guys are already married and like to keep their personal lives private. But most of the rest like to brag about their recent conquests and to go into all the gory details of their sexual exploits. I listen to all this and realise that either there's a lot of exaggeration going on or that I've lived a very sheltered and naive life so far. I don't like to admit it to the rest for fear of being ridiculed but the truth is I am still technically a virgin. I've had several girlfriends, Jilly being the last. With them, we've got around to kissing and cuddling but I've never actually got to the winning post. I listen to some of the tales being told and can't help but feel envious. I hope that my turn will come in the near future, though confined as we all are in Le Marchant Barracks, Devizes, it's certainly not going to be any time soon!

Last week, we were all marched in to a classroom that's been converted into a cinema and were required to watch a film about venereal disease. It included sections on syphilis, gonorrhoea and other sexually transmitted diseases with infected penises shown in graphic detail, albeit in black and white. I was nearly physically sick just watching this film. I suppose it is designed as a big warning to us all not to rush off and get cheap back street sex. Some of the guys seemed quite relaxed about the film's contents but it certainly worked as far as I'm concerned. Naively,

I'd never even heard the term "venereal disease" before having to watch the film. Needless to say, the subject was the major topic of conversation in our barrack room that evening.

During this phase of our training, we've been concentrating on learning about the weapons that will be part of our equipment as infantrymen. We've already had instruction on the Self-Loading Rifle (SLR), which is to be our basic weapon. We've been taught about its characteristics, how to strip it down, clean it and reassemble it. We now each take the gun on the parade ground, march with it and carry out specific drills such as "shoulder and present arms". We've been told that we'll be going to the ranges next week to fire and "zero in" this rifle.

This morning, after our routine inspection and breakfast, we form up in our three ranks as always and are marched round to an open area next to the armoury. We are told that "what we're going on with now" is an introduction to the Bren gun. This weapon is a particular favourite of Sgt Beck who is giving us an introductory lecture. Our platoon is required to form a semi-circle around a trestle table on which the gun has been laid out. In almost reverent terms and in his individual style, Sgt Beck tells us:

"Without doubt, this gun is one of the finest light-machine guns ever made. It provides the main fire power for the platoon and was used with great distinction by the British army throughout both the Second World war and by our troops in Korea. The gun's basic design has remained the same since it was originally produced in Czechoslovakia in the 1930s. The only modification has been for it to fire the NATO standard 7.62 mm calibre bullet rather than the .303-inch calibre round that was used before. This gun in front of you is designated "Bren L4A2". Today I'm going to TEACH you how it WORKS, how to STRIP it down, CLEAN all working parts, and REASSEMBLE it."

With great panache, Sgt Beck then proceeds to take the gun to pieces, explaining to us the precise name of each part and its role. He ends his tutorial dramatically by telling us:

"Right, that's your first introduction to the Bren. We're now going to TEACH you how to STRIP and REASSAMBLE this weapon and the different carrying and firing positions you will HAVE to adopt. Next week, you will each also FIRE the weapon on our first day at the ranges.

It is my job to MAKE SURE you all understand exactly how to HANDLE and FIRE it. I will even make you correctly ASSEMBLE all the parts blindfold. TREAT it as your best friend because one day it could SAVE your life!"

We are then marched off to the armoury, draw out another eight Bren guns and are formed into groups with four men per Bren. For the rest of the morning session, we concentrate on learning all about the weapon, and being taught by our corporals how to take it apart and put it back together again. We are required to repeat this drill many times with Sgt Beck keeping a beady eye on us all. It's not exactly taxing but I've learnt that it's not a good plan to be seen to learn too quickly as I could then be construed by Sgt Beck as being too much of a "smart Alec". Better, I've learnt, to make a couple of early errors, on purpose, then to miraculously get it right so that the good sergeant can feel my progress had been solely due to his brilliant instructional technique!

Photo: Bren gun training

Our Bren gun training goes on until our lunch break. We're then allowed a half-hour free time after we've cleaned up mess tins and eating irons. As I'm leaving the mess dining room, Darrell Roberts sidles up beside me and indicates he wants a private chat. We move away from the rest of our guys to a spot where we can't be overheard. This time Darrell hands me two letters and again asks me to read the contents. I look at the handwriting on the envelopes, I can recognise one is in Tracey's fair hand. I'm genuinely intrigued to see how she's responded to the letter to her that I composed for Darrell. I don't recognise the handwriting on the second letter.

Darrell is keen for me to read them for him. I start with Tracey's and read out:

"Dearest Darrell. How wonderful to get your letter. I had no idea you could write so beautifully! [hmm, hmm, little do you know, I'm thinking!]. I'm missing you so much and can't wait till the army lets you come back home to Portsmouth. Love and kisses, your Tracey"

I say to Darrell: "You seem to have hit the jackpot with your Tracey. You're definitely in with that one!"

I open the second envelope and find a letter written by another of Darrell's old flames. I read it out to him:

"Darrell. I was so sorry to have missed you before you had to go to the army — as you know my parents insisted I went with them to stay in the horrid new Pontins caravan park in Morthoe. I hated every minute and wished I could have been with you and shared your farewell party at the pub. Let me know when you can get back to Portsmouth. I'll be there to greet you. Love Martha."

Oh dear, one Darrell, two loving girls!

I turn back to Darrell and say to him: "You're a popular guy with the ladies, Darrell, you've got them both lining up for you. If you want me to reply to them, you'll have to let me know how you want to play it: you could string them both along, keep one and drop the other or cool it with them both? I'll need to know so that I can find the right words to reply. What's it to be?"

Darrell doesn't hesitate. "Yeah! I want to keep them both."

"OK, I understand. But what do you want to write to each of them?"

"I dunno, but you're good with words, mate, can't you just write something to keep them both sweet? You know, like what you wrote to Tracey. That worked good."

I feel I'm getting too involved with Darrell's love life but there you go. So far, he's kept his side of our deal as he's cut out the rough stuff in the barrack room. But not so his chum Rik Parfitt. Rik continues to be a pain in the butt, always trying to play the hard man. I tell Darrell:

"All right I'll think of something. But remember our deal was for me to write your letters to Tracey? Now you want me to write to Martha as well. OK, but I need you to rein in Rik Parfitt. Tell him to cool it. Yesterday, he was threatening to beat up Chalky White, the guy in the next bed-space to mine. He's got to lay off his bully boy tactics. Deal?"

Darrell agrees and I tell him I'll write the letters and show him what I've done before they're posted off to these poor unsuspecting maidens. As I prepare for our afternoon training session, I can't help thinking about the irony here. I'm supporting Darrell's love life with his two girls while I haven't yet had a single reply from Jilly, my own ex. I tell myself I'll write to her once again and see if she answers. I suspect her father has persuaded her to give me up for good.

This afternoon, CSM Willis forms up our whole platoon and gives us some unexpected news. He says to us:

"Right, listen in! An important parade is taking place on the Isle of Wight tomorrow. The Wiltshire Regiment is amalgamating with the Berkshires to form what will be known as the Duke of Edinburgh's Royal Regiment or DERR for short. His Royal Highness himself will be presenting the new regiment's colours and a lot of other bigwigs will be there. The senior officers have decided they need more soldiers on parade to fill out the ranks. That will be you lot! It will be best uniforms and best boots. You've now had nearly six weeks here to get you to look something like real soldiers so this will be your first test to show what you're made of. That's all. Sergeant Beck, Carry on!"

I think this news has even caught Sgt Beck and our training corporals unawares as they take some time to adjust and decide how best to prepare. We learn that we are supposed, for tomorrow, to be extra members of either the Wilts or the Berks regiment, whereas our uniforms have Royal Hampshire shoulder flashes sown onto them.

Having collected himself, Sgt Beck decides to abort our previous training schedule. Instead, we are sent back to our barrack room to give an extra glow to our kit and be ready for inspection before lights out this evening. Our preparations include unpicking our Hampshire shoulder flashes and temporally sewing on Wilts or Berks flashes as issued by our corporal.

Our morale is given a boost. First, we're being entrusted to be on a major parade alongside fully trained soldiers. Second, at least we'll have a day out of barracks doing something different. That can't be bad.

Chapter Six

It's the morning of 9 June 1959: a fine sunny summer's day. I'm on parade at Albany Barracks on the Isle of Wight. I'm wearing my tailored "best" uniform, now with the Wilts regimental shoulder flashes that I was required to sew on last evening. All of us from the Devizes recruit platoon were driven down to Southampton this morning, across on the ferry to Cowes and then to Albany Barracks. We travelled in our denim lightweights with shirt sleeves rolled up in regulation summer "shirt sleeve order" while our parade uniforms, boots, rifles, etc. were all individually marked and taken by separate transport. These were delivered to the barracks' gymnasium where we were all reunited with our own kit. We then stripped off and put on our smart parade uniforms. It's the first time I've experienced the military system of getting men and supplies brought together with co-ordinated logistical efficiency. I'm impressed.

To make the numbers look more impressive for the parade, our guys have now been inserted into the ranks of the fully trained Wiltshire and Berkshire regiment soldiers from Albany Barracks. The places where we've been told to stand seem to be based on our height. I'm in the second (middle) rank of the centre platoon of what I've learnt is part of C (Charlie) Company. On my right is Jeff (Nobby) Stiles who is from the same Devizes barracks as me. Nobby is six foot three, a couple of inches taller than me. He's at the end of our row. On my left is a guy from the regular regiment who I've not seen before. We have not had the chance even to exchange names let alone to have a chat.

We've been inspected several times and we've practised our drill, particularly a movement called "Advance in review order", which is to be a centrepiece movement of the parade ceremony. It involves marching directly forward counting fifteen steps and halting exactly in time with no other word of command. Very impressive, provided we all halt in unison — a bit of a shambles if we don't! Poor Nobby Stiles is having difficulty with this precision counting so I'm saying the numbers out loud, just enough for Nobby to hear. It seems to be working so far.

A novelty for us Devizes recruits is the arrival of a military band. As they strike up their rousing march numbers, the music instils in us a sense of pride and occasion. Somehow, we all seem to respond and put extra spark and gusto into our drill. With the band helping us to keep the step and timing of our movements, we practise the parade procedure many times over, until at last our drill instructors seem satisfied.

As the parade square clock approaches midday, the parade regimental sergeant-major (which we now know is abbreviated to RSM, and is a rank even superior to our CSM Willis) now gives the command "Fall in the officers", whereupon these officers march onto the parade ground, all carrying their swords held in the upright position. They take up their posts in front of our three ranks. I can see three lieutenants, one is our own Lt Fleming, but I've not seen the others before. Then there's a captain (three pips on his shoulder) and in front of all these is a major, who wears a crown emblem on his shoulder. He's a very imposing officer whose name, we're told, is Major Stone. There are five companies in all, each commanded by a major and a similar number of supporting officers. Finally, the most senior officer, a lieutenant colonel, marches on parade. He is the commanding officer (CO) and we're told he will receive the new Duke of Edinburgh's Regimental colours from His Royal Highness, Prince Philip, himself.

The parade square has been immaculately cleaned and the whole barracks is spick and span in preparation for today's great event. Across the square, we can see many guests have arrived and have been seated on raised stands facing our formed-up ranks; gentlemen wearing either suits or uniforms with medals, ladies all adorned with smart hats. I have no idea who they all are and we've not been told: but I assume they are civic or political dignitaries and senior military personnel. It's all very grand!

As the clock begins to chime out twelve o'clock, a convoy of three vehicles drives up in front of the raised stands and comes to a halt in front of a dais in the centre of the stands. From my position in the second rank back, I can't really see much and have no idea who most of the passengers are. There is only one individual I instantly recognise from the many newspaper pictures of him — it is the dashing young Prince

Philip, Duke of Edinburgh himself. He is also wearing a military uniform. We are given the order to come to attention, to "shoulder arms" then to "present arms", the latter being the equivalent of saluting, but while carrying our rifles. In front of us, we see the prince returning our salute.

Now, the parade gets underway. First the prince walks along our ranks accompanied by the commanding officer and a couple of other officers whose position and role are not clear to me. During this "inspection" we are ordered to stand firmly to attention — head up, eyes looking straight ahead, chin in, shoulders back, stomach in, knees together, feet at a "five to one" angle with the tip of our rifle touching the edge of the toecap of our right boot. Holding this position, it is not possible to see the progress the prince is making along our ranks. In the background the band is playing. I hold my "at attention" position with my eyes remaining fixed straight ahead. After some time, I hear the sound of the inspection party and the prince's voice as he occasionally stops and has a word with one of the soldiers. At last, out of the corner of my eye, I see the prince himself. I hold my "attention" position as I've been trained. For a moment, the prince pauses as he reaches me. I wonder if he's going to speak to me. He does not. Then he moves on along the ranks and my chance of a royal word is gone!

Holding the "attention" position is tiring and I suppose all of us on parade are quite relieved when the prince finishes his tour of the ranks and returns to the dais in front of the parade. At last we are given the order to "stand at ease", then to "stand easy" — a much more relaxed position. The ceremony then continues with speeches from various dignitaries all of whom have played some part in the history of either the Berkshire or the Wiltshire regiments. I have no real understanding of all this background stuff, nor, I imagine, have most of my fellow soldiers on parade. Finally, the prince himself takes to the microphone. He compliments the CO on the high quality of the soldiers on parade (hmm, hmm, I'm proudly thinking!) and what an honour it is for him to be the first colonel-in-chief of the amalgamated regiment to be named after him. There is then the poignant moment when the prince presents the CO with the new regiment's first set of colours.

Now again, it's our turn. We have to perform the "advance in review order" drill we had been practising earlier. The band strikes up again. Then it's the CO who gives the orders. Firstly, he brings us back to "attention", next to "shoulder arms": then: "Parade will advance in review order, forward — MARCH!" This is it! I count the steps out loud enough for Nobby to hear: one-two-three-four-five-six-seven-eight-nine-ten-eleven-twelve-thirteen-fourteen- HALT! I think we've made it as I can hear the sound of all our boots coming to a halt in unison. I think there was a late shuffle somewhere on my left but it wasn't Nobby or me! On the fifteenth step, the band also halts playing abruptly, emphasising the precision of the movement. I think we all inwardly breath a sign of relief that we didn't fluff the moment. Then comes the order: "Royal salute — present arms". We've also practised this move and carry it out with snappy precision. Finally, we "march past" the royal dais giving an "eyes right" as we pass the prince who returns our salute. During this "march past" the band strikes up the tune of "To be a farmer's boy", which, we're told, has been adopted as the new regimental march. It has really catchy tune, easy to keep step to, so we all proudly march along to the beat and continue off the parade ground. And that's it — parade over!

After we've been dismissed from the parade, our Devizes group is again reformed and we troop off to the gymnasium, change back into our denims and hand over our rifles and "best uniforms" for separate transportation back to Le Marchant Barracks. We're then marched over to the cook house where a late lunch has been prepared, then it's back into our transport and the home journey back to Devizes.

I think we all have mixed reactions to today's events. As ever, there are the cynics amongst us who think the whole amalgamation rigmarole was a waste of time and money. They're right, I suppose, but, being completely honest, I find the day very impressive; we recruits had managed to mould into the squad of fully trained soldiers without letting our side down and it had been genuinely moving to have been part of the history of a newly formed regiment and to have participated in a parade in front of the husband of our queen. As we travel back to Devizes, I know I will never forget this day.

We're now into our eighth week and at last we've got to fire the rifles we've been training with for the past few weeks. We've stripped and reassembled them, cleaned and oiled them, spent hours learning to drill with them. But today, we're on the ranges at Salisbury Plain and are firing our rifles with live ammunition.

We were brought here by truck early this morning and we're told our range time has been booked for today and tonight. Sgt Beck and our Cpls Andrews, Warburton and Pitcher are all here but they all defer to two sergeants called Mitchell and Jenkins, who are specialists in range firing procedures. We're told they come from the School of Infantry, based at Warminster. The sergeants have given us a lecture on range safety and have made it very clear that we are to follow their instructions to the letter.

We start our live firing from the 100-yard point. In front of us are targets in the shape of an enemy figure. I think we all feel a buzz when we experience the kick of our SLR rifles as we squeeze the trigger to fire our first live rounds. Suddenly, all our training has a serious meaning. We are handling lethal weapons. Following our instructors' direction, we all fire the full twenty rounds from the rifle's magazine, show our instructors that the rifle breach is empty and made safe, then we move forward to inspect our targets to see how accurately we have fired. In the first session, most of us found our shots were erratic; one or two have hit on or near the "bull" in the centre of the target, but others were scattered around the outer rings or some shots had missed the target completely. Our instructors counsel each of us in term, explaining what we have done wrong and how to improve our accuracy.

We repeat the same exercise several times, learning to control our breathing, to feel more confident in holding the gun and gently squeezing the trigger, not snatching at it. Gradually, throughout the day, our accuracy improves. When they are satisfied by this phase, our instructors show us how to "zero" our guns to maximise their accuracy relative to our individual firing characteristics. As the day continues, we move back to the 200 yard point, then again to both the 300 and 400 yards firing points, again checking the results of each set of firing sequences.

Later in the day, we each have a turn at firing the Bren gun, the light machine gun much beloved of our Sgt Beck. We start by firing single shots, then bursts of two or three rounds, finally a burst of rapid fire. We soon realise how accurate and effective the Bren gun is and its importance as an integral weapon in an infantry formation.

We're staying on the range throughout tonight and as the darkness finally arrives on this mid-June day, our instructors organise a firing demonstration including a mix of normal and tracer rounds. They explain how effective tracer can be in indicating and highlighting enemy targets, particularly at night.

It is now fully dark. We are now required to fire our weapons while moving slowly forward between the 300 and 400 firing points. Our instructors control the safely of this exercise very tightly. Next to me is Rik Parfitt who has been told to carry and fire the Bren gun. Rik can sometimes be his own worst enemy and a couple of times earlier during the day had been showing off and pretending to aim his gun as if he was in some American war movie. Each time the instructors shouted at him to stop and to follow the correct safety procedures. Now Rik is at it again. He is supposed to keep in line with the rest of our squad but instead he goes on ahead and fires off a rapid burst with his Bren. Immediately, Sgt Mitchell gives a loud blast on his whistle — a sign that we all are to stop where we are and unload our weapons. Sgt Mitchell shouts out to Rik:

"Right, you with the Bren, what's your name?"

Rik realises he's in trouble and sensibly stands to attention and replies:

"Recruit Parfitt, sergeant."

"OK, Parfitt, I could have you arrested and put in closed detention for your behaviour there. You need to learn that you're handling a lethal weapon and to treat it with respect!"

Sgt Mitchell then tells the rest of our squad to keep our positions and then orders Rik to strip down the Bren and lay out all the individual parts on his groundsheet and report when he has finished. Rik complies and reports back to Sgt Mitchell who comes over with his torch to check that the gun is fully stripped down. Then he tells Rik:

"Right, smart ass, now reassemble your gun and report again when complete. You've got three minutes. Go!" Sgt Mitchell turns off his torch and moves away.

I am still standing next to Rik and, although it's pitch-black, I can tell he's struggling and nervous. I kneel down next to him and can tell he's not even reassembled the breach mechanism let alone refitted the barrel. This is a procedure we practised many times with Sgt Beck. It's no big deal but it seems that Rik hadn't been paying enough attention. I push him aside and get all the parts reassembled correctly then pull him back in front of the gun and whisper to him to report back to Sgt Mitchell. Rik calls out:

"Bren reassembled, sergeant!"

Sgt Mitchell comes back to Rik's position, turns on his torch and inspects "Rik's" work. When he's satisfied that the gun is correctly reassembled, he tells Rik to watch his step, in future. That's all. We now carry on with our training exercise.

We're now back in our barracks after the range training. Rik singles me out and asks:

"Back there on the range, you knew I was in the shit with the Bren. Why did you fix it for me? I always thought you didn't like me and Darrell."

I tell him: "Well Rik, we've all been together now for seven weeks. We have to help each other out. We're a team, aren't we?"

Later, I ask myself the same question. Rik is a bully and pain in the backside. It would have served him right to have been disciplined for arsing about on the range. Why did I help him? I have no answer. Perhaps I'm learning.

The next day, we're given a lecture by Lt Fleming. Subject: British Army operations overseas. The lieutenant gives us a summary of all the countries and war zones that our British forces have been involved in since the end of the Second World War until now. He tells us about the continuing stationing of garrisons in Germany. He gives a résumé of our heavy commitment and sacrifices in the Korean War and of our not so glorious involvement in Suez three years ago. He continues:

"Today, our forces are still pretty stretched. We, the Royal Hampshires, will shortly be heading for the West Indies as you've already been told. We're looking forward to that but, be under no illusions, there's a job to be done there and it's likely we'll be seeing some action, particularly those going to Jamaica. But you must realise that the British Army is still heavily committed in other parts of the world. In Cyprus, our operations have been principally against the Greek-Cypriot EOKA. This has already cost nearly four hundred British soldiers' lives, but hopefully our commitment there will reduce with Cyprus independence this year. In Aden, we still have many troops deployed with still no sign of a political solution and so far, some 150 British soldiers have been killed. Our troops are also engaged in Kenya where for some years we've been in operations against the Mau Mau. In Malaya, we are optimistic that we are at last winning the war against communist terrorism. It has been a long slog there since the emergency began in 1948.

"The main reason I choose to highlight these operations is for you all to understand there is a real purpose to your training and to your instructors' insistence that you fully master all the skills of being a trained infantry soldier. It's for the future protection and safety of yourself and your fellow soldiers. You have just completed your first full day of live firing on the range. I hope you now appreciate how vital it is that you are totally skilled in all the aspects of your training here — your fitness, your cohesion and morale, your weapon handling. As national service soldiers, you continue to be an essential asset to the defence and security in our national interests around the world."

I find I'm quite fired up by the lieutenant's lecture. It's all beginning to come together. All our square bashing, discipline and following orders now seems to have a real purpose. I begin to understand what it's all about. We need to be ready, to be fit and to contribute to all the amazing sacrifices that our predecessors have given in the service of our country. I feel quite humbled and I'm now beginning to regret helping Rik to reassemble his Bren gun. At the time, I thought I was being kind to help him out. Now I think I was wrong.

Chapter Seven

It's Wednesday, the day following our live firing day on the range. After Lt Fleming's lecture, we're back on the parade square back in Devizes. We're to be given some important news. CSM Willis calls us all to attention and turns to salute a senior officer who has come to address us. I recognise him as the major in command of the company we reinforced at the amalgamation parade on the Isle of Wight last week. We are ordered to "stand at ease", then to "stand easy". The major then says:

"You may remember me from the Isle of Wight parade. My name is Major Stone and I've just been sent here to Devizes to replace Major Dickson as your commanding officer. Over the next few weeks, I will get to know you all much better as you reach the end of your basic training and get ready to join your regiment, the Royal Hampshires, in preparation for their tour of the West Indies. For now, I congratulate you all on how well you did at the Isle of Wight parade — and, of course, this is also a compliment to your instructors, CSM Willis, Sgt Beck and the rest of the training staff. Subject to your passing a drill test, to be judged by CSM Willis, I am authorising that you may take a twenty-four-hour pass to leave the barracks during this coming week-end."

Major Stone's comments instantly create a buzz of excitement amongst us as this will be the first time, we might get to leave the barracks on our own since we first arrived here seven weeks ago! CSM Willis shouts out, "Quiet in the ranks" then brings us back to attention. He salutes Major Stone who is now leaving the parade square. CSM Willis then says: "About Saturday, this is the score. You will be given a twenty-four-hour pass, as the major has told you, but on two conditions. One, you will all be individually tested on a short drill procedure. Two, those who pass the test will be allowed out of barracks on the strict order that you will continue to wear your uniform in public at all times."

He continues, "Now, about the drill test. This will be held on the square on Saturday morning — time to be decided. You will wear your best uniform and boots. When your name is called, you will individually march onto the square, then march smartly to the centre where Major Stone and I will be standing. You will come to a halt one pace in front of the major, you will salute, give your army number and name, salute again, then take one pace backwards, about turn and march off the square. I will be judging your performance and will advise the major who has passed and may be granted the twenty-four hours out of barracks and who has failed. Those who fail will remain in barracks for the whole weekend. Any questions? — No? OK, carry on Sgt Beck!" After we've been dismissed, the weekend pass possibility dominates our conversation.

It's now Friday evening and we've been dismissed from our last parade of the day. Right now, like most of our free time since learning about the chance of a twenty-four-hour pass, this subject has dominated our conversation. Most of us seem pretty confident about the quality of our marching and drill. What's worrying a lot of our guys is remembering the army number we were given during our initial induction at the QM stores on Day One. The number has been embossed on the "dog tags" we wear round our necks at all times. They consist of eight numbers and CSM Willis has made it very clear that if we don't shout out these numbers correctly, we'll have blown our chance of freedom at the weekend.

Now, we are doing another practice in our barrack room and for some reason I seem to be the one chosen to test the others. My number is: 23636241. I find there's a sort of rhythm to it: 23.63 seems to stick easily then the 62.41 follows. I'm pretty sure I've got it. We've compared numbers and find that everyone has the same six number start: 236362 I suppose because we are all from the same intake. After that everyone has a different ending. We rehearse the numbers together and I make up a little lilting song as we all say together: 2363 dah dah 62. Seems to be no problem there and everyone is in sync. Then we have the last two numbers which are individual to each of us. I try to test each of our guys separately on their own last two digits. Darrell has been one of the keenest to get the procedure right and even got me to blast off a quick note to his Tracey to meet him on Saturday night. His chum Rik is also taking his preparations seriously and seems to have got his number sorted as have Chalky White and Keith Hignett, my two nearest bed-space neighbours.

It's Saturday morning and we're all lined up along the edge of the parade square. CSM Willis is calling us out in alphabetical order. Clive Allen goes first and seems to be OK but we can't hear exactly what is said from this distance to the middle of the square. Kevin Barrow is called next and I get myself ready as my name as a "C" is next in the alphabet.

"Chambers!" bellows out CSM Willis. I reply "Sir!" as I come to attention then set off towards the middle of the square. I come to a halt one pace in front of Major Stone as we've been instructed. I salute him then shout out "23636241 Recruit Chambers, sir!" Major Stone returns the salute and says, "Carry on Chambers." I salute him again, about turn and march back to my position on the edge of the square. I'm thinking to myself, "That was pretty straightforward. Let's hope we all pass and can get home as we've been promised."

It takes the best part of an hour for each individual to perform his march-on procedure, Chalky White being the last to be called. Then we all wait while our performances are confirmed. At last, Major Stone leaves the parade ground and CSM Willis comes over to us. We can tell he is not pleased.

"Right, listen in" he begins, "On the whole, that was pathetic. The marching was average but far too many of you fucked up your regimental numbers. You've been told many times that it is essential for you to remember them. As a result, the only personnel to have passed are, "Allen, Chambers, Parfitt and White. You four can report to admin and collect your train warrants. The rest are denied any home visits this weekend. That's all. Now fall out!"

Only four have passed! Of course, I'm pleased to have got through but it would have been so much better if all of us had done so. I can imagine the effect on our squad morale this will have. I also fear for what state my kit will be in when I get back. Then there's Darrell. He failed but his big mate, Rik Parfitt passed! And I imagine poor Tracey waiting in vain for Darrell to turn up! I can't help feeling that it would have been better to have failed myself — just for our squad cohesion.

I have a word with Darrell and tell him that when I get out and can find a phone, I'll call his girlfriend and tell her he can't now come. I also tell him to ensure he protects my kit while I'm away — or else no more letters. Darrell says OK but I'm not a hundred per cent sure I can trust him.

Frankly, my first day of freedom turns out to be a big disappointment. As soon as I'm allowed out of the barracks, I find a phone box and ring my mother to tell her I'm coming home. She sounds pleased, of course, but tells me my father is away. Next, I call Tracey, Darrell's girlfriend, and tell her the bad news. She doesn't sound too disappointed. I then turn up at Devizes station, exchange my free travel warrant for a return ticket to Bath Spa station and head for home.

It's my first night of "freedom" but it feels strange to be back in my own bed at our home in Saltford after seven weeks away. I can't sleep. It's the same mattress as I've slept on for years but it seems far too soft after the army metal framed bed and thin paillasse mattress that I've now got used to. After I'd got the number thirty-three bus from Bath back to Saltford, I spent a couple of hours talking to my mother. She was as supportive and interested as ever but, somehow, I found it difficult to describe adequately the army life I am now living. I'm now in such a different world from the one I left eight weeks ago. Later this evening, it was even worse when I went out to my local village pub. It had been impressed on us that it was mandatory to wear our uniform at all times we were out of the house and I didn't dare to disobey. Johnny Fisher was there as were a lot of my chums from the village. I don't know what I had been expecting, perhaps a fulsome reunion as I was welcomed back into the fold of our village life. It didn't happen like that. Yes, everyone seemed to be pleased to see me again but also, they sort of distanced themselves from my new image — short haircut, military uniform, precise creases in my trousers, shiny black boots. It seemed to put a psychological barrier between us. We had a couple of rounds of beer together — I had no money to buy another — but the normal relaxed friendliness I had always known with these guys was missing. It was as if I had become another being. I was now part of an institution, no longer the free individual I was before. After an hour or so, I made the excuse that I had to leave early next morning and said my goodbyes to my village chums. I walked home feeling strangely empty.

As I lie here in my own bed, I wonder what the fuck is going on. I feel confused and mixed up. I've only been away eight weeks yet already I feel somehow different. I try to rationalise my thoughts. In eight short weeks, the military system has taken over my life — everything I own and wear is now military property. The discipline, the marching, our whole existence has been part of a regime that is all consuming. I have always had an independent side to my nature and I thought I could preserve that throughout the basic training. Now I don't know anymore. And the amazing thing is that I feel content with this type of benign indoctrination. I'm fitter than I've ever been. I feel part of an organisation that is efficient and knows what it's doing. Suddenly it's my village chums who seem passé. I feel in some way I've now outgrown that life. Now I'm thinking about all my new colleagues from our barrack room. I regret that we had to be separated today because of this stupid drill test. I'm uncomfortable to be here while the vast majority are still back in barracks. I miss not being there with them.

The next day, I spend a long slow breakfast with my mother. I tell her about all the practical things we have been taught as part of our basic training. I don't tell her about my confused thoughts from last night. I don't think she'd fully understand. I don't think I understand myself.

I catch an earlier train than is necessary from Bath back to Devizes and get back to the barracks in time for Sunday lunch in the cookhouse. Everyone asks me if I enjoyed my day of freedom. I don't know how to tell them that I felt awkward and out of place. So I just say it was great and leave it at that. I tell Darrell that I squared it with his girlfriend. He seems relieved. I had been worried that the lads would have messed up my kit while I was away. But no, everything is present and stacked in the tidy pile I left it yesterday. Perhaps Darrell had seen to that.

Chapter Eight

At last, we're now in our twelfth and final week of recruit training. Major Stone and our platoon commander, Lt Fleming, have become much more involved in our training and judging our performance than during the initial few weeks. They've given us lectures about the regiment we are soon to join, its composition, it's history, its battle honours. We've also been called out for one-to-one interviews with one of these officers. I was told to see Major Stone and was surprised by the detailed questions he asked about my background. I found the major to be an intelligent and perceptive officer and enjoyed talking to him. I felt relaxed with him and forgot all about my stammer.

Since we started here at Devizes nearly twelve weeks ago, no one has dropped out through illness or injury despite all the strenuous physical work we've done. We're all much fitter than when we started, not just in marching and running but in upper body strength through the time we've put in on the obstacle course. I've noticed that the barrack room bullying seems to have stopped. Darrell and Rik are the same characters, of course, but both seem to have settled down and are no longer always wanting to throw their weight around. There's a cohesion about our work. Our drill is now smart, sharp and together. The accuracy of our shooting on the range has improved significantly since the early range days and most of us are now shooting to "Marksman" grade with both our SLR rifles and the Bren Gun.

Our barrack room is now always kept neat and tidy. No one needs to be told what to do. No one turns up late for parades anymore. We all know that we are approaching the end of this phase of our training. We still have our jokers in the squad and still the same "barrack room lawyers", but overall there's a sense of achievement that together we have successfully come through a tough transformation from being a disparate, motley group of eighteen-year-old civilians to becoming a group of fit, smart young soldiers. We are now part of a well drilled team. We share the common value of what we have achieved. There is one word that now best describes our feelings — a word that perhaps none of us would have thought remotely possible twelve weeks ago. And this is it. We have a sense of pride — in ourselves and in the regiment we are soon to join.

During this last week here, there is a feeling of excitement as we prepare for our recruit passing out parade. The parade won't be as grand an affair as the amalgamation parade held in the Isle of Wight. We don't have a band to march to, for a start. And there will be no stands for VIP visitors, although written invitations have been sent out to our parents/partners. I told my mother not to bother to attend. I don't know why. We're told we will carry out a series of drill moves on the square and will be inspected by a lieutenant colonel from the Royal Hampshire Regiment. We will then be granted a few days home leave before joining the regiment directly in Lemgo, Germany or in the UK transit facility. We are told that the regiment is due to leave Lemgo in November and will then spend three months in UK before sailing to the West Indies from Southampton in early February.

It's our final day here, Thursday 23 July 1959. We've cleaned out our barrack room for the last time and our kit is packed ready for our home leave. We are now still on the parade square having just completed our prepared passing out marching drills. The inspecting officer now passes through our ranks and each one of us is presented with a Royal Hampshire hat badge, signifying that we are now trained soldiers and members of the Regiment. From now on we are no longer to be called "recruits".

After the parade, we march down to the armoury and check in our rifles; then CSM Willis tells us to fall in again for an address by Lt Fleming, our platoon commander. The lieutenant tells us to stand easy, then he says,

"Firstly, I want to congratulate each one of you for your smartness on parade today. But much more than that I want to say how proud I am to have been your platoon commander for the past twelve weeks and how impressed I've been by all the hard work you have put in during that time. I know that you are not volunteers for the army and that for some it has been difficult to adjust from your civilian lives. All I can say is that the hard slog of initial training is now behind you and you will soon be joining our regiment as we sail for the West Indies early next year. I know we will be in for a demanding time over there but it should also be exciting and worthwhile for all ranks."

The lieutenant then tells us that, after our four days' home leave, we are to return to duty in one of two locations. He then reads out the names of those who are to go to Lemgo, Germany, to join the regiment there. He says travel warrants have been issued and personnel will travel as a group to Lemgo next week. I note my name is not included. Then he reads the list of those who will remain in a transit area in UK on preparation duties prior to the whole regiment sailing from Southampton next February. Again, my name is not included. He ends by saying:

"I have one further announcement to make before you will be dismissed and begin your leave. Having consulted your training staff, I have the authority to promote two of you to the rank of lance corporal. These are Privates Wight and Jackson. Congratulations to you both. LCpl Wight will be in charge of the group going to Lemgo."

I'm pleased for these guys — Chalky Wight particularly — as he has become a good friend during our training and I know how hard he's worked during our twelve weeks here. I don't know Gary Jackson well as he's been in the other barrack room but he seems a good guy as well. However, I have to wonder why my name has not been called at all: but then, finally, Lt Fleming says:

"Oh, and one last thing. Private Chambers is to report to Major Stone soonest. Now carry on, sergeant-major."

I'm asking myself what is going on. Why have I not been given a future posting location and why have I got to report to the major? We are now dismissed by CSM Willis. There's a general buzz of conversation as farewells are being said by some and "see you in four days" by others. I can't join in as I don't know what my future is to be.

I can't see Major Stone about but I'm told he's in his office in the headquarter building. I haven't been in this building before and it takes me a while to find his office. I knock on the door and he calls for me to come in. I walk in, salute and stand to attention in front of his desk. He tells me to stand at ease, then says:

"OK Chambers, this is the score. You're not going to join the regiment with the rest of the squad — at least not yet. We've been looking at your record and the way you've been conducting yourself during the basic training. We've decided you are 'officer material' and we've applied for you to attend the next War Office Selection Board or WOSB as it's called. This will be at the end of this month or early August. You will be notified of the details. Until then you will be given other duties here in Le Marchant Barracks. Of course, you may not pass the WOSB but you must give it your best shot. If you do pass, you will be sent for officer training at Mons Officer Cadet school in Aldershot and, again, if you pass that, then you will re-join the regiment as a second lieutenant. So well done Chambers and good luck!"

I salute and march out of the major's office. My head is in a whirl as this new development is completely unexpected. I had not the slightest idea that I might become an officer. I've been comfortable with the recruit training and have been looking forward to the whole West Indies experience serving alongside the guys I've got to know so well during the past weeks. I really don't know anything about being an officer and I don't even know if I want to be one. I know I've got to complete two years of military service. What difference does it make what rank I have? In many ways I think I'd prefer to remain a private soldier like most of my mates from our training here in Devizes. Now I've got to hang around here while I'm waiting for this selection business, whatever that entails.

By the time I get back to the barrack room, its deserted. All the guys have gone, some heading for the station, others have arranged to be picked up by parents or friends. I collect my packed kit bag and head for Devizes station with my travel warrant for Bath Spa station. There's no sign of any of my chums. They must have got earlier trains to their home destinations or left with their parents or partners. Because of my interview with Major Stone, I didn't even get to say goodbye to them. I wonder when or if I'll catch up with them again.

I don't know what job they will give me when I get back to Devizes to wait for my WOSB selection. I hope it wouldn't be in the Quartermaster's Store issuing out kit to the next lot of recruits. After my four days' home leave, I report in to the headquarters at Le Marchant Barracks and ask what I am supposed to do. I am told I am to report to

RSM Holland. The RSM is the most senior of the non-commissioned officers, a post senior even to our CSM Willis. The RSM is, in effect, the head of discipline — the most feared and/or respected individual in the whole of Le Marchant Barracks.

I find the RSM's office, tap on his door and wait to be called. I stand to attention in front of him but do not salute — I now know that we only salute commissioned officers. RSM Holland has a formidable reputation. He is a tall man with an imposing presence. His uniform is immaculate and his deportment ramrod straight. I wait in some trepidation in front of him. To my surprise, he is quite benign. He says:

"Ah, Chambers, I heard you were in limbo while you await the WOSB. I'm told you're a bright lad so I've decided to make you my clerk. There's a lot of paperwork to be sorted. You can get stuck into that. My office also issues out all our guard and other duty rosters so you can look after those as well. You can start right now. I have other duties so I'll leave you to it." That is all he says as he gets up and marches out of his office

It takes me a while to adjust. Sort out his paperwork. Do the guard rosters. I look around the office and see that it's a real mess. Papers strewn around his desk, some typed, some handwritten notes. No clear filing system. Where do I start?

I've now been the RSM's clerk for three weeks. I've learnt a lot. First, the RSM has an immaculate outward presence but is fucking useless at administration. It's taken me all this time to get some sort of order to his files and general admin. I can tell that he's an outdoor soldier, his strengths lie in man management and leadership in the field. In the office, he's lost. During our time together, I've tried discretely to tidy up his office affairs and introduce a simple but effective filing system. There are no longer papers strewn all over the place but all are either on named clipboards, filed away or destroyed. His office is now as neat and tidy as his uniform. He hasn't actually said anything but I can tell he's pleased and relieved that his office is now in order.

I've also learnt that my temporary post as the RSM's clerk gives me unexpected power. I'm now working out the rosters for guard and other duties including who is to be on guard over the weekend. I issue these rosters under the RSM's signature and authority. I'm now being approached everyday by someone who has a special request — "Chambers, I need to get home this weekend, so can you please not put me on duty?" or "Chambers, I can't stand cleaning out the cook house. Can you swop me for the fire picket instead?" I'm still only a private soldier, but being the RSM's clerk has suddenly given me influence, way above my humble rank.

I've found this duty a good little niche job here that could suit me well for the rest of my two years' service and I'm not too chuffed when I get the notification that I am to attend the WOSB selection at Barton Stacey next week. I'm informed I am to report by 18.00 hours on Tuesday 18 August. The selection tests will last two full days and we will be told whether or not we've passed at the end of the process — on 20 August. If I should pass, I'm told there will be a demanding sixteen-week officers' training course at Aldershot. If I should fail, I'll carry on, at least for now, as the RSM's clerk. I'm not sure how hard I'll try to pass.

Chapter Nine

The last few days have been rather a blur. I tried to find out what goes on at the WOSB and what, if anything, I should be doing as preparation. My best source has been Lt Fleming. He told me of his own experiences at WOSB a year or so earlier. It all sounded like a weird mix of physical and academic tests for which it seems impossible to prepare. The lieutenant told me just to be myself and not try to bluff the selectors. He also advised me to beef up on current affairs — not so easy in Le Marchant Barracks. I've had access to only one TV in the barracks and that seemed to be tuned either to sports programmes or such epics as *Dixon of Dock Green*, *Opportunity Knocks* and *Crackerjack*. I don't reckon any of these would prepare me adequately for the WOSB! As far as newspapers were concerned, it's been difficult to find anything deeper than the *Daily Mirror* until Lt Fleming provided me with old copies of *The Times* and *The Daily Telegraph* when they were discarded by the officers' mess. I read these avidly so that I have some idea about what has been going on in the world during our incarceration here in Devizes.

So here I now am at the War Office Selection Board at Barton Stacey, near Andover. I managed to check in by the 18.00 hours deadline. It's Tuesday 18 August 1959. I travelled here in my battledress uniform and brought my denims and PT kit as instructed. I'm directed to the main reception office, where my identity is checked by a smart and fit-looking sergeant who issues me with a red bib type garment with the number twelve embossed on both the front and the back. The sergeant then directs me to a barrack room, allots me a bed-space and tells me to change into denims and PT shoes. He says that I must wear the "number twelve" bib at all times. It all seems very strange. I begin to relax when I meet up with other guys who are also checking in. We're all in the same boat. We realise we're under constant observation by the selection staff, hence the individual numbers on our bibs. I suppose even how we just walk around — important to walk straight, not slouch or have our hands in our pocket

— is all part of a comprehensive review of our suitability to be an officer.

Before the first official briefing, the sergeant reappears and leads us to a mess hall for a light supper. Here we find that members of staff, mostly captains or sergeants, are interspersed with us candidates so that even how we hold our cutlery seems to be noted. I even find a captain has accompanied me when I go for a pee. I'm not sure what notes he makes of my urinary performance there!

After supper, we're required to assemble in a small conference room. There are some twenty-odd of us all duly wearing our bibs. We jump up and stand to attention when a group of officers enter the room. At their head is a senior officer who says:

"Gentlemen, be seated." He pauses while we sit back down on the wooden chairs provided. He continues. "During the next two days, my staff and I will be assessing each of you to determine whether or not you have the potential to be officers in the British army. We will be giving each of you a number of tests — some to check your mental and speaking capabilities, others to see how you perform in academic and psychological assessments, then others in both collective and individual physical tests. At the end of this programme, my staff and I will decide who will go forward for officer training and who will return to your present duties with your regiments. Should you pass, you will shortly be posted to Mons Officer cadet training school in Aldershot. Should you fail, you can be proud that your regiments have felt you fit enough to recommend you to my board. Right, I wish all of you good luck. Do your best and we will see how each of you performs."

The officer, whose rank flashes show him to be a brigadier, then turns and leaves the room. We all stand up to attention again and wonder what is going to happen next. Another officer, with a major's rank badges, then tells us to retire to our beds in the barrack room and get some sleep. He says we will be woken in the morning with instructions for the tests that will follow.

We've been told that the next day will be busy: that is an understatement! After breakfast, the major we met last evening divides us into three groups of eight and tells us we'll remain in these same groups for the duration of the selection tests. I find that I've been put into the same group as numbers 9 to 16, a couple of the guys I had been chatting to last evening and who seem to have a similar background to my own. That gives some comfort. I've not met the other five guys before.

An officer, who introduces himself as Capt Shields, tells us he is the director of our group for the first phase of our tests. He is a rather studious-looking man with spectacles. His shoulder flashes read "Royal Army Education Corps". Capt Shields leads us to a classroom-type room, which is furnished with desks, paper and pens. He makes a few introductory remarks then starts us off with a series of written tests. First, we're given a page on which is written a number of subject headings, I think about six in all. The subjects are all totally different. For example: one subject is "Your favourite sport", another is "Your last holiday" and yet another is "General de Gaulle". Capt Shields tells us to write short one-page essays on each of the subjects and gives us one and a half hours to complete this test. I really don't know quite how to handle this project but I see those around me are starting to scribble away so I do the same. I don't remember what I write, mostly gibberish I suspect, but at least I fill the required one page on each subject and finish just in the allotted time.

We're then given a short "leg stretch" break before returning to our desks. Capt Shields then gives each of us a set of indistinct photos and tells us to write a paragraph on the idea they convey. I haven't got a clue what some of these pictures are about so I just put down the first thought that comes into my head. I suppose this exercise is part of what the brigadier had called psychological tests. I have no idea how I'll be judged by what I've written.

The final written part is referred to by Capt Shields as "numerical reasoning". It includes some arithmetical questions, some involving percentages and charts and, finally, some puzzling shapes that have to be pieced together like a jigsaw. Maths has never been my strong point and I make heavy weather of this section and can't even finish fitting the jigsaw shapes together. I'm sure I've failed this section. All these tests take us up to lunchtime.

We spend the afternoon out of doors tackling what are called "command tasks". We form up in front of a set of iron scaffolding, much of which is painted red. In front of it is a large sand-filled wooden crate.

It looks heavy. Our group director for this phase is a very fit-looking guy from the Army Physical Training Corps. He's dressed in a white T-shirt, blue trainer trousers and PT shoes He introduces himself as Sgt McKay. He tells us to gather round him then he says:

"Right listen carefully. Your first task, as a group, is to take that sand-filled wooden crate over the iron scaffolding obstacle in front of you and on to a marked point beyond the obstacle. You have to start behind that line which, as you see, is a good yard from the scaffolding You will see that the scaffolding itself is mostly painted in red. The key point is that you are not allowed to touch the ground either side of these lines or, and this is crucial, any part of the scaffolding that is painted red. Your challenge is to work out a system or technique which will ensure that all your group with the crate are able to climb over the scaffolding and beyond the far line within the rules I've explained. If you do touch either the ground or the red painted parts of the scaffolding, I will stop you and you'll have to return to the beginning and start again. Now sort yourselves out. You've got half an hour from now!"

We realise that what at first seems an easy exercise is, in fact, very complicated and will take careful planning, coordination and execution to achieve within the rules laid down. A variety of ideas are floated then dismissed. Then one of our group decides this is his moment to show his leadership skills. He nominates himself spokesman and leader and starts to organise the rest of us. I don't know the guy's name, only to call him "number ten" as per the number in his bib. I don't much take to him because he seems rather snotty and brash. OK, so he wants to be the leader for this task but I think he's got the wrong approach as he's nominated only one of our group to carry the crate. I don't think that's feasible due to its weight and awkward shape. In my opinion, the crate needs to be manhandled by several of our group as we form a human chain over the obstacle. I tell that to number ten but he insists on his method, so fine, I join the rest of our group in trying our best to support him and follow his instructions. We get the crate midway up the scaffolding when its weight and shape become too much for the guy tasked to carry it. He slips, steadies himself by clutching onto a red painted portion of the scaffolding and the crate crashes to the ground. Sgt McKay immediately blows his whistle and calls out:

"Stop! That's a foul! Now, all of you get back behind the line and start again."

I think all of us, except perhaps number ten, have learnt from this — take your time, don't rush to push yourself forward, work out a plan that involves using all the team in a coordinated way and making use of any other equipment that we can legally use. Then and only then, put forward your idea and get agreement from the rest of the group before putting the plan into action. I know we should all be helping each other but I, and by their gestures, the rest of the group feel rather smug that number ten has fucked it up!

Our next effort at the crate-carrying exercise is much better! Six of us climb up onto the "safe" part of the scaffolding, then the two remaining on the ground pass the crate up to two perched on the lowest rungs. The crate is then passed to the next two of our group who are at the top of the scaffolding while the remaining two, climb down the other side and jump out over the final marked point. From there, they are in a position to support the crate when it is lowered down to them. Finally, the rest of our group scramble over the non-red parts of the scaffolding and jump down beyond the final marked point — so the crate and the group are all safely beyond the far marked point without touching red or the ground.

Sgt McKay again blows his whistle and this time he judges that our task has been successfully completed. We see he's writing a lot on his millboard. Except for number ten, we're all quite chuffed with ourselves.

We're not done yet — far from it! Sgt McKay moves us on to a fresh area where we are again faced with another "command task" obstacle. It's similar in nature to the first crate-carrying test but the layout is different and this time we need to transport heavy logs over the obstacle. After the first test, we take our time in analysing how best to achieve our mission and our group works much better as a team in reaching our solution.

Sgt McKay gives us several such tests throughout the afternoon where we are required to work out our solution as a group activity, then the rules change again. The sergeant tells us:

"Right, up till now, you've had to work out amongst yourselves how to complete each task. We're now going do some more of these tests but this time I'm going to nominate one leader. The rest of you may offer him suggestions but it will be his decision what system he uses to achieve the task. Right, number nine. You're the leader for the next task. Over to you!"

The guy wearing the number nine bib realises this is his big moment. He gets the rest of us together and we all consider the task and how it can best be overcome. He then asks for our views and we all chip in. Having listened to us all and found there is a good degree of consistency, number nine calmly makes his decision, outlines his plan and gives each of us a specific role. We all fall in behind the lead he has taken and between us we complete the task successfully. Personally, I'm impressed by number nine's approach and determine to adopt that style when my turn comes to be the nominated leader. To be honest, I'm enjoying this activity as it combines using both reasoning and physical abilities.

Number ten, the guy who had earlier rushed to try to prove himself a leader, seems also to have learnt that leadership is as much above listening as talking and when his turn comes as nominated leader, he does quite well, although, again, he can't seem to resist his impulse to boss the rest of us around. Perhaps I am just lucky but when my turn comes to be the leader, I find it quite easy to work out the best approach. After listening to other's views, I explain my intended plan to the rest of our group and they all agree. In this case, it involves carrying a number of poles and jerry cans over the obstacle. We get all the required material and ourselves over in one piece, without touching red or the ground and in pretty good time. I see Sgt McKay writing his notes and feel it went OK.

Chapter Ten

We're all pretty knackered after these "command tasks", which have occupied all afternoon. We were lucky that the weather was dry as they would have been much tougher if it had rained. We'd been rotating the obstacles with the other two groups but now we all join back together for our evening meal in the mess hall. I think everyone is pleased that the "command task" phase is now completed. The meals we had last evening and at breakfast today were taken in near silence as we were all nervous and apprehensive. Now the atmosphere is much more relaxed. We're no longer so conscious of being judged all the time.

After our meal, there's no free time. We're told to collect, in the same groups, in a series of smallish rooms laid out, not with desks and hard chairs, but with comfortable chairs arranged in a semi-circle. We're told to take a seat and wait there. Shortly after, an officer with a major's crown insignia on his uniform, enters and takes a chair facing us.

"OK guys," he says. "We're now going to have a discussion. I will introduce a few subjects and I want you to give me your thoughts about these. To get us going, I'll nominate one of you to start off but, as we proceed, do feel free to chip in with your own views. Relax and just speak your mind as you choose."

The major then turns to bib number fifteen, a rather scholarly looking guy who, frankly, hadn't excelled when he was leader on his "command task". He'd been very hesitant in his approach there. "Right you can set the ball rolling. What are your views about what is being referred to as the "space race"?

"Blimey!" I'm thinking, "Glad he didn't ask me. I think I've read something about it in one of Lt Fleming's cast-off newspapers but I'd really show my ignorance if I'm asked my views about that subject"

However, number fifteen seems quite at ease. He says, "Well, sir, looks like there's going to be quite a race between the Americans and the Soviets as to who gets the first manned space flight. The Sovs notched up the first victory when they launched their artificial satellite called

Sputnik into the Earth's orbit a couple of years ago. Since then, it looks as if the Americans are catching up fast."

"How come?" says the Major. He looks round the room and his gaze fastens on bib number thirteen. "What's your view?"

Number thirteen gives a pretty good answer, He says, "Well this year NASA, that's the American National Aeronautics and Space Administration, introduced the first human astronauts to the world's press. I understand that NASA is dedicated to beating the Sovs to manned space flight. At present, I believe they're carrying out an astronaut selection procedure in Albuquerque."

Then bib number ten interrupts. He says, "You're right that the initial selection was in Albuquerque but it's now been moved to the Wright Aeromedical Laboratory in Dayton. Ohio. I understand there are about thirty potential astronauts left. Meanwhile, the Sovs have themselves not been hanging around and also preparing to put a man into space. That could be as soon as the next year or so."

Phew! I'm impressed with these guys' knowledge except I can't help feeling that good old number ten is trying again to show how clever he is — or he thinks he is. But from my side, I realise I can't just keep quiet all the time or I'll definitely be losing points in the officer selection process. I try to remember the subjects I had read up on — the space programme was not one of them.

The major then widens the discussion by saying. "Let's stick to world affairs. Would any of the rest of you like to raise a subject?"

I think it's time to open my mouth. I remember reading in the press about Nixon's visit to the Soviet Union a couple of months ago. Seems like a good topical subject.

I say, "While we're talking about the Americans and the Sovs, I was interested in the visit in July by Vice President Richard Nixon to the Soviet Union and his discussions with Nikita Khrushchev, which the press labelled the "kitchen debate". The talks were held behind closed doors and each side was coy about the details but I do think it's a good thing that the two major superpowers are at least talking to each other."

I'm glad when bib number eleven chirps up beside me, talking about the Soviet forces arriving in Afghanistan earlier this year, as I've just about said all I know about this subject. Number eleven goes on to wonder if this is a start of a new push for Soviet global expansion.

Our "guided discussion" carries on for about a couple of hours with subjects including: the situation in Cyprus after the granting of its independence earlier this year and Archbishop Makarios' return to the island after three years, the resignation of Mao Zedong as Chairman of the People's Republic of China after the disastrous failure of "the Great Leap Forward", Castro's proclamation of a new Cuban constitution, and the swearing in of Lee Kuan Yew in Singapore and that island's remarkable economic achievements. I manage to contribute to some of this and I'm so relieved I'd read those cast-off newspapers in Devizes. I reckon, though, that the major can see through my shallow comprehension of world affairs but at least I don't sit there like a lemon or don't say anything too ridiculous.

At last the major winds things up and thanks us all for our contributions to the discussion. He then continues: "Right, now for something completely different! I'm going to give each of you a subject about which you will give a short talk. You will have one and a half hours this evening to prepare your talk. Paper and writing materials are available should you wish to use them. Your talk should relate solely to the subject you are given and will last not more than twenty minutes. You will be giving your talk after breakfast tomorrow morning."

The major then gives each of us a slip of paper with the subject written on it. I look at mine. It reads: "Your Home Town." That's all.

I just can't get to sleep. I'm worrying about tomorrow's talk. Not about the subject matter — that's easy. I'll be talking about Bath — my home town. I went to school there for seven years and know almost every street, square and back lane and alley of this beautiful city. I also know most of the main talking points of its Roman and Georgian history and culture. I can give pretty accurate dates about Bath's post Roman history, about the rebuilding of Bath Abbey, the founding of my own school in 1552 and the beauty of the Royal and Lansdown crescents that tower above the city. Last evening, I drew up my primary visual aids — the first had the bold heading: Bath Spa. Under this I wrote its Latin name *Aquae Sulis* (the waters of Sulis). On a separate sheet, I listed Bath's main features: the baths, the abbey, the crescents, the circus, Pulteney bridge, the Kennet and Avon canal and I intend to speak about each of these. I have almost too much information and during the evening I refined it down to what I reckon will fit my allotted twenty-minute slot.

It's certainly not the content of the talk about Bath that's bugging me and keeping me awake: it's my stammer! I seem to have got it quite well under control when I'm actively participating in something. For example, I wasn't even aware of stammering at all during the "command tasks". Even the discussion group went OK I think, because I wasn't conscious of the precise words I was going to use before joining in during the discussion group activity. But I find I have a big problem giving a structured pre-planned presentation that contains many words I find so difficult to get out. Even the title word: Bath. I have real angst over any word that starts with a "hard letter", for example the "B" in Bath, the "P" in Pulteney, the "K" in Kennet. I also struggle with "D" and "L". The trick I find that works best for me is this: when I know I'm about to have to use one of my bugbear words, I try to slide into it by joining a preposition or another lead-in word immediately in front of the hard letter word. For example, I try to say "in Bath", or "at Bath" by stressing the "in" or "at" and relegating the sound of the bugbear word as if it's a subordinate part of the "in" or "at" lead-in word.

I also have another technique. When I'm faced with a bugbear word, I do all I can to find a replacement or alternative word or phrase that means the same thing. This can be mentally tiring and doesn't always work. For example, how can I give a talk about Bath and not use that word? But at least searching for alternative words has given me a wide vocabulary of the English language!

It's also strange that, during my school days, I often acted in plays. I even got rave school revues for my interpretation of Edmund the Bastard in Shakespeare's King Lear. When acting, for some inexplicable reason, my stammer disappears. Also, when I sing. So now I'm trying to work out if I can act a bit when I give my Bath presentation tomorrow. In my restlessness, I'm trying to practise saying "in Bath" and "at Pulteney bridge" and also trying to work out how I might get into an acting mode without it appearing to be over the top. Not easy.

I know I'm not going to solve this issue tonight and that I need to be sharp tomorrow. It's not just the presentations. I know there's other tests still to come before the end of the selection process. Eventually, I can feel myself becoming drowsy and try to get off to sleep.

Wow, I made it! I've just finished my piece about Bath. I had been worried about this right up until the moment came. In our eight-man group, we listened to each other's presentations under the supervision of the same major who lead our discussion session last evening and with another couple of officers, captains I think, sitting in.

We were told to give our presentations in the numerical order on our bibs with number nine going first. He did a good job talking about his hometown of Sheffield — clear, informative and interesting. He brought his piece to a conclusion ending pretty much on the twenty-minute deadline. Next, number ten. As usual, he was in confident mood, you could say overconfident. He told us his home town was Henley-on-Thames. He had no written notes and had made no visual aids. He spent a few minutes talking about Henley, more about its annual regatta and even more about his school days in Eton, how many chums he had there and how well he did. He was still in full flow when the major interrupted him and told him he had run out of time. I could tell the invigilating officers were not impressed. Nor was I.

It's odd how mood matters. I could tell that number ten had totally misjudged the requirement of this test. Our invigilating officers couldn't give a stuff about how brilliant he thinks he is. What is required is a well-structured twenty-minute piece, sticking to the subject of "Your Home Town". Listening to number ten and watching the officers' reaction to it, gave me confidence to do my bit and overcome my speech impediment. Before my turn, Number eleven gave his presentation. This was OK but the guy mumbled a lot and I don't think he really knew many facts about his home town, Reading. But, though limited, at least he stuck to the subject and was on time.

I then heard the major say, "OK, number twelve. Now your turn, you've got twenty minutes, starting now!"

I had got up and stood in front of the group, picked up my paper headed "Bath Spa: *Aquae Sulis*" and got straight into it. I had started, "My subject is "a Bath" Spa and I'm lucky to have been brought up in such "a beautiful" city. No problems there. I had then got into my subject and used enthusiasm as a way of masking my fear of getting stuck on the hard letters. After the first few minutes, I had found I had nearly forgotten my stammering problems and was able to cover the headings I had drafted. I had rounded off with an offer to be tour guide "to Bath" to any of those present. I could see the major was looking at his watch and so I had used my final moments to thank everyone for their attention and returned to my seat.

That was it! I felt I had got through what for me was the most difficult task of the selection procedure. I'm sure the officers would have been aware of the hesitancy of my speech with some of the hard letters but I don't think it was any big deal! I sat through the remaining four other presentations with interest — 13, 14 and 16 were all OK but nothing special but the scholarly number fifteen gave a great exposition about his hometown, Leeds. The whole session had lasted over two hours. Time for a leg stretch and on to the next test.

After our break, we are called to different offices in the barracks for what is referred to as "individual interviews". In my case I find myself facing the same major again who had taken our earlier presentations. I learn his name is Clark. I think I'm in luck here because Major Clark tells me that Bath is one his favourite cities. We talk about Bath and my presentation. He had picked up on my stammer, hardly surprising, and he asks if I find it a major handicap in other aspects of my life. I tell him it's not generally a problem but I do get concerned about giving formal presentations. I'm relieved when he says,

"Don't worry, our last king, Winston Churchill and General Montgomery all suffered from speech impediments and managed their lives pretty well so you're in good company!"

This is quite a boost to my morale and I learn from this experience to try not to get too fussed about my stammer in future. The rest of our conversation went well. Of course, aged eighteen, I have hardly travelled at all so the range of our conversation is limited. However, I find that I like Major Clark well enough and feel quietly confident that our interview went OK.

After these interviews, our group is now told to change into our PT kit and prepare for our final test. This is to be an "individual obstacle course". We are taken out to another area of the barracks where Sgt

McKay is ready for us. He explains,

"Right, this is the score. I'm going to take you around the course and show you what you will have to do."

He's not kidding. Sgt McKay is an extremely fit man. While the rest of us look on, he demonstrates each of the obstacles. Another lesson here. Don't just tell soldiers what to do, show them! The obstacles are given letters. They are, A — a running jump to scale an eight-foot wall. B — climb a ramp and balance along a narrow pole then run down the ramp at the end. C — wriggle under a row of pegged out barbed wire. D — climb a scaffolding construction, jump out and cling onto a rope, then lower yourself to the ground. E — jump over a water filled obstacle approximately six feet wide. F — climb a five-yard rope ladder to a wooden trellis then slide back down to the ground. G — give a member of the staff (hopefully not one too porky!) a "fireman's lift" for twenty yards and finally, H — climb through an open aperture (or window) set into metal scaffolding without touching a line set a few feet in front of and behind the scaffolding.

There they are — eight obstacles in all. Sgt McKay demonstrates them and makes them all look easy. But the rest of us know they are not! I watch Sgt McKay's technique and try to remember how he tackles each obstacle. Some seem quite straightforward and not unlike the obstacles we did during our basic training at Devizes. But there are two that look real brutes. D looks a devil — we have to jump out to clutch onto the rope, which is positioned a good yard from the scaffolding, which itself is about fifteen feet high — if you miss it you're in for a hell of a drop! Then there's the last one, H. I see that Sergeant McKay takes a flying jump through the scaffolding "window" and does a forward roll at the other side. Oof! I don't know. I'm sure he's right but you have to be very fit (and daring) to do that.

We don't have a lot of time to think about it when we're called out individually to tackle the course. We're called out in our normal bib number sequence. We're lucky to have number nine as our trail blazer. His number is called and he's away. From our starting point, we can't see the end of the course so we don't know how our group members do on the last three obstacles. Our colleague number nine seems to be doing well. He's a good guy who seems to take everything in his stride. I watch him tackling obstacle D. He goes for it and jumps well out from the scaffolding and gets a good grip on the rope. He's fine with that. I switch attention to our number ten — the guy who has been a bit of a pain so far. But he's also doing well. He might be a bossy type of guy but he's certainly fit.

Number eleven is then told to start and off he goes. I then have to stop watching the others as it's my turn next. I decide, no matter what, I'm going to go for it. What the heck! I'm thinking that even if I fail the course, at least I'll have tried my best. I hear Sergeant McKay calling out:

"Number twelve. GO!"

That's it. I know my basic training at Devizes has toughened me up and produced muscles that I never before knew existed. I also realise that, apart from needing to have guys who are basically fit, the board is also challenging us to dare. OK, I'm up for it. I'm away!

Obstacles A, B and C are no problem — just like another session at Devizes. Now for obstacle D. I whip up the scaffolding construction in no time. Then I come face to face with the need to jump out for the rope. Go! OK I've got it. I lower myself down to the ground and keep on running to obstacle E. Over the water jump — also no problem. Onto F, up the rope ladder and down the other side. Got it, done it! On again to G, "fireman's lift". The guy I'm to carry is average weight but by now I'm so pumped up I just don't care. I push my shoulder into his tummy, lift him then we're off up the twenty-yard course. I don't treat him too gently but there you go! I've now got my sights on the eighth and last, obstacle H. I don't stop to think too much about it otherwise I might chicken out. I run up to the line in front of the scaffolding and, like I saw Sgt McKay demonstrate, I take a flying header into the metal "window". I just make it but whereas Sgt McKay landed with a neat forward roll, I land awkwardly in a tangled heap on the other side of the obstacle. I had bitten into my cheek and had jarred my knee. I don't care. I've completed the course.

Later, I find out that our number thirteen had fallen heavily at obstacle D and had to retire from the rest of the obstacles and poor old fifteen had struggled all the way through and needed medical attention when he nearly knocked himself out at obstacle H.

We are given a half an hour after the obstacle course to go back to our rooms, shower, change and pack up our kit. We then reassemble in the cookhouse where we meet up again with the other two groups. We're all pretty hungry by this time and get stuck into a solid lunch of beef stew.

Now we're all lined up in the main administrative hall wearing our battledress uniforms and with our kitbags ready to return to our units. It's been an experience I shall remember for the rest of my life. I've never been so tested and pushed before. With what purpose? Have I got what it takes to train to become a British Army officer? I have no idea but I, like the rest of us here, have been put through an extensive series of tests — academic, psychological and physical that will soon end in a judgement. We've been told we will be given the results before we leave. There are three alternatives. We either get a PASS, which means we will then go to officer training school in Aldershot, or a FAIL, which means we will return back to our original unit, in my case Devizes, or we will get a DEFERRED, which means the selection board feels we have the potential to pass but not yet and should reapply at a later stage.

We snap to attention as the brigadier, who had given us the opening address, arrives accompanied by his senior staff officers. On his command, we "stand at ease" then he says,

"Gentlemen, you have now reached the end of the selection course. My staff has been thorough in analysing your performance throughout the many varied tests you have undergone in the past couple of days. It's now time to give you the results. You can be assured that we have made our decision after much deliberation and objective analysis. If you've passed, congratulations and good luck in your future officer training, if you've failed, we wish you well back in your regiment. Should you get a deferred result, we look forward to seeing you back here again for another try. My staff will give you your results."

That's it. We all stand to attention again while the brigadier leaves. We never did learn his name. Major Clark calls us out individually. He uses our bib number but, for the first time, also uses our name. As bib number twelve, I'm in the middle of the pack to be called. I wait, then hear,

"Bib 12. 23636241 Private Chambers P J."

I march up to Major Clark, salute and he hands me an envelope. I salute again and take my place back with the others. Those in the line ahead of me are opening their envelopes. I can see number nine, he looks content. I'm sure he's got a PASS. He deserves it. Then there's number ten. I can't read his expression but I can tell he's pissed off. I guess he's got a FAIL.

I open my own envelope. Inside is a short note. It reads,

"23636241 Private Chambers P J.   PASS."

Chapter Eleven

It's Saturday evening and I'm in my parents' house in Saltford. After the WOSB selection board in Barton Stacey, I had returned with my warrant by train to Devizes and reported back to my holding unit at the barracks. I was told that they had already been informed that I had passed the WOSB and that I was to join the next officer training course at Mons, Aldershot, starting in ten days' time. The staff were now busy with training the next intake of recruits, I had sorted out the RSM's admin for him and I had become surplus to requirements. I had a good interview with Major Stone who congratulated me on passing the WOSB and wished me luck with the officer training. He said he hoped he would see me back with the regiment as an officer after the training. Meanwhile, I could take home leave until I have to report for the training in Aldershot.

I'm thinking about Jilly and wonder if I still have a chance with her. I decide to give her a call. It's Jilly who picks up the phone. I don't know why I'm nervous, but I am, and this makes my stammer much worse.

"Hello J-Jilly. G-Good to hear your v-voice. Are you f-free to talk?"

Bloody hell! Why am I stammering?

There's a pause on the line. I hear her drawing breath. Then she says,

"Well — umm — hello Peter, it's been a long time. Yes, I can talk for a few minutes but I have to go out soon. How's the army?"

I can hear resistance in her voice. That's not good. I say:

"Oh — the army's OK, really sort of enjoying it. L-look Jilly, I'm on l-leave and b-back at my p-parents' house for a w-week or so. I was just w-wondering if we might g-get together for a d-drink or something. 'Fraid my scooter had to be scrapped after our incident b-back in April. I could get a b-bus into Bristol and we could find a b-bar there. W-what do you think?"

For a while, Jilly doesn't answer. I can hear her breathing at the other end and can tell she's thinking about the right words to reply. I then ask her:

"Is it your f-father? Has he b-banned you from seeing me?"

"No, it's not that, it's — well it's a bit difficult right now"

I think I'm beginning to get the picture and suddenly I find I'm losing my stammer. I tell her:

"I've been wondering why you haven't answered my letters." Then I come right out with it and ask her: "Are you seeing someone else?

Jilly again takes her time to answer. Then she says:

"Well, er, yes I am. And Peter, I don't think I can see you any more. At least not for a while. Please understand you've been away a long time. I hope we can still be friends but — well — you know!" Her voice trails to a stop.

I suppose I had been expecting this and, under the circumstances, I can't blame her. But the fact is I've become very fond of her, I've missed her, and I just hoped we could get back together after my army training. I can't help but ask her:

"Has he got a car?"

"Well, yes, he has actually and he's coming to pick me up shortly. Look Peter, I'm sorry but I've got to go. Good luck with the rest of your time in the army!"

That's it! I hear the phone disconnect.

I still have no transport except my bike but I had hoped that I could pick up again with Jilly. No such luck! I'm pissed off that I've been given the heave-ho but if I'm honest with myself I can't blame her. Months away, no transport, her father dead against me. Then along comes another guy and he's got a car! And me stammering away in the background. I had no chance.

I'm not going to hang around the house moping so I decide to take the number thirty-three bus from Saltford into Bath. I'm now allowed to wear my civilian clothes again. As it's a fine August evening, I decide to wear the blue Lee jeans and T-shirt that I had bought just before my call up. I get off the bus at the terminus, just off Charlotte Street. It feels great to be back in Bath again where I have spent so much of my youth, and to be free for a while of my uniform and of the formality of the military life. I make my way along George Street and The Paragon, past St Swithin's Church and on along the London Road. I stop at the Roundup, the jazz club where I used to take Jilly on Saturday nights. I wonder who I might know there today. I go in and pay the two-shilling entrance fee. It's nine o'clock and it's heaving with people. There's a live band and they're really going for it — and so are their fans. I struggle through the masses, make it to the bar and manage to get myself a beer and enjoy getting into the mood of the music — the instrumentalists are obviously Miles Davis and Charlie Parker fans and are giving a very fair rendition of "Bloomdid", "Au Privave" and "Walkin"! Then a blonde singer in a tight silver dress comes on, the music tempo slows and she gives a sultry interpretation of "The touch of your hand" and "Somebody loves me". A lot of couples take to the floor. The blonde singer gets them in the mood for smoochy dancing. I stand near the bar and watch. I'd like to find a girl to ask to dance. There are plenty here tonight but they nearly all seem to be paired off with other guys. There are a couple of girls standing alone who might accept my invitation. Neither of them is bad looking but — I don't know — neither is my type and they're not attractive to me. Sod it, I'm missing Jilly and I'm not enjoying being here without her!

At last I recognise someone I know. His name is Chris Waters. He was in the same form as me at school but we lost touch after our "A" levels. He also seems to be on his own. We make eyeball contact and try to talk but it's not practical competing with the music, particularly as the band has now picked up the tempo with their version of Bobby Darin's "Mack the Knife". Chris points to the exit. I down the last drops of my beer and follow him out.

We greet each other outside the club where at last we can talk. Chris is not tall but he's muscular and chunky. We had got on well together at school and had both played in the first rugby fifteen, him in the front row of the scrum, me at outside centre or on the wing. We agree that, as we're without girlfriends this evening, the club's not for us. We decide to go to a pub we both know in Bath city centre. We get into easy conversation as we walk back down Walcot Street and to the pub in Upper Borough walls. This used to be our "regular" during our sixth form days and it's just round the corner from our old school in Broad Street. We go into the pub, which like the Roundup club is crowded but at least we can hear ourselves talk. We're at the bar. I'd like to buy Chris a drink but, frankly, I'm pretty skint as my thirty shillings a week national service pay doesn't go far. I'm relieved when he gets the first round of pints. There are a couple of bar stools free so we take these.

Chris asks me about my life in the army and I can tell he's not sympathetic. He says:

"Look, Peter, why didn't you get an exemption? I've just finished my first year at Bristol university. I've got a minimum of two more years and by then, this national service business will be finished. During this time, I hope to end up with a degree but you'll have slogged away in the army and have nothing to show for it at the end of your two years. I don't understand why you didn't go on to the uni after school like the rest of us."

I can see Chris's point. I tell him:

"I've now done four months as a squaddy, so I guess I missed out and it's too late to change."

"I don't see that Peter. What grades did you get and what subjects?"

"Phew! I've got to think. Yeah OK, I remember now it was an "A" in English, a "B" in history and a "C" in geography. Cambridge needed straight "As" so that's why I dipped out."

"Heh, those grades were better than mine but I got into Bristol without a problem. Actually, I was also offered a place in both Birmingham and Sheffield. There're all good establishments."

"I understand, but it's too late for me now anyway as I'm already doing my army bit."

"I don't see why. What's the bloody point of you marching up and down the barrack square in a system which is about to finish when you could be studying. Look I've got a good relationship with my tutor in Bristol who I'll be seeing for prelims next week. Do you have any objection if I talk to him and see what he might come up with?"

I don't know quite where this is going but I can't see any harm in what Chris is suggesting so we agree that he will talk to his tutor and give me a call. I tell Chris I've still got another week's leave and we exchange phone numbers. I get the next round of beers and Chris and I spend our time chatting about our former fellow pupils, about rugby (Chris is already in Bristol University's first team) and girlfriends. Chris has a steady relationship with a fellow undergraduate who is now on holiday with her parents. I tell him about being ditched this evening by Jilly. Chris insists on buying another round to drown my sorrows.

I can't believe how the time has flown. I suddenly realise it's 10.35 and the last number thirty-three bus leaves at 10.40. I down the remains of the beer, say a hurried goodbye to Chris and sprint out of the bar heading towards Charlotte Street. I'm too bloody late! I just catch a glimpse of the green bus with the number thirty-three sign illuminated on the rear panel. I'm a good runner but I can see there's no way I can catch up with the bus as it picks up speed along the Bristol Road. Just in case the timetable has changed I carry on to the terminal stop and check the board. As I thought, the last bus is at 10.40. I catch my breath. OK it's six miles to my home in Saltford, it's a dry warm evening, so I'll walk; no problem.

I'm about to set off when I see there's a young girl standing alone at the bus stop. I notice she's slim and petite. She's wearing a cotton summer dress and carrying a light sweater. She looks about seventeen or so — I also notice she's very pretty. Much more my type than those two unattached girls in the Roundup club. I don't know her and I don't know whether she might be upset if I speak to her. It's dark now and perhaps she'd think I'm trying to pick her up.

I need not have worried about that as she makes the first approach. She says:

"I'm sorry to trouble you. I want to catch the Bristol bus and think I may just have missed the last one. Do you know if it's gone yet?"

"Yeah, I'm afraid it has. I've just missed it as well."

The girl looks distressed. Nearly in tears, she tells me:

"My parents will be so worried. I've been in Bath to visit a girlfriend and I promised my folks I would be back in time for that bus. Now I'm too late. I suppose I could try to phone my father to bring his car but my mother isn't well and I know he won't want to leave her. I really don't know what to do."

"Where do you live?" I ask her.

"I live in Saltford, that's a village about six miles from here"

"Me too." I tell her. "My name's Peter Chambers by the way, what's yours?"

"I'm Linda Snow. I live at the bottom of the village near the Bird in Hand pub."

"Do you know a guy called Johnny Fisher, about my age? He lives near where you do? Yes? Well he's a mate of mine and knows your parents. Johnny talks about you often but somehow, we've not met before. Don't worry Linda, I'll make sure you get home but I'm afraid we'll have to leg it as I don't have a car or a motorbike."

Linda looks relieved. I'm very happy to help a young damsel in distress, and this pretty one in particular. But after my experience with Jilly's father, I'm cautious about just turning up late at their house without warning. I want her to feel more relaxed with me so I suggest we go to a phone box and call her parents. There's one nearby and we squeeze inside the box together. I put three pennies in the slot and Linda calls out her parents' number while I dial. It starts to ring. I hear a man's voice, press button "A" and hand the phone to Linda. I listen to her telling her father her story and saying she will be walking home. When she tells him she is with me, I ask her to pass me the phone. I say:

"Good evening Mr Snow. My name is Peter Chambers and I also live in Saltford. You may know my parents who are friends of your neighbours, Mr and Mrs Fisher and their son Johnny. You do? That's good. Look, I also missed the last bus home and by chance have just met up with your daughter, Linda. I will escort her to your home. We will be walking so it might take up to a couple of hours but don't worry, sir, I promise to look after her well."

Mr Snow had sounded suspicious at first but I felt he was relieved about his daughter when he knew who she was with. At least I hope so! I'm also pleased I managed to get through the phone call without stammering. Strange how it comes and goes.

There are two ways to get to Saltford from Bath. One is to take the same route as the number thirty-three bus — via Bathampton over the old Avon bridge and along the A4 to Corston then turn right, past Saltford railway station, up the hill into Saltford village. The other route is via the back road through Kelston and down through the fields, over the old LMS railway bridge and into Saltford village by the river. I decide on the Kelston route, not only slightly quicker on foot but it ends up close to where Linda lives.

I enjoy the walk with Linda. She's a slim fit girl with an easy walking action. She's wearing low shoes, which don't seem to trouble her during the long walk. We talk easily together. She tells me she's still at her grammar school in Bristol with another year before her "A" levels. She doesn't yet know what she wants to do after school. I tell her about my school days and my first few months in the army. She's a good listener. I don't tell her about Jilly.

When we reach Kelston, we have to turn off the road and follow a track down through the meadows towards the river Avon. I know the route well as I regularly include it in my cross-country running training. It's a dark night with only a sliver of moon. The heat of the August day has cooled and there's a tingling freshness about the air. At one point, we have to climb over a gate. I go first then turn back to take Linda's hand, help her over and lower her to the ground on the other side. I continue to hold her hand as we walk on through the fields. She doesn't take her hand away. She walks close beside me and I feel the warmth and freshness of her body. We reach the old LMS railway line and cross over its bridge which spans the river Avon. This brings us to the bottom of Saltford village. We are still in darkness but I can see the village street lights up ahead. Her house is just up this road. I stop for a moment and we turn to face each other. It is a memorable evening and I've enjoyed every moment of my walk with this enchanting young girl. It is achingly difficult to resist drawing her towards me and kissing her. But I don't. I had promised her father I would look after her well and to kiss her would be going too far.

We walk on up the short hill and to her house. The lights are still on and Linda's father opens the door as soon as I ring the bell. He kisses Linda, shakes my hand and thanks me for escorting his daughter safely home. I walk away feeling almost virtuous. I have resisted temptation. I have met a very lovely girl and have nearly forgotten about Jilly.

Chapter Twelve

True to his word, Chris Waters calls me at my parents' house on Monday evening. He tells me:

"Hi Peter. I've just left a meeting with my tutor at Bristol University. Actually, we didn't talk much about next year's study programme, more about next season's rugby as, Professor Paul Radfern, that's his name, is also chairman of our university rugby association. Although we don't resume our formal studies until the end of September, we're planning to start up our rugby training from next week. Point of my call is this: I mentioned your situation to Paul and told him about your "A" level grades and subjects. I also praised your rugby skills as a strong centre, wing or perhaps a future full back! Paul was very interested — he reckons the army business can be annulled. He said he would like to meet with you. I told him you're on leave at present and at your folk's home in Saltford. He asked if you could make it to his study in the Faculty of Arts tomorrow afternoon. How about it?"

I'm not sure how to react. I remember my conversation with Chris last Saturday but I suppose I thought he was only partly serious, maybe just winding me up. I hadn't thought any more about it since until this call. I tell him:

"Thank you for remembering my situation Chris. But I'm not sure I'm that keen to be honest as I explained to you at the weekend."

"Come on Peter, snap out of it! This could be a great solution for you. What have you got to lose? Look, I've done my bit but I'd appreciate if, only as I matter of politeness, you give him a call yourself and take it from there."

I realise that I'm probably being too negative to Chris who has taken the trouble to try to help. I thank him again, take down the professor's home and university numbers and agree to call him. Chris says his girlfriend is due back tomorrow and between seeing her and starting rugby training he'll be tied up for the rest of the week.

I put the phone down and wonder where this is going. I've reconciled myself to completing two years in the army. I've already got through the basic training part and am quite chuffed with myself for having passed the WOSB. Of course, I hadn't told Chris about that and what was involved, but I don't think it would have changed his opinion about the virtues of university life versus, in his view, wasting my time in the army.

I decide to sleep on it and to phone Professor Radfern in the morning.

I've chosen to wear my suit. I've only got the one: it served me well while I was working in the Bristol department store before my call up. It feels loose on me after all the army fitness training. I spoke to the professor this morning and we arranged a meeting in his study at four-thirty. He gave the address as 16 Priory Road, Bristol. He told me this road leads off Elmdale Road and Tyndalls Park Road. Getting there from Saltford is easy; the same number thirty-three bus right through to Bristol city centre then a walk up the hill to Priory Road.

When I get to the address, I find it's heavily populated with university establishments but is quiet as most staff and students are still on vacation. Professor Paul Radfern is clearly a well-known figure and I'm shown directly to his study by an elderly gentleman I meet at the entrance to number sixteen.

I knock on his study door and receive a loud "come in" call. I enter and am greeted by the professor — I reckon he's in his mid-fifties, he's about the same height as me, six foot one, or perhaps a little taller, fit looking and wiry. He has a mop of black hair with only tinges of grey around the edges. He has the ruddy complexion of a man who has spent much of his life out of doors — not behind the desk where he now is. He bounds to his feet and comes around his desk and pumps my hand.

"Peter Chambers? Glad you found us OK. I must say you have a strong supporter in Chris Waters who was here yesterday singing your praises. Take a seat and let's have a chat."

The professor is an engaging speaker, positive and enthusiastic. First, he explains the basic structure of the university with its faculties of arts, engineering, and the various science disciplines. He says he belongs to the School of Humanities, which embraces classics and ancient history, English, history (historical studies), history of art, and religion and theology. He then tells me he's "taken the liberty" of phoning the secretariat of the Cambridge University examination board, the authority that controls our school's "A" level exams, who confirmed the subjects and grades I had got last year. He continues:

"This is the way I see it, Peter. National military service in UK will be finished in a couple of years and the government is going through the motions of continuing to hold young men for a service that has now become an anachronism. My offer to you is this: let me try my hand at getting you off the hook with a quick discharge from the army. This is something I've done successfully for other lads like you. Then we'll start you on a foundation undergraduate course this autumn, see how you take to that, then mainstream you into either the English or history department to complete your degree. How does that appeal?"

The professor speaks with such enthusiasm that I find it difficult not to go along with his ideas. I'm trying to think how to respond when he starts up again.

"That's not all Peter. I like all I'm learning about your rugby ability — not just what Chris Waters told me. We have scouts out covering local school's rugby and I've heard nothing but praise about your speed and handling skills. I tell you. We need to beef up our three-quarter line. You might be just the guy for our university first team!"

I've never before met anyone quite like Professor Radfern. He's brimming with enthusiasm. I suspect he carries this zest into the lecture hall and is a great motivator for his students. It's difficult not to just roll over and go with the flow of his logic. I'm seriously impressed. But in the back of my mind, I feel a certain resistance. Something I can't yet define but strong enough to stop me from instantly saying "yes" to his proposition.

I'm trying to get my incoherent thoughts into some sort of order. I realise that Professor Radfern has stopped talking and is waiting for me to respond. I try to get a grip. Unfortunately, my confusion brings back my stammer in my mind so I resort to the system I developed and used for the WOSB presentation. I try to put an "a" ahead of all those hard letters I struggle with. I reply:

"Professor, I really appreciate your generous offer. I'd like to think about it. Can I please call you before the end of the week?

Professor Radfern seems surprised by my reticent reply. I certainly don't want to offend him as I'm sincerely grateful that he should be so interested in me to make this offer. I realise it could well be just what I need to get back on the path of academic study and a useful degree. I'm confused.

I shake the professor's hand, again thank him and promise to phone him back in a couple of days.

It's Thursday and the fine August weather continues. I'm still unsure what to do about Professor Radfern's offer. To clear my head, I decide to go for a run. I take one of my favourite routes — down through Saltford village, cross over the river via the old LMS bridge, take a circular route along the far river bank to a point opposite the Jolly Sailor pub, then climb up through the fields and woods to come out onto Kelston Tor from the Lansdown racecourse side. Distance so far: about four miles. I cover this route at my usual pace but try to push myself on the uphill slopes — good for the cardio vascular system I'm told. I get to the top of Kelston Tor, take a pause and sit down on the grassy bank.

I look back down towards the Avon valley and Saltford on the far bank. This is my home turf. Saltford, the village of my birth, is on one side of the Tor and Bath, where I spent my schooldays, is on the other. I love this country. I bless the fact that I was born here and that, by such good fortune, I had won a scholarship to my school in Bath. However, I realise my life has already moved on. I'm just not sure in what direction I want it to go. I had made no effort to resist my call up for national service. Now I have another chance to change direction again. My head is still full of my conversation with Professor Radfern. His proposal is very tempting and I can't fault his logic that I could be wasting my time by serving out the rest of my two years in the army while the political decision has been taken to end conscription. I could then find I'm discharged at the end of what could have been two wasted years.

But I've a strong nagging doubt. I've spent enough time in the army to appreciate the positives that military service can bring. I think back to my first days in Devizes and my initial meeting with my fellow recruits — we were a disparate group of young lads from totally different backgrounds and upbringing. We had nothing in common. No one wanted to be there. Yet, through the training we were given, after twelve weeks, we were transformed. We supported each other. We were physically fit, more mentally alert and worked together in a cohesive positive way. I felt a real sense of loss when I was told I was not joining the rest of "my new mates" in being sent to form up with the Royal Hampshire Regiment in the West Indies. It's even more than that. I know most of my ex-school friends look down on national service and see it as a waste of time compared with bettering themselves by studying at university. That is also Professor Radfern's line. But I find myself at odds with this opinion. I feel patriotic about my country. Although we came through the World War on the right side, just about, that was down to the sacrifices of our fathers' generation. Our country still faces external threats and, to survive in the future, we need to retain a trained reserve of our military. At the moment, our country is involved in operations in Cyprus, Aden, East Africa and elsewhere. There's also the looming menace of the Soviet Union and its Warsaw Pact allies. We can't all opt out of these threats and hide behind the walls of university life. What's more, I've learned to like the military life. It suits me.

I know I'm not going to solve my dilemma right now and, in any case, I need to get going again before I stiffen up. The quickest way back to my house from here joins up with the route that Linda and I took last Saturday evening. I decide to go that way. From Kelston, I head off through the meadows leading down towards the river. I get to the same gate that I had helped Linda over. I think about that evening. I remember us holding hands and the sweet warmth of her body next to mine. I know I'd like to see her again.

After I cross back over the old LMS bridge and get down to the bottom of Saltford village, I can't resist but to take the short detour past Linda's house. Who knows, she might be there. I see a lady do some light weeding in the front garden. It's not Linda but she looks just like an older version. I'm sure it's Linda's mother. I can tell she's seen me so I go over to speak to her:

"Excuse me but I think you may be Mrs Snow, Linda's mother. I'm sorry if I seemed to be snooping — it's just that I came here last Saturday when Linda came back from Bath."

I wasn't sure how she would react. She says:

"Ah yes of course. You must be Peter Chambers. I know your mother, we're both members of Saltford Women's' Institute. Thank you, Peter, for seeing Linda safely home."

I feel this is going quite well so I risk it and say:

"It was pleasure. Mrs Snow, forgive me asking but I wonder if Linda might be free. I'd love to go for a walk with her this evening — that is, if she would like to and if it's OK with you and Mr Snow."

She gives me a smile, which I think, at least I hope, is of approval. She replies:

"Yes Peter, I'm sure she'd like to walk with you. I'll tell her." She looks down at my sweaty T-shirt and continues:

"Say in about an hour, that'll give you time to change and for Linda to be ready. Make sure you look after her. OK?"

I whip back home, go to our bathroom and strip off. We don't have a shower so I do a sort of half bath in our tub. I brush my teeth and comb my hair. It's quite the fashion to wear a heavy hair gel like Brylcreem but that's not my style. At least my hair is growing back to a decent length after being shorn at the start of my army training. I've only the one pair of jeans that I wore last Saturday but they'll have to do. Fortunately, I do have a clean shirt and my day walking shoes are reasonably clean.

Linda is waiting for me when I get back to her house. She's wearing a different dress from last time. Her dark brown hair is glistening as if it's been freshly washed. She looks great. I ask her if she'd like go anywhere special but she says she'll leave it up to me. I lead her down towards the river along a path which runs above but parallel to it. I know this path well as it's here that my father often comes to paint. At home, we have a number of his creations, many showing the view from this very spot — views up towards Kelston Tor then to the right looking down over the river and its meandering route towards Corston and Bath. The view is a blend of river, and meadowland interspersed with woodland and the occasional farm building. The evening sun is throwing up shadows that highlight the contrasting rural colours. Very scenic. By the time we reach the little wooden bench that overlooks this view, we're already holding hands. There's just room on the bench for us both to sit down.

We sit close together. Our conversation is light and natural. I learn more about Linda, her family, her school, her likes and her dislikes. I haven't yet told my parents about Professor Radfern and his proposal. I don't know why but I feel I want to share it with Linda. She's a good listener but quite rightly she tells me it is a decision that only I can make.

Linda decides to change the mood. She looks very directly at me and says:

"Peter, do you remember when we stopped just before we got to my house on Saturday evening? Did you want to kiss me?"

I have only one answer: "Yes Linda I did. Very much"

"Well why don't you stop talking and kiss me now?"

So I do. I put my arm around her shoulders, pull her towards me and we kiss. The feel of her lips, the delicious warmth and scent of her, the bond of our bodies as we explore each other for the first time. I'm lost in the thrill of these moments. My big decision dilemma is forgotten for now.

We realise that we've lost track of time but are brought back to reality when another couple walk along the path right next to us. We see that already the darkness of night has descended. It's time to take Linda home. We don't talk much anymore on the way. I know I want to see her again and I'm confident she feels the same. We make no great declarations to each other. We're both young and have time on our side. I leave her at her front gate and make my way back to my parents' house.

It's now Thursday night and I'm lying in my bed. I can't sleep as I mull over and over again my great dilemma of whether I should follow Professor Radfern's proposal to try to abort my army service and reboot my academic studies or whether to stick with my life in the army and see it through until the natural end of my national service. As my wakeless thoughts proceed, more and more I lean towards a decision that in my heart I felt I was always going to follow. And it's this: of course, I would like to have a good degree and explore the higher world of academics. But, but, but I like doing my duty as a soldier, of having already proved to myself that I can handle difficult social challenges. I like the whole environment of military life, it's real, it's today, it's involved with our nation's security and protection. I like the possibility that, if I can get through the Mons training, I will be an officer in the British army. I'm both concerned and excited how it might be to see operational action, to experience bullets fired at me. How will I react? Will I handle myself with control or will I fold up with fear. I don't know but I need to find out. There's only one way to do that. My mind is made up. Decision made. I'm staying in the army. At last I can now get to sleep. And tomorrow I'll call Professor Radfern, thank him for his proposal but tell him not to proceed with requesting my discharge. I intend to complete my two-year commitment as a national serviceman. On Monday, I'll report to Mons Officer Cadet School in Aldershot as instructed. No going back.

Chapter Thirteen

There've been times during the past few weeks when I've seriously wondered if I had made a mistake not to follow Professor Radfern's advice about getting out of uniform and into university. But we're now only three or four weeks away from our passing out parade and I'm now determined to stick it out till then.

The only real difference between being an officer cadet and a recruit soldier is that we get to wear a white disk behind the hat badge in our berries. The rest is much the same in terms of the constant barrack room inspections, guard duties and rigorous attention to timings. In many ways, we've been treated even worse than when we were recruits.

It had started back in September when our intake of twenty-six guys formed up together at Mons Officer Cadet School at Aldershot. All of us had earlier passed the WOSB selection board. Any thoughts that we might, in some way, be rather special were quickly dispelled. RSM Holland at Devizes was an impressive guy but here at Mons, RSM Kincaid is really something else. He's a very tall gentleman with a large girth. He must weigh something approaching twenty stones but despite this he is remarkably light on his feet. He is always impeccably turned out with glittering brasses on his waist belt and with boots that gleam like glass. He always carries his pace stick as if it's weapon about to be launched at any one of us. He's from the Irish Guards and, conforming to the tradition of his regiment, the brim of his hat slopes down parallel to the ground, stopping just short of his large nose. His bright beady eyes stare out from either side of the brim in a way that makes you think he's glaring directly at you. A formidable individual!

At our initiation parade at Mons, RSM Kincaid had addressed us in his broad Ulster accent. His voice is deep and rich with the volume of a foghorn. He said:

"Gentlemen, you will find this is a very strange place. I call you 'sir' and you call me "sir". There's only one difference. You mean it — but I bloody don't!"

Apart from the initial blast from RSM Kincaid, we had been given an opening address by the commandant, Brigadier Hopkins. He had made it clear that all of us could pass the course but we should be under no illusions. The regular army was well resourced for officers and any new commissions would only be granted to those who meet the very high standards demanded. The brigadier also introduced us to the training staff of officers and senior NCOs. The training major was Major Mathews-Clegg, Coldstream Guards. Capt Shepley, Royal Green Jackets, was responsible for our intake. RSM Kincaid who had already introduced himself was responsible for drill and camp discipline.

We all realised that if we could get through this phase of training, there should be more interesting days ahead for the rest of our national service. We were all of similar educational background and age and the strict discipline bonded us together. It was apparent that the requirement for more young officers to be commissioned was not great and four from our squad were dismissed from the course early on, often for seemingly trivial reasons, and sent back to their original units. The dreaded term used is RTU'd, standing for "returned to unit". This is really hard on the individuals concerned. I'm determined to do my best not to let it happen to me.

Photos: Mons Officer Cadet School, Aldershot.
September 1959 intake and rifle drill practice.

While we were still in the barracks or out in the neighbouring Hampshire hills, we were taught a range of skills relevant to becoming young officers. We learnt advanced map reading and how to use the prismatic compass. We were perched on hilltops and taught how to "describe the ground" in order that we could identify and tell our future soldiers exactly where to go or where to aim their weapons. We were taught the composition and roles of each of the members of an infantry platoon and how each had to do his job: riflemen, members of the Bren-gun team, light mortars, signallers. We learnt about communications and basic first aid. We threw grenades and made simple explosives. We had to practise each infantry role to the satisfaction of our instructors.

We were allowed very little time to ourselves but we did have every other Saturday free. This caused a split between us. Some of our fellow cadets come from well-off families. Some have their own cars and can drive off on their own for the day, others have parents who come and pick their sons up. The rest, me included, have no parents on hand or our own transport. But I was lucky in that one of my new-found chums, Patrick Harrington, is a mechanical genius. He will probably later be assigned to the REME (Royal Electrical and Mechanical Engineers). Patrick has somehow built himself a car from scraps he acquired from various wrecks he had found. He made the outside chassis out of aluminium but I have no idea what comprised the engine and other moving parts. It has no roof so if it rains the occupants just get wet. But it works and goes like a rocket. Not very original, but Patrick's car is called "The Harringtonmobile".

On one of our free Saturdays in late October, Patrick suggests that he drives me and another couple of officer cadets up to London for a night out — a journey from Aldershot of about an hour or so. The other two were Michael Cooper and Ian McKay. Michael is probably the brightest of our intake, with a very sharp wit and an easy disposition. In all our time together at Mons so far, nothing ever seems to faze him or get him down. We all admire his temperament and brain. Ian McKay's parent regiment is the Argyle and Sutherland Highlanders. Ian is a credit to his regiment. He's undemonstrative and speaks with a quiet Scottish Highland brogue. He's a big man with an imposing physique, the sort of guy you want to have on your side.

We all readily accepted Patrick's invitation but admitted we had no money to enjoy the flesh-spots in London's West End. We were all in the same boat — broke but with just enough between us to buy petrol for Patrick's thirsty car and perhaps the odd beer. A total of about fifteen pounds between the four of us.

We set off and Patrick demonstrated his brainchild's manoeuvrability and zip. None of us knew about London's nightlife but we'd all heard the word Soho and somehow, we found our way there. Patrick parked up with great panache. We were all quite scruffily dressed as all we had with us in the Mons barracks at Aldershot, beside our military kit, were a few strictly casual civvy clothes — jeans, shirt and sweaters. Strictly no jackets and no ties. Despite being skint, we didn't care!

Michael had heard that there was a new jazz club opening about now, called Ronnie "Somethings". He knew it was located in Gerrard Street so we made finding it our first mission, then to see if it was open and try to gate-crash. We were in luck. It was either the opening night or close to it and not only was entry free but we were all given complimentary drinks to celebrate the opening. We spent a good couple of hours there for free, absorbed in some of the best live jazz and blues music we'd ever heard. It certainly outclassed the Roundup club in Bath!

Michael was on great form and, as we wandered round Soho, we passed a place with the rather seductive name of The Rose Petal club. Michael suggested we give it a try. It had a rather grand entrance. I thought about our meagre funds and the scruffy way we were dressed but Michael insisted and forged on ahead. The rest of us were content for him to take the lead. Inside, there was an entry vestibule where a young lady was taking coats (we had none) and standing by was a young man wearing a long red satiny coat, drainpipe trousers and "winklepicker" shoes. He seemed to have some sort of management role. He came towards us but before he could speak, Michael summoned him over, saying:

"Hi, how are you today? I'm Michael and you are?"

"Um, Vincent. What are you —"

Michael cut straight back with:

"Good to meet you Vincent. Look, my associates here are looking to relax for a while. We're staying at the Ritz but right now we slipped over to Soho to drink a little champagne and maybe have the pleasure of the company of some of your young ladies. Kindly show us to a quiet corner where we can enjoy your floor show with our drinks."

I was learning from Michael. If you want to bullshit, do it with style! Vincent seemed stunned by Michael's air of total confidence and he meekly led us inside the club and found us a corner banquette. The seating was a thick purple colour velour in a half-moon shape. The background lighting was dim in order to create an intimate atmosphere. In front of us was a small stage. There was quiet background music playing. In the gloom, we could only see a few other customers. It was probably early yet by Soho's nightlife standards.

We were approached by a young lady holding a silver tray. She was wearing, well, not very much — black fishnet stockings, under a red top which just about contained her voluptuous breasts. Her hair was tucked up and held with a large black bow. She addressed herself to Michael while Vincent still hovered uncertainly in the background.

"Good evening, sir, welcome to the Rose Petal. What can I get you gentlemen to drink?"

Michael maintained his urbane and relaxed manner. He looked the waitress up and down (as I think the rest of us did!) and said:

"Good evening my dear. You're looking very glamourous this evening. As I was telling our friend Vincent here, we'd like to drink a little champagne. Have you a list?"

We could only marvel at Michael's cheek, acting as if we were wealthy young men used to this lifestyle. The waitress, whose name she told us was Viola, brought the list and presented it to Michael. He took his time, pursing his lips as he studied the list.

"Let's see. Hmm, yes, I quite like the look of the Bollinger; and the Veuve Clicquot looks promising. Ummm, no I think we'll start off with a bottle of your Dom Perignon. Fifty-three was a good year."

The waitress had given all of us the champagne list, which also advertised the club with its address and phone number. I looked at the prices. The one Michael had chosen cost over fifty pounds — for one bottle! My god, what the hell were we doing here? We only had fifteen quid between us. I could tell that Patrick and Ian were also concerned but

Michael — not at all. He seemed completely at ease as if a fifty-quid bottle of champagne was a mere drop in the ocean.

Viola came back with the bottle and put it on a table in front of us with eight, not four, glasses. We wondered why but did not have long to wait as four young ladies appeared. They were dressed as skimpily as Viola. It seemed they had been herded there by Vincent who by now had satisfied himself that the club was going to have a profitable night. He probably fancied a good tip from Michael for himself.

The girls squeezed themselves in between us. I was sitting in the middle of the banquette and found myself wedged between a blonde and a brunette. One was stroking my left knee, the other had turned her body towards mine and was brushing her ample bosom against my shoulder. I'd never experienced anything like this. Both girls wore heavy perfume. I had no idea whether it was Dior or from the local Woolworths but it had a heady impact. I felt quite carried away. These were exotic girls who were experienced in arousing their clients. They were certainly succeeding with me. My relationships with girls like Jilly and Linda in Bath seemed so pure and innocent by comparison. I felt tempted to relax and let this situation flow but I realised the girls were here for one purpose only — to extract as much money from us as possible. I had no idea how we were going to get out of this.

Before Viola had brought the champagne, I noticed Michael talking quietly to Patrick. Now, just as we were getting settled on the banquette, Patrick extracted himself, got up and left the room. I supposed he was heading for the "gents" and I settled back to continue to enjoy the attentions of these nubile and sexy girls.

A short while later, Vincent was back. He rushed up to Michael and told him:

"Sir Michael, there's a phone call for you from the Ritz hotel. Your father, Lord Douglas, needs to talk to you urgently."

Michael took this in his stride, made a fulsome apology to his lady escort and followed Vincent out to take the phone call. Ian and I stayed put wondering what the heck was going on. A few minutes later, Michael was back. His face was full of regret as he beckoned to Ian and me to leave our gorgeous girls and follow him back out to the vestibule. There was no sign of Patrick. Michael was in earnest conversation with

Vincent. I heard him say:

"This is so annoying Vincent, just as we were beginning to enjoy ourselves. And the floor show hasn't even started yet! It's my father you see. He's instructed me to return back to the Ritz — something to do with checking on the Middle East investments we made today. I'm sure it's nothing really but I suppose with his wealth, he expects us all to jump whenever he calls. I'm sure we'll get this sorted quickly so we can come back and watch the show. Look Vincent, let the girls stay where they are and finish off that delicious champagne. And put another bottle on ice for us for when we get back. Oh, and Vincent, you're doing a great job. We'll see you again very soon."

With that, Michael calmly ushered Ian and myself out of the club before Vincent had a chance to react. We turned right and quickly mingled with the crowd as we were joined by Patrick who had earlier nipped out to the phone box across the street and initiated the spoof call to the club. He got the number from the champagne price list. We walked on briskly for some minutes till we came to a simple local pub. We went in, checked that no one had apparently followed us, looked at each other and burst out laughing. Michael had played a blinder. We had enjoyed a glass of champagne while we were propositioned by some gorgeous girls and got an idea of Soho's night life. All good sport and a bit of light relief for four eighteen-year-old officer cadets! We used up the rest of our funds on a pint of beer apiece then reckoned we had had enough excitement for one night and decided to retreat back to Aldershot

We re-found Patrick's "Harringtonmobile" and all piled in. The downside was that it had started to rain heavily. Ever inventive, Patrick had a small locked container in the car from which we retrieved our army issued groundsheets, which also doubled as ponchos. These kept some of the worst of the rain out as Patrick deftly drove us back to Aldershot.

Chapter Fourteen

Our trip to Soho was some weeks ago. Now we're on manoeuvres in the Sennybridge training area in the Brecon beacons, Mid Wales. It's December and the weather is as miserable as it can be. It's cold and during most days there's a persistent driving sleet or wet snow, which gets into every crevice of our bodies. We've been here already for ten days and still have another week to go.

This phase of our training involves carrying out a series of infantry tactical manoeuvres such as: advance to contact, attacking from the front and the flank, set piece defence and tactical withdrawals. We repeat these phases many times over but each time our individual roles are changed. Sometimes we are required to be a simple section rifleman, at others we might be the platoon commander, sergeant, mortar-man or signaller: these changes are designed to ensure that we fully understand and are tested in every job that exists within the standard infantry platoon. Within the first hour of every day out in the training area, we get soaked through. I've decided the best approach is to grit my teeth, take any instruction I'm given and get on with it. When I'm tasked with a responsible leadership job, for example as platoon or section commander, I try to raise my game to show our instructors I'm up to the job. Seems to be working OK so far.

After the long day's training and exposure to the elements, we're all knackered. Our accommodation is in "Nissen" huts. Our camp beds are lined up along the sides of the hut. In the centre is a coke-fuelled stove. We take it in turns to fetch the coke and we try to keep the stove permanently burning. When we return from training each evening, we first grab our supper in the canteen then we retreat to the hut, strip off and try to dry out our combat kit. With ten of us in each hut, drying our clothes generates a thick haze of steam, which we endure through the night. In the morning, our kit is only ever partly dry. We repeat this procedure daily except when the phase of our training requires us to carry out night simulated operations. These often involve long night marches, which we navigate by compass as there's rarely any moonlight to assist our night vision. It's on one of these days, 10 December, that I realise it's my nineteenth birthday. I'm sure my mother will have sent me a card but we're not allowed personal mail until we get back to our barracks in Aldershot. I also wonder if Linda from Saltford has written. I'll have to wait to find out.

It's a Saturday and at last we're given an evening off as a concession to acknowledging our training has reached the required standard. We've learnt that there is a dance being held in Ystradgynlais, a small town a few miles from us here in Sennybridge. What's more, our chief instructor has authorised the use of two Bedford three ton-trucks, plus drivers, to take us there. Apparently, the town is well populated with young ladies. That's the attraction!

We scrub up as well as possible but the only clothes we all have with us are our combat uniforms. These are mostly still damp but they'll have to do. Army boots are the only footwear we have with us. I wouldn't pick them to go dancing but there's no choice. There's no obligation to go this evening but we get a hundred per cent turnout. Probably some are more keen than others but I reckon everyone has had enough of our steamy Nissen huts and this is a chance to have a break from them, albeit only for a few hours.

We all mount up in the back of the Bedfords and are driven through the sleety rain to Ystradgynlais, timing to arrive at about nine-thirty when we hope the dance will already be in full swing. We have a minor navigational problem en route when, embarrassingly, our driver has to enlist the help of a local policeman to guide us to the dance hall. But we pull up outside it in good shape. We've given no prior notice to the local organisers of our participation.

We decide to make our entrance something of a spectacle. In true military style, we line up in three ranks and march into the dance hall. Understandably, this causes some confusion and concern in the hall. The music, which had been playing at high volume is immediately silenced and everyone stands around wondering what is going on. In hindsight, I think our "grand entrance" was a mistake as we want to have a friendly relaxed evening and our militaristic style didn't set the right tone.

Thereafter, we have to work hard at a charm offensive to persuade the local inhabitants that the army has not commandeered the town.

The first good news for us when we enter the hall is that it's warm and dry. The second is that several rows of young girls are lining the walls. There are a few young men there but they are heavily outnumbered by the girls. This confirms our earlier intelligence that the local watch factory indeed employs almost exclusively female staff due to the fact that their intricate work requirements are best carried out by deft, small female hands. As the watch factory is the only major employer in the town, many of the young men have left to find jobs further away.

Michael Cooper, our natural spokesman, soon settles the atmosphere by saying:

"Ladies and gentlemen, we must apologise for our heavy-handed entrance. Let us explain. We are in training at Sennybridge up the road from here. We've only our army uniforms so we're incorrectly dressed for your dance. However, we've been given a few hours off from our training and we'd be so pleased if you will allow us to spend it with you — to enjoy some music and, we hope, to have a few dances."

As always, Michael hits the right tone. In no time, the DJ starts up the music again, the girls seem to relax and readily accept invitations from our guys to dance. We seem to be creating a steady output of rising steam as our soggy uniforms begin to dry out in the dry warm atmosphere of the hall. Also, our body cleanliness is not of the highest hygiene standards after two weeks with minimum washing but these nice girls seem to be very forgiving. We thought we might meet opposition from the local young men but the reality seems to be that they are quite relieved to have extra male support as they have difficulty coping with the large female ratio. We're in a win-win-win situation. We get to have a good break from our training, the girls get some fit young guys to dance with and the local guys get some relief from having to cope with the preponderance of the female sex.

I'm really starting to enjoy the evening as the music settles everyone down. I get to dance with some charming girls. There's a bar in the corner of the hall that sells beer and soft drinks. It's also good to be socialising with my fellow students who I've spent the last thirteen weeks with, as we've progressed through the phases of the officer cadet training course.

Most have now become good friends, not least during our time here in Mid Wales as we've all suffered together the effects of the wet and cold weather. Here at last it's warm and we can relax for a couple of hours. I also realise it was a good psychological move by our instructors to give us this time off. Our sinking morale has been restored and we should return to our training with renewed enthusiasm.

I think we've timed the evening well. At eleven-thirty sharp, the DJ brings the last number to a close and makes his concluding comments. The dance is over. Everything went fine. Perhaps if it had gone on for another hour or so, the beer or personal passions could have degraded the atmosphere. As it is, we leave with due decorum, thanking the DJ who organised the evening, kiss the charming girls politely on each cheek and shake the young lads' hands. We pile back into the back of our trucks and head back to our Nissen huts at Sennybridge.

It's now Monday 4 January 1960. I'm finding it difficult to grasp that I'm at last into the final session of our training. After all the months, first through basic recruit training and now, since September, at Mons Officer Cadet School, we've been told the date of our passing out parade — next Thursday 14 January. It's been a long journey.

The final week at Sennybridge had been no easier than the first two. During the week, two more of our intake were RTU'd, reducing our intake to twenty. The final exercise required us first to establish a fully prepared defensive position. In my case this meant digging a five-foot-deep foxhole. Fortunately, I was sharing this with my chum Ian McKay, the Argyle and Sutherland Highlander. With his strength, we soon got the job done. We occupied this trench during the night as we constantly bailed out the seeping rain water. Our simulated "enemy" was provided by soldiers from the Royal Anglian regiment. Our task was to defend our position against a very realistic "attack", which involved flares, stun grenades and rapid fire (fortunately using blank ammunition!). The "attack" was deemed by our instructors to have been successfully repulsed and we were then ordered to mount a counter-attack against the "enemy" force. My role was changed at that point and I was made the platoon sergeant and later, when our cadet platoon commander was deemed to have been "killed", I was told to assume command. The exercise was very realistic and, despite the cold and rain, I actually found I was enjoying it. I must be a glutton for punishment!

We had returned to Mons, Aldershot, shortly before the Christmas break. Our first priority had been to wash and dry all our sodden kit and clean up our other equipment. We also took time out to attend to our personal hygiene! We then returned to the parade square to be knocked back into shape by RSM Kincaid. Eventually, we were allowed four days off to spend Christmas with our families. I managed to get a train back to Bath and then home to Saltford. I was pleased that my sister, her husband and my now three-year old niece manged to join us from their home in Essex. It was good to have a traditional Christmas Day and to feel normal again even if for only a few days.

Once again, we're back in Mons. We've just attended a presentation by a colonel we've not met before. He told us that when we're commissioned (I like it that he said "when" not "if"), we would be offered other options for us other than to re-join our original regiment — in my case the Royal Hampshires. The colonel said that display stands had just been put up by representatives from various other commonwealth countries who were short of young officers and were interested to recruit from our intake. We needed to visit these to get the details of what each had to offer.

I find the colonel's information interesting and take the chance to visit the display stands. There are representatives from countries ranging from Malaya, Hong Kong, Kenya, Nigeria, Ghana and, I think, a few others. I get a briefing from each. I don't really know why but Nigeria sounds fascinating. I've never been overseas and, somehow, the idea of Nigeria has great appeal. The officer on the stand tells me that, if I were to join them, I would get a substantial secondment credit (i.e. more money!) plus a higher rate of pay than if I stay with the Royal Hampshires. They need an answer by this Thursday, 7 January, in order that the paperwork can be completed before the passing out parade next week. I leave the stand undecided what to do but I know I need to make a decision quickly.

I can't get to sleep because I'm worrying about what is the best thing to do. Until this briefing today, I hadn't thought much about the next phase of my army service. It was quite enough to concentrate on getting through the officer training and I didn't want to get ahead of myself. When I had last talked to Major Stone, back in Devises, he had told me that, if I passed Mons, I would re-join the Royal Hampshires who would then be based in the West Indies. That sounded pretty exciting to me but at that time there were still so many hurdles still to overcome. There's no one I can consult. My parents wouldn't be able to advise me nor would my former chums. If I could call Major Stone, I'm sure he would tell me to stick with the Hampshires. If I called Professor Radfern, he wouldn't want to know me after I declined his offer to get me a deferment. So, it's up to me. I still think going to the West Indies sounds great but I've been told the pay for a second lieutenant is four pounds sixteen shillings a week. That's not going to get me very far. I'm concerned that I might find myself based in some exotic spot where everyone around me is rich. I'd be physically there but too poor to join in the social highlife. On the other hand, Africa in general and Nigeria in particular, also sounds an exciting place to be but without the same touristic element. What's more I would get an immediate cash credit, earn more and not have so many expenses. All my life I've been broke and this is an opportunity to get something in my bank.

Eventually, I can feel myself dropping off to sleep. I've decided to opt for Nigeria! I'll go and tell the representative at that stand tomorrow.

The first time we were on the square for a passing out parade was just after we had started our course here. Then our intake was at the back of the parade square and there were three intakes in front of us. The front intake comprised those being commissioned as second lieutenants on that day. Progressively we've moved further forward. Today, we are the front intake. It's Thursday, 14 January 1960. It's our turn to be commissioned.

The "passing out" ceremony has great style and panache. A band has been provided and is already into its repertoire. RSM Kincaid is in his element and has got all of us on parade in impeccable order. VIPs and a large gathering are assembled. We have rehearsed our drills so frequently that we automatically move in unison. My mind is in a blank as I go through the parade programme on autopilot. The inspecting officer, a senior general, walks through our ranks and returns to his dais as we stand at ease. I don't concentrate on his address. He speaks with a "far back" lispy voice and it's starts with something like:

"I remember, many years ago, receiving my first pip. It was a great honour to me then, as I know it is to those of you being commissioned today. I'm sure that each one of you will wear your uniform with pride and carry out your duties as officers of Her Majesty's forces with distinction."

My mind switches off his speech and I regret I don't recall what else he said. As I'm standing here in the front rank, I marvel that at last this phase of my service is about to end. I continue to hold my stance correctly and to maintain the required expression on my face. When the general's address ends, we are brought back to attention, the band strikes up and our intake marches off parade while the remaining intakes remain and give a "general salute". Once we are clear of the square, we halt and are dismissed from the parade. That's the final action. I now hold the rank of second lieutenant. I'm an officer in the British Army.

Chapter Fifteen

We're dismissed from the parade and, as soon as we have handed in our SLR rifles at the armoury, we are free to leave. Already our personal kit has been packed and left for collection on our tidied bed-spaces, ready for a quick getaway. There is no final end of training party, we had that last evening. It was a low-key event held in our local NAAFI. Just a few beers, feeling relieved we had got through the course but remembering those who had been RTU'd along the way. Our intake, which had started with thirty officer cadets, had been whittled down to nineteen. We knew that this was the final tally, and all we had to do the next day was perform through the parade, but somehow, we all seemed apprehensive and somewhat superstitious that at this eleventh hour, something might still go wrong. But it didn't and here we are!

I suddenly see my parents. I had told them about the "passing out" parade and that parents were welcome but I didn't expect them to come. They are accompanied by a friend of my father, who is somewhat more commercially minded and actually owns a car. My time so far in the military has been a totally separate world from my home-life in Saltford and I'm so pleased to be able to show my folks just a little of what army life is about. I'm proud that they had come, and, particularly, on this special day.

I've now been home on leave for a few days. All we've been told is that we will shortly be receiving our joining instructions for our new regiments. I've been watching out for the post and this morning a letter arrives. I think back to the last time I received a letter with the envelope marked "On Her Majesty's Service", which told me I was to be called up for national service. This letter is a complete contrast. It reads:

"Dear Sir,
    It is hereby confirmed that you have been granted a commission as an officer of Her Majesty's Land Forces in the rank of second

lieutenant. You are assigned to the Royal Hampshire Regiment with secondment to 2nd Battalion the Queen's Own Nigeria Regiment. Your seniority date is 14 January 1960. You will receive your joining instructions and an information pack by separate mail.

I have the honour to be, sir, your obedient servant.

James Ogilvy

Under secretary, Ministry of Defence."

Wow! How my life has changed in just a few days. Back in Mons, Aldershot, RSM Kincaid had been shouting at us till the final parade and was still calling us "You 'orrible little men". Now I'm addressed as "Dear Sir" and "I have the honour to be, sir, your obedient servant". That's going to take some getting used to!

The next post brings a bulky envelope addressed to Second Lieutenant P J Chambers. This confirms my secondment to the 2nd Battalion, QONR, based in Dalet Barracks, Kaduna, Northern Nigeria. The letter tells me I am to report to battalion headquarters there on Thursday 28 January 1960 and encloses a BOAC air ticket reservation from London at 18.30 hours on 27 January. The ticket shows a one-way flight from London Heathrow to Kano, Nigeria, with an onward connection from Kano to Kaduna.

Apart from the air ticket, the envelope also contains a short summary about the regiment and a leaflet about Nigeria. It also informs me that:

- I must acquire Paludrine tablets from my chemist and start taking one a day straightaway as a safeguard against malaria.
- I must report directly to the quartermaster at Topsham Barracks, Exeter for the issue of tropical uniforms. A return rail warrant from Bath to Exeter is included.

That's all. All very neat and organised but, to me, a totally new experience. My mother has an old atlas and I find where Kano and Kaduna are — way up in the north of the country. I'm finding this new information exciting but also daunting. I've never been out of England so far and my only visit to London was last year with Patrick in his "Harringtonmobile" with my other chums from Mons.

I manage to get a phone number for the quartermaster in Exeter and arrange to go there the next Monday. I get to speak to the QM himself.

He sounds a regular guy and is not at all phased by my request for tropical uniforms. He says he's been informed about my kit requirements. He asks for my basic measurements — height, waist, inside leg and tells me he'll get the kit ready.

I don't have much time left before I leave for Nigeria. I'd like to have spent time with some of my chums both from my old school and from our village. But it's mid-January, the weather's pretty shitty and all my chums are either back at university or working during the week. In any case, none of my former friends have done national service. For the past eight months, I've been living such a different experience to them and now I find it difficult to relate to them so freely or at least to renew the easy relaxed friendship we had before. The military is an alien world to them and talking about our training, the discipline, the weapon systems, the rank structure, et cetera is all beyond their knowledge and, frankly, their interest.

I also wonder if I should try to contact any of my "girlfriends" before I leave. I feel like some female company before my new adventure to Nigeria. Jilly is a no-go. I've already been given the heave-ho by her so that's it. There is another girl I think about who was always great company. Her name is Diane. She's very sporty and fit. She's also very beautiful! I met her when I was working at the department store in Bristol. This was just before I started going out with Jenni. I remember I took Diane one weekend on the back of my motor-scooter to an athletics championship. We had both entered for the main track events. It became embarrassing as I managed to win all my races — the men's 100, 220 and 880 yards and Diane cleaned the board with all the ladies' events. Our logistic problem was that we had won so many cups and medals, it was difficult to carry them all back with us on the scooter! On a whim, I decide to give Diane a call and see if we might meet up for a drink in Bristol.

It doesn't work out with Diane either. I eventually get her on the phone. She sounds friendly and happy to chat for a while. I tell her I'm now doing my national service in the army and will be going to Nigeria shortly. She enthuses about that and wishes me good luck. But when I suggest we get together for a drink, I can hear the resistance in her voice. She doesn't actually say "no" but none of the dates I suggest is suitable.

Ah well! It was worth a try!

I think perhaps I had used Diane as a smokescreen to forestall me contacting Linda, the girl who I escorted back to our village after we'd both missed the last bus from Bath. She's a sweet girl and has certainly not given me the brush off. I've been thinking about her often since I kissed her the last time we met when we were sitting on the bench on the Saltford side of the river Avon. I also remember how she had responded. I call her house and her mother answers, recognising my voice straightaway. She passes the phone to Linda and we have a short chat but she tells me she's needs to finish off a homework assignment before her school the next day. She asks me if I'm free on Saturday and I tell her it's my last weekend before I leave for Nigeria and, yes, I'd love to see her then. We agree to go for a walk along by the river in the afternoon, weather permitting. If not, we might take the bus and go to the pictures in Bath or perhaps Brislington, on the way to Bristol. We can decide later.

It's Saturday and it's a sunny winter's day, mild for mid-January. I call for Linda at her house at three o'clock as arranged and we agree on a walk. That seems to be our main activity together. We retrace the route we had taken on the way back from Bath via Kelston and this memory brings us together. We cross the river Avon by the old LMS bridge, then decide to take a path that leads up to the woods that are bisected by the disused railway line. The woods are leafless now but, in the spring, they are an abundance of wild bluebells and daffodils. It's been a favourite place of mine ever since I can remember. At one point, deep into the wood there's a clearing with a fine view looking down over the Saltford weir by Shepherd's Boating hire station and the rowing clubs that line the river up towards Corston and Bath. I take off my anorak and lay it on the grassy bank. Linda and I sit down together and look at the view that has formed so much of our childhood lives.

For a while we sit there without talking. I'm pleased to be here, in this very spot and I know I'll treasure this moment and hold it in my memory no matter where and what I may be doing in the future. I don't look directly at Linda but I feel her closeness next to me. I like this girl, how she looks, how she moves, the soft timbre of her voice. We seem to have an easy rapport that is natural and comfortable for us both. We're only just getting to know each other but now I'm about to open a whole new chapter in my life. I'm feeling very attracted to Linda but I know this is not the time to start a deep relationship. I have no idea what my life now has in store, what I'll be required to do, who I'll meet, how I'll feel about Linda when we'll have had no direct contact during the months and maybe years ahead. And Linda, she's still so young and hasn't yet experienced anything beyond her family and school life. I'm jolted out of these thoughts when Linda says:

"Peter, I know you're leaving next week. I need to tell you that I'll miss you terribly. I don't want you to go."

I take my time to answer. I don't know what to say. In the end, I choose to tell her exactly what is in my mind. Anything else could lead to later regrets. I tell her:

"I think we're very good together and perhaps we both want it to lead to something more. But Linda, I also think we both know it would be wrong to get too involved right now. That wouldn't be fair to either of us. From my side, next week I am going to a country whose name I've only recently heard. I know nothing about how my future may turn out. From your side, you still have your "A" levels and then you, too, will be entering a new phase of your life — university, a gap year with travel? Who knows? Let's hold today in our minds and take it for what it is — a wonderful memory."

Linda is silent for a while. She looks away from me and I can see she's disturbed and saddened. My instinct is to put my arm around her and draw her in towards me but I feel it best to let her take her time. Eventually, she turns to face me, her face brightens to a smile and she says:

"Yes Peter, of course you're right. But you can't stop letting a girl dream!"

I'm so touched by Linda's attitude. This time I do hold her and draw her close. These past few minutes have meant so much. We know how we feel right now but we both have to accept that it's best we leave everything light — no declarations of love, no promises for the future, no continuous letters. We're both young and our lives are yet to develop. I know we'll always be friends, Linda and I. Anything more than that is for the future. For now, we have to follow what our destinies will bring.

Already we can feel the shadows lengthening and the coolness of the January evening descending on this quiet wood. We stand up and straighten our clothes. I pick up my anorak and we turn to retrace our path back to the village. But not immediately. First, I take Linda in my arms, hold her close to me and I kiss her, gently at first but, as she responds, with more passion. I can feel the outline of her slim body pressed against me and the arousal of my loins. We hold this embrace for a while then I very slowly pull away. We look earnestly into each other's eyes. Then I tell her in a soft whisper.

"One day, Linda, one day!"

There's nothing more we need to say. We walk slowly back towards the village as the winter light fades. I continue to keep my arm around her not only out of affection but also to keep her warm as the temperature drops in the gathering evening gloom. We reach her house and find her mother is alert and waiting for us. I can tell she has taken to me and asks me in for tea and cakes. I accept and we spend a half hour or so chatting. My posting to Nigeria is, of course, a major topic. I didn't tell either Linda or her mother about becoming an officer but it seems Linda's mother had learnt this from my mother. I can tell she's pleased. I leave their house with mixed emotions.

It's Tuesday night and a lot of thoughts go through my mind before I can go to sleep. Tomorrow, I will leave my home in Saltford, take the train to London then to Heathrow airport and my flight to Kano. I'm nervous as this will be a totally new experience. I'm also excited by the prospect of what lies ahead. I've been told that although I'm being seconded from the routine national service two-year cycle with the British Army, I will still only have to serve for the same period, meaning I will finish my service obligation at the end of April 1961. By then I'll be twenty years old. Who knows after that? I have no job to come back to, no university course to join, and no other commitments. I've been thinking a lot about Linda. It has all the signs of becoming a deepening relationship. I think we both want that. But now, I'm convinced it was right to leave it open. It's better this way. By the time I get back from Africa, who knows, Linda and I could be very different people.

I'm now ready for a new page in my life. I've been to Exeter and collected my tropical uniforms, I've started taking the anti-malaria Paludrine tablets and, last Sunday, my parents invited our neighbours for a social evening at our house as a farewell.

My kit is packed. Tomorrow I will say a final goodbye to my parents. I'll take the train from Bath Spa to London, then to Heathrow. Then I fly to Nigeria. I'm ready.

Chapter Sixteen

I'm sitting three seats down on the left-hand side of a little propeller driven aircraft flying between Kano and Kaduna in Northern Nigeria. Every one of the twelve seats are taken, six down either side. Apart from the pilot, also aboard are his co-pilot/assistant/steward, who calls himself Moussa, and two smelly goats. The latter are tethered at the back of the plane. All of us passengers have window seats. The view has been of a flat arid red coloured landscape stretching far into the distance, interspersed by small habitations — villages or simple farmsteads. My fellow passengers, all male, are dressed in long white cotton robes that cover most of their bodies. Their heads are covered with neatly folded turbans. One feature is that the only white skinned person on board is me.

Moussa has gone forward and is talking to the pilot through the open hatch to the cockpit. They are in conversation and Moussa is nodding his head as if to say: "OK, I'll tell them." He turns towards us passengers and shouts out something in a language I don't understand. Then he turns to me and in decent English, he tells me:

"We'll be arriving at Kaduna in five minutes, sir. Put your seat belt on and prepare for landing. The local time is two p.m."

Already the aircraft is descending and I try to get myself mentally prepared for what is to happen next. Apart from the name of the Dalet Barracks, I've been given no further information and I couldn't find anyone to consult. My kitbag is safely stowed and I've still got a few UK pounds in my pocket. I hope there may be a taxi or something to get me to the barracks.

We land safely on the single runway and I let the front few passengers disembark through the forward door. I line up just in front of the two anxious goats. The sun is now high in the sky and I am hit by the force of its heat and glare as I climb down the steps onto the tarmac runway. At the bottom of the steps, I see a black-skinned army officer. He is immaculately dressed in a starched light khaki shirt and shorts, long socks with puttees and black boots. He's wearing a wide brimmed bush hat with a green hackle. As he sees me, he moves towards me and says:

"Lieutenant Chambers? I'm David Edozi. I'm here to meet you. I hope you had a good flight."

David's English is excellent and I'm relieved that my onward travel is being taken care of. I immediately take a liking to David. He's my introduction to my new regiment — indeed to Africa, to Nigeria. We shake hands and I reply:

"Yeah, I'm Peter Chambers. And, yes, the flight was great. I'm glad to meet you David. What's the score here?"

"Score? Oh! I see what you mean. We just have to wait while they offload your kit then we'll be away. I'll signal to our driver and he'll bring the Land Rover to pick us up."

It doesn't take long to offload the baggage from the back of the aircraft. While we wait, I watch as the two stubborn goats, encouraged by a few sharp slaps, are ushered down the steps and then prodded up a little ramp fitted to the back of a pick-up truck that's been reversed onto the aircraft apron. The owner gets up front with the driver and the party roars off with a trail of exhaust smoke. I can only wonder what their journey from Kano was all about.

I reclaim my kitbag when it appears from the back of the aircraft and David gives a wave to the driver of a military Land Rover that is parked on the edge of the airfield. David ushers me to the front passenger seat, jumps up in the back with my kitbag and off we go. The Land Rover is open topped except for a small overhead canopy. This allows us to experience fully the outside environment and I'm aware of the heat, the dust and, to me for the first time, the smells of Africa, unlike anything I've known before. David points out some key landmarks — town hall, shopping centre, football stadium as we pass by. There are masses of people everywhere, most of the men in T shirts and shorts, the women in long colourful robes. Many of the women are walking along beside the road carrying pots or other loads on their heads. It's noisy and I have to strain to hear David's running commentary. He explains that we have only a short drive of about thirty minutes to get to our barracks.

He tells me: "I propose that we go straight to our officers' mess and have a light lunch. It's pretty quiet at present as most of the battalion is out on manoeuvres. Only our unit, C Company, is in barracks on holding and defence duties. After lunch, we'll get you settled in with accommodation, kit et cetera. Is that OK with you?"

I reply: "Sounds good David. Of course, I've got so many questions but I guess they'll keep till later. This is my first time in Africa and I'm excited just to absorb the atmosphere and try to orientate myself to your world."

The road leading from the airport to the barracks is tarmacked and in quite a good state. In what seems a short time we see the barracks up ahead. The driver turns right and pulls up at the guard room entrance. There is a large sign, which reads, in English: "Second battalion Queen's Own Nigeria Regiment." Then written in another language, which David translates, are the words: "All visitors are to report to the guardroom." A smartly dressed young soldier appears and he and our driver exchange greetings. The barrier is raised and we proceed towards the officers' mess. This is my new home and the start of a new phase of my life.

Map of Nigeria, highlighting Kaduna, home of 2nd Battalion, Queen's Own Nigeria Regiment

Northern Region

Lake Chad

Kaduna

Nigeria

Western Region

Lagos

Eastern Region

Cameroon

Gulf of Guinea

0   200 km

I'm still in a sort of dream world. Our driver drops us off outside a large rambling building; brick walls and a corrugated iron roof. David tells me this is the officers' mess. He introduces me to the mess steward and some of his staff. Also, there is a British officer who I guess is in his forties. He greets me, introducing himself as George Riley, the battalion quartermaster. We arrange that I will meet him later in his stores to "make sure I'm properly kitted out".

David and I both help ourselves to a light lunch from a side table containing platters of meat and fruit. David then summons up the Land Rover and driver and takes us on a mini tour of the barracks. David points out the battalion headquarters building, the main parade ground and the separate lines allocated to the four rifle companies — A through to D. David is from C Company and he tells me I will also be joining the same outfit. This is commanded by a fellow Brit, Major Sutter who, David says, I'll be meeting soon.

Our tour continues to include the soldiers living accommodation, rifle range, armoury, ammunition store, sports pitches and stables. We then drive out of the main training ground and take a trip around an area of well-built houses, which David explains are the married officers' quarters. Close by are lines of smaller houses, which are the accommodation for married soldiers and their families. It's all very neat and tidy and gives an impression of a professional and well-disciplined set-up.

"I've left the best till last!" David says as he tells our driver to pull up by a collection of small individual huts. At least that's what I think he says because I don't understand the language he's speaking. David explains: "These are the single officers' billets. You've been allocated this one and mine is just over there. You'll find they're not de-luxe but adequate for simple living. I'll leave you to settle in. Two things you should know. One is that we are allocated personal orderlies who take care of our basic domestic needs. Your guy is called Private Usman Pele. He's been told to report to you this afternoon. The other point is that Major Sutter has invited you to meet him for supper this evening. A driver will collect you at 18.30 hours. Oh, and you are to report to our C Company lines tomorrow morning at 08.00 hours sharp."

I suppose I should be tired after the long flight from UK but I'm far too excited and want to explore my new world. My billet is small, built partly in wood but with a tin corrugated iron sloping roof. It's raised above the ground on some supporting pillars so I have to climb up four steps to reach the veranda that runs along the front of the building. Inside, there's one room containing a single bed and bare mattress. The bed is surrounded by a wooden frame from which a large white mosquito net has been erected. Other than the bed, the room is quite sparse but there's a wardrobe with hangers for uniforms on one side and drawers for smaller clothes on the other. There's also a small table, a high-backed chair and a writing desk. The room has working electricity with a lamp on a small bedside table and an overhead light. The room leads to a small annex, which contains a shower and a lavatory. I also notice another small cubicle with a fridge (empty!) and a kettle. Outside, on the wooden veranda, are two wicker chairs.

While I'm in the midst of the initial inspection of my new home this afternoon, there's a knock on the door. I look up to see a black soldier wearing a similar uniform to David's but with no badges of rank. He is tall and muscular. When he sees me, he immediately snaps to attention and smartly salutes. In clear but very limited English, he announces:

"Lieutenant Chambers, sir. I am Private Usman Pele. I am your batman and have been detailed to look after your requirements. I have brought sheets and pillow cases for your bed. Shall I make this up now?"

It takes me a while to adjust. After being treated like shit for the first months of my army service, it's a total change in my fortunes to be allocated the support of this young soldier. At first, I don't know quite how to respond but I realise I must quickly adapt from being a private soldier myself to becoming an officer. Private Usman Pele remains standing to attention, waiting for me to reply. I stammer out:

"S-stand at ease — er yes, go ahead and make up the bedding." I watch as Pele expertly moves the mosquito netting aside, prepares the bed and replaces the mosquito netting. He then says:

"My orders are to escort you to the quartermaster's stores and ensure you have the correct uniforms for tomorrow's parade."

This is my introduction to Private Usman Pele. He speaks adequate English but he tells me he is a Hausa man, which is the majority tribe in the battalion and Hausa is the most spoken language here. I ask Pele about his family and he tells me he is married, has four children and he and they are all accommodated in the soldiers' quarters nearby. As we talk, I realise I will be depending heavily on this guy at least until I learn the protocol here and what my own duties will involve. I also find I like Usman Pele. He has a warm personality and I look forward to getting to know him better and working with him. Usman tells me that the Hausa word for "house" is "*gida*". I like the sound of that word and decide always to use it when referring to my new abode.

Usman Pele leads me over to the quartermaster's stores with my kitbag full of all the tropical uniforms I had been issued with in UK. Captain George Riley, who I had met in the officers' mess at lunchtime, was there. The first thing he does is scoff at my UK-issued kit, throwing it all in a heap on the floor, exclaiming:

"Bloody rubbish — can't think why they still have that stuff. I'm going to get you looking like a real officer of the Nigerian army! You remember how David Edozi was dressed? Well, we'll set you up like that in time for your first parade tomorrow."

George takes my basic measurements — I'm six-foot one-inch tall, have a thirty-three-inch waist and take size nine boots — and he sorts out a series of uniforms. He explains I will need a normal daily working uniform consisting of sand-coloured shirt, long shorts and an official parade dress outfit with a tailored longer jacket. With both, I will wear long green socks (our battalion colour), light coloured puttees and black boots. I will be provided with the same wide brimmed bush hat that I've seen David wearing with the green hackle. I will also require a set of long combat trousers for "field" training and a "mess kit" for formal evening functions. I've brought a "Sam Browne" belt that I had acquired in UK. George examines this and grudgingly passes it as being OK provided, he says looking at Usman Pele, it gets "a fucking good" clean.

Later, at 18.30 hours precisely, a driver arrives outside my *gida* to take me to the married officers' quarter of Major Sutter, who will be my company commander.

The major is a tall man in, I would guess, his late thirties. He has blond hair bleached even paler by the sun and has a small moustache. This evening he's wearing sand-coloured slacks, a white shirt and regimental tie. I notice he's deeply tanned, which contrasts totally with my lily-white English winter skin. He looks to be a very fit and active guy. I'm rather nervous as this is my first meeting with my new company commander but I find him and his wife, Carolyn, to be charming. They have gone out of their way to put me at ease. We drink beers and Mrs Sutter produces a light supper, mostly salads and an exotic array of local fresh fruit. Our conversation is relaxed. Major Sutton gives a brief overview of the battalion's mission this year — first training for operations in the Cameroons for a three-month tour of duty there, then our participation in Nigeria's independence ceremonies on 1 October. He keeps to a broad outline of our activities and tells me I will be getting much more detail later. After our supper, he tells me we will meet tomorrow at C Company lines for first parade at 08.00 hours.

Now, here I am on the veranda of my *gida* enjoying a beer that somehow Usman Pele has managed to put into my fridge. Above me, the clear night African sky is illuminated with a myriad of stars. I had long ago dispensed with my suit jacket. It's now after 23.00 hours and still warm with a balmy light breeze. I realise I will be on show tomorrow as I go on my first parade as an officer. I will meet the soldiers of my first platoon. Usman Pele will ensure I'm awake by 06.45 hours and now it's time to get to bed. I finish my beer, go inside, strip off, brush my teeth, have a pee and a quick wash. I just about make it to my bed before I crash out. My last thoughts are of a mix of apprehension and excitement about tomorrow.

Chapter Seventeen

I come out of a deep fog of sleep. I check my watch and see it's 06.45 hours, exactly the time I have to wake up. I guess Usman Pele must have discretely woken me. I struggle to get up and the first thing I see is that the uniform that Captain George Riley issued me yesterday has been transformed. The droopy creased shirt and shorts are now crisply stiff and starched. On each shoulder tab of the shirt has been attached one metal pip — the designation of the rank of second lieutenant. Someone, Usman Pele I suppose, has laid them out on the little table. Next to this are my now gleamingly polished boots, high socks, puttees and waist-belt. On the top of the table is a smart new bush hat with its prominent green hackle.

I stagger across the room of my little *gida*, find the toilet, take a leak and more. Then I stand under the shower and turn on the tap. The water flows freely — there's no hot/cold control but that's absolutely not a problem. The outside temperature here, even at this time of day, is quite warm and I find the shower is refreshing and wakes me up. I dress in the uniform that Usman has laid out for me. It's so strange but everything fits well including the size of the bush hat. I do a visual check in the mirror with all my new uniform on including the bush hat. I find I'm looking at someone that I can't yet recognise. But that's the new me!

I arrive at the C Company lines just before 08.00 hours. There are single storey buildings forming three sides of a square with a mini parade ground in the centre. The company headquarter building is clearly signed and I report there as told by Major Sutter. Facing me, as I approach, is a tall slim immaculately dressed soldier carrying a pace stick under his arm and wearing the rank badge of sergeant-major. He snaps a salute, as smart as any from Mons or Devizes, then extends his hand saying:

"Lieutenant Chambers? Major Sutter detailed me to welcome you here to C Company. My name is Company Sergeant-Major Kabala. I'm just known as the CSM. I'm going to show you how the company is organised and then introduce you to your platoon. You will be the platoon commander of Number Two Platoon of C Company. We're short of officers at present as Lieutenant Buhari is acting as the battalion patrol expert and is advising the commanding officer out on manoeuvres. So, for the present, we've divided the company into only two platoons instead of the usual three. There are forty-two soldiers in your platoon."

I find I immediately like CSM Kabala. His English is good, spoken with a soft engaging Nigerian timbre. As he continues his briefing, he speaks with knowledge and confidence. I know I have a lot to learn from him.

CSM Kabala suddenly raises his voice to parade ground volume as he shouts out; "Number Two Platoon, fall in at the parade ground at the double!" He also gives what I presume is the same order in the Hausa language. Groups of soldiers who I had noticed carrying out various duties around the camp, immediately stop what they were doing and run into the centre of the company parade ground. They form up in three lines under the orders of a sergeant. In front of me, I see a mass of black faces and I wonder how I'm ever going to differentiate between individuals. They all stand stiffly to attention while the sergeant marches out and reports to CSM Kabala.

"Sgt Yerima Bado reporting sir. Number Two Platoon on parade and ready for your inspection.

CSM Kabala replies. "Thank you, sergeant. Now I introduce you to Lieutenant Chambers, your new platoon commander."

This is the first time I meet "my soldiers". I feel a mix of apprehension and pride. I know we will have to get to know each other well both here in the barracks and later, as we face the operational tasks Major Sutter outlined last evening. I wonder how I will be able to learn all their names and hope I can gain their trust. I have to start at the beginning not only as being an officer but also being a white guy in a black man's world.

My first morning with C Company is busy. Major Sutter arrives and we have a formal interview following our more relaxed chat last evening. He tells me that I need to get to know my soldiers as quickly as possible as we will be leaving for manoeuvres next week with the aim of practising all the skills we will need to perform our operational role during the plebiscite in the Cameroons. The battalion will deploy there at the end of February for a three- to four-month tour. Major Sutter also tells me that the battalion needs to improve the leadership skills of all our junior rank NCOs (i.e. corporals and lance-corporals) and he has nominated me to run a course for all these NCOs from the whole battalion. I am therefore to produce a full training programme for the CO's approval shortly after we return from manoeuvres.

My head is full of Major Sutter's instruction as I spend much of the rest of the morning with CSM Kabala and Sgt Bado looking through the photo printouts of all the Number Two Platoon soldiers. They tell me the name of each, which tribe he's from — e.g. Hausa, Fulani, Tif, Yoruba or Ibo, what training each has had and a summary of their performance — good or bad!

I make two pledges to myself. The first is that I must quickly learn the correct name of all of my soldiers and study their service records. The second is that I will do my best to learn to speak at least passable Hausa as soon as possible. I think I'm going to ask CSM Kabala to be my language tutor.

I'm now three days into my new life as a second lieutenant in the 2nd Battalion Queen's Own Nigeria Regiment. Yesterday, the rest of the battalion rolled into camp in an assortment of vehicles, mainly Land Rovers and three-ton Bedford trucks. Their return was orderly and very impressive but the dusty and mud-stained condition of the vehicles showed they had been out on non-tarmacked roads for long distances. With their return, the barracks immediately filled up and I feel I'm now part of a large military force.

Last evening, there was a gathering in the officers' mess. I was pleased that David Edozi and George Riley were both there and, patiently, they made the introductions to the officers from the other companies who had just returned for manoeuvres. Most were Nigerian officers whose names I'm still struggling to remember but I noted that there appeared to be a mix of the tribal backgrounds. There were also some fellow Brits. First to introduce himself was a guy called Bill Holding who told me he was a second lieutenant national serviceman like myself, who had also undergone similar training including a session at Mons Officer Cadet School. It seems he was some two intakes ahead of me there and has been with the battalion here for about nine months. He told me he has only about another nine more months to do before he'll be demobbed back to UK. He said his job in the battalion is Motor Transport Officer, or MTO as it's called. Bill and I obviously have a lot in common and I feel he and David Edozi are likely to be my closet chums in the battalion.

I was also introduced to an older British officer called Major Charles Sedgewick. He's a florid faced man, aged I would guess, about fifty. He has a large waistline and seems already to be tackling not his first whiskey of the evening. He told me he's the commander of what's called Administrative Company. He was friendly enough and treated me in an avuncular manner, insisting I come to the local Kaduna club on a Saturday evening. Not knowing what else to say, I, of course, agreed. Major Sutter was also there, mostly keeping company with two other British majors, who I was told were the commanders of A and B Companies. Our commanding officer, Lieutenant Colonel Johnson was not there as, apparently, he was dining with the British high commissioner in Kaduna. I was told I will meet him tomorrow. After the dinner was completed, we all adjourned to the anteroom where the beer and whiskey flowed freely, the noise volume increased and everyone relaxed. I enjoyed the evening.

Today is the first time I've been rostered as battalion duty officer. I've been given a full briefing about this duty from both David Edozi and CSM Kabala. Looks like we can forget about getting much sleep during the night. In summary, this is it. We have to perform all our own duties during the working day then at 18.00 hours, we inspect the guard and ensure all ranks are clear about their duties during the night. One section is tasked to patrol the barracks, respond to any intrusion and inform my command post, another section moves to the high commissioner's residence in Kaduna town and mounts guard there for the night. A third detachment is sent to guard an ammunition store some twenty kilometres from here. The duty officer stays/sleeps in a separate designated billet, checks on the three guard detachments at various times during the night and responds to any incident that may occur during the duty period. The duty lasts until 06.30 hours in the morning after which normal daytime duties are resumed.

So far, so good. I've carried out the guard 18.00 hours inspection and ensured that the three guard detachments are correctly allocated and briefed. I've now retired for the night in the duty officer's billet. This consists of a small office with both landline and radio communications and an adjoining bedroom, which I don't see myself using much tonight. I have despatched both the high commission detail and the ammunition store guard with their own dedicated vehicles. I have also two Land Rovers in reserve to use as I see fit.

I'm just settling in during the early evening when I'm visited by one of the corporals who is a section commander from "my" platoon in C Company. I've learnt his name is Cpl Aiki Riba. He's short for a Nigerian and I'm told he belongs to the Tif tribe. I'd already noted he has several etched facial (tribal) markings and a set of spiky filed teeth. He's a tough little guy and has acquired a reputation as being a skilled and loyal soldier and an accomplished tracker. He has very limited English and my Hausa has yet to get going so we have some communication problems between us. His main message though is clear enough as he is accompanied by his heavily pregnant wife. Aiki tells me his wife is about to give birth and asks permission to use the duty Land Rover to take her to the local Kaduna hospital. This is my first "out of routine" task and I'm keen to assist in my soldier's personal problem. I summon the duty driver, help (Mrs) Aiki Riba up into the back of the Rover next to her husband. I decide to accompany them personally and I get up front next to the driver and off we go.

I've been told that Kaduna hospital is on the outskirts of the town, some twenty miles from the barracks. I don't know the procedure there, of course, but I'm keen to ensure we do whatever's necessary to assist the poor lady's childbirth. This is absolutely not my area of expertise!

We must have driven not more than half way to the hospital when Cpl Aiki Riba asks me to stop the Land Rover. I don't know what's going on but I tell the driver to pull over to the side of the road. Cpl Aiki Riba helps his wife down and they disappear off into the bush. I suppose his wife has to respond to a call of nature, so we discreetly wait for her and her husband to return. Our wait continues and it is probably a full half an hour before the pair return. I say pair but I notice Cpl Aiki Riba is carrying a bundle in his arms. We all get back aboard the Rover and I tell the driver to continue to the hospital but Cpl Aiki Riba tells me it's now not necessary as his wife, with his assistance, has already given birth while they were out there in the bush. He asks if we can now go back to the barracks. So we do. That was the only out of routine incident that I had to relate in my first duty officer's log!

The next day, I attend my normal "in barracks" work but the incident of Cpl Aiki Riba's wife has been playing on my mind. After our daily duties, I decide to follow up. I find the "other ranks" married quarters and am directed to Cpl Aiki Riba's *gida*. It's very clean and well presented. Cpl Aiki Riba is at home and I ask if I can see his newly born. He invites me into his home and, as we approach the entrance, we pass a lady sweeping the yard. Inside the corporal's delightful little house, there is a baby wrapped in a lightweight blanket. Cpl Aiki Riba plays the proud father, scoops the baby up, a little boy, and we both admire how healthy he seems to be. I'm relieved that my duty the previous day had ended so well. But I have to wonder about the mother and I anxiously say to the corporal:

"I'm so pleased about your baby — he seems very healthy but, tell me, where is your wife?"

"But sir," he replies with surprise, "You just passed her as we came through. She's the lady you saw sweeping the yard:"

Indeed, he's correct and when we come out of the house, I recognise his wife from the evening before. When I speak to her anxiously to ask about her health, she puts down her broom and just smiles. Husband and wife seem surprised that I'm asking about her with such concern. I realise I have so much to learn. In Europe, childbirth is rated as a big deal. Women go into labour then give birth either in the maternity ward of a hospital or at home with the help of a midwife. The mother then has a period of recuperation and maternity before life returns to normal. Even the husband gets some time off work. But not here. Not in Nigeria. It seems that childbirth is regarded as a normal routine business. The Aiki Ribas' baby was born yesterday. Today is just another day!

Chapter Eighteen

I've now been here in Kaduna for nearly three weeks and am beginning to find my feet. It's been a steep learning curve both from the military and social sides. So far. I've hardly been out of the barracks and I'm tempted when, earlier in the week, Major Sedgewick pressed me and Bill Holding to come to the Kaduna club on Saturday evening. I'm undecided but Bill says to me privately:

"Look, Peter, Major Sedgewick is a bit of an old bore but he's part of the furniture of the battalion. It would be diplomatic to spend some time with him there. But I should warn you that he likes his whisky and really knows how to throw it back. We could eat in the officers' mess earlier then join the major for drinks at, say, about eight-thirty. Why don't we take my car to be independent? We could then leave when we choose."

It sounds like a good plan and I'm intrigued to experiment with Kaduna's social life so I readily agree. I still haven't managed to do any shopping since I landed in Kaduna but George Riley has been kind enough to kit me out with a couple of pairs of lightweight slacks, white shirts and a pair of sand-coloured desert boots. George tells me that this combination is acceptable to wear both in the officers' mess in the evenings and in the Kaduna club as it more or less conforms to what is known as the "planters order" dress code.

I'm concerned that I won't be able to pay my way for drinks, etc. this evening as my first salary as a British officer hasn't yet come through. Everything in the barracks has been put on a tab. Bill tells me not to worry, it takes time to grind through the system. He offers to give me a float, which I can square up with him later. He explains that the new currency of Nigerian pounds (divided into shillings and pence as per the UK) was introduced last year in preparation for independence.

Bill's car is an elderly Wolseley. As he's the battalion Motor Transport Officer (MTO), he can ensure it's kept in good mechanical condition. He drives with fluency and after about a half an hour heading in towards Kaduna town, we arrive at the club in good time for our rendezvous (RV) with Major Sedgewick.

Photo: Bill's Wolseley

How to describe the club? I suppose it's much like I had imagined a British colonial social establishment to be — here we're in northern Nigeria but I suspect these clubs are not much different in, say, Kenya or India or Singapore. The club exudes an atmosphere of calm stability, permanence and British gentility. There's a perimeter fence around the estate, with a smart sentry at the entrance access point. We show the sentry our military ID cards and tell him we're Major Sedgewick's guests. He accepts that, salutes and raises the barrier. Inside the perimeter, there are car parking spaces then a path leading through well-manicured lawns and trees to the club entrance. The building is a semi-circular shape with the entire frontage open to the elements allowing fresh air to cool the interior. Inside is a restaurant, separate bar and a large "sitting out" area with tables surrounded by wicker-framed chairs with large comfortable cushions. Overhead fans hang from the ceilings to add additional cooling. There is an orchestra stand with a cleared space for dancing.

When Bill and I enter the club, it's already quite full. We can see the restaurant is well patronised and most of the chairs in the "sitting out" area are also occupied. The "orchestra" is a grand name for what, in reality, is a small ensemble, consisting of piano, saxophone, drums and double bass. They are giving a rendition of "Stardust" as we walk in. I can't help but notice that most of the club members are white but there are a few exceptions. I see one family whose appearance suggests they are of Indian origin and I'm also pleased to see that David Edozi is there with another Nigerian. Both are wearing their traditional robes.

I ask Bill who are most of the members. He explains:

"Well, I'm not an expert but I believe most of the membership is composed of resident Brits from the British administration here — civil service, judiciary, police and military. There are also a number of civilians working for British or international companies such as banks, the construction industry and so on — some on long-term, others short-term contracts."

The staff is all black. The waiters are impeccably turned out wearing white uniforms with red cummerbunds and red fez caps. I suppose this "white skinned members" and "black skinned staff" is logical as we are in British colonial Africa. But in my ignorance, I would have thought that by now there would have been a more equal mix of cultures, considering that Nigerian independence will take place later this year. I find this preponderance of white-skinned people, myself of course included, slightly unsettling.

Major Charles Sedgewick spots Bill and me and beckons us over. He has a glass of whisky in front of him. I'm sure it isn't his first! There are two other Brits of similar vintage sitting next to him. The major does the introductions:

"Right you two, come over here and meet a couple of my old chums. This is Edward Southerby who runs our local bank. I know young Bill here is already a customer so no further intro is necessary. But I also want you both to meet James Heathcote from the British high commission. You'll find that James will feature prominently in all of our lives later this year when we have to face up to this tiresome independence business. We three have known each other for many years. Isn't that right? What!"

The two gentlemen both nod their agreement and the major continues, talking directly to me: "Now young Peter, this is your first time here at our club, right? You should make the most of it while it remains half way civilised."

He points over in the direction of David Edozi and continues: "Already you see we're being infiltrated. I know we have to accept African officers into our regiment but at least we should be able to continue to keep our social lives to ourselves! Anyway, enough of that for now. Make the most of the evening and why don't you invite some of our charming young ladies to dance?"

The major stops his diatribe. He raises his hand, clicks his fingers and waves across to a waiter who instantly comes over to our table and hovers ready to take a drinks order. The major brusquely tells him:

"Bring these two gentlemen whisky and the same again for my colleagues and myself."

That's it. My introduction to the Kaduna club and to Major Charles Sedgewick in full socialising mood. I've only once before tried drinking whisky and I didn't enjoy the experience. I would much prefer a beer but I haven't been given the choice. I realise I'm very new to the colonial scene here but, somehow, I find the major's disparaging remarks about our Nigerian officers distasteful and unnecessary. It's the first time I've experienced any such antagonism. I decide to say nothing. Yet again, I realise I've got a lot to learn.

Major Sedgewick had mentioned having a dance. That at least sounds interesting and also will avoid having to keep pace with the whisky-drinking rounds, which seem likely to continue if we stay for long at the major's table.

There are several couples on the dance floor and I wonder how I can get involved. I find the music very — well — old fashioned! The band leader seems to be a great fan of Mantovani because all the music so far has been from that era. We've had: "Moon River", "Charmaine", "Smoke gets in your eyes" and now we're into "Misty". The dancing is very formal — either waltz, quickstep or foxtrot — I haven't learnt any of these — very different from my jazz club back in Bath where we do our own thing with rock and roll and jive. I try to work out who are the unattached girls as I don't want to create some social misdemeanour by trying to pick up some guy's wife. It isn't too difficult as most of the couples are considerably older than my nineteen years and I watch them return together to the same table. Then I spot two much younger girls who seem to be with their parents and not attached to a partner. One is quite pretty and could be about my age. I had earlier seen her dancing with one guy and now she's with a different chap. I wait till the end of the number — another Mantovani classic — and watch them return to her table. I see her dancing partner thanking her for the dance and saying a "thank you" to an older couple who I take to be her parents. Now's my chance.

I don't know the etiquette but I think it best to play it ultra-formally. I go over to her table and say to the father:

"Excuse me, sir, may I have your permission to ask your daughter for a dance?"

He doesn't answer, just looks me up and down and nods. His wife, though, does give me a smile. At least that's something positive. I turn to the girl and say:

"Hello, I'm Peter Chambers. May I have the pleasure of this dance?"

She doesn't exactly spring to her feet. She gives a rather resigned sigh, stands and allows me to take her hand and escort her to the dancefloor. The new music number is a tune I don't know but it's in the same genre as the rest. I recognise it's a waltz tempo. I don't know how to dance a waltz properly but I do know you have to keep to a one, two, three, one, two, three, one, two, three rhythm. It shouldn't be too difficult — so off we go. I ask her name, and she tells me it's Annabel, I ask her how long she's been in Kaduna and she tells me two weeks staying with her parents then she's soon going back to uni in UK. I ask her if she likes Kaduna and she says it's OK. She doesn't ask me anything about myself and doesn't look at me directly. At one point, I lose the waltz rhythm and she glares at me, as I step on her toe. I realise I'm on a loser with Annabel. At the end of the dance, I escort her back to her parents' table, thank her and her parents and head back to the bar. When the next dance starts, I see that Annabel is back on the floor with another guy.

There's still one other girl of about my age who also seems to be unattached. I suppose I could have a go at asking her to dance but, after the Annabel experience, I don't fancy the prospect of another brush off.

Bill has been observing my pathetic pick-up attempt. He says:

"Hey Peter, couldn't help watching you there. Guess you dipped out with Annabel. I don't even bother with the British girls here. There's so few of them and they are heavily outnumbered by guys like us. They can afford to be very choosy, which I find a real turn off."

"Yea, I'm beginning to understand," I reply. "I thought I'd have a go on the dance floor but I was a real flop there. From the start, I could tell she wasn't the slightest bit interested in me. She's a pretty girl but, to be truthful, no fun to be with. It was as if she was doing me a tremendous favour to dance with me. I'm really not into that."

I'm beginning to get restless. The Kaduna club is in a beautiful setting and seems to be very efficiently organised. I realise I'm still very new here and have yet to adjust fully to the lifestyle of living in British colonial Africa. But after Major Sedgewick's remarks, his heavy whisky drinking, the boring music and the lack of girls to dance with, I'm feeling that I just don't belong in this scene. Bill can sense this. He turns to me and says:

"Peter, why don't we take off. While you were doing your thing on the dancefloor, I had a chat with David Edozi. He suggested we go with him and his friend to an African club. It's not far from here. There's great music, not at all like this, and real Nigerian night life. We could say a polite goodbye to the major and bugger off. How about it?"

Well done Bill! I tell him. "You're on Bill. Let's go!"

As a point of courtesy, we go over to Major Sedgewick's table to say goodbye. I thank him for inviting us but I'm not sure how well it registers with him as, by this stage, he doesn't seem to be focussing too well. I'm concerned about how he's going to get back and I check on this with Bill who says:

"Oh! don't worry about that. Remember, he's one of the old school, who's lived in Africa for much of his service. He has good contacts here both with the ex-pat community and with the Nigerians. Despite what you might have gathered from his comments, it's amazing how popular he is with the locals. I think they see him as some sort of avuncular icon. You can rest assured someone will see he gets home safely."

We meet up with David Edozi and his colleague in the car park where he has also left his car. He tells us to follow on in Bill's Wolseley. There's not far to go and soon David pulls up, gets out and indicates for Bill to park up behind his car.

The scene is a total contrast to the genteel Kaduna club. We're in a dimly lit back street. David leads us along a series of narrow alleyways and stops at a door set into a high rough wall. He pushes the door open and immediately we hear loud music blaring out from inside the building. There is a guy just inside and David gives him some coins, which we find entitles us to go through.

Inside, the place is packed. We find ourselves in a large roofless building. There is a moon tonight and it shines brightly through. Together with a myriad of stars, the full moon provides the main illumination. We are surrounded by a throng of Nigerians — some in traditional dress, others in T-shirts and shorts. I can tell there's no fixed dress code here — anything goes! There's a band at one end of the building hammering out a hypnotic rhythm. The central area is packed with dancers all locked into the power of the music. Around the perimeter walls there are also many people. Although not actually dancing, they are instinctively moving in time to the music.

David Edozi comes up close and shouts into my ear:

"Welcome to our club, Peter and to our Nigerian 'highlife' music. How do you like it?"

I'm finding the scene difficult to take in. It couldn't be more of a contrast to the Kaduna club. The atmosphere and the music are mesmerising. I shout back to David.

"This is amazing David, I love it. Would it be a problem for me, as a Brit, to dance like I see everyone else is?"

"Not at all Peter. That's what we do here. Wait a moment. I'll be right back."

David slips away and I wonder what he's up to. Then he reappears with a young woman wearing a traditional floral Nigerian costume. I notice two other things. One is that she's taller than most of the other girls around her and very pretty, the other is that she's smiling widely

135

and directly at me. Her even white teeth contrast with the ebony texture of her skin. David again puts his hand to my ear so that I can hear him against the roar of the music. He shouts to me.

"This is Assibi, the sister of Mamadu who was with us earlier in the Kaduna club. She saw us come in and would like to show you how to enjoy our 'highlife' music. When you're done, I'll have a beer ready for you!"

David doesn't need to say anything more. I just give him a big "thumbs up" sign, turn to Assibi and we're away. She takes my hand, leads me to the middle of the dance area and we're straight into the music. It's loud, it's raucous but I find it totally infectious. It's impossible not to pick up the rhythm. As I dance with Assibi, she looks up at me, smiles, and nods encouragement as our bodies move and sway in unison. I look directly at her face and realise she is not just pretty, she is truly beautiful. Her face is as if it's chiselled out of marble — small straight nose, high cheek bones. All her movements as she dances are not only rhythmic, but also have an attitude that's proud, almost noble. I'm captivated. All around, I see happy, smiling faces. I notice that Bill has also taken to the floor holding another young woman. I don't know where he found her! We are the only two white skinned people here. I suppose I could have found this intimidating but all around us I feel friendliness in the eyes of these people and warmth in their attitude. And being with Assibi, I feel safe, relaxed and content.

I don't know how long I dance with Assibi. We can't talk over the music but even so I find her manner, and just her presence, infectious. Eventually the band takes a break and Assibi and I walk hand in hand back to where we had last seen David. When we find him, he's standing with Bill and the guy who was with him in the Kaduna club and who he told me was Assibi's brother. David's holding a couple of beer bottles and says:

"Glad to see you enjoying yourself, Peter, and I can tell Assibi is as well!" He hands me one of the bottles and continues: "Oh and have a go at our local beer. Not quite like your British bitter or larger but it suits our Nigerian taste. While you're having a swig, let me introduce you to my good friend, Mamadu Baldeh. Like both of us and Bill, Mamadu is also an army lieutenant. He's on detachment in the Zaria training school at present but will soon be back with the battalion."

I shake hands with Mamadu and thank him for the introduction to his sister Assibi. He just smiles broadly and replies:

"No problem, I can tell she likes you Peter! We Fulanis and Hausas are very broad-minded people — you can see we're even friends with David here and that's a pretty rare thing between us and Ibos as no doubt you'll be finding out!"

I don't understand what he means by that comment but I let it go. The evening is too relaxed to get into a discussion about tribal differences. I notice the band is packing up their instruments and the crowd is starting to drift away. Bill indicates it's time to go so I finish off the beer and we thank David for luring us away from the Kaduna club. I hope we can come here again. I also hope that Assibi will be here.

Bill and I trace our way back to his Wolseley and then head for our home in Dalet Barracks. Neither of us says much on the drive back. We both have our own thoughts. It's been an evening of contrasts. I need time to assess these new experiences and how this will affect my attitudes and values. But that's for another day.

Chapter Nineteen

We are now into March and tomorrow our C Company goes on field manoeuvres. I've been told that much of the rest of the battalion will also deploy with us but it'll be C Company who primarily will be tested during the manoeuvres. This training is in preparation for our operational tour of the Cameroons, which we deploy to in three weeks' time. We'd been told that when we're there, our companies will be well spread out covering a large geographical area. It's hoped we can fulfil our role without confrontation with the communist-backed insurgents that we've been briefed are aiming to disrupt the political plebiscite process. But we need to be fully prepared. The aim of our manoeuvres is to train for any eventuality that might crop up in the Cameroons, including having to fight well-armed insurgent forces. This is the first time that I've had to face the possibility of coming under fire. I'm not sure of my reaction, perhaps more apprehension than fear. But also, some excitement. How will I cope if there are bullets flying around me? Will I be able to keep calm and lead my soldiers effectively? I now fully realise the importance of training.

I have a near disaster late on the Sunday morning, the day before we leave for our manoeuvres. I've just got up after last night's socialising in Kaduna when a soldier turns up in a Land Rover outside my *gida*. He jumps out, salutes smartly and informs me that he is delivering the Land Rover to me as my personal vehicle for the manoeuvres. This is news to me. He hands me a set of keys and leaves. I feel quite chuffed that I am to have my very own transport but there's one major problem. I've never driven a vehicle with four wheels. I've got a licence for my now defunct Lambretta scooter but this is a whole new dimension. I don't know how to react. If I go to Major Sutter, my company commander, and tell him I can't drive, I don't know how he will react. Will I be relegated to some minor role for the manoeuvres? I don't want that and I don't want to admit my driving limitations.

In the end, I decide to give myself a rapid self-teach instruction course and hope for the best. I get in the driver's seat, find the ignition, put in the key and turn it. There's a throaty roar as the LR starts up. Now, what to do? I know the principles of driving (who doesn't?), and where all the pedals, etc. are but there's a big difference between principle and practice. I release the hand brake then depress the clutch pedal with my left foot and push the gear lever from the neutral position into first. I then try to press on the accelerator with my right foot while slowly easing up on the clutch. First time, the LR lurches forward, then immediately the engine stalls and cuts out. Try again, same result. I'm beginning to sweat realising that it's going to take time to master the technique. On the positive side, this is Sunday and a "stand down" from routine duties. There's a rear entrance to our barracks, which leads onto open bushland. I reckon if I could manage to coax the LR out of the rear gate, I can practise out of sight and sound and not return, until I feel confident I can drive reasonably OK. I try the starting off procedure again — same result, a lurch forward and the engine stalls. On the fifth or sixth time, I seem by chance to hit it right with the accelerator cutting in as I let the clutch out. At last we're moving. I head off towards the rear gate not yet daring to try to move up into second gear. The distance to the gate is about a quarter of a mile and I reach it without stalling the engine again. I'm in luck. The gate is open with a single sentry standing next to it. I aim at the entrance and shout a friendly greeting to the guard. He seems to recognise me and snaps to attention as I drive through. I don't stop and carry on still in first gear until I'm several hundred yards into the bush and well out of sight of the barracks.

Now I have all day to practice without an audience. I hadn't planned for this ordeal and I set off wearing only a T-shirt, shorts and my new trendy flip-flops. They might be trendy but they're bloody hopeless for driving! Too bad — I'm stuck here now! As I press the brake pedal to stop, the LR judders to a jarring sudden halt and the engine cuts out again. I start up again, clutch down, gear in first, slowly letting up the clutch while pressing down on the accelerator. Same as the first time — the LR lurches forward and the engine stalls and cuts out. I calm myself down by taking a few deep breaths.

"Come on, you stupid bugger," I say to myself. "Get a fucking grip on yourself and learn to drive, it's not exactly rocket science!"

I try again — clutch down, gear stick into first, clutch slowly out again as I press down on the accelerator. Same fucking juddery stalling and engine cutting out! I start again. At last, after the umpteenth time, we're away. I drive further into the bush, keeping in first gear. I try to change up into second gear but all that happens is a grinding sound, the engine cuts out and we shudder to a halt again. I start again, OK now into first but the same as before when I try to change up to second gear. I can't seem to grasp how to change up to second or any other gear. I swear out loud both to myself and to the LR.

"I can't drive this bloody thing all the way sticking in first fucking gear!"

For some time, I sit in the driving seat trying to contain my frustration. Then I remember someone, could have been Patrick Harrington back at Mons, saying that Land Rovers don't yet have synchronised gear boxes and that you have to, what he called: "double the clutch" or something. I think that means you have to press on the clutch twice with each gear change, once to move the gear stick into neutral, then as you put it into the selected gear.

I start over again. Gear from neutral into first slowly letting out the clutch and depressing the accelerator. Fine, we move forward nice and smoothly this time. We gain speed and now for the big new experiment! Clutch in, gear back to neutral, clutch in again, gear to second, clutch slowly out and depress the accelerator slowly again. Eureka! It works, we gain speed again and I use the same technique into third gear. Again, no problem! We're now going quite fast over the shrub of the bush. There are no roads here and I'm having to concentrate on steering between bush trees and trying to keep to even ground. I dare not even attempt to go into fourth.

I drive on then, using the "double the clutch" technique. I successfully change down from third gear to second, then slowing and back down to first, then to neutral. The LR calmly slows to a stop. I take my foot off the foot brake and apply the hand brake. I heave a sigh of relief. At last I'm beginning to get the hang of simple driving. I practise this technique several times — all OK. Then it occurs to me that we won't always be going forwards — there will be times when we'll need to reverse. So, taking care to look for obstacles behind me, I use the same technique with the reverse gear position. Wow — it works! Under reasonable control, at last I can go both forwards and backwards!

I reckon I spend about two hours just driving around in the bush. My feet are getting sore due to my flip-flops but too bad! Starting off smoothly and under reasonable control, going through the gears, learning how to coordinate the actions of clutch, accelerator and brake. Starting, changing gears up and down, stopping again. Sometimes going forwards — sometimes in reverse. Repeat, repeat, repeat. At last I feel I've got it!

Next to the gear stick are two levers, one yellow and one red. I think they are something to do with changing the gear ratio to enable the LR to traverse steep slopes or to get extra grip in wet terrain. I try to experiment with these levers but they don't seem to respond. I reckon I can master these later. My priority right now is to be able to form up tomorrow with my LR and stay in convoy with the other company vehicles as we drive from our barracks to our manoeuvre training area.

After all this driving around, I'm quite disorientated and it takes me some time to find my way back to the barracks. It's already well into the afternoon when at last I sedately drive back to the rear gate and neatly park my LR outside my *gida*.

I feel the need to relax after the trauma of learning to drive. Also, my feet hurt after being so bloody stupid to wear my flip-flops while trying to drive. I sit on my terrace and look at the LR that's now parked neatly right outside. I still don't feel totally confident that I'm going to be able to handle it OK tomorrow. I suppose I'll be marshalled into the convoy line and just have to follow on. We've been told that the first leg is a few hours' drive then there's a refuelling point that the MT team have pre-positioned. I'll try to concentrate, keep to the flow of the convoy and hope for the best!

It's far too late for lunch in the officers' mess so I grab a beer from my fridge and spend about an hour trying to master the Hausa vocabulary that I've written down during the language training sessions I've been having with CSM Kabala. He's been very patient with me and has concentrated on the words and phrases I'm most likely to need when talking to our soldiers. Everything we've done so far is verbal as I haven't yet acquired a textbook of the Hausa language. I try to write everything down using phonetic pronunciation as I hear the words from CSM Kabala. Hausa words have little similarity to English but, as far as I've learnt so far, the grammar is pretty basic. For example, there are no "le or la" or "der, die, das" genders as in French or German. CSM Kabala has taught me that our battalion, which comprises a mix of all the main Nigerian tribes, has adopted a "lingua franca", which some call "barracky Hausa" as it also contains some Yoruba and Ibo words.

I stick at the Hausa training for a while until my mind starts to wander and I'm finding I can't concentrate anymore. I'm getting hungry but I can't be bothered to get showered and dressed to go to the mess for supper. I also need to check the kit I'll need for tomorrow's manoeuvres. I go over to my own little fridge to see what I can get by with for tonight and a quick breakfast tomorrow. There's not much left there. Some milk and cornflakes — there's also some eggs, which I could fry on my primus. That's about it. But nature is kind to us here as, for example, there are some pawpaw trees about fifty metres from my *gida* and I often find freshly fallen fruit there. They make a fleshy and nutritious meal. I wander off there in search of some fresh pawpaws to supplement my supper and am in luck. As I pick up a couple, I'm approached by a scruffy little dog. This is quite unusual. Several British officers here do own dogs but they keep them under close control. There are many stays in the nearby villages but I've seen very few here in the barracks.

I head back to my *gida*. The dog follows. As I climb up onto my terrace, it tries to follow me again. I turn and try to shoo it away saying: "Off you go, you don't live here!"

The dog has other ideas. Very decidedly, it climbs the steps onto my terrace, comes directly to me, wags its tail, sits down next to me and looks directly up at me with its appealing eyes. I don't know where it's come from, I see that "it" is a "she", and she is making it very clear she wants to be with me. I can't help being attracted by this animal. I lean down and stroke her head. She responds by pressing against me and wagging her tail again. I run my fingers over her coat searching for ticks or other parasites. I find none. As I sit down in the folding canvas chair on my terrace, the dog comes and lays down next to me. I stay sitting there for a while and the dog stays lying there. Sometimes she looks up at me and flutters her tail then lies back as if sleeping contentedly.

I tell the dog: "I guess I'm stuck to you this evening but I'm going off on manoeuvres tomorrow and you certainly can't come too!"

My hunger gets the better of me so I go inside my *gida* and prepare my simple supper of cornflakes and milk followed by eggs fried on my primus and then the sliced pawpaw. I carry my food back out onto the terrace on a tray. The dog looks at me appealingly and I can tell she's hungry too. I go back inside, bring an extra bowl and we share our supper. I don't know if this diet is good for her constitution but she scoffs it down. She then settles down again at my side.

I've got to concentrate on tomorrow and make sure I've got all the kit I'll need. We've been told we'll be away around ten days. This will be my first "out of barracks" training and I know our company will being tested rigorously. The commanding officer (CO) of the battalion, Lt Col Johnson, and his headquarter staff will require us to show our proficiency in all the military skills we'll need in preparation for our Cameroons deployment. I've now met the colonel on a few occasions. He seems a straightforward guy but he correctly sets high standards and comes down hard on anyone who he feels is not up to them. I hope I'll measure up to those standards. I feel apprehensive about the manoeuvres but also keen to see how we all perform. Most of all, I'm looking forward to spending a concentrated period with the soldiers of my platoon and training with them under field conditions. I think I've now learnt all of their names but this will be the first chance to get to know them as individuals.

I see that my faithful Usman Pele has been in my *gida*, presumably while I was juddering around in my Land Rover in the bush this morning, and has laid out my basic kit for tomorrow. He will also be coming with us. I do a sort inventory check: boots, field puttees, long light weight trousers, khaki shirt, bush hat, lanyard with whistle and prismatic compass, webbing belt with attached water bottle and ammunition pouches, webbing small pack with spare shirt, washing kit, mess tins, knife, fork, spoon, small towel, toilet paper. All seems fine to me. Entrenching tools, jerrycans for water and fuel, rations and cooking kit will all be organised centrally.

Before we leave barracks tomorrow, we'll be collecting our weapons. The platoon section commanders and I will be armed with the

Sten machine carbine 9 mm, mark three. It's got a thirty-two-round magazine. It's pretty much the same as the version used during the Second World War. I've familiarised myself with this weapon in the barracks. It seems very old fashioned compared to the Sterling L2A2 machine carbine we trained on back in UK during my time at Devizes and Mons. I've been told the Nigerian army has ordered Sterlings to replace the Sten but it seems unlikely we'll get them before we go to the Cameroons. Our soldiers are mostly issued with the bolt action Lee Enfield .303 with its tiny ten-round detachable box magazine. This also seems so old fashioned compared with the British Army but it's what we've got. Again, we've been told the new NATO standard FN, Belgian-made rifle is being negotiated but we're not likely to get them in the battalion any time soon. When we are issued with them, I guess there could well be an administrative problem in changing from the .303-inch ammo to 7.62 mm. For safety reasons, live ammunition is banned during this training period so we'll be taking blanks plus additional non-lethal thunder flashes to simulate grenades. After the manoeuvre, we'll have several sessions at the range firing live ammunition so our weapons will be zeroed in before we may have to use them in action.

I turn in quite early tonight to be ready for the morning's parade. I hope my newly acquired driving skills don't desert me! I'm about to get into bed when I remember the dog. She's been following me around ever since supper. She's still hanging around now. I think she wants to lie down next to the bed but I don't think that's a good idea. I lead her out onto the terrace and shut her outside. I expect she'll be gone in the morning.

I'm wrong. In the morning, the dog is still here. She must have slept on the terrace all night. I pour out the last of my cornflakes and milk and share them with the dog. I dress in the kit I'd checked through last evening, load my small pack in to the Land Rover and go back into my *gida* for a final ablution. When I come back out, the dog has jumped into the back of the vehicle. I have to be firm with her. I lift her out and point my finger at her in a "stay there" sign. She doesn't seem to understand because as I drive off, smoothly thank heavens, she starts to follow on. As I accelerate away, I see her in my rear-view mirror running behind for a while then slowly giving up and stopping. My last view of her is seeing her dejectedly turning back towards my *gida*.

I reach my company lines and am directed into convoy position by one of Bill's MT marshals. I park up with a sigh of relief that the Land Rover didn't stall. Next, we need to draw out our weapons from the arms store, inspect the soldiers of my platoon, and be ready for the "off".

The convoy is now fully lined up. It's very impressive. In the front are the vehicles of the reconnaissance platoon. They're equipped with scout car-type vehicles, which I believe are called Ferrets. It's the first time I've seen them. Next is the command group with the CO's long wheel-based Land Rover. The vehicles of B Company are behind the CO, then our C Company vehicles follow on. All formations of the battalion are now present, less A Company who will remain to guard the barracks while the rest of us are away. My own platoon consists of my Land Rover then three Bedford RL three-ton trucks loaded with our three sections and platoon headquarters personnel, all forty-two of them, plus our stores. At last I feel part of a fully kitted out military formation. It's good to be here.

Chapter Twenty

The MT marshals at the front of the column wave their white batons, the reconnaissance lead vehicles move off, followed by the CO's group and steadily all the vehicles in front of my platoon start moving. My turn comes, I release the hand brake, engage gear and, with a sigh of relief, my Land Rover moves smoothly forward. Behind me, I can see the Bedford RL's coming on. We're off. The 2nd Battalion Queen's Own Nigeria Regiment is on the move.

The tarmac road soon ends and we're driving on a rough reddish coloured surface, which I'm told is called laterite. There hasn't been any rain since I arrived in Kaduna at the end of January and our convey is driving through a haze of red dust due to the dry weather. The lead vehicles are proceeding at not more than about forty miles per hour so we just follow on. Bill's MT section has a couple of guys on motorbikes who constantly patrol up and down the column ensuring we're all keeping station. I'm slowly beginning to relax about driving as my gear changing becomes more fluent and automatic. I can't think why I had made such a meal of it yesterday.

After driving for about a couple of hours in our convoy, the MT marshals direct us off the main road and onto a smaller track in open bushland. A few miles along this track, we see signs for the Nigerian Military School, Zaria. The marshals direct us to a large open area at the side of the school, which has been designated as our vehicle bivouac point during the start of our manoeuvres here. Each vehicle is directed to park up in a pre-marked space. I pull my Land Rover into its allocated spot and our three platoon Bedford trucks come in alongside. Our spaces are signed: Number 2 Platoon, C Company, 2 QONR. All around us, the other vehicles are parking up. We find ourselves inside a compound protected by a barbed wire fence. Outside, armed guards are on duty.

We all dismount and are directed to form up in an area of open bushland that forms a natural amphitheatre shaped space facing onto a raised mound which simulates a stage. The whole of our party: Battalion

HQ, Admin company, B and C Companies are on parade, lined up in our company groups, all turned out in our full combat kit. I reckon that's about 600 of us. When our numbers are complete, Capt James Thompson, the adjutant, brings us all to attention, turns to Lt Col Johnson, our CO, salutes and reports to him:

"2nd Battalion Queen's Own Nigeria regiment on parade and awaiting your instructions, sir!"

The colonel turns to face us and orders: "Battalion, stand at ease!" Then: "Stand easy!"

I wonder what is going on. I met the colonel on my initial arrival at the battalion and have briefly spoken to him in the officers' mess but that's been all so far. He is a tall, slim man with a small moustache. Beneath his bush hat, I can see his aquiline features and his rather large prominent nose. Like the rest of us, he's wearing full combat dress. He seems rather aloof and distant but he's held in great respect by the other officers.

He continues: "Soldiers of 2 QONR. It's good to see all ranks here in battle order. It's fitting that all the battalion is here together, less A Company, who I shall be addressing separately. This is a good opportunity to tell you about several important matters that will be affecting the lives of all of us this year."

The colonel pauses and a Nigerian officer, standing beside him, translates these words into Hausa. The colonel then continues: "In three-week's time, we will be leaving for the British Cameroons. Our Battalion HQ will be based in Bamenda and our companies deployed in widely separated areas of the country. We will have a major responsibility there to ensure that the political plebiscite to be held later in the year is carried out peacefully. To achieve that, we need to maintain security throughout that country and combat the threat from insurgents whose aim, we believe, is to cause major disruption to the peace process. Our tour of duty in the Cameroons will last three to four months."

Another pause for translation. The colonel then continues: "I know I can rely on you to perform your duties in the Cameroons with distinction. To help to ensure that we will be as well prepared as possible, we are here now to practise our military skills. I shall be giving each company tasks to perform, both in offensive and defensive tactics and I and my team of invigilators will be checking that satisfactory standards are achieved. During this training, C Company will act as "own forces" while B Company, with additional support, will play the role of "enemy insurgents". Detailed orders will be given shortly."

Again, a translation pause. I'm listening to the colonel, our CO, with close attention, wondering what tasks we will be given. This will be the first time my platoon and I will have worked closely together as a single unit. The colonel then continues:

"I also want to share with you all some other important matters. First, concerning right here in Zaria. This year, 1960, the training school celebrates its elevation from its former title of 'Boy's Company' by being renamed and reconstituted as the Nigerian Military School. This is part of the transference of responsibilities as your country moves towards it's full independence on 1 October. I can now also tell you that our battalion has been honoured to provide the main parade force in Northern Nigeria on that day when the independence ceremony will be performed in front of the governor designate of Northern Nigeria and a member of the British royal family. Our preparations for this parade will commence shortly after we return from the Cameroons."

Translation pause again. This last information is news to me and I'm wondering how I'll be involved. The colonel turns to a very smart Nigerian officer — a new face to me and I think to most of the rest of us. He continues:

"Before we disperse, I want to introduce you to Capt Musa Katsina. He is joining our battalion to take over from Capt Thompson as our new adjutant. His important appointment is part of the progressive process of appointing more Nigerian officers in place of British. By the time of independence, most of our officers will, quite correctly, be Nigerian. This will include my own appointment as your CO."

When translated, this causes quite a reaction from our soldiers. I can't tell whether they're pleased or what. I'm also wondering if this means I'll be sent home before my two years' service is up. The colonel now concludes:

"I'll now hand back to your company commanders to give specific orders for the remainder of your training here. I shall be regularly visiting you in your exercise locations. Remember that the harder you work during this training, the better prepared you will be for the challenges you will face in the Cameroons. Good luck to you all!"

After translation, Capt Thompson calls us up to attention and salutes the colonel who then leaves the parade. His speech has given us much to think about but right now, I'm determined to do my best to perform well during this training period.

It's 18.00 hours and I've just finished my rounds of all the three rifle sections of my platoon before it gets dark in about forty-five minutes' time. The ground I'm to cover is on a slight promontory with clear views over the most likely attack lines. I get back to the central sector where I've established a small platoon HQ. We've posted sentries but the rest of the guys are busy digging their defence trenches. Major Sutter, our company commander, is waiting for me there. He's come to inspect us. He asks me:

"Right Peter, this is your first time out in the field. Tell me how you've deployed your platoon."

"OK sir," I reply. "You told me to ensure that I provide all-round defence of the sector you allocated with my platoon covering our left flank and our Number 1 Platoon on the right. I've deployed my guys with two sections covering the forward most vulnerable approaches and the third covering the rear. Here, we're in my platoon HQ location where I'm also holding our radio operator and the two-inch mortar team. All sections and our HQ element will dig-in fully to safeguard against artillery attack or air strikes. We're lucky that the natural folds in the ground make this task feasible to complete before it gets fully dark."

"What about machine guns?"

"As you know, sir, you allocated me an extra Bren gun section, making four in total so I've deployed one to each of the rifle sections as per routine and am holding the fourth in reserve. Should we be attacked, I shall commit this team to where I assess the most threatened area to be."

"Who is responsible for allocating the individual rifleman's arc of fire. Their section commanders?"

"No sir, I have just come back from visiting all three rifle sections. With their section commander present, I've spoken to each soldier and personally given them instructions on arcs of fire to ensure that these overlap, not only within each section but also between the three sections. I'm confident we have complete, all round defence cover."

"Right Peter, I'm satisfied with that so far. Of course, this is just a training exercise but we need make it as realistic as possible. In the Cameroons, this could be for real. Our CO hasn't given much away but I think you can be sure that the exercise controllers have got some pretty lively surprises for us so you'll need to stay very alert. All I do know is that it's likely we'll be attacked tonight or tomorrow morning. What instructions have you given about sentries, meals, rest, etc?"

"Sir, the guys are still digging in and will continue until their fire trenches are completed. Sgt Bado, our platoon sergeant, has already made sure all our guys have had food rations from our platoon supplies and all have individual water bottles, which were filled earlier today. That will last them till tomorrow morning. I've ordered section commanders to ensure that one soldier per fire trench remains on alert sentry duty at all times. We've practised 'stand-to' procedures in barracks. I've reminded everyone of these today."

"OK Peter, that covers all main points. In theory, I would have liked us to have been able to reinforce our defences with wire and flares deployed forward of our positions but this is not practical during this exercise. You are to ensure that my company HQ is informed if you suspect an attack is imminent. Make sure radio procedures are fully checked this evening."

As the major leaves, I'm tempted to salute him but saluting is not accepted when in this field deployment. I breathe a sigh of relief that my briefing went OK. I'm really impressed by the way all our soldiers have acted. They all seem keen and well-motivated. So far, I've managed to make myself understood using a combination of the English language, lots of hand gestures and even some words of Hausa that I've remembered.

It's been dark for some hours now. I look at my issued fluorescent watch. It's 05.45 hours. The guys finished digging soon after dusk and we all assumed our defence positions. Who knows how long we might be here? Now it's very quiet. We're waiting. I decide to go to our forward sections. I talk in low tones to each of the three section commanders in turn and together we check on each of the two- or three-man trenches. Everything is as ordered. One man per trench is awake and alert, the others are resting.

I get the feeling we're just passively waiting to be attacked and need to be more proactive. I'm lucky to have three members of the Tif tribe in my platoon. They're renowned for their tracking ability. One of these is Cpl Aiki Riba (the guy whose wife gave birth in the bush recently!). Earlier, I had instructed him to move forward with his team to recce the ground ahead. I've learnt to appreciate his phenomenal skill as a tracker. I've been out with him on an earlier night exercise from our barracks. I had tried to move stealthily but I sounded like a clumsy elephant next to Aiki Riba. He moves soundlessly like a cat. He's just the man I need for a night recce of possible "enemy" approaches. I'm waiting in his section lines when suddenly he and his team reappear. I didn't hear them come. He reports:

"Sir, we've located the main 'enemy force'. They're now forming up at the head of the ravine on our left flank. Mostly riflemen but also, we saw three light machine guns. We counted about sixty-five to seventy men. Their officers were getting them into battle order and we assess they will be ready for a full attack on our position in about thirty to forty minutes. We also covered the other possible approaches but found no evidence of movement there."

I thank Aiki Riba, put our entire platoon a "stand to" and report his findings to our company HQ giving "enemy" location and strengths with our assessment that an attack is imminent, probably to coincide with first light at about 06.45 hours.

In fact, the attack comes in at 07.00, so our assessment was pretty accurate. I'm impressed by the coordination of the "attacking force", which is well directed at our defensive layout. I order our troops to hold fire until the leading attackers were within fifty yards of our position. Then, on my order, we open up with rapid fire, using the "blank" training ammunition and throwing thunder flashes to simulate grenades. Earlier, I had deployed our reserve Bren gun team to reinforce the attacked front. From their position, they could fire at enfilade into the attacking force.

There are exercise controllers accompanying the "enemy force" and they quickly order a complete cessation of all firing. This phase of the training has been concluded. The "attackers" are ordered to withdraw back a hundred metres and our troops are forbidden to follow up with a counter attack at this stage so there is no physical contact. This is after all, only a training exercise. I see Lt Col Johnson, our CO, is with the controllers. He had followed the approach of the "enemy force" and now he comes over to my side and orders me to show him the full defensive layout of our platoon. He asks several questions similar to those that Major Sutter had asked the previous evening. Finally, he asks how it was that all our soldiers were alert and ready for the "attack" and why the reserve Bren team had been deployed facing the main attack force. I explained about Cpl Aiki Riba's team forward recce patrolling and what he had reported back thus enabling us to assess time and direction of the "attack".

The Colonel tells me he is satisfied with this phase of our training. He and his team of invigilators have judged that our defences had been well organised and that the "attack" on our position would have been repelled. I see him now talking to Major Sutter. Looks like my platoon and I have just passed our first test together!

The simulated attack on our platoon is just the first of a series of training tests that our CO puts us through. We also practise, "advance to contact", rapid deployment in response to a surprise attack, deep patrolling at section and platoon level both during the day and at night. Sometimes, we mount up in our vehicles and drive to a specified grid reference, at other times we move on foot using tactical bounds section by section. One final test is a thirty-mile cross-country march using the issued 1:25,000 scale maps and "my" prismatic compass to navigate point to point to a specific grid reference. This was through bushland with few distinguishing landmarks. The only way is to set a bearing from start to end point and follow the compass needle precisely for the whole of the distance. This test takes us about sixteen hours to complete. We were told we are to RV with our vehicles at Milestone 64 on a road shown on our map. When eventually we end up hitting the road, I can hope we have followed a true route and our vehicles are close by. I can see no sign of a milestone marker. I tell one of our soldiers to turn right, walk down the road, get to a mile-stone and come back to tell me what it says. I tell another to turn left with the same instructions. The first to reappear is the soldier who had gone right. He tells me: "It says Milestone 63. The soldier who turned left soon returns reporting he had seen Milestone 62. So, we all turn right and find our vehicles waiting for us just over one mile up the road at Milestone 64.

Photo: Approaching milestone 64

After sixteen hours covering thirty miles navigated solely on a prismatic compass bearing, we were one mile off course — not too bad!

After ten days of training, we climb back into our vehicles for the last time and begin the long drive back to our barracks. As we trundle along, I go over in my mind what we have achieved. First, I'm relieved I seem to have come through all the tests OK and I realise how much that is due to all the weeks of being bashed around during basic training in Devizes and as an officer cadet at Mons, Aldershot. I now feel quite at home here in Nigeria. I've fully acclimatised and am as tanned and fit as any of my fellow Brit officers. But most important to me is that I feel at ease with my soldiers. At first, I was hesitant, as a nineteen-year old Brit, giving orders to Nigerian soldiers, most of whom are older and more experienced than me. But as we have spent time together, particularly during this concentrated time away from barracks and other distractions, my soldiers seem to appreciate that, as far as infantry skills are concerned, I do know what I'm on about. They see that I regularly consult the seniors in the company such as CSM Kabala and Sgt Bado. They know I care about their welfare. When I first arrived in the battalion in January, I remember seeing a mass of black faces and wondering how I would ever tell them all apart. But I now know all of their names and have learnt about their individual characters. I no longer think about our different colour. We are who we are and colour is irrelevant. We are now blending into a close-knit team. We are supporting each other. I feel they now accept me as their platoon commander. This gives me a good feeling.

It's mid-afternoon when our dust-covered convoy rolls back into Dalet barracks. We all dismount and return to our respective company lines. I tell Sgt Bado to fall our platoon in on our C Company parade square. I tell my soldiers how proud I am that our Number Two Platoon has performed so well, which should set us up for our tour of the Cameroons. Before we dismiss, I inspect all weapons to ensure they are clean and oiled before we return them to our armoury. An NCO from the MT section arrives to reclaim the Land Rover. I'm relieved that it's still in one piece.

I pick up my kit and walk the short distance back to my *gida*. I can't wait to have a beer and a shower. As I approach my house, I see a scruffy little dog lying on my terrace. She sees me, leaps up and bounds excitedly over to me. She must have been here all this time, waiting for me to come back. I climb up the few steps to my terrace. The little dog follows. I go inside, find a beer from the fridge, bring it back on the terrace, sit down on my canvas chair, snap open the can and take a good swig. The little dog sits next to me. She puts a paw up onto my knee. I fondle her head. She looks up at me and wags her tail. That's it — I know I can't send her away. I guess I've got myself a dog. I look right at her and say quietly:

"OK, I suppose you'd better have a name. I first saw you when I went to collect fruit from the pawpaw tree so I think I'll call you 'PawPaw', no, let's make it "Pawpy". From now on we'd better stick together. You agree Pawpy?"

She looks up at me and wags her tail again. I know she agrees. But what about our four months in The Cameroons? I don't know anyone who would look after her while we're away. She'll just have to come too!

Photo: Pawpy's first day on parade!

Chapter Twenty-one

It's 28 March 1960 and most of the battalion has now arrived in the British Cameroons. There's still the rear party en route — they're somewhere between Enugu in eastern Nigeria and our location here. I arrived here, driving all the way from Kaduna with a convoy of Land Rovers. We had three-night stops, including a drunken one in Enugu with fellow officers of the battalion based there. I managed to spirit "my" Pawpy away in my Land Rover. Private Usman Pele is looking after her while I attend our CO's briefing.

Our Battalion HQ has been established in Bamenda, the regional capital and our CO has gathered all the officers into a room in the local police headquarters. In addition to our CO, the local police commissioner and several of his staff, there's a stout florid-faced middle-aged British gentleman. Despite the sticky humid climate, he's wearing a light-coloured suit, shirt and tie. The rest of us are in our combat short sleeved shirts, khaki for us military, dark blue for the police.

The CO gives a short introduction, saying he's pleased the battalion is now almost complete in the Cameroons and is in good shape to carry out our vital role during our tour of duty here. He then introduces the civilian gentleman as Mr Johnathan Brierley from the British Foreign and Commonwealth Office and asks him to brief us all on the local political situation. Mr Brierley begins:

"Gentlemen, you arrive here in the British Cameroons at a most pivotal time in this nation's history and particularly concerning Britain's relations with our African colleagues. As you know, our prime minister, Mr Harold Macmillan, last month made a speech concerning the British government's decisions about many of our colonies and plans for their national independence. The expression he used 'a wind of change is blowing through Africa' has been widely quoted. This change directly affects all of you here when Nigeria achieves its own independence on the first of October this year.

"Now to focus on the Cameroons and the reason you're here. Our friend and ally, France, granted independence to the French Cameroons on the first of January this year, within the French trusteeship and on the twenty-first of last month the new nation, formally known as La Republique du Cameroun, held a constitutional referendum. As a result of this, we expect the first president to be Mr Ahmadou Ahidjo. We all hope that the transition from colonial rule to full nationhood in the new Republique will be smooth and peaceful. But there are problems. For many years, an organisation called the UPC, standing for Union des Populations du Cameroun, has opposed the legitimacy of the former French rule and of the newly constituted Republique. The French army has been involved in major operations against the UPC, which has resulted in scores of deaths and caused ill-will amongst sections of the population there. To complicate the situation, both the Soviets and the Chinese have been giving aid to the UPC as these states attempt to increase their influence in the region."

Much of this information is new to me and pretty mind boggling. Mr Brierley is a rather pompous little man but he obviously knows his stuff and it's really important we understand the background so that we can do our job here effectively. He continues:

"Turning to the British side, a plebiscite is planned to be held here under the auspices of the United Nations, on 11 February next year, 1961. British Cameroonians will be asked whether they wish either to join the newly independent Nigeria or whether to join La Republique du Cameroun. For the British Cameroons to have their own independence, separate from both Nigeria and La Republique, is not considered to be a viable option and that question will not appear on the plebiscite questionnaire. That decision has not gone down well with certain factions here and there is a splinter organisation of the UPC who aim to disrupt the administration of British Cameroons at this delicate period. This group is known as Cameroon freedom fighters or CFF for short. We suspect this group is also supported and armed by the communist powers.

"So you see, gentlemen, during this year we are faced with a very delicate situation as various factions jostle for power. The UPC and its affiliate the CFF do not recognise the border between La Republique and the British Cameroons. Our intelligence people assess that, encouraged by the communist powers, the UPC/CFF groups now pose a serious threat to the stability of the region."

Turning to our CO, Mr Brierley concludes. "Colonel Johnson, we look to you and your soldiers, working closely with the police, to ensure that peace and stability are maintained as we move towards the plebiscite early next year which will decide the future direction of our Cameroon brothers."

I noticed that Mr Brierley was sweating heavily during his speech. I'm not surprised as already I'm realising how different the climate here is from Kaduna. Up there, on the vast north Nigerian plateau, it's hot but it's a dry heat and the air is normally fresh and clear. In Bamenda, it's also hot but a humid sticky type of heat. It's not raining right now but already we've experienced some heavy downpours and I'm told this country has one of the highest annual rainfall totals in the world. We're going to have to adjust quickly to this climate change.

Our CO now takes over again. He says:

"Gentlemen, on behalf of us all, I want to thank Mr Brierley for his most informative speech. It's a complicated situation here but Mr Brierley has so clearly and succinctly summed up the main points we all need to understand. Before we proceed, I want also to introduce Police Commissioner Obadike. Our role here is to support the commissioner and his staff in maintaining security and allowing all citizens to live in peace during this turbulent period in their national history. I have already had full discussions with Commissioner Obadike and we have agreed a *modus operandi* between us. A police detachment has been allocated to each of our companies and will accompany all of our patrols to ensure that the law is always correctly observed in any conflict situation we may experience. Be very clear, we are not at war here and it's the military's job to act purely in support of the police to ensure that law and order is maintained. There may be frustrations due to the circumstances but we must contain any emotion and, where necessary, defer to police decisions. This is not our country, we are here at the request of the British Cameroon authorities and our job is to support them at all times. There may, of course, be times when it will be necessary to return fire if we are directly threatened by an armed rebel force. I shall be issuing you clear rules of engagement to ensure we use minimum force while at the same time safeguarding our security."

I'm thinking to myself: "Police in charge, we support. OK, that's clear!" I'm wondering what my job will actually be. My platoon and I are all here — present and correct. I've now spent the best part of a year in training — at Devizes, at Mons Officer Cadet School Aldershot and here with the battalion in Kaduna. Now at last, our training is over and we are about to engage in live operations. I have mixed emotions. Mr Brierley's description of the rebel forces is daunting. But this is now the real thing. Let's get on with it!

The battalion has now dispersed and fanned out into our designated company areas. C Company is based on the small settlement of Ndop, some thirty miles on rough road east of Bamenda. Major Hugh Sutter and his C Company HQ staff went ahead of the rest of us and set up our accommodation and operating headquarters. We are being housed in a new build school, which is scheduled to open to the schoolchildren sometime next year. The officers have been allocated a building, designed to be the school staffroom, located on a raised area overlooking the rest of the complex. Major Sutter, David Edozi and I will be billeted here plus Bashir Buhari, who has newly returned to our company. I'm also pleased that CSM Kabala will be housed with us here.

Photo: Temporary Officers mess in Ndop

Photo: C Company base at Ndop

A separate small building has been allocated to our sergeants. These comprise Sgt Yemima Bado, from my platoon and three other C Company sergeants. The main school classroom area has been allocated to the rest of our soldiers. Each of our platoons is billeted in individual classrooms. In charge of the room where "my" platoon soldiers are billeted is Cpl Aika Riba. Already defence positions, to guard against any surprise attack, have been established and CSM Kabala has produced a roster for guard duties.

When we've all arrived at Ndop. Major Sutter gets all his officers together and gives out his orders. He begins by saying:

"Welcome to our new home! This will be our base for the next four months so make sure your soldiers and yourself are settled in as well as practical. We have been given a large geographical area to cover. This is how we'll operate. My company headquarters will remain here and I will maintain regular contact with our CO in Bamenda." He then turns to Bashir Buhari and to CSM Kabala and continues:

"Bashir, we welcome you back to our company and I want formally to congratulate you on your promotion to captain. You are now our company second in command. Your main duty, apart from being my deputy, is to establish and maintain the closest possible liaison with the local police force/forces based in Ndop and the rest of the area of our operational responsibility. CSM Kabala, your main task is the defence of our headquarters here, camp discipline and routine. We need to ensure that, above all, we operate from a strong, secure base."

Major Sutter next turns to David Edozi and me. He tells us:

"I intend that we will create a very active presence in our area starting forthwith. The two-platoon division of our company will remain, i.e. that each platoon will be forty-two soldiers strong. From tomorrow, one of your platoons will be on patrol, while the other remains here in camp. When the first patrol returns back to base, there will be a quick debrief then the second platoon will deploy, thus we will maintain a permanent patrolling presence at all times. This evening, a detachment of police will arrive and be based with us throughout our tour here. We will treat them as if they were members of our company and involve them fully in all our activities. David and Peter, I am allocating one policeman to each of your platoons. Get to know these guys well and fully involve them in your duties. Apart from handling legal aspects, they know the area intimately and also the local personalities and sensitivities. Learn from them."

Then, turning to me, the major says:

"Peter, you are to take out the first patrol. At this evening's meeting with the police, I will allocate your specific patrol area. With the police in attendance, I will also clarify precisely your rules of engagement, should you make contact with an armed rebel group. Your platoon will set off at 08.00 hours tomorrow morning. As this is our first patrol, keep this one short, say only a couple of days. We'll extend the duration once we see more clearly how things work out."

That evening, after meeting with our police augmentees, Major Sutter tells me that my platoon's first patrol is to make contact with the FON of Bafali. I'm told the word "FON" stands for chief or head man. Bafali is located between Ndop and the British/Cameroun Republique border, a strategic area where the CFF rebels are believed to operate. We now have our first operational mission.

We leave on schedule at 08.00 hours and move steadily but cautiously on our route to Bafali. We trained for this type of patrol during our exercise in Zaria last month and we use the same *modus operandi* of a leading scout point section. My small headquarter group then follows, now with John Abdalah, the policeman attached to my platoon. I've taken to John. He's not a big man but he seems fit and wiry and well able to keep up with our progress. I find him to have an engaging personality. He doesn't seem to be bothered by either my white skin or the rest of the soldiers who are not from his country. He speaks English well enough and clearly has a very good knowledge of the local area and issues. I know that this knowledge will be an invaluable asset.

Photo: John, "our policeman"

The further two sections follow behind. Every two hours, we pause while I change over the lead point section thus keeping that section as fresh and alert as possible. After much soul searching, I decided to bring Pawpy along, although I didn't tell Major Sutter as I thought he would disapprove. She stays close to me at all times. Today, there are several differences from our training in Kaduna. The first is the terrain/climate. Here, there is a mix of tight jungle trails and more open tracks with views of distant mountains. There's high clammy humidity and I find I'm permanently sweating. I'm glad we've brought a good supply of water. Second, when we drew out our weapons from the armoury this morning, we were also issued with live ammunition. Before now, this has only been when we were on the firing range. And third, this situation is for real. We've been told we could bump into a rebel group at any point, so the utmost vigilance is required.

So far, it's been without incident. We've encountered several persons on our route, some in groups, some individuals. Each time, we have stopped them and John, our policeman, has questioned them. In each case, he has been satisfied they were all local people with routine innocent reasons for being here. As we approach Bafali, John explains that he has once personally met the FON who has a formidable reputation. His village is tightly run under his direct control. John has difficulty in describing the FON's personality telling me that I will find out for myself soon enough!

Photo: En route to Bafali

The evening dusk is beginning to draw in when John tells me that we are now nearing the edge of Bafali village. My first thoughts are how clean everything looks. The trail here has recently been cleared and swept. We reach small houses, all constructed from local jungle materials. As we approach the centre of the community, we pass several people. All bow their heads as we pass. John knows that they are Bafali residents and doesn't stop to question them. I let myself be guided by John's knowledge and experience. In the centre of the village, there is a wide cleared area, which, like the trail we've just used, is immaculately swept. In the centre is a larger construction, which I'm soon to learn is the focal point of the village. John leads me to the entrance of this building, while my soldiers fan out into our practised defence positions.

I don't have long to wait before a gentleman comes out of the building. He has a tall imposing figure, is wearing long orange, yellow and black flowing robes and a floral coloured turban. I can't help but notice he's wearing polished leather black shoes, gleamingly clean, almost like dancing pumps. No socks — just these shoes. This seems incongruous as all the other villagers are bare-foot. He comes directly to me and shakes my hand. I'm rather stunned by the fluency of his English as he addresses me:

"I was forewarned you were coming to see us, lieutenant. You are welcome. Please honour me by joining me in my home where we can talk and I can offer you some refreshment. I will also see your soldiers are brought drinks. Oh, and I see you've brought your dog with you. How interesting!"

At first, I'm taken aback by this impressive man — by his excellent English, his air of calm confidence and his style. We go into his "domain" and he summons over a young woman. She approaches him with a bowed stance. When he addresses her, she puts her hands over her face before answering. He tells her to bring drinks. She withdraws backwards and it's only when she is several yards away that she turns around and leaves the room. The FON then gives instructions to others of his subjects. They all respond in the same manner, approaching him in a bowed stance, covering their mouths as they answer him and withdrawing backwards from his presence in the same bowed fashion of total subordination. But strangely, although the FON seems to be the all-powerful leader of Bafali, I don't get any feeling of animosity towards him by his "subjects". Quite the reverse, he seems to be revered and regarded with affection and devotion.

The girl he ordered to bring the drinks reappears with an assistant and, again with their stooped approach in front of the FON, place glasses, real glasses in front of us, then carafes of water and a substance that looks surprisingly like beer! They even bring a bowl of water for Pawpy! They then discreetly withdraw. I'm in rather a dilemma. I can tell how powerful the FON is and how important it will be to keep a close liaison with him. He's likely to be a major ally and source of information through the contacts I suspect he has. But my mission is to be self-sufficient and alert. I'm not sure how reliant I should be on his hospitality. I'm pondering on these thoughts when the FON surprises me by saying:

"Lieutenant, it's a real pleasure to meet an Englishman. I have met so few from your country. A few years ago, I received a visit here by a Mr Harold Chapman, who was then the British resident in Bamenda. Do you know him?"

"I'm afraid not, sir. This is my first time in your country." I call him sir because I don't know how else I should address him. In fact, at my age, I find it easier to call almost all older people sir"

The FON continues, "Mr Chapman invited me back to visit him in his residence and I found myself fascinated to learn more about your country. Other than Bamenda and visiting some of our other local FONS and chiefs, I have never actually been far from my village here. In any case, there's always much to do with my people. So whenever I get the opportunity I read English books and magazines. I love the style of your English, or should I say British, architecture and the customs of your people. Now you are here and I can learn more form you"

I'm flabbergasted. I'm sitting next to a wise and all-powerful gentleman and now he's asking me, a nineteen-year-old Brit, to teach him! Our conversation continues on the theme of British culture and history. I do my best to answer but my own knowledge of this subject is limited to my simple Somerset upbringing. I thankfully drink down the water that has been brought. It's refreshingly cool. The FON then tells me the other liquid is a local brew of beer. Very tempting but I'm conscious that I'm now on my first day of an operational patrol. So no beer for me today and I have to politely decline.

After our surprising academic conversation about British culture, at last I manage to turn to the reason for our visit today. I tell the FON about our mission to provide security during the period leading up to the plebiscite in February next year, 1961. I find he is well informed about this and he offers his full support. We discuss possible rebel aims and I ask him if he has any specific information to assist us in our mission. The FON tells me that he believes that the rebels regularly use the local markets as a means of distributing their weapons through the country. He tells me where and when markets take place and the main route leading to those villages. We pause while I ask for our policeman, John, to join us as his wider knowledge will assist.

After our discussions, we make a plan. There's a village some ten miles from here where a large market is due to be held tomorrow. It deals in a wide range of goods, all the basic foodstuffs but also cooking and building materials and utensils. Based on the FON's informants and John's police intelligence, it is assessed that arms could be smuggled into this market from one of the main tracks leading from the Republique du Cameroun. I decide that we should lay an ambush on this track tonight and see if we can intercept an arms haul. I will take all my soldiers to a holding location close to the track then, with John and a ten-man patrol, I'll lay an ambush on that likely route. We need to leave directly as already it's dark and we need to be in position by midnight at the latest. The FON offers me a guide to assist John in navigation.

Before leaving, I thank the FON for his assistance. He insists I come and visit him again soon. He tells me that he would like it if, next time, I and my soldiers would stay in his village. I hope that we can.

I get our section commanders and Sgt Bado together and tell them about our ambush plan. We leave the village at about 20.00 hours. I'm apprehensive but also excited. I have no idea how tonight will work out.

Chapter Twenty-two

It's nearly 22.00 hours when we get to a small settlement that our policeman John knows well. He assures me the villagers here are loyal to the government. It's about one mile away from the point on the track where we plan to set up our ambush. It seems a safe area to leave the rear party for the night. I leave Sgt Bado in charge and tell him to set up a guard roster then settle everyone down for what is left of the night.

I choose Corporal Aiki Riba and nine soldiers from his section to be the ambush group: with John Abdalah our policeman and me, we're a total of twelve — plus one dog: Pawpy! I check that all weapons are loaded and we're carrying spare ammunition. We set off, guided by John, and with Aiki Riba's natural tracking sense, we quietly move forward in the dark until we reach the track that leads from the frontier to the village where the market will be held the next morning. Here, we are in thick jungle. It's still dry, but at ten minutes to midnight, it's as hot and clammy as it's been during the day. It's pitch-black. Above, the canopy of foliage conceals any glimpse of the moon or stars. We have brought several torches but for now we'll have to rely on hearing to detect any movement along the track.

We set up the ambush with soldiers on both sides of the track. We're all linked together by twine tied to our wrists. Our ambush is now set and all we can do is wait. But as soon as we settle down, the mosquitos come to life — in their trillions! We cover every exposed part of our skin with netting but still they are omnipotent. It's not just me, with my British white skin, that's affected. All around I can sense our soldiers straining to protect themselves against these insidious insects. And the collective noise they make! It's so loud, I can't hear another sound. With both sight and sound impaired, I wonder how on earth we can gain surprise if a rebel group ventures down this track. Tactically, it would have been prudent to have posted a couple of our guys some hundred yards further up the track to keep well out of sight but to alert us by radio should the rebels use this route tonight. A simple walky-talky set would have been useful but we don't have one. Our only radio in the platoon is a B47 Larkspur but that's for us to communicate back to our Ndop company HQ.

Then I find that, after all, we have a secret weapon. For reasons I can't understand, I notice that my Pawpy isn't troubled by the mosquitos. She's lying right next to me, seemingly unconcerned. She now has to be our eyes and ears — our early warning system.

Time passes very slowly as we wait in our ambush formation. By 02.00 hours, no one has used the track. Same at 03.00. I'm seriously wondering if we are wasting our time here. Perhaps the FON's informants were wrong. Perhaps they got the wrong day or the wrong track. Despite covering myself with netting, the mozzies are still getting through and I'm itching all over my arms and face. I bless the fact I've been keeping up with taking the daily Paludrine tablet to warn off the threat of malaria. I'm trying to keep alert and concentrated but my mind is starting to drift. I'm even wondering if we should abort the ambush tonight and get more specific intelligence about these smuggling routes before we try again.

Sometime between three and four o'clock, Pawpy suddenly bristles and lets out a low growl. I quickly check my watch. It's 03.46 hours. I put my hand over Pawpy. She's fully alert and still growling. I say: "Shhh! Good girl," which seems to calm her. I then pull hard on the twine attached to both my wrists. I get responding tugs so I know our guys are also alerted and prepared.

We wait. Still nothing for about a minute. Then they come. They're moving steadily along the track seemingly unaware of our presence. I count them as they pass. There are four, then another two, then again two more. That's eight altogether. I can't afford to let them proceed beyond the end stop of our ambush. After the eighth guy, I can't tell if there's more but I can't wait any longer. So I decide to spring the ambush. I fire one shot in the air with my Sten gun and at the same time John Abdalah shouts out an order: "Put your hands in the air. Do it now!" He uses the strange pidgin language that is widely used here. Our soldiers are now all on their feet and advancing towards the smugglers. They aim their guns directly at them.

We achieve total surprise and the smugglers instantly freeze, drop their headloads and put their hands in the air. That is — the first six do. The last two in the group don't have headloads. I see one of them reaching for something and I see, or at least I think I see, him pulling out a gun. It's still dark and I can't be certain it's a gun. The "rules of engagement" flash through my mind "Only fire at an individual if directly threatened by an armed rebel". This is my first major decision since I became a soldier. I must do something. I can't wait. I decide to fire but not to hit him. I squeeze the trigger of my Sten and let off a short burst of rapid fire, aiming between the guy "with the gun" and his companion, who is standing about two yards further away. It does the trick. He drops the weapon and raises his hands. The guy next to him also puts his hands up.

Our soldiers now move forward and check the smugglers for weapons. We can now turn on the torches we brought so we can at last see properly who we are dealing with. The first six have nothing more than the type of knife or machete they would normally carry in this terrain. We confiscate these and I tell two of my soldiers to tie their wrists with the twine we used in the ambush cordon. Now for the other two guys. I shine a torch directly at them. Even with my inexperience, I can tell there's something different about these two from the other guys. Neither was carrying a headload and they seem to be less agitated than the other six. John and I move directly up to them, covered by a couple of our soldiers. John carries out a detailed body search of them both while I recover the weapon that had been dropped when I had fired my Sten gun. It is a pistol of a type I'm not familiar so I handle it with care. I shine my torch directly on it. It's about six inches long and not dissimilar to the Browning pistol we were taught to use in Mons. I work out how to detach the magazine and pull it out from the butt of the gun. I then point it away from our soldiers and pull the trigger. The gun instantly fires a round. With the chamber now empty and the magazine detached, it is now immobilised. I'm relieved that my decision to fire earlier was fully justified. If I hadn't, one of our soldiers could have been killed.

John gives an exclamation as he finds and relieves the second guy of a pistol. He hands it to me. It's a similar model to the first and I carry out the same procedure to immobilise it. During his body searches, John also uncovers some papers. I shine my torch on them and see a mass of writing and what looks like sketch maps. We'll take these back to police headquarters for later examination. I tell my soldiers to tie the hands of these two and to guard them closely.

Now for the headloads. I don't know what I had expected to find — weapons I suppose and other military supplies. I'm completely wrong. All are filled with cartons of cigarettes, dozens of them, and we also uncover bottles of whiskey! No guns, no explosives, no other military supplies. I ask John what he makes of our find. He takes his time to reply, then says:

"Very strange! The cigarettes are either Gauloise or Gitanes. The whiskey seems all to be Johnny Walker brand, that's British-made but I know it's much cheaper on the French side than here. All I can conclude at this stage is that the first six guys in the line were smuggling in smokes and booze from the French Cameroun to sell at the market later today. The other two are different. I've never known smugglers around here carrying weapons, and certainly not pistols of this type. I don't know what they're up to but we need to get them back to our headquarters for questioning."

It's time to leave. We ensure the two who were armed have their hands tied behind their backs and are closely guarded. They are a surly pair and we need to watch them closely. The other six still seem scared and agitated. I order the hands of the six smugglers to be untied and for them to pick up their headloads. I position them in the middle of our patrol. In this order, we make our way back to the settlement where we had left our rear party. We reach it as the first signs of dawn are appearing.

Sgt Bado is here to meet us with the soldiers detailed for guard duty and shortly the rest of my platoon, who had been resting, all appear. There's a buzz of excitement when they hear about our unusual ambush. They're eager to know all the details, how we couldn't hear a thing because of the mosquitos and how my Pawpy had warned us of the smugglers approach. She's now a little heroine in the platoon.

By now it's light and I have the chance to examine the two pistols we've acquired. I'm still not sure of their make but I notice what I think is Cyrillic writing on the side of one, suggesting it's of Soviet origin. They both look quite new and are in a good state of repair. I recognise the cartridges as 9 mm but they're shorter than the ones the Brits use in the Browning pistol. I feel sure that they will be of considerable interest to our intelligence experts, as will the papers, John confiscated during his search.

John has been talking in detail to the six smugglers and the other two guys. It seems the smugglers are willing to talk openly about themselves. John tells me:

"The guys said that they are working for a gang who acquire goods in the Republique du Cameroun. Their boss tells them where and when to take the goods. Last night, they were on route from the Republique village of Kinbali to the village in British Cameroon near where we ambushed them. They were to meet with a guy there at 06.30 hours and deliver the goods to him. He would give them a receipt chit for them to take back to the boss in the Republique. They would then be paid off and wait for the next load."

I ask John. "What about the other two?"

"They're not talking and the six smugglers say they don't know much about them. They only met up with them last evening shortly before they left with their headloads. Their boss told them they were to lead the two guys to the village where the market was to be held. That's all they say they know about them and they had no conversation with them during the route. I believe them. I really think they are exactly what they seem — simple smugglers trying to earn some money. They're still really frightened about what will happen to them."

"Well we certainly need to take those two back to our base and hand them over to your police headquarters. I think they're quite a prize. But, John, we've also got to decide what to do about the six smugglers. If we take them back with us and hand them over to your police chief, what will happen to them?"

"They'll be charged with smuggling and be given a few months in jail. Then we'll let them go and they'll probably disappear and start smuggling all over again."

"And what about the goods in their headloads — the ciggies and booze. What will happen to that?"

"Well to be honest, I suspect they'll be consumed by the police. They certainly won't be returned to the Republique."

I have an idea. I know it's not exactly legal but what the heck! I ask John:

"Do you think it's really necessary that we take the smugglers back with us? How important are they to the police?"

"Not at all. In fact, it will just create more paperwork while their cases go through the legal process. Quite frankly, the police have got better things to do."

John's answer helps me to make up my mind. I go up to the six guys, who are now sitting in a group guarded by our soldiers, and I ask John to translate when I tell them:

"Look, you are all guilty of smuggling. If we take you back with us and hand you over to the police, you will be charged and sent to prison. But I am prepared to let you go free. What is it to be?"

It takes them a while for my remarks to sink in. I tell our soldiers who are guarding them to stand aside and rest their weapons. Then the smugglers realise I'm serious. They no longer hesitate. They stand up and start to walk back towards the ambush trail then they break into a run. They disappear into the jungle canopy. They're gone.

I can see John is smiling as he understands. We look down at the heavy headloads left behind. They'll be enough cigarettes there to keep the platoon in smokes for quite a while. I'll have to decide later about who gets the whisky. I say to John:

"I think our soldiers will feel it was worth braving the mosquitos last night!"

I need to send a report back to Major Sutter. We set up our Larkspur radio and I manage to get through to our HQ. I make the report brief. I tell Major Sutter about my meeting with the FON, his tip off about the smuggler trails and how we picked up a couple of armed guys. I recommend we return back to base now to hand the two guys over to police headquarters. Major Sutter agrees. I don't tell him about our "loot" — yet!

As we make our way back to base at Ndop, I recap on the day and night's events. This was my first contact with an armed adversary and I can't help but feel good about the way it worked out. I'm feeling confident with the ability and, I hope, the loyalty of all the soldiers of my platoon. I now know them all as individuals. Some are brighter than others, they have different characters and skills. But they are "my" platoon and I'm proud of the way they operated on this patrol. I trust them and I like them. I hope they trust and like me too.

We arrive back in base by late afternoon. Following our earlier radio conversation, Major Sutter has arranged for a police team to be here and we hand over the two guys and the documents that John had uncovered. I also give them the pistols and the full magazines we had taken from them. I ask if they could identify the guns and let me know. I then tell Sgt Bado to fall the platoon out while I report to the major. He is to keep the headloads under supervision. They are not to be opened without my authorisation.

I head up to our officers' billet and report to Major Sutter. Both Capt Baldeh and David Edozi are also here. I tell the major:

"Sir, since our earlier radio check, there were no further incidents. The two arrested men have now been handed over to the police. All our men are back safely and, with your permission, I will dismiss them from this duty. I have two follow-up points. The first is that I found the FON of Bafali to be a very intelligent operator and I believe he will be a most useful source of further assistance to our mission here. He expressed a great interest in 'all things British'. I wonder if we could somehow obtain copies of magazines that I could take to him on a further visit. Something like *Homes & Gardens*, that sort of thing."

Major Sutton tells me he will see what can be found. Then he says:

"OK Peter, good job so far. We'll liaise closely with the police concerning your two arrestees. You said you have two follow-up points. The FON's request is one. What's the other?"

Now for it. I don't know Major Sutter well enough yet to know how he will take it. Here goes:

"Sir, we didn't only apprehend the two, armed guys. We also captured six smugglers. We questioned them but found them not to be threatening so, with policeman John's agreement, I let them go."

"But what about the goods they were smuggling. What was it and what happened to it?"

"Well sir, actually it's a quantity of cigarettes and, er, whisky — Johnny Walker to be precise. We brought it all back with us and it's now sort of homeless. With your permission, I intend to distribute the cigarettes among my soldiers as a small reward for their good work."

Major Sutton's face goes firm and I don't know how he will react. Then he asks:

"And what about the whisky?"

"I was thinking of giving John some bottles to share with the police. And, er, to crack a bottle with our fellow officers this evening."

Major Sutter reflects on this suggestion, then says:

"It would be a waste just to pour it all away. OK, Peter, go to it and compliment your platoon on a good first patrol."

I go back to our parade square and tell Sgt Bado to fall the men back in. The headloads are to be produced. When all are present, I say to my soldiers:

"Well done all of you. Major Sutter is very pleased that the ambush was successful. When I give the order, you are to file past me. Now, platoon, DISMISS!"

My soldiers turn to the right, salute and, as they pass me, I hand out a couple of packets of either Gauloise or Gitane cigarettes to each of them. Only a few are smokers themselves, but packets of cigarettes, especially French, make excellent exchange currency here in the Cameroons. By our soldiers' expressions, I don't think there'll be a shortage of volunteers to go on patrol next time!

Chapter Twenty-three

It's refreshing to have a shower and a change of clothes. I even give my Pawpy a good wash. She's quickly becoming a star in the company after everyone learns about how she sprung our ambush. She seems to understand. Although she always sticks closely to me, she's also very fond of Private Usman Pele, my orderly, and she also likes CSM Kabala. Perhaps the fact that he is in charge of our food distribution has something to do with it.

I spend my first evening back after the patrol in our converted officers' mess with Major Sutter, Capt Mamadu Buhari, David Edozi and CSM Kabala. David will be leading our next patrol and he, and the rest, insist I give them a detailed debrief about the FON, the ambush and everything else we experienced during the last couple of days. The bottle of whisky goes down very well even with Mamadu Buhari and CSM Kabala who I know are both Mohammedans. After our supper, the conversation gets around to Nigeria's independence in October this year and what immediate impact that could have on Nigerian life in general and in our battalion in particular. The main speakers are, of course, our Nigerian officers with CSM Kabali making a few discreet comments. Major Sutter and I find it best to be listeners rather than participants. Our Nigerian colleagues are concerned that there could be political friction as the three main tribal groups — Hausa, Yoruba and Ibo, vie for prominence and power after the British have left. The Hausas and other northern tribes have by far the largest population in the country but there are prominent well-educated Yorubas and Ibos who will be demanding to be fully represented in the distribution of top government and civil service jobs after independence. Mamadu and David say that, already, there is a strong movement in Enugu, the main city of the Ibos (the word Ibo is sometimes spelt in English as Igbo). This movement is making it clear they will resist aspects of Hausa political dominance and even the decision to keep the national capital in Lagos, a Yoruba heartland.

I previously knew precious little about these potential rivalries and clashes within Nigerian tribal groups and it makes disturbing listening. Capt Mamadu Buhari says he's even worried about the effect on the battalion when most of the British officers leave later this year. I remember our CO, Lt Col Johnson, told us he will be leaving but Mamadu says that most of our British company commanders with the rank of major will also go. He asks Major Sutter about his own future in Nigeria. I can tell that the major is uncomfortable to be spotlighted. He gives a diplomatic answer, saying:

"Well, I haven't yet been given details about my next posting but, of course, it is only right that most key positions after independence will be filled by Nigerians. I just hope that the transfer of power and responsibilities will be carried out amicably and that all sections of the Nigerian population will grasp their new status of freedom and independence in a peaceful manner in all sections of society — the new government, the civil service, the legal system and of course within our military. But, gentlemen, although we can speculate, I think we should leave these higher-level matters to others and concentrate on the job we are tasked to carry out here in the Cameroons for the next few months."

I can tell Major Sutter is anxious for the conversation to move on from internal Nigerian politics. This is the first contact I've personally had concerning this sensitive issue and I now realise that tribalism could surface when independence occurs and even in the build-up months. I think about my own platoon, which comprises a mix of all Nigerian tribes. It hadn't even crossed my mind that there could be tribal conflict between them. I feel I'm gaining the trust of my soldiers for now but what of the future? Yet again, I realise I still have much to learn.

I'm still troubled by this evening's conversation when we retire to our beds at about midnight; but after having had no sleep last night and, perhaps with the afterglow of the Johnny Walker, I hit my pillow and that's it. I fall asleep immediately and dreamlessly.

Next day, we're all up early to witness David's platoon leave on patrol. We've had information from the police that the CFF, the Cameroon Freedom Fighters rebel group, are concentrated in the mountainous frontier area, some fifteen miles east of Jakari. David's mission is to move his platoon into this area, question local villagers there and see if he can gain more details about the rebel activities in this area. He's taking a local policeman as per our standard operating procedures and also a civilian from the Jakari area to act as a guide. Major Sutter tells David to follow up any leads he may gain and to send regular situation reports back via the Larkspur radio.

This is my platoon's in-barracks time but I don't intend for our soldiers to hang around and get bored. Although we're billeted in an area where the rebels could operate and we need to take defensive precautions, I'm determined we keep fit and, each morning, as a platoon we do a couple of hours of exercises even getting out onto the trail next to our base and running as a formed squad. I'd like to do some live firing to hone our shooting skills but Major Sutter doesn't agree to this for fear of frightening the local villagers. We do, however, refresh our tactics such as anti-ambush drills, advance to contact and attacking in both section and platoon formations. I'm now confident that all my soldiers know exactly what their duties will be if we do come face to face with a rebel group. We still don't know enough about our potential foe but each time we go out on patrol we're learning more about the organisation of the CFF rebels and their *modus operandi*.

Apart from using this time to continue my Hausa lessons with CSM Kabala, I'm slowly realising that the local language here is not as alien as I had first thought when I listened to villagers chatting away. In fact, I now understand that what I'm often hearing is a form of English or French but in an accent generically referred to as "pidgin". I've learnt, for example, that the term for God phonetically is something like "*Na bignabig master ho come from up*". This is usually said in reverence and with the hand pointing to the heavens. There are similar expressions using pidgin French. It's quite complicated, so I think I'll stick to John's interpretations and concentrate on my Hausa lessons.

David's platoon has only been out for a couple of days when he reports back by radio that he's had an armed contact with the rebels. He says he has taken casualties to his platoon and is heading back. That evening he and his soldiers arrive back at our base. His men are carrying three improvised stretchers. On two of them are our own soldiers. One of these is conscious but has his arms and chest wrapped in bandages. The other is lying on his side. His shirt is blood stained and he's not moving. On the third stretcher lies what can only be described as the remains of a human being. Much of his face has been shot away and one of his legs appears to be missing. The stretcher is covered in congealing blood.

Following David's radio report, Major Sutter has arranged for a police detachment to be here when David arrived and had requested a medical team and ambulance from our battalion headquarters to assist. They turned up this afternoon and are standing by. Our first priority is the well-being of our wounded and the medics immediately take over and attend to them. Their first diagnosis is that one has only a shallow wound and he should recover quickly. The second is more serious and will need urgent attention in Bamenda Hospital. The wounded are carefully loaded into the ambulance, which then heads back to Bamenda. It's too late to save the third guy. David tells us he was one of the rebels that had ambushed his soldiers in the foothills of the mountainous area east of Jakari. His soldiers had fought bravely and had driven the rebels off. After the contact, David had searched the rebel's ambush positions. This was where the shot man had been found. David insists that the rebels had fired first and that his men had therefore stuck to the rules of engagement that had been laid down by the authorities.

We have a sombre evening meal in our officers' mess. No whisky today! David's experience has brought home to us the seriousness of our mission here. Apart from reporting about the armed contact with the rebels, David also tells us about a village they had earlier visited during their patrol. Apparently, the villagers had welcomed his soldiers, had provided them with a meal and given them information about the rebels. When David's platoon returned to the village on their way back, they found three of the villagers had been shot dead, and the rest had fled into the bush. David had to conclude that the rebels had seen his soldiers being given hospitality and had gone there and taken reprisals. The police have been informed and hope to get help there as soon as possible.

I now realise that my own first patrol had been lucky to have chanced only upon a group of smugglers and not of armed rebels. Next time, it could be very different. I also wonder if I should avoid returning to visit the FON of Bafali for fear of putting him and his villagers at risk. After all the months of training and make-believe, David's experiences today have made me appreciate that being a soldier is a serious business. I wonder what will happen on my next patrol. David is very calm and he and his platoon seem to have handled the situation very professionally. So far, I have not yet come under direct fire and have not had to give out clear orders in a calm manner. I wonder how I will respond.

Early next morning, Major Sutter gives me my orders for the next patrol. My platoon is to deploy to an area close to where David had been ambushed yesterday. The police intelligence assessment is that the area to the south of the Oku mountain range is a likely rebel forward operating base. I am to proceed with caution and ascertain whether there is still a rebel presence. If not, then I'm to proceed to the mountain frontier area to search for fresh rebel-made trails. I am to ensure strictly to stick to our side of the border. The Major doesn't give me a time limit for the patrol — that will depend on what we find. I am to report back by radio at regular intervals.

We leave at 08.00 hours. Policeman John is with us again but, in addition to my own platoon, I have also been allocated two medical orderlies who had arrived yesterday from headquarters — a sensible reinforcement after David's experience. I sincerely hope their expertise won't be needed.

We make steady progress for the first few hours. We stay clear of local villages after David's report yesterday. Most of our route is still in jungle terrain and often we have to wade through areas of swamp. I have the only map in the platoon — it was first drafted some fifty-odd years ago. It's proving quite accurate for the main topography and I now appreciate all the map-reading training we did at Mons. The scale is only 1:50,000 so it lacks detail and many of the villages we encounter must have sprung up after the map was made. I want to get us up from the jungle base to higher land where we can start our ascent towards the Oku mountain range.

Just before we're due to move out of the jungle, it starts to rain. It's like a tap being turned on. A vast cascading tap. I've never known anything like this. Someone told me that the Cameroons has a very high annual rainfall. They weren't kidding! The rain appears to be falling in vertical rods. There's no way we can continue our tactical formation. We just have to hunker down and ride it out. We carry ground sheets, which double up as rain-capes, but they don't even start to keep us dry. My platoon is stuck in a morass of driving, beating rain.

Photo: Cpl Jamil's section.

I'm trying to survive as well as I can when I see a hunched figure approaching. It's Sgt Bado. He comes up close and has to put his mouth right to my ear so that I can hear him against the racket of the torrential rain. He shouts out:

"Sir, the rain is causing this place to flood. If we stay here any longer, we risk being swept away."

"Yes, I can see that. What do you suggest?" I shout back.

"I recommend we should turn right towards the east and make for higher ground. Even being in the open would be better than here in this rising swamp."

Sgt Bado is right and I agree. Using hand signals, we get the platoon moving again, sloshing our way through the battering rain. After about a half an hour we emerge out of the jungle cover and start the climb into the foothills of the mountain. Rain water continues to swirl around us but at least it's flowing away from us back down into the jungle swamps.

Then, as quickly as it had started, the rain abruptly stops. I look up and see a line of blue sky appearing out of the blackness of the rain-clouds. In no time, the darkness has vanished and we are swathed in hot sunshine. Our sodden clothes and kit are soon steaming as the water begins to evaporate. It won't be long before we dry out. I realise we will have to adjust to this climate and adapt our patrolling disciplines accordingly.

One advantage of being out of the jungle is that we can now see the features of the Oku mountain up ahead. It has a prominent skyline and we can pick out individual peaks, which are all clearly marked on my sodden but still just readable map.

When we have sorted ourselves out after the storm, we resume our patrol, now again back into tactical formation. I manage to identify the track that we had been aiming for before the rains and we are now back en route. We've lost some time and I want to get to an area where we can set up a bivouac for the night. But by now we are firmly in "rebel" territory and I'm not prepared to move faster due to the terrain and the threat of a rebel ambush.

Corporal Jamil is leading his section on point. Suddenly he signals us to halt. We go to ground. Jamil comes back to my position and whispers his report:

"You see them there? There must be at least twenty in the group. Look, there's one up in that tree, he seems to be an alert sentry. I don't think he's spotted us yet but I can't be sure."

I can't see precisely what they're doing but I can see movement and several of them together. Perhaps it's an orders group. I decide we need to act quickly if we are to surprise them before they can react and organise their defence. I immediately despatch a Bren machine gun support team to our left to an enfilade position to provide covering fire. I will then take a fire group forward. John indicates he wants to be up the front with me. I'm glad to have his support. I hope we can get them to surrender and I will need John to interpret. I can feel the adrenaline starting to flow. My fear is that this situation could lead to a shoot-out due to the number of rebels that seems to be here.

We prepare our assault group and I signal the advance. We move in, weapons cocked and at the ready. We get within twenty yards of the rebels when Jamil urgently shouts out:

"Stop. Hold your fire!"

I wonder what the fucking hell is going on. I'm tense and strung up. What's up with Jamil? Then I realise what this is about. Our "dangerous guerrilla rebels" are, in fact, a family of gorillas. We have disturbed their slumbers. When they see us, they get up as a group and amble away into the bush. Of course, no shots are fired. We are overwhelmed by the anti-climax. We had been all set to fight our way through this seemingly threatening situation; then abruptly, we realise there is no threat at all, quite the reverse. It is our group who have threatened this beautiful family of gorillas whose natural habitat we have disturbed.

All we can do is to fall about laughing. The joke is firmly on us. These are gorillas not guerrillas!

Chapter Twenty-four

We need to get a grip. Not just my soldiers but me as well. I'd got myself all strung up as I thought this could be the first time I would be tested under fire. It didn't happen. But next time? Sgt Bado is calming our soldiers down and getting them back into formation. I value Sgt Bado's experience and steadiness. I'm lucky to have him as our platoon sergeant.

We re-set our tactical formation and set off again. Now we're climbing up into the foothills of the Oku mountain. The rain clouds have completely cleared and although it's still hot, we've lost the sticky humidity of the jungle below. The air is fresher and cleaner up here.

My soldiers' morale seems to be good, as far as I can tell. We make steady progress up the foothills and, so far, there's been no sign of the rebels. We've been moving tactically and there is no reason to suspect we've been spotted. I now have to think about where we can set up our bivouac for the night. It will start to get dark soon after six o'clock and we need to find a suitable place well before then. Up here, we're in "rebel" country so we must ensure we have good all-round protection. I discuss this with Sgt Bado and together we discuss options. Finally, we find an area that we reckon is suitable. It's a reasonably flat clearing, in between jagged rocks. There's enough room here for all the platoon, and the rocks can form part of our defence perimeter and allow us observation while being out of the line of sight from the tops of the mountain. The location is also central to the area we are to patrol during the next few days.

We get organised in our bivouac and I post sentries to cover all possible approaches. I also make contact with company headquarters on our radio and give a short "sitrep". I'm surprised the radio still works OK after the drenching it got in the rain earlier. I give our current location as well as I can work it out. I don't mention our party with the gorillas! Meanwhile, Sgt Bado gets our evening meal underway. We have to stick to our cold rations for now so as not to emit cooking smells and we supplement our issued rations with bunches of plantains that the soldiers picked up while we were in the jungle. I organise the night guard roster, which Cpls Aiki Riba and Jamil will supervise. It's still very early but we're all tired after our long approach march and those not on guard duty can get some sleep. I tell my guys to keep everything quiet and no torches or fires. My little dog Pawpy has been softly padding along all day. Now she's relieved to be able to settle down beside me as we drop off to sleep.

I wake up; it's completely dark. My luminous watch tells me it's only 22.15 hours. The first thing I notice is that it's cold — very cold. This is the first time since I landed in Kano in January that the temperature has been anything other than either hot or warm. It must be the altitude. I hadn't realised how high we must have climbed and that this would affect the night temperature so radically. We're in the middle of west Africa, for fuck's sake! I'm sleeping on my groundsheet but decide I'd prefer to lie on the rough ground and put the groundsheet over me. It might relieve the worst of the chill.

I'm still tired and I must have dropped off to sleep again when someone shakes my shoulder. It's Cpl Jamil. He reports:

"Sir, our sentries have seen lights up on the mountain. We think they are from torches as people are moving on a trail."

I get up. I ask him: "How far away and in which direction are they moving?"

"They're some way further up the mountain. Perhaps about two miles but it's hard to tell."

I tell him: "OK, I'll come and have a look"

I go over to where the sentry is positioned. I can also see the lights. There are about ten lights spaced evenly apart covering a distance of perhaps forty or fifty yards but, as Jamil says, it's very difficult to judge. In the sky, there's a half-moon giving some light but it's still just a guess. about exact location. As we're watching, we see another group of lights moving towards the first. They seem to converge at one point then both groups are stationary. I can only estimate that what we are looking at are two groups carrying torches to guide them. They now seem to have met at some pre-arranged rendezvous. Perhaps it's their camp for the night.

There's nothing more to do except for our sentries to keep observation. I take a bearing of their rendezvous point with my prismatic compass. We'll take a patrol up there in the morning. I'm about to go back to my makeshift bed when Sgt Bado appears and says:

"Sir, the men are very cold and ask if we can light a fire to make a hot drink and try to get some warmth."

I have every sympathy with them. I'm also bloody cold and I'm a northern European. It must be much worse for these guys who've probably never experienced cold like this before. But I have a problem with their request. I believe the rebels have not yet spotted us. We now have the advantage of surprise and I need to keep it that way for as long as possible. I snap back at Sgt Bado:

"No, I told you already. No fires or lights. We'll just have to put up with it."

"Yes, sir," Sergeant Bado replies but I can tell he's going to have a hard time relaying that to our soldiers.

I go back again to my improvised bed-space. Pawpy tries to close up. I know I need to sleep now as I have no idea what the morning will bring. I can't settle. In my mind, I begin to question everything. I'm nineteen years old. I'm a British national service conscript. Like the rest of our guys, I'm cold. Earlier today, I thought we were going into action where bullets would be flying only to find we were facing a bunch of monkeys, for heaven's sake! But now, all the signs are that we could well be involved in a shoot-out tomorrow. I'm alone with my Nigerian soldiers. I'm so grateful that they seem to have accepted me as their leader and until now there's not been an issue about that. I am their platoon commander and they accept my position and, what a crazy word to say! they accept my *authority*. In retrospect, I wonder if my insistence about no fires or lights was justified. At that moment, I thought it was the right, the professional thing to do, but now I just don't know. Why should I try to play the great military expert when I have no idea what really is right or wrong? I'm confused. But thinking like this doesn't get me anywhere. Tomorrow, I'll take out a patrol group and see how our fortunes will pan out.

I almost can't wait for the dawn because I can't sleep anymore. I'm still cold, cramped up and still troubled by our situation here. I'm eager to get going again. I want to get up to near the summit of the Oku mountain and try to flush out those CFF guys. I know I've got to stick with the rules of engagement but, after David's report about the rebels murdering innocent civilians, I think we now have more latitude to take the initiative. I'll make sure I have policeman John with us to witness and, I hope, approve anything we do. He's a good guy and I think he's on my side.

I take Cpl Aiki Riba's section plus our radio operator with me on the patrol. It's 06.45 hours, just light and I'm eager to get going. I check again the grid direction that I'd saved of the lights we saw last evening. The terrain here is rocky with deep crevasses between our present location and what I believe is probably the rebel base. I plot out a route that I hope will get us up there but should still keep us under cover from their observation. I leave the rest of the platoon under Sgt Bado's charge. I tell him to secure the bivouac and wait for further instructions. Yet again, I wish we also had a VHF short-range radio or simple walky-talky so that we could communicate with him while we're out. But we don't, so we have to get on with it.

As we climb on up the Oku mountain, we move into an area of bamboo forest. The tall straight trees raise high above us and, like in the jungle, the sky is obscured. We're now following a steep track with the mountain side raising up above us on our left and falling sharply away on our right. There's an earie atmosphere here. It's quite windy and these tall bamboo trees seem to moan and whistle as they sway under the strength of the wind. I try to hold to the route I've planned but the contours of my map don't seem to relate precisely to the ground. My compass tells me we're still heading in the right direction but our exact position is a matter of guesswork.

It's taken longer than I thought to reach the high peaks of the Oku. But I'm confident we've found the track where we saw the lights last night. Once on this track, we keep going east but we have to be cautious. I can't afford for us to stumble right into a rebel position. I decide to take over the lead position myself with Cpl Aiki Riba up behind me. I estimate we must now be close to the place that we assess was the rebel rendezvous last night. We've already been out several hours since we left base today. It's difficult to maintain full alertness for long periods but here, on this trail, in the middle of a bamboo forest, I feel tense and wary.

There's no prior warning. We come around a bend in the trail and suddenly we're face to face with a rebel group. The lead man immediately raises his gun and fires at me. I fire back. The difference is — he stays standing while I drop to the ground as I fire. The result: he misses and I hit. Our Bren machine gun team know what to do. We've practised so often for this situation. They run up the hillside to our left and engage the rear of the rebel group with rapid fire. It's effective and lethal. I can't hear any further firing from the rebels so I shout to our guys to cease fire. We do a quick check. On their side; three dead, one with a flesh wound in his arm, eight who've dropped their weapons (all Kalashnikovs as far as I can tell) and raised their arms in surrender. Our side; one has a grazed shoulder where a bullet must have whipped past him. He's bleeding but still conscious. The rest of us are all intact. I tell Cpl Aiki Riba to take a couple of his men to do a quick follow-up along the trail to see if there are more rebels. He's soon back to report no further sightings.

This was for real: my first contact with an enemy group! It all happened so quickly I didn't have time to feel any emotion. I just acted as I'd been trained to do as did the rest of our guys. Now that it's all over, the reality starts to sink in. We've been through a kill or be killed situation and we've survived. I feel myself shaking. We could have been killed ourselves.

I try to get control of my emotions. As per our procedure, I need to report this contact to headquarters. I do a quick check with my map and work out where I think we now are. Our radio operator establishes communications and tells me Major Sutter is on receive. I try to keep my voice calm, stating the details of the contact and giving our grid reference. There's a pause on the line. Then I hear Major Sutter voice snapping back:

"I hope you're wrong, Peter, the position you've given is two miles over the border into Republique du Cameroun. You have no right to be there and certainly not to engage rebel forces. This could cause a major international incident."

Until now, I'd been chuffed that we had done a good job but now I realise this was a potential serious breach of regulations as Major Sutter had clearly told me I must not cross the border. The only thing I could think to say was:

"Will recheck grid and call back." I use the pressel switch to end the call.

I then recheck my map. Major Sutter is correct. I must have climbed further up the Oku feature than I had intended. Although there had been no sign of the border, no marking or border posts, I now realise that the trail we're on is indeed in the Republique. I'm in a panic but force myself to calm down and assess this new situation. Other than my soldiers and the surrendered rebels, there is no sign of another human being in this area. There are no villages nearby and no border markings. This is a completely isolated place.

I decide what to do and say to Cpl Aiki Riba:

"OK, we need to get moving straightaway. Keep our prisoners guarded and they can carry the three dead guys. Make sure we take all their weapons and personal kit with us. And post a rear guard to watch we're not followed."

We retrace our route back along the trail then I find another track leading back down the Oku feature. I follow this for about three miles then stop and recheck my map. Looking up, I can clearly see a ridge line along the top of the Oku with a particular shaped series of peaks. These are clearly marked on the map. We're now at least one mile inside the British Cameroons. I double check to be certain. Yes, we're definitely back on our own soil. I tell our radio operator to re-establish communications with our headquarters and to ask for Major Sutter in person. When he comes on the line, I tell him:

"Reference my earlier contact report. Correction on grid reference." I then read out the grid of our present location. Again, there's pause. I suppose the major is checking his own map. He then calls back, saying;

"Right, I thought you must have been mistaken earlier. Good job Peter, and congratulate your platoon!"

Phew — the situation is retrieved and I'm no longer a potential war criminal!

Our progress back to our bivouac base is slow. Our walking prisoners don't try to resist. They seem quite weak and dispirited. We have to keep goading them to keep up. The wounded guy is obviously in considerable pain and is bleeding profusely. We frequently have to stop to attend to him. We carry simple field dressings as part of our basic kit and do our best to bandage him up: but none of us have had much medical training and I'm not sure we're doing the right thing. The two stretcher bearers back at our camp are trained medics so we can give our prisoner better treatment there — if he survives that long. We're also slowed down by having to carry the three bodies and all the rebel weapons in addition to our own. Our own casualty seems to be doing fine. He's a strong Hausa man named Jalloh. He seems already to have shrugged off his injury.

After the adrenaline of the contact, and then the threat of being arrested for transgressing over the border, I'm now feeling something of an anti-climax. It's been another long, tiring day and I'm pleased when we finally make it back to our bivouac camp. There'll no longer be the need to conceal where we are. First, we must ensure sentries are set for our defence. Then I plan to get a fire going, prepare some hot food and try to keep everyone warmer tonight. We'll have to stay here for one more night then we'll move back to our base in Ndop tomorrow and turn our prisoners and three dead bodies over to the police.

Chapter Twenty-five

As soon as we get back to the camp, I realise something is wrong. I had expected Sgt Bado, and all the soldiers who had remained in the camp, to greet us back and be eager to know the story of our day. Everything seems to be in order. Everyone is there. But there's an atmosphere I've not experienced before. I arrange for the prisoners to be safeguarded and check with Sergeant Bado that a sentry roster has been made for the night. I then ask Bado to tell the two medics to see me so that we can arrange the care of the wounded prisoner. Bado says:

"Yes, sir. They want to speak to you. I must warn you, sir, they're trouble!"

I've no idea what Bado means by saying "they're trouble". I confess that until now I hadn't given the medics much attention. There had been so many other priorities. The two of them now come to where I'm standing in the middle of our base camp. I can see at once that their manner is surly and arrogant. Before I can say anything, one of them says:

"We've been waiting for you, white man. Why have you taken us to this hell hole? Who do you think you are to order us about?"

I'm stunned. What is this? Since I've been with the battalion, everyone has been totally co-operative. I've been trying to do my job as well as I can and treat all my soldiers fairly. I don't understand. Before I can remonstrate, the medic continues:

"While you've been away all day, we've been talking to the soldiers here. We are Nigerians. We are soon to celebrate our country's full independence and we will run our affairs in our own way. We don't see any point in us being here in the so-called British Cameroons. It's nothing to do with us. Now you've been shooting our African brothers and you expect us to clear up your mess. I've told the soldiers here that they shouldn't obey you anymore. Why don't you go back to Britain where you belong?"

So that's what this is about. I glance around and see that my platoon soldiers have closed in to witness what is going on. I'm completely on my own here: miles from anywhere. We're on operational duty and what the medic has just said amounts to treasonous behaviour. I should have the two of them arrested immediately. I again glance around at my soldiers and try to read their attitude. They are watching closely. I can't say they look antagonistic towards me but neither do they intervene. They seem neutral. I feel that if I order them to arrest these medics, I can't be sure they will obey me.

There's got to be another way. Inwardly, I'm really scared. I can't believe that, after all that my soldiers and I have been through together in the past few days, I would find myself in this situation. I know I *must not* show my emotions. At all costs, I mustn't appear to be intimidated by them. If they think they've frightened me, I'm done for. I must try to keep up the pretence of being calm in front of them. I struggle to get my breathing under control then say to them in what, I hope, is a steady voice:

"You two are only here to do your medical work. We have a badly wounded man. Go and attend to him, and do it now!"

They pause, then it's the second medic's turn to get involved. He looks around at my soldiers and gives a sort of smug grin. Then he moves up close to me and says:

"We'll do our medical work but when *we* decide, not you. It's time you left, white man!"

I'm now stuck in total confrontation with these two medics. If I try to reason with them, I'm sure it'll only make things worse. I've no option but to stand firm and challenge them to make me go. Perhaps I'm crazy but all I can think to do is to confront the two of them and hope for the best. The second medic moves up close to me. Instead of retreating, I move even closer towards him so that we are standing face to face only about two feet apart. I say:

"I stay here with my soldiers. What are you going to do about it?"

He hesitates, then pulls out a pistol, cocks it and points it directly at my face. I have no weapon as I'd given my Sten to Usman Pele to be cleaned.

He snarls: "Leave us, white man. This is not your world."

I take my time to reply then I tell him:

192

"Shoot me if you will. But if you do, my soldiers will then either shoot you both straight away or take you to the police where you will be convicted of treason and then shot. Either way, you both lose."

My little speech is of course just bravado. I have no idea if my soldiers will act against them. Again, I know if I show fear or weakness, I'm lost. My guts are churning but I must-not-show-it-or-give-way! I stand up straight and look directly at the medic. I fix my stare at his eyes. I don't look at his pistol, I stare at him. We're in a sort of impasse, standing there almost like two statues. I refuse to do anything but keep on staring into that man's eyes. I don't know how long this goes on. I only know I'm into this now and can't back out.

After some time, I've no idea how long, I sense he's uncertain what to do, whether or not to squeeze the trigger. I continue to stare at him, to try to bore into his eyes. I see he's beginning to lose it. He's bewildered. He looks round at his medic colleague for support, I suppose. This is my chance. I lean forward and, gently not firmly, take hold of the muzzle of his pistol and turn it down towards the ground. Then, with a sharp tug, I rip it out of his hand. I then point the pistol at both of the medics and say:

"That's enough from you two. You have your work to do. Sgt Bado, take these two men to the wounded prisoner and see that they attend to him. That's why they're here."

I can tell that it wasn't just me who had been emotionally involved. I see that my soldiers begin to relax, to shuffle in embarrassment, then to smile and, by their attitude, to show how relieved they are by the outcome of this stand-off. They start to rally round me. Instinctively, they line up as if on a formal parade. Sgt Bado quietly calls them to attention. Then he steps forwards and salutes. I'm really moved by this gesture. Without words, my soldiers give me their support, their loyalty. I'm still in some sort of shock from the face-off with the two medics. Now I see my soldiers are on my side. I'm close to tears but just manage to continue to hold myself together. I try to continue to play the role of the platoon commander. All I can manage to say to Sgt Bado is:

"Carry on sergeant, and dismiss the men to their duties."

Life soon gets back to normal. Now that I've authorised fires, my soldiers light one in the central space of our bivouac camp. They busy themselves preparing foodstuffs they have brought with them all this way but that has been left uncooked until now. The whole atmosphere has changed. I can tell the crisis is over. My soldiers are now back to being their normal, happy, contented selves.

I need to take some time to adjust. I find again the space I had occupied last night and lie down. My darling little dog, Pawpy, faithful as ever, flutters her tail and comes over to me and licks my face. She settles down next to me on the hard rock surface of our make-do bed. I know she also feels the emotion that I've experienced this evening.

I reflect on what has been the most stressful day of my life — the shoot-out under the whistling bamboos when one shot either way could have killed me, my navigational fuck up, which could have caused an international crisis, and now, having to face a potential mutiny right here in our camp. I know I have more to do before I can sleep, but right now, I'm physically and emotionally drained. I need a few quiet minutes to let my system adjust. I know I'm very close to tears: of emotion, of relief, of exhaustion. Weird images flash through my mind. I think about my school friends from Bath, those now settling down to university life in UK, none of those could possibly imagine my situation here on this mountain having to face what I've experienced today. My thoughts go back to the instructors in Devizes and Mons. How they had hammered away to ensure our weapon handling skills, our tactics, our fitness were all up to their high standards. Their persistence really paid off today. I don't know why, but I also think about the dead rebels and, I suppose, especially about the one I shot and killed myself. They were our enemy, if we hadn't shot to kill them, they would surely have killed us. But all these guys had lives, family, wives, children who would never see them again. In a strange way, I mourn for them.

I think about this final episode. When I was being threatened at gunpoint by the medic, I was praying my soldiers would intervene to save me: but at that point they didn't move. I then realised I was completely on my own. I could count on no one else. I had to draw on some inner strengths I didn't know I had. Perhaps that was the moment when I ceased being a youth and began being a man!

I can't continue to indulge myself in these thoughts any longer. There's still work to be done. I find my inner shaking has eased, at least for now. I'm still holding the pistol I took from the medic. It's a 9 mm

Browning. I check the breech and find there's a round in the chamber. The rest of the magazine is full. The medic wasn't kidding. If he'd squeezed the trigger, I would be dead.

I get up and go over to where the wounded prisoner is lying. The soldiers have rigged up a makeshift bed for him. His bandages have been changed and he seems to be more comfortable. Perhaps he'll survive provided we get him back to Ndop tomorrow and then to the hospital. The medics have finished their job. Elsewhere, the soldiers seem to have completed their evening meal and are preparing for the night — some on guard duty now, others later on. Now is the time I have to move and re-establish my authority here. I can't just pretend nothing happened this evening.

I tell Sgt Bado to do two things. First, formally arrest the two medics. Second, form the men in again as I need to talk to them all. Bado does as I tell him and all my soldiers, line up in front of me. I stand near the light of the fire so that my face will be clearly visible as I speak. I also insist that the two medics, with their hands firmly tied, are close to where I'm standing. I try to speak in a clear voice using simple English, and now some Hausa words that I hope they all will understand. I begin:

"Most of you saw the incident earlier this evening when these two men held me up at gunpoint. They said that you should no longer obey my orders and that I should leave. I want to thank you all for not supporting them. Let me just say this. I am here at the request of the Nigerian authorities. I have been trained to be an officer and to take the decisions that are needed in this operational situation we face today. My position is the same as Lt Edozi and Capt Buhari, back in Ndop. What is different is that I am British and white skinned. Edozi and Buhari are Nigerian and black. We are all soldiers and we are here to carry out the tasks we are given. Later this year, Nigeria will have complete independence. All major political and military decisions will then be made by Nigerian people. Perhaps the new Nigerian authorities will require the British officers to leave right away. Or maybe we'll stay on until there are sufficient trained Nigerian officers. Until that time, our job is to work together and support each other. I have now been four months in the battalion, in C Company, in Number Two Platoon. We have all got on well together. We are a team. You are my brothers. *Mu'yan wasa ne ku yan'uawa*! We function well as a unit. Until today!"

I now point directly to the two medics. I continue:

"These two men were allocated to our platoon to assist in medical requirements. Indeed, I've just checked that their work on the wounded prisoner was well carried out. But that was all they are here to do. Instead, while our patrol was out risking our lives and carrying out our mission, these two men were stirring up trouble and trying to persuade you to reject my orders. They threatened to shoot me when I was unarmed. There actions cannot be tolerated. They have no place here. *Ba su da wani wuri a nun. Ba su da sojoji!* They will remain tied up and under arrest. Tomorrow we are returning to our base in Ndop. *Muna goyan bayan juna banda laurin fuskokinmu*! I am writing a report about their treasonous behaviour, which I will sign and Sgt Bado and all our corporals will also sign as witnesses. That's all. Sgt Bado, fall the men out!"

It was a long speech but I felt I had to make it one hundred percent clear to all my soldiers that the actions of the medics were totally unacceptable. I hope and pray that I will never again have to face such a show of racism.

As my soldiers are dismissed, I feel genuine warmth and support from them. Perhaps the best gem of the whole evening comes from Cpl Aiki Riba. He smiles deeply, and says: "*Da kyau, Sir, duk nuna goyon bayanka.* Sir, those two are just couple of ignorant Ibos. We knew they were talking typical Ibo rubbish."

Well, I'm thinking: "Racism comes in many different forms!"

I do a final round before we settle down for the night. My morale is now much improved, partly by the attitude of my soldiers who are almost falling over themselves to please me, and partly because I needed to make my little speech and shame the two medics. I go to check on them and find that their hands are tied together and they have been put among our rebel prisoners. I'm not too keen on that so I have them moved to be next to the three dead bodies. Somehow that seems more appropriate.

We keep the fires going during the night, which wards off the worst of the cold. I tell Sgt Bado to get an early breakfast organised because I plan to leave on the dawn at around 06.00 hours. I'd got a message through to Ndop last evening and I said we hope to make it back before dark and to have ambulances standing by. It's a long haul to do the trip from here back to base, lugging our prisoners and wounded with us, and still have to move in tactical formation. How much easier our lives would be if we could summon up a helicopter or two but unfortunately these are not available to us.

Our return patrol works nearly to schedule, the only delay being yet another rain deluge. We ride that out as before but I make sure our prisoners are closely guarded throughout the storm. The rains have again caused the jungle trail to be swamped and we find ourselves waist high in water until the rains recede again. I'm relieved when at last our dishevelled group struggles back to the safety of our base camp in Ndop.

I had reported by radio our main situation but had not told Major Sutter about the two medics (nor of course about my cross-border blunder!). When we have attended to the rebel prisoners and I've made a report with John to the local police commander, I ask to speak privately to Major Sutter and for Sgt Bado and Cpls Aiki Riba and Jamil to attend. I recount the story of the two medics and ask Bado and the others to make comments. They all confirm my account. I say I will produce a full written report and request the two men be returned to the headquarters in Bamenda under close arrest. I want them both to be charged with whatever the Nigerian military legal service deems necessary.

There's another point of interest that evening. The police had been examining the weapons we recovered from the rebels. I had thought they were Kalashnikovs. The police now confirm this. Apparently, they had been manufactured in Russia only two years before. This find is of great interest to the intelligence organisation.

At last, we have completed all our end-of-patrol duties, the ambulance and other transport have left and I've dismissed my soldiers for the night. I re-join my fellow officers and manage to uncover another bottle of whisky from our earlier smugglers' haul. During the evening, Major Sutter tells me that Bamenda have sent down copies of English magazines that I had reported were requested by the FON of Bafali. The major suggests my next patrol should be to revisit him and renew our liaison with him.

"Certainly, sir" I reply. "I would very much like to see the FON again. But right now, if you'll excuse me, sir, I need to go to bed."

I'm excused, I stagger to my bed. I can hardly remember hitting my pillow before I crash out.

Chapter Twenty-six

Major Sutter doesn't even have me woken up for first parade when David Edozi's platoon leave on patrol. Their mission is to check out an area west of Bafut. The police have learnt, from their interrogation of the two armed guys we captured in our earlier ambush, that more weapons are planned to be smuggled into the British Cameroons via the village markets. Last evening, I'd been discussing with David how we laid out our ambush. But I told him he couldn't take my little Pawpy dog to assist!

When I do wake up it's already after 09.00 hours. I feel refreshed and ready to go. Major Sutter tells me that yesterday he sent a report to our CO,
Lt Col Johnson, about my confrontation and arrest of the two medics. This morning, the colonel has said he wants to see me personally about the incident. I'm to report to him in Bamenda tomorrow. For me, this is bad news. What happened, happened. I dealt with it as well as I could and my soldiers supported me. Now it seems the whole business is escalating to a higher level. The last thing I want is to get embroiled in local racial and political issues.

I speak to Sgt Bado and tell him to take charge of the platoon for a couple days until I'm free to continue my duties. I then spend the rest of the day writing up my account of the incident, getting it typed up by our company clerk and having Sgt Bado and Cpls Aiki Riba and Jamil sign that they confirm my report is accurate. I give a copy to Major Sutter and prepare a second copy to take with me tomorrow.

Next morning, I take one of our company Land Rovers and drive myself from Ndop to Bamenda. The police tell us that the security threat assessment requires that all journeys on that road should be with an armed escort so I take Usman Pele, my orderly. He's armed with his Mark 4 rifle and I also take my own Sten gun.

In Bamenda, I report to Capt Thomson, the adjutant at Battalion HQ, and hand in my report. I'm told to wait in a separate room to be called.

It's a long wait. While I'm sitting there, I hear the arrival of a group of people in the adjoining room, which I presume is the CO's office. I can hear greetings and the muffled sound of conversations, then a long silence then, again the conversation recommences. At last, the adjutant puts his head round the door and tells me:

"Right, Lt Chambers, the colonel will see you now. Make sure you march into his office and salute." I'm thinking he doesn't need to tell me that. What is this? I'm the innocent party here, for fuck's sake!

I get up, assume a marching mode, enter the CO's office, halt and salute as required. Lt Col Johnson is sitting behind his desk but also in the room are two Nigerian officers. By their rank badges, I see they are also both lieutenant colonels. The CO acknowledges my salute and says;

"At ease, Chambers. Come and take a seat. I want to introduce you to Lt Col Kagara, who will be your next CO, replacing me in October and to Lt Col Abraham, who is head of the legal service of the Nigerian military forces. Both officers flew in from Lagos today after I informed them of your report about the two mutinous medics during your patrol. We take these issues extremely seriously particularly in these last few months before Nigerian independence. Now, we've all read your written report but we'd like to hear about it in your own words."

Phew! I'm not expecting to be put on the spot like this. I'm glad I had spent good time writing up the report as it made me concentrate on remembering the whole sequence. I trot out the events as clearly as I can, trying not to stammer over the hard vowel sounds. I end my description by saying:

"All I could do was to try to protect military discipline and the chain of command. I want to emphasise that I feel I have an excellent relationship with the soldiers of my platoon. These two medics were attached as late additions. My platoon soldiers told me later that they had been trying to stir things up from the start. They also complained about the cold at night on the Oku mountain. I wanted no trouble with them but it seems they were intent on trying to incite my soldiers, as they felt they shouldn't be taking orders from me who they racially called 'white man'. That's all I can say."

The CO and the other officers are quiet for a while. I just wait for a response and am surprised when it's Lt Col Kagara who speaks.

"Lt Chambers, I regret that we should meet for the first time under these somewhat strained circumstances. The situation you experienced is not unique, but my country is determined to carry out peacefully the transfer of powers and responsibilities when we gain independence later this year. For now, I think I can speak for both Lt Col Johnson and myself in saying that we appreciate the action you took regarding the two medics and the clarity of both your written report and verbal summary. You can rest assured the two medics will be charged with mutiny and will face trial. You may have to be called as a witness by the court but we'll try to protect you from that. Meanwhile, you are to return to your duties in C Company and carry on the good work you are doing. We will be sending an explanatory note to Major Sutter."

I salute, leave the office, and go to find Usman Pele and my Land Rover to get back to Ndop. It's now mid-afternoon and although I've had no lunch, I just want to get going.

On the drive back, I reflect on this meeting. I'm intrigued by Lt Col Kagara saying the situation I experienced was not unique. Perhaps I should have asked him to clarify this but I didn't think it appropriate. Regarding the colonel himself, I'm really impressed. He seems to be a highly intelligent Nigerian officer and, although I've had no problems so far with Lt Col Johnson, it will be interesting to see how life in the battalion develops when most if not all the senior officers will be Nigerian. For now, I just want to put the whole two medics incident behind me. I'm keen to get back to my platoon and to resume my normal duties.

I report to Major Sutter as soon as I get back to Ndop. He tells me he's already spoken to the CO who said that he and Lt Col Kagara were completely satisfied with my account of the medics' incident. He continues:

"Peter, as you know, David is still on patrol with his platoon but I'm expecting him back tomorrow. Then I'd like you to pay another liaison trip to the FON of Bafali. I've been talking to the police about security. You are to take precautions, of course, but the police assure me that the rebels are highly unlikely to attack his village due to the historic ties he has with the FONs of Bafanji and Bafut and the power and influence these three, hold over the whole community in this area. So, it serves our cause to maintain good liaison with the FON. For some reason, he seems to have taken to you and has specifically asked for you to visit. I've had a message sent ahead to the FON to suggest you visit again tomorrow and have received his reply. He welcomes you, proposes that this time you spend the night in his village. He will arrange accommodation for you and all your platoon. Just make sure your security patrols are still mounted but otherwise, accept his goodwill invitation. He's an important ally Peter, so make sure you treat him well."

That's fine by me. I enjoyed my earlier meeting with the FON and, also, going to his village is a damn sight easier than flogging up Mount Oku again. I need to get myself genned up about British up-market life so I spend much of the day reading through the magazines sent down from Bamenda. There are pictures of English stately homes and articles about the British aristocracy. My problem is that I've never been to these places and haven't moved in such upper-class social circles. Other than looking at the pictures with the FON there's not much I can tell him. Eventually, I find two lifelines. One is a potted history of Hampton Court. I've never been there but it did crop up during my "A" level history syllabus when we were studying Henry VIII as part of a Tudor period project. Then I find a long piece about Bath. Hooray! I can certainly bang on with authority about my hometown.

Late that evening, David Edozi is back with his platoon. They're not alone. David has hit the jackpot. He wheels in six forlorn-looking prisoners under heavy guard. Their hands have been tied with twine. Behind them, David's soldiers are carrying two improvised stretchers. We learn that they're carrying one of our own soldiers who was shot during the ambush of the rebels. I can see he's been hit at least once in the abdomen, has been bleeding profusely and appears to be unconscious. He will need urgent medical care. The other stretcher is supporting one of the rebels who is obviously dead. David reports that he was shot and killed during the fire fight. In anticipation of David's return, Major Sutter has organised an ambulance with medics (not the pair who mutinied against me!) and a police party to take care of the prisoners. That's not all. Bringing up the rear of the platoon are several villagers who David has co-opted as porters. All are carrying heavy headloads. David gets them to lower the loads to the ground and somewhat triumphantly opens them up to expose a small arsenal of weapons. There are rifles that I recognise as Kalashnikovs, a few pistols, similar to the ones my platoon captured earlier, plus a mass of ammunition, some hand grenades and even a machine gun.

First priority is to get medical support for our wounded soldier. It doesn't look good. He seems too weak to be moved by ambulance to Bamenda straightaway so CSM Kabala will organise a temporary first aid facility here in our camp. We have to pray he will make it.

The police take charge of the prisoners and the weapons. They also arrange for the dead rebel to be taken to a morgue facility in Ndop village. They tell us that the intelligence they are likely to gain from David's haul should make a valuable contribution to controlling the flow of rebel infiltration into the British Cameroons, at least our sector of it, and to maintaining the peace and stability of the region.

Tempered by the sadness about our wounded guy, everyone is buoyant about David's successful ambush. In the few weeks we've been deployed here, we now seem to be understanding and dominating our area of operational responsibility, and fulfilling our mission.

Next morning, it's my platoon's turn again. This time I leave my little dog, Pawpy, in the care of CSM Kabala. She likes him, especially when he takes her to the cookhouse. We leave early on our route back to Bafali. We experience yet another soaking as a storm batters us and we squelch our way along the half-submerged tracks. However, by the time we reach the Bafali compound, the sun is out again and our steamy uniforms have pretty much dried out.

We have the same experience as last time when we enter the village. We are welcomed by a small delegation of villagers who escort us to the cleared centre by the FON's residence building. On a complete whim, I decide to form my platoon as if on a formal parade. I think the FON might appreciate the gesture. As if on cue, the FON appears at the entrance of his residence. He is resplendent in his flowing robes and wide turban-shaped headdress. As on our first time here, I can't help noticing his black shoes. The rest of the villagers are barefoot, this is the norm in this area. But not the FON. Again, he's wearing a pair of shiny leather shoes but with no socks. They gleam in the evening sunlight. I suppose they are a mark of his authority but I wouldn't dare to ask him. As the great man descends the steps of his residence, I bring the platoon to attention, march towards the FON, halt, give a snappy salute and report:

"Number Two Platoon, C Company, 2nd Battalion Queens Own Nigeria Regiment, on parade and ready for your inspection, sir."

The FON seems to be suitably flattered and plays his role like a connoisseur. Together we walk the ranks of my platoon, he says a word or two to some of my soldiers then returns to the front of the paraded platoon. I salute again and give the order to stand at ease and stand easy. The FON invites me to join him in his residence, which I accept but ask for a few minutes to ensure my soldiers are settled and that our security is organised for the night. Everything seems to have been well organised to accommodate all the soldiers of my platoon. Sgt Bado tells me that food has been laid on for everyone. Despite the overwhelming hospitality of these delightful villagers, I still feel it right to ensure we maintain a roster of patrols throughout the night.

The light is fading as The FON and I enter his residence. He invites me to sit on a large ornate wicker chair facing him. The room is adorned with rich multi-coloured tapestries. There is an air of opulence, which, combined with the FON's immaculate robes, makes me feels decidedly shabby in my creased army fatigues. As on my last visit, as soon as we sit down a servant approaches with glasses and jugs of water and the FON's favourite beer. There's a unique aroma in the room, at least unique to me. A sort of mix of flower blossom and other perfumes. It's not at all unpleasant.

The FON puts me at my ease by asking questions about my health, my soldiers' welfare, and how we're adjusting to our lives here in the British Cameroons. All innocuous small talk as we toast each other with his local beer, which on this visit I feel I can sample. I find it tastes not at all like British bitter or the Nigerian larger I'm now getting used to. I find the first taste rather daunting but after a few sips it starts to go down well. In any case, I feel it my duty to accept my host's hospitality. I'm also thinking the time is right to make my presentation.

I'd been protecting the magazines I'd been saving for this evening by carrying them in several layers of canvas. I'd managed to keep them dry even during the torrential rains earlier today. Now is the moment: I make quite a performance of unwrapping them in front of the FON. I place the magazines on the small table between us and say to him:

"Sir, when we last met you expressed an interest in my British culture. Here are some magazines that I hope will illustrate the type of buildings, countryside and social events that you asked me about."

I lay out the magazines in front of him: old copies of *Homes & Gardens*, *The Tatler*, *Country Life* and a couple of others. I'm amazed by the FON's reaction. His eyes light up and he seizes on each of the magazines, turning the pages reverently. It's as if I'd brought him a set of the crown jewels. During the next hour or so, he bombards me with questions such as:

"How is this building made?" "What are these bricks and what are they made from" "How do people get from the bottom to the top of these big houses?" "What are these men and ladies wearing" "Why do they have hats like that?" "All the pictures are in black and white — what are the real colours?"

And so on. The FON seems transfixed by the magazines. His questions are in one way so simple and naive and yet in another so deep and intelligent. I realise I am listening to a man who has rarely moved far from his village yet has a thirst for knowledge about the world beyond his experience. I try to answer his questions as well as I can and am relieved when he lets me guide him to the features of Hampton Court and then Bath.

Midway through our discussions, two young servant girls approach carrying trays with dishes of food — a plate of roast pig, followed by a platter of fruits — mangos, papayas, plantains, guavas. And constant refills of the beer. We eat with our hands as is the tradition here. The FON indicates for me to help myself but he seems intent to continue his research through the magazines. Throughout, I've had to struggle to give adequate answers to his searching questions but at last he lets me talk about Bath. I give him a short geographical piece about the Somerset hills and the flow of the river Avon through the city, its Roman origins as Aquae Sulis, it's rebirth during the Georgian period and I show him pictures of the Royal and Lansdown Crescents, the Abbey and Poultney Bridge. I find a street plan and tell about the layout of the old city. The

FON even interrogates me with enthusiastic interest about the location and structure of my old school building.

Our conversation lasts the whole evening as our empty plates are discreetly removed by the servants. I realise I'm in the presence of a deep thinking and highly intelligent man. I've never met anyone like the FON. He's quite remarkable. As I had noticed on my first visit, his subjects approach him with complete deference. He is a total authoritarian in his village, a despot, a dictator. Yet all I see on the faces of his subjects and in their demeanour in his presence is genuine warmth, affection, even love. Although he is in total command of his village, he retains a freshness and a thirst for new knowledge.

After giving me an exhausting but exhilarating grilling throughout the entire evening, at last the FON closes the pages of the magazines and places them carefully on the table between us. He also has been drinking the beer throughout the evening and, as he gets to his feet, I notice a slight unsteadiness. He tells me:

"Lt Chambers. I thank you for bringing this excellent gift, which I will keep as a treasured possession. Also, I thank you for bringing the pictures to life with your eloquent descriptions. Now I'm going to retire. You will be sleeping in my residence tonight and will be well looked after."

I'm wondering what will happen next. Then the FON claps his hands loudly. This is the cue for his wives to appear — all twenty of them! They line up in front of the FON as if on a military parade. They vary in their ages ranging, I would guess, from their thirties down to teens. They have some things in common. All are beautifully dressed in their coloured robes, all exude a feeling of freshness as I suspect they have all recently bathed and scented their bodies, and all are looking lovingly (and I feel hopefully) at the FON.

The FON takes his time then begins his "tour of inspection", slowly walking down the line of his wives. He says a little word to each as he passes and I see nervous pleasure on their faces. Then he pauses in front of one, indicating he has chosen her to accompany him this evening. He continues down the line, en route selecting two others also to join him later. At the end of his tour, he turns towards me and says:

"Lieutenant, I have chosen three of my wives for myself tonight, but there are seventeen others. Please feel free to choose as you wish. They will be so honoured to assist you to have a pleasurable night!"

He then turns away and leaves the room with his three chosen ladies. He doesn't look back. All this happens so apparently routinely. I turn towards the remaining young ladies. After their initial disappointment at not being chosen tonight by the FON, they are now all looking at me with a mixture of coy shyness and expectation. I'm totally confused. For a long time, I've been rueing the fact that I'm still a virgin and now, suddenly and totally unexpectantly, I'm faced with seventeen colourful African ladies hoping I might choose one or more of them to sleep with me tonight. This is crazy! I'm embarrassed. I had thought that one day I might find a girl, probably white skinned like me, and if the situation developed OK, and she was willing and agreeable, we might come to having consensual sex together. But this is totally different. At first, I feel I should discreetly decline the FON's offer. These are his wives for heaven's sake! But he was very specific in his offer. I also have to remind myself that Major Sutter told me I was to gain a close liaison with the FON and "treat him well". Perhaps he would be offended if I were to decline.

I look again at the ladies. I see no animosity towards me. Only a shy expectation — dare I say, even hope, that I will choose at least one of them. I am nineteen years old and like most of my age, I have a healthy attraction and desire for the female sex. I have to decide. What an offer! What an opportunity! OK, for the sake of Queen and Country, let's go with the moment!

I copy the FON's method of walking down the line smiling at each of the ladies as I pass. One of them stands out. She has beautiful soft skin and, as I pass, she gently puts her tongue between her lips and gives me an inviting smile. I choose her. Near the end of the line I see another girl. She's younger that the rest, perhaps about seventeen. I feel an instant attraction to her so I choose her also.

The two I've chosen step forward. The rest look slightly crestfallen but accepting and without a word they file out of the room. I'm now left with the two I've chosen. I feel I'm now committed. I ask myself what the hell am I doing?

My two chosen ladies come up to me. They gently take me by the hand and lead me through to an adjacent room. It's dark but there's a small paraffin lamp in one corner. On the floor, I see a large bed made of the local raffia material. There's also a bowl and a jug of water. The ladies seem to know what to do and I just let it happen. First, they take off my dirty uniform, socks and underpants (I had removed my boots when I first entered the FON's residence.). Then they take off their own robes, all of them. When we three are all naked, they wash me, every part of my body and dry me down with soft cloths. I just give myself to their soft and expert hands.

My mind is in another place. I feel slightly drunk, partly from the FON's beer, but mostly my mind is lost in the blissful wonderland of lying naked between these two enchanting ladies. This is as close to paradise as I've ever been!

Chapter Twenty-seven

I wake the next morning with the sun filtering through the slats of the side panels of the building. I'm still naked but covered by a crisp clean white sheet. My two, night companions have left. My watch tells me it's six-fifty. I get up and use the toilet, which is set off to the side of the room. I notice the paraffin lamp still burns brightly and the jug of water is full. Both must have been recently refilled but I didn't hear a thing. There's another wonder. Next to the bed I find my uniform, underpants and socks. They are all freshly laundered and neatly folded. I can't understand how this could have been possible in the few hours of the night.

I get dressed and go through to the main room where I had spent the previous evening with the FON. He is already there, installed in the same chair. He's dressed immaculately in a fresh set of robes. He sees me and calls out:

"Lt Chambers, or may I now call you Peter as I feel we know each other better? I hope you had a comfortable night and are now rested."

I reply: "Yes sir, very comfortable. And I must thank you for arranging for my scruffy uniform to be transformed!"

"Oh! It's our pleasure, you are our guest here Peter."

That's the only reference he makes to my magical night's activities. There's nothing more to be said about that. My arrival must have been anticipated as two servants appear with a breakfast spread of scrambled eggs, some sort of sausage and bowls of fresh papaya and guava. They set trays down in front of the FON who beckons for me to join him.

After our last evening's concentration on British society and culture, I detect the FON is in a different mood this morning. He tells me:

"A messenger came during the night. He regularly links the exchanges I have with my colleagues in Bafut and Bafangi. We like to keep ourselves informed. He confirmed all you had told me about the operation your colleague had two nights ago against the Cameroon Freedom Fighters. We refer to these guys as the CFF who, as you know, are an affiliate of the UPC fighters from the French Cameroon. We discussed the wider implications of that successful operation."

I can't help wondering how he had manged to fit this meeting into his night and also be entertained by three of his wives but of course I don't ask him. The FON continues:

"My fellow FONs and I exchange views regularly with the police in both Ndop and Bamenda. The assessment now is that the presence of your soldiers and the successful patrols you have carried out since you came here has already had a major disruptive effect on the CFF activities. We are grateful to you all for making us feel safer here. Our information is that much is happening on the French side of the border and the UPC is still very active there operationally against the French army despite the granting of independence there this January, under French trusteeship. We are still concerned that the conflict there could still spill over to our side. What is your view about this Peter?"

My role has been to carry out the tasks I've been given and I get only a limited insight of the bigger picture. It's fascinating to know that the FONS have their own intelligence network and, again, I'm full of admiration that the FON is so well informed. I say:

"Sir, there's not much I can add to what you've just told me. I'm glad to know that you feel we've been successful so far and I'll be pleased to pass this on to Major Sutter, my company commander. I need to get back to Ndop today. As soon as we've finished this delicious breakfast, I'd like your permission to gather my soldiers together and set off. We aim to be back before dusk this evening. Once there, I'll find out from Major Sutter what my new orders will be."

"Yes of course you need to get back to your duties today. But before you go, I want to give you a little present as a reminder of your stay with us."

The FON claps his hands and his servant appears again, this time carrying a raffia package, which he places on the table in front of us. I'm impatient to see what it contains and I see the FON gesturing that I should open it up. I pull the raffia apart. Inside is a statue carved in some sort of hard wood. It's of a hunter, standing poised to fire an arrow from his bow. It is immaculately carved — an exquisite piece of work. I'm stunned by its beauty. The FON is smiling as he says:

"This was sculpted recently by one of our villagers. It shows you how we used to feed ourselves and survive in the olden days. Now, I suppose we've got soft as much of our foodstuffs comes from the local markets. Do you like the statue Peter?"

I find it difficult to give an adequate reply. Before I came to Bafali, I suppose I had thought of these village people as somewhat backward. I was so wrong. Not only have I found the FON to be a highly intelligent man but this example of artwork shows such sensitivity and skill. The people here are so much more cultured and refined than I had imagined. Their cleanliness and good manners are an example to many so-called developed civilisations. And what a wonderful gift. All I had managed to give the FON were some tatty old magazines. I tell the FON:

"Sir, this is a magnificent statue and I am so honoured that you should give it to me. May I first show it to my soldiers, then have it wrapped safely for us to carry it back with us to Ndop?"

Last evening, I had told Sgt Bado to have our platoon ready to leave by 08.30 hours and already I can hear them assembling outside the FON's residence.

There is one more surprise before I leave the building. I had left my boots at the entrance when I came in last evening. They are still where I had left them but now, they are polished and gleaming as brightly as the FONs own black shoes! I know the shine won't last more than a few hundred yards along the track but I find the FON's attention to detail is remarkable.

I go outside to find all the soldiers of my platoon lined up. Sgt Bado reports that everyone is present. They all look well and contented and I'm sure they were well fed and entertained by the villagers last evening. I call them to attention and hold up the statue explaining it is a present from the FON. It is passed along the ranks and I hear much admiring "ahhs and ums". I don't know how much they really appreciate the skill of the art work but they make all the right gestures.

While the statue is being securely rewrapped to survive the rigours of the trek back, I have a final, few words with the FON, thanking him for the hospitality he and his villagers have given us and promising to ensure that close liaison between us will be maintained.

Finally, I bring the platoon to attention and give the FON a formal salute in the present arms movement. Then we adopt our patrol formation and leave, with the villagers escorting us to the edge of their territory. As we make our way back along the trails to Ndop, I know I will never forget the night we stayed in Bafali. I have now got to know a most remarkable man and am humbled by the smooth, friendly efficiency of the way he runs his village. I can't think I will ever again meet a man who rules with such total dominance, yet is revered and loved by his people.

We make it back to our camp in Ndop just before dark. I check in to Major Sutter, report all the events of the patrol and show him our statue. My patrol report does not include how I slept last night! Major Sutter tells me that things have moved on since I've been away. Our mission has now been expanded and we are to operate in support of French forces. A meeting has been arranged tomorrow here at Ndop when a delegation will arrive, comprising French military and diplomats, together with liaison staff from our battalion headquarters and the police. All our company officers are to attend.

I spend the evening chatting with David and rest of our officers; our future new role being the main topic of conversation. Everyone admires the FON's statue and we resolve to safeguard it well and take back to Kaduna at the end of our tour. Personally, I'm delighted to be reunited with my little dog, Pawpy. She looks well but I think she's putting on a bit of weight. CSM Kabala must have been spoiling her!

A long convoy of vehicles grinds to a halt at our camp in Ndop mid-morning the next day. Before then CSM Kabala has been organising our soldiers to ensure everything is clean, tidy and ready to host our visitors. We have never been so full. Apart from the visitors, the Ndop police have also sent representatives and our two platoons, David's and mine, are unusually both in camp at the same time.

Major Sutter has directed that we use the space of our officers' quarters for the meeting and by 11.30 hours we are all assembled and settled down together. I'm sitting in the back row next to David Edozi. We are very much the junior members of this gathering. I try to identify all the senior guys up front. I see Mr Brierley, the British FCO chap who gave us our initial briefing in Bamenda when we first arrived in the

Cameroons. He's not wearing a jacket like the last time but he's still got his shirt buttoned up and a smart diplomatic tie. Then there's Lt Col Johnson, our battalion commander who is accompanied by another British officer called Captain Thomas Pitcher. He's the battalion Intelligence Officer or IO. There's also another Brit officer from the battalion called Major Bob Hardwick. He's the OC of our "B" company which is deployed some forty miles east of our own area of responsibility. I wonder why he's here. There are four Cameroon police officers, one of whom I recognise as Mr Obadiki, the police commissioner. The others are from the local Ndop station. Finally, there are three Frenchmen, one in civilian clothes, the other two in uniform. Then we have our home team of Major Sutter, Capt Bashir Buhari, David and, at the back of the room, me. It's quite a gathering!

Lt Col Johnson welcomes everyone and thanks Major Sutter for hosting the meeting. He says the French civilian is M. Dumoulin and one of the military guys is called Commandant Lagarde. I don't catch the name of the other one. He then turns to Mr Brierley to give a political update. He begins:

"I was pleased to talk to many of you when you first arrived in the British Cameroons in March. Events have moved on somewhat since then. You will recall that La Republique du Cameroun was established as an independent country under French trusteeship on 1 January this year. It has been a very volatile period there since then with major clashes between the ruling Cameroon Union party (known in French as the UC) and the opposition Union des Populations du Cameroun or UPC as it is known. The UPC is well armed and is now in open rebellion. Prime minister Ahmadou Ahidjo, who has just been elected president, has requested French military assistance to combat the UPC rebels. In one major clash last month in Douala, the capital, twenty-five rebels and four government policemen were killed. In another UPC attack, nineteen individuals were killed and some five thousand people have been displaced. French forces are now actively engaged and have managed to drive the main rebel force away from the capital. The French are now engaged in "search and destroy" operations but are concerned that the rebels may now try to cross over into our British Cameroon territory."

Mr Brierley now turns to Lt Col Johnson and continues:

"Colonel, this is where your soldiers are needed. The French request that your men act as a block to deter the UPC rebels from crossing the border into our territory. They propose that French troop advances will be coordinated closely with your soldiers so that the rebels will be squeezed between the two elements. Her Majesty's government and the Nigerian authorities have been consulted and concur with the French proposition."

So, this is to be our new mission. The senior officers then proceed to discuss the details of how operations will be coordinated. We are to set up one or more semi-permanent base camps on the Oku and other mountains close to the border and operate patrols from these bases. David and I have been mere bystanders during this process but at last we are asked to comment. I've been trying to imagine how the new procedures will work on the ground and I remember being stuck in the freezing cold up on mount OKU so I say:

"Gentlemen, please appreciate that temperatures at the higher altitudes of the OKU feature are very cold, which most of our soldiers have never before experienced and we have no cold weather clothing here in Ndop. I strongly request that, if we are to maintain base camps in the mountains, that our soldiers are provided with suitable clothing."

I thought my comment might seem rather petty but I'm pleased that I get a sympathetic response. In particular, Commandant Lagarde nods his head vigorously and I see our CO is making a note.

The meeting is formally closed with a decision that we will start our operations in support of the French from tomorrow. My platoon has the task of setting up the first base camp on the Oku. It has to be fully protected with all-round defence positions. From there, we will launch border patrols in conjunction with the French "search and destroy" operations. Communication links are to be established. I'm not too sure how we'll manage with our different languages but we'll just have to get on and make it work.

Lunch and drinks are brought up to us, organised by CSM Kabala. There is a spirit of goodwill between the British and French delegations but I notice the Nigerian officers are quiet and keeping to themselves. I can't help feeling uneasy about our new mission. The ex-French part of the Cameroons is already independent yet the French still seem to be the major military force there and are dictating operations. The people of the British Cameroons will be holding their own plebiscite next February and should be preparing for their future without involvement in the affairs on the ex-French side. Nigeria is on the brink of its own independence yet now our soldiers are about to get involved with this new mission outside its country. We seem to be getting drawn into politics where too many decisions are being made by the ex-colonial bosses. We are in Africa here. It's a time of great change and I feel that it's for the African people to be making the major decisions about who supports which party — even who is to be considered the legal authority and who is called a rebel. I even wonder whether the UPC guys should be categorised as rebels or as freedom fighters.

These are my private thoughts but I realise that it's certainly not my place to express them to anyone. I'm basing my opinion merely on the briefing by Mr Brierley and what I've learnt since we've been here in the British Cameroons. I wonder what the FON of Bafali would think and I wish I could have the chance to talk to him openly about this. But I know I must keep my opinion to myself and get on and carry out the duties I'm given. I just hope we can get some warm clothing for my guys when we're back up on the Oku.

Chapter Twenty-eight

Next morning, Sgt Bado gets our platoon ready to move off. We've got the full complement of our forty-two men reinforced platoon. I reckon it's going to take about one and a half days march along the same trails we used last time to get up onto the Oku feature. John, our Cameroon policeman, is with us as usual and I've been told we will also be joined by a French liaison guy. His task will be to communicate with French forces on the other side of the border so that we can coordinate our patrols with their operations. Until now, he hasn't turned up and we're still without any cold weather kit.

We need to get moving if we're to reach our base camp area before dark on the second day. By 10.30 hours, without our Frenchman, Major Sutter tells me to get going. He instructs me to give frequent communication checks using our Larkspur radio.

Photo: On the way to the Oku mountain

We set off in patrol formation. Although the intelligence reports are that this area should be clear of CFF rebels, we don't take chances and I ensure our point and rear guards are alert. All our weapons are loaded and can quickly be brought into action. We've only been moving for about three hours when the inevitable Cameroonian feature arrives: torrential rain! By now we're all quite used to this event and we hunker down as best we can and wait it out as there's absolutely no merit in trying to struggle on through the vast torrents of water. Apart from it being impossible to define the track amidst all the flowing water, there is a serious risk of being swept away by the rising water levels.

Two hours after the rain starts, it suddenly stops as if some controlling god has just switched off the tap. We emerge from our make-shift shelters into the hot sunshine, at least the amount that can penetrate through the jungle canopy. As before, our clothes steam as they dry out. In addition to the steam, there's a strong human odour emitting from our now sweating bodies.

We resume our trek towards the Oku but I'm concerned that our enforced delay will mean we'll have to reduce the duration of our night stop if we're to reach the planned base camp location before dusk tomorrow. Our trail now begins to slope upwards and by early evening we emerge out from the jungle canopy into more sparsely covered terrain. I find a cleared area suitable for an overnight bivouac and delegate positions to all our sections. Sgt Bado also sets up a temporary cookhouse and quickly there's a smell of cooking meat. I take the chance here to establish contact with our company HQ using our Larkspur radio and give my best guess of grid reference location. Major Sutter comes on the line and says:

"I note your location. Is there sufficient space for a helicopter to land there?"

I ask him to "wait out", get up and study the ground around us. We're in an area of dispersed trees but to one side there's a relatively flat area with only a few small shrubs within its circumference. We can easily chop these down with the machetes we have with us. I go back to the radio, re-establish the link and report back:

"Affirmative. We can prepare a heli at our present location."

It's Major Sutter again: "Right, hold at that location and prepare to receive a heli tomorrow morning. ETA between 09.00 and 10.00 hours"

We sign off and I despatch a team to clear the ground for the landing. I'm wondering what this is all about. We've never had helicopter support before and I didn't know there were any in the British Cameroons. I'm still wondering about this as we settle down for the night.

Next morning, we get packed up and are ready to move but we now wait, with anticipation, for the arrival of the helicopter. I get a couple of guys to position themselves in the centre of the cleared area, hopefully to direct the chopper down safely. We've got flares ready in case the pilot has difficulty finding us. It's nearly 10.00 hours when we hear the distinctive throbbing beat of the chopper's blades. Soon the heli comes into view, spots our clearing and lands safely.

First out is Major Sutter himself. Behind him I see CSM Kabala and another soldier who I don't recognise. The major comes straight over to me and says:

"Right Peter, well done, we found you OK and this is a good site for our landing."

He turns to the soldier who was in the helicopter and continues: "I want to introduce Warrant Officer (WO) Bréchignac, from the First Foreign Legion Battalion of the French Army. He will be your liaison officer while you're on patrol here. Also, you'll be pleased to know that your plea for cold weather clothing didn't go unheeded. The French military had anoraks and other warm clothes flown in to Ndop yesterday. These stores are now on board the chopper and we've also thrown in some sandbags, which will help you to reinforce the base camp. Also, I'm redeploying CSM Kabala to your platoon for the duration of this mission. He has also brought along a team of guys the police recruited for us in Ndop to act as porters. We need to offload everything here as I'm under pressure to return the helicopter back to the French today"

This is great news. Not only are we going to be able to stay warm on the mountain but we don't even have to cart all the kit there ourselves. Things are looking up! As Major Sutter was speaking, several guys are getting out of the chopper, carrying packages that I presume contain our cold weather clothes. When it is all offloaded, Major Sutter says:

"OK, Peter. I wanted to come out myself just to ensure all is going OK at this stage. Just be clear. The base camp must be well organised for

218

all-round defence. It looks like there's a lot building up on the other side of the border so take all precautions. I need to get back now as Colonel Johnston requires my presence at a meeting this afternoon. Good luck with your new mission and keep in radio contact as per the regulations."

Major Sutter then shakes the hand of the French soldier, gets back into the helicopter, which immediately lifts off. We shield ourselves from the down-blast as we watch the heli wheel away on its route back to Ndop. Suddenly there's silence, then, as our ears adjust, the familiar sounds of the jungle uplands reassert.

Photo: On the Oku mountain

We make it up to the same area of the Oku we used the last time we were here and I mark out a section of ground that I reckon will give us all-round observation but which we can reinforce to form a strong defensive perimeter. The centre of the position is quite flat but is surrounded by sharp rocky outcrops: we can exploit these as part of our defence. Beyond our position, the ground rises up toward the summit of the Oku. The border between the British Cameroons and La République du Cameroun runs along this summit. Beneath us, the ground falls steeply down toward the jungle treeline. I can see no possibility of a heli being able to land nearby but, if one could become available, it could hover over our position to provide resupply and, possibly, carry out casevac (evacuation by air). I'll check this out in more detail later.

We spend our evening here settling in. I allocate each section an area of responsibility, both for defence and sentry duties and for their sleeping "quarters". I check arcs of fire and ensure we have the whole area covered in general but concentrate on the most likely approach routes. Our porter team assist by filling sandbags, which we use to plug any gaps in our perimeter defences.

Latrines are always a vital facility. If we're going to have to occupy this area for some long time, it's essential we get these prepared hygienically straightaway. Sgt Bado gets on with this project and proposes a site well clear of our main sleeping area but also covered by our defence shield. A pit digging team gets to work and by dark they've completed a clean facility.

When all this work is done, we can revert to more congenial activities. First, we open up all the packages that the porters have so valiantly struggled with all day. Inside, we find everything we will require to keep us warm up here during the cold nights: anoraks, woollen sweaters and blankets. I count up to sixty of these, enough for each of us, including our porters. I'm delighted with these treasures. The anoraks are all of French manufacture. Our Nigerian soldiers are not familiar with them and we spend some amusing moments while they try them on and give little whoops of satisfaction when they find how warm and protective they are. This gives me the chance to thank WO Bréchignac and formally to welcome him to our platoon. He's also brought with him a heavy radio set of a type that is new to me. It seems to operate on HF (high-frequencies) similar to our Larkspur. We'll have to spend a session later getting familiar with each other's communications. During my training at Mons, I learnt that, for security, we should be using one-time pads for encryption but these are not available here; we'll have to keep our comms to essentials and hope they're not being intercepted by the rebels.

As the short tropical dusk fades, I feel we've now got ourselves properly established here. CSM Kabala and Sgt Bado have organised the evening meal, sentry rosters have been allocated and our soldiers can settle down for the night. By wearing the woollen sweaters and anoraks and covering themselves with the blankets, I'm confident they will be able to sleep in relative warmth and comfort.

I've been lucky to find a spot where four rocks form a square at bench height and, with some simple rock moving, I construct a natural flat-topped stone table. As always, my orderly, Usman Pele, is with us and he proposes to serve my evening meal of stewed meat and fruit here. I like the idea but first I prefer to join our soldiers in the centre communal area so that we all eat the main meal together. I'm pleased to find that the morale among the soldiers is good. After the trek up here and the heavy work in preparing the defences, our guys can now relax and wind down for the evening. It's now fully dark but the moon has not yet risen. Our few paraffin lights give an atmospheric ambiance. As I look around, I see our soldiers in animated conversations. There are big smiles as they model their new anoraks to each other. After my close shave with the two mutinous medics the last time here, it's heartening to think we are now a great, well trained and rehearsed team. I can't help feeling proud about that.

After the main meal, I invite CSM Kabala, John our policeman and WO Bréchignac to join me at my homemade table and seats. Usman Pele rustles up a pot of coffee and four metal mugs. I would personally love to have a beer but we never bring alcohol on operations. I'm pretty sure WO Bréchignac would like to join me with a beer but, of course, CSM Kabala is a devout Mohammedan.

I'm thinking how lucky I am to be with this group, many miles from any human habitation. WO Bréchignac is a French foreign legion paratrooper. He is, perhaps, in his forties — old enough, I suppose, to be my father but I'm not a good judge of people's ages. He's a short man but lean, wiry and seems very fit. I suspect he's had some incredible war experiences. I'm also very pleased that CSM Kabala is with us. I really appreciate his calm efficiency and the respect that all our soldiers have for him. John, our policeman, has been with our platoon since we arrived in Ndop and has shared all our experiences here in the Cameroons. It's good for him to be here now.

CSM Kabala, John and I manage to communicate well together — mostly in English but my Hausa has now got up to working level standard and we're all picking up some of the local Cameroon pidgin language. I'm keen to know how we'll get along with our "Frenchman". These are three men who, in totally different environments, have lived full lives. For me, as a nineteen-year-old Brit, here in the Cameroons in 1960, my life so far has been school in Bath, England, conscript training and these few months here in Africa. I'm eager to learn from these guys. Somehow, I think I'll get a broader perspective of life from these three gentlemen than from Mr Brierley or the ex-colonial Brits from the club back in Kaduna.

I find that WO Bréchignac speaks passable English. I tell him we're having trouble pronouncing his surname so he suggests we use his first name — Yves. We can all remember that! It was only this morning that he jumped down from the heli on the edge of our jungle route. Straightaway, he seems to have connected with our soldiers, our style of operating — to fit in and accept who we are — a platoon of Nigerian soldiers here in the Cameroon mountains with a young white boss — that's me! He doesn't seem phased at all by our situation here and I can tell he's pleased that he's included now in this group. I don't want to put him on the spot but I can't resist asking him if he could share with us some of his experiences. I think he's trying to compose his words in the English language. Then he says:

"*Eh bien*! Where do I start? Perhaps I should tell you, Lt Chambers, that when I was your age my life was perhaps very different from yours. I was born in Marseilles in an area that in English you would call a "slum". My father had no regular work and was always drunk. My mother had to look after my four brothers, my two sisters and me. *Quand j'étais un* — when I was a teenager, I, how you say, 'hung out' with a gang who, like me, were very poor and lived by stealing from what, who and where we could. I never went to a proper school. I was first arrested by the police when I was fourteen. When I was released with a warning, I didn't learn my lesson and went straight back to my life of petty crime. My gang was not alone and I remember we had to assert our authority over rival gangs, which involved fights, mostly with our fists but sometimes also with knives. You had to be sharp to survive in those days."

Yves pauses and looks around to the other three of us. I can tell that both CSM Kabala and John have been fascinated by his opening life story. We all three want to know more. I say:

"Yves, please carry on. How did you become a French Legionnaire?"

"*Alors*, that's just it. It was soon after my eighteenth birthday. My gang and I got into a fight with a rival group, which ended with us all using knives. I found myself facing a brute of a guy. In order to survive I stabbed him in the abdomen. He collapsed and probably died. I don't know. All I did know then was that I was already wanted by the police and if they were to arrest me again, I would face a long time in prison. That night, I left Marseilles and hitched rides to the Legionnaire recruitment centre and signed up. *Mon dieu*, that was back in 1936. I've been in the Legion ever since. They've given me training, an education, everything. The Legion is my life.

"You will realise that this was a bad period for France with the rise of Nazi Germany and the threatening prospect of war. After parachute training in Corsica, my regiment was sent to Morocco, where I spent most of the war years. There was much confusion as we had many German nationals in our ranks and allegiances varied, particularly after the Vichy government took over in France. My regiment supported the Allies when Operation Torch was launched in November 1942. This operation involved an invasion of west North Africa by US and British troops aimed at preventing the Germans from taking control of Vichy France territories."

I can't help interrupting Yves by saying:

"I have to tell you Yves, I was only just born then! And it's now 1960. Where have you and your regiment been more recently?"

"You're right, lieutenant, that all happened a long time ago. To move on. After the World War, France was struggling to hang on to its colonial possessions, particularly in the Far East. In 1947, my regiment was sent to Indo-China and we stayed until the end, when we were eventually forced out of Dien Bien Phu."

"You were there?" I exclaimed. "I know the basics of that from lessons at school. How was it for you personally?"

"There's only one word in English to describe it — hell! You need to understand that the French Army had already endured seven grinding years of guerrilla war in Indo-China before the Dien Bien Phu defensive garrison was established. My regiment was 1BEP (that's the First Battalion Étranger de Parachutists). In October 1953, we took part in an operation we called 'Mouette' in the South Delta Basin of Vietnam and that was the first time I saw real concentrated warfare. My battalion lost several men killed but the death toll of the communist Viet Minh was much higher. The French politicians and senior military brass considered it to be a victory for us."

Yves sees we are still in rapt attention listening to his story, so he continues:

"Later that year we parachuted into Dien Bien Phu, a ten thousand strong French garrison established in a jungle valley in the north west of Indo-China, deep in communist Viet Minh enemy territory. Our own sector was based on a defence feature we called Claudine 6 on the edge of the Naam Youm river. You probably know the outcome of our battles there. General Giap, the communist Viet Minh leader, managed to mass a force of some fifty thousand men with modern artillery. This force formed an ever-tightening ring around our garrison which finally was forced to surrender in May 1954. Our troops were being systematically rounded up to be marched away to prison camps. A colleague of mine and I decided that was not for us and we manged to escape through the enemy cordon"

CSM Kabala, John and I are riveted by Yves story. We can't let him stop there. I ask:

"And what happened? How did you manage to survive?"

Yves pauses. He seems to be mentally reliving this experience, then he continues:

"I guess we were very lucky as, afterwards, we learnt that very few escapees survived. In our case, we avoided the valleys for fear of meeting local villagers who we thought would be hostile and contact the Viet Minh. We kept to the crests of hills and steadily headed south and east. We must have been about three weeks on the trail when by chance we met up with a French patrol near Muong Sai. From there we were airlifted back to Saigon. We were both sick of malnutrition and disease and we spent some weeks' rehabilitation in hospital. By this time, the French were withdrawing from the country and we were taken by sea back to the

Algerian naval base at Mers-el-Kéber. Then it was almost immediately back into action as French forces were engaged in Algeria against the Algerian National Liberation Front or FLN as they are known. This campaign is still continuing but General de Gaulle has recently declared that Algerians have the right to self-determination. I don't know how things there will end up but there was still a very tense situation in Algeria when I was posted to the Cameroons last month."

Yves looks around at the three of us, smiles and concludes:

"Yesterday, I was ordered to come over to the British side as a liaison link between our forces. So, messieurs, that's my little story and here I am now!"

We all take a pause to reflect on the amazing life this guy has lived. I don't know how long we'll be tasked to hold this base camp but I really want to learn as much as I can from him. At this moment, I smell coffee and look up to see Usman Pele appearing with very welcome refills to our mugs. I find it difficult to gauge CSM Kabala'a reactions. I ask him how he has spent his military years.

Kabala takes his time to answer. He has a deep voice and a slow and measured delivery. His English is good but very much his second language. He begins:

"Yves, I don't know whether to be envious that you have had such an amazing life or pleased that mine has been much simpler and nothing like as exciting as yours! I am a few years younger than you but to our Lt Chambers here I suspect I don't look it. This is my story. As you may know, in World War Two, the Nigerian army fought initially in Kenya and Italian East Africa before being sent to join British forces in Burma. I joined the West African Frontier Force, as it was then known, in 1945 when I was nineteen and was earmarked to join our forces in Burma. But I missed out completely as the war in the Far East ended in 1946 so I was never sent. In fact, until being here in the Cameroons, I have never been out of Nigeria. During my service, most of our missions have been in internal security in support of the police. One highlight was being on parade when Queen Elizabeth visited Nigeria in 1956. In recognition of our service, we were renamed The Queen's Own Nigeria Regiment. I suppose for us Nigerians it is the future rather than the past that interests us the most. We wonder how it will be for us to become a fully independent country later this year. We are so used to being part of the British Empire, and proud of it, that it is quite daunting to think we will be soon managing all our national affairs. I suppose it must be similar for you, John."

John Abdalah, our policeman, had been listening to the conversation with concentrated interest. He's a quiet man and indeed I'm interested to know how he'll respond. He says:

"Well, I'm not so sure the British Cameroons is similar to Nigeria because although we're having our own plebiscite early next year, we're not given the choice to become an independent country. I suppose it makes sense because we are a very small colony and it would be difficult for us to sustain our own economy. All we're being offered is to choose either to join Nigeria or the Republique du Cameroun. To be honest, I don't find either very appealing. I hope that the FONs will give us direction as what they say is likely to influence most of the rest of us."

I realise it's now getting late and there's a lot to do in the morning. So, regrettably, I suggest we abort our conversation for today. I hope we can continue tomorrow. With handshakes and, I feel, a warm atmosphere between us, Yves, CSM Kabala and John make their way to their bed-spaces in the centre of our camp. I nip off for a quick pee, then settle down for the night. We're all sleeping on the hard bedrock and, as always, it's cold up here in the mountains but now with our woollen sweaters, anoraks and blankets, we should be able to sleep OK.

I lie down on my back and see the moon has risen and the stars are shining brightly overhead. As I start to drift off to sleep, I have two enduring thoughts. One is how lucky I am to have the benefit of hearing such amazing stories, first hand from such diverse characters. My other thought is that in these weird circumstances, I am in charge here. I'm nineteen years old, I'm still very naive and inexperienced. But this is my platoon, I am responsible for all that goes on here and for all my soldiers. I vow to do my best not to let them down.

Chapter Twenty-nine

We'll all up for "stand to" half an hour before dawn. We haven't even tried to conceal our base camp. Our intelligence from the French is that several of the rebels have crossed over the border to seek some sanctuary on our side but at present they are assessed to be in disparate groups and not likely to attack our base — for now. Even so, we must be prepared and organised for a possible future attack. Our "stand to" involves all soldiers being awake and manning their defence positions to provide all round protection.

There's an increase in our communication traffic this morning. Yves is busy on his own radio. I notice he's using a "one-time pad" encryption system and sending/receiving his messages by key rather than voice. Our battalion doesn't have any form of secure comms. Major Sutter now informs me that our time at our base camp is likely to last much longer than I was first told. The initial plan had been that we would alternate with David Edozi's platoon and change over perhaps once a week. That has now changed. Major Sutter tells me that David is now en route to set up another base camp further to our east and that our B Company is also establishing base camps close to the ex-French border. This will form a defensive ring around the most viable crossing points from the border. We're likely to be stuck here for some long time. It concerns me that our conversation is in clear voice. It's not my place to push it with my company commander but I think I know a way we can be much more secure. I try to be discreet when I say to Major Sutter:

"Sir, I don't know if the rebels can listen in to our communications or even if their English is up to it. But would it be a good idea to be more secure if we all speak only Hausa on the radio?"

Major Sutter just replies: "I understand. Will inform you later."

I don't hear from him for a while, then I get a message from his call sign. A voice speaking Hausa says:

"We have a new instruction. All comms on this net are to be in the Hausa language only." I guess I've scored with that. I can now hold my own in Hausa providing it's not too complicated. In any case, I've got Hausa-speaking support all around me, especially CSM Kabala.

We're not here to sit around all day so we get on with sending out patrols up towards the border. I plan to take the first one with Cpl Aiki Riba's section and add a second Bren gun to ensure we have good fire power if we bump a rebel outfit. Before that, though, we need to make our camp more secure if we have to stay here longer. We'll also need resupplies of food, ammo and further defence materials. Then we get some good news. We're informed that a British-made Westland Whirlwind helicopter has been acquired from somewhere and this will be used to resupply our base camps. I task CSM Kabala to compile an inventory of our requirements and send it through to our Battalion HQ.

I can't help feeling uneasy about our changed role here in the Cameroons. We started out with the very clear task of being here purely in support of the local police to ensure stability in the lead up to the plebiscite. But now we're stuck up here on the Oku to act as a backstop to the French ops on the other side of the border. This seems like what I've heard the Americans call "mission creep", but what do I know?

By mid-morning Cpl Aiki Riba reports his section is ready so we set off up the mountain, John our policeman and Yves joins our patrol group. I don't know whether we'll get a contact but Yves tells me that his French contacts assess some fifty "rebels" have crossed the border in our area during the past week but little is known about what weapons they were carrying or whether they've had casualties from their fighting on the Republique side. The ground here is steep and rocky: there are precipitous drops and relatively few places where humans can pass. I reckon we've got them well bottled up in this rugged terrain. We move with caution and explore the most likely areas where the rebels might hole up or indeed plan to ambush us. After several hours, we've seen no one: nor have we found any trace of recent human activity or movement. So I decide to pack it in for the day. As we near our return to our base camp I fire a flare to let our guys know it's us approaching and not a rebel group.

We heard the distinctive sound of chopper blades while we were out and when we get back to camp, I'm chuffed to find we've had our first delivery of support stores. These include wire and flares to reinforce our defences and already CSM Kabala has organised strengthening of our perimeter and deployment of the trip flares forward of our position to alert us day and night of anyone approaching our camp. The rations include some fresh meat and fruit so we're going to be well fed besides keeping warm at night. For a soldier, this is luxury.

During the months I've been in Africa, I've been getting regular mail from my mother updating me on all the local gossip. In return, I've been trying to describe our life first in Kaduna and now here in the Cameroons but I'm not much of a letter writer and I don't know if she can really picture this strange world where I'm now living. Recently, the post reaching Ndop had pretty much dried up but to my surprise today's heli drop includes another letter from my mother. She doesn't have any startling news but it's comforting to read her neat handwriting and to feel everything is much the same at home.

We've now been here for nearly four weeks and have developed a steady routine. After "stand to" before dawn, we settle down to breakfast, then we send out a patrol to cover likely rebel routes. A couple of times our patrols have come under fire but it's been sporadic and from long range. We've returned fire but have not been able to assess either the strength/composition of the rebel force or whether we've caused them casualties. In camp, we've organised some light exercise drills to keep us fit: then the highlight of our day is to enjoy our evening together before settling down for the night. Personally, I've enjoyed further conversations with Yves, CSM Kabala and John and have learnt a lot from them all.

Today our routine changes. From first light, I notice that Yves is very involved with his radio comms, mostly he's on receive. When he signs off he tells me:

"Lieutenant, that was the CO of one of our forward bases in the Republique. He informs me there's been a major push against the rebels. Several have been killed but others have fled across the border opposite our sector here. He warns us to be alert and block any attempt they may make to break out on our side."

I then get a call from Major Sutter. He also reports the French offensive but adds that a French major is en route in the Whirlwind heli.

Shortly after closing down the radio, I again hear the distinctive thumping sound of the Whirlwind's blades. Our guys are now experienced in directing it and it's soon hovering over our base camp. A French military guy is winched down and Yves and I go to greet him. The heli also lowers down our daily stores resupply, then rises up from its hover and banks away back towards the jungle canopy below us. When the sound of the helicopter dies down, Yves introduces us. He says:

"Lt Chambers, this is Major Souquet from 1 BEP, my own battalion, which has been carrying out the offensive over the border."

Like Yves, Major Souquet is quite short in height. He has a dark skin and his upper lip sports a small moustache. He is armed with a sub machine gun of the same type as Yves. He seems to bristle with confidence and has a sort of natural authority. I sense he's used to giving commands and getting his own way. I can tell he wants to get straight down to business so I lead him to my self-made rocky seating, Usman Pele brings us all mugs of coffee and we wait for the major to address us. His English is limited but, with Yves' occasional intervention, we understand him well enough. He says:

"Gentleman, I need to inform you that we had a successful operation against the CFF rebels yesterday. We had several kills and have destroyed their main military capability. We pursued the remnants of their unit up to the border but we had to stop there as politics forbids us to cross. However, the rebels, of course, do not recognise the border and many crossed over and were therefore beyond our reach. We assess there are some fifty of them but they may now have split up into smaller groups. We have no way of knowing that. But they're now boxed in here between the border and your camp. Lt Chambers, by agreement of your commanding officer, I am now here to co-ordinate rounding up these rebels. I must warn you they still are well armed and will be desperate to fight their way clear. We need to get after them straightaway. I trust I can rely on the assistance of your soldiers."

I hear the major out and understand his requirement. But I feel very uneasy about this task, which is a long way beyond the police support role we started out with. I can't help feeling we are being dragged into a war that doesn't concern our Nigerian troops. I'd like to clear this new mission with Major Sutter but I worry what his response would be. I suppose I just need to get on with the job and not think about it too much or ask too many questions.

Before we can organise a patrol, one of our outlying flares is tripped. Our soldiers react by manning our defence perimeter and our "on duty" patrol commanded by Cpl Jamil prepares for action. I grab my Sten gun and join him. I tell Cpl Jamil to get his men in the dispersed patrol order we've practised many times. The ground here is rugged and there are very few trails that men can use along the precipitous cliff edges. Cpl Jamil leads on point and I follow close behind. He peers around the corner of a bend in the narrow trail then stops, goes to ground and signs to me that he's spotted rebel movement. I crawl slowly forward up to Cpl Jamil's position. He uses sign language to show me that he's a mere ten yards from the first of a group of guys — some fifteen to twenty. They're positioned along the edge of the trail, guns at the ready but standing still. They are looking warily in our direction. We're in a sort of stand-off situation. So far, no shots have been fired. I inch back to find John Abdalah and motion for him to come forward with me. I whisper in his ear to call out to them in French and English pidgin to throw down their weapons. John doesn't hesitate. Even with my limited knowledge of this local language, I totally understand him when at the top of his voice he shouts out in pidgin:

"Drop your weapons and put your hands up! Do it NOW!"

There's a pause, nothing happens. John then shouts out again:

"Drop your weapons and put your hands up" Do it now or you'll all be shot!"

Another pause, then I hear the sound of guns being lowered then dropped — at least I hope that's what's happening as I can't yet see. It's now time to move. Cpl Jamil, John and I cautiously around the corner of the bend in the trail. Here, there's only room enough for movement in single file. Our weapons are cocked and ready to fire. As we'd hoped, we see a gaggle of young men with their hands held above their heads and a pile of guns on the ground around them. They seem to be in a poor state. Keeping them covered, we inch slowly forward along the cliff edge. As we go, it's tempting to kick their dropped weapons out over the edge of the track and down the steep precipice below. I resist this and, carefully, we retrieve their guns and pass them back to our soldiers behind us for safekeeping. They'll be needed as evidence in any future enquiry. When three of our soldiers have passed beyond the last of the rebels, they search on up the slope to check for signs of any more rebels. They report back that the track ahead is empty. I order body searches to be made of the guys we've captured. I worry for the safety of our soldiers here as we have to operate in the confined space, close to the perilous edge of the track. By now, the rebels are cowed and subdued. They offer no resistance. We find knives and spare ammunition, which we confiscate, but no other hidden weapons or grenades. I'm confident these men are now unarmed.

Major Souquet had been at the rear of our patrol. But now he pushes forward to come up to my position on the ledge. He calls to me:

"*Tuez-les, tirez tous ces rebelles maintenant*! Kill them, shoot all these rebels now!"

As he's saying this, he points his own sub machine gun at the first guy and I think he may be about to shoot him himself. Something inside me flares up. These so-called rebels are all young men. I know nothing about their background, what organisation they belong to or what they may have done in the past. But here and now, they are just a bunch of frightened young guys. We've disarmed them and we will ensure they pose no further threat up here on the Oku. I turn to Major Souquet and tell him:

"Major, put down your gun. No one will be killed here."

Major Souquet stares at me as if in disbelief. He sees me aiming my own gun at him. Usman Pele is right behind him and senses the tension of the moment. Usman raises his own gun and pushes it in the major's back. Quietly, I tell him:

"Major Souquet, sir, you are to drop your gun now!"

He knows he has no option and slowly lowers his gun. I take it from him, extract the round that's in the breech, detach the magazine and put it in my ammunition pouch. Then, silently, I hand the gun back to him. He's not done yet and tells me.

"Lt Chambers. *Vous êtes insubordonné à un officier supérieur*. You are being insubordinate to a senior officer. I will report you to Major Sutter and demand you are charged."

I think he's bluffing but at this moment I don't care. I tell him:

"Major Souquet, I realise you outrank me but I am in charge here — not you. These are Nigerian soldiers and our mission is to support the local police. It is not to murder unarmed men. And it would be murder as these guys have dropped their weapons and are our prisoners. As such we will protect them while they are in our charge. When we can, we'll get them transported back to your jurisdiction, then you can do with them what you will. But until then, we will treat them with respect. You can report me for insubordination if you choose, but if you do, I have witnesses here who will testify that you planned to commit a war crime."

The last bit is bluff but it seems to have had the desired effect. I can tell Major Souquet is seething but he's realistic enough to accept the situation.

We return to our base camp escorting our prisoners. When we do a detailed headcount, we find there are twenty-two of them. They are now quite docile and follow our instructions. Back at the camp, we ensure they are loosely tied and I allocate a section to keep them under constant guard. Two of them have gunshot wounds, which seem to be going septic through lack of medical attention. Cpl Jamil is also a trained medic and does a good temporary job of dressing their wounds. Sgt Bado has organised a lunchtime meal and we arrange for all the prisoners to be fed with the same rations as ourselves. It seems to be the first food they've eaten for some long time and they all tuck in ravenously.

The next issue is how to get them transferred to the French authorities. I report our contact to Major Sutter and ask if the Whirlwind could be sent to winch them up from our camp. I get a negative reply as it's assessed that winching is not feasible at our forward location. The heli would need to hover for too long and would be exposed to possible rebel small arms fire. I was told to recce a location further to the rear where the heli could land and on-load directly without winching. A protection party would be needed to cover the area while the heli was in the ground.

This proposal is feasible as we had already earmarked a place some two miles down the Oku that has a space sufficiently flat to land a heli. I report this, saying it would take approximately two hours to get there with our guarded prisoners and to mark out the strip for landing. I was then given an RV time — 15.30 hours. I reckon we can make the trip and prepare the LZ in time and. hopefully, return camp before nightfall. I radio back to confirm.

The prisoner transfer operation onto the heli goes OK and by 16.00 hours the last of our prisoners is on board. Major Sutter has sent a protection party so they will be guarded during the return trip to Ndop. I have no idea what will happen to them after that. All I do know is that, while we were responsible for them, we treated them fairly. Major Souquet has accompanied us to the Heli LZ. We haven't spoken to each other since our altercation on the mountain. As he's about to get on board, I hand him back the magazine I had confiscated from him earlier. We face each other without speaking. I give him a rather exaggerated salute. He then boards the heli and I turn away to avoid the down-blast as it lifts off and wheels away back towards Ndop.

I gather the escort party together and we make our way back up the mountain. I'm relieved to be back and to have discharged our duty in disarming the rebels and offloading them safely back to our HQ. Yves Bréchignac had remained at the base camp during our trip down the mountain. Earlier, he had witnessed the face off I had had with Major Souquet and I wonder what his reaction would be. But I need not have been concerned as he comes up to me, salutes, then shakes my hand. He says:

"Lieutenant, I salute you for what you did on the mountain. You should understand that although the major is my superior, he is not a professional legionnaire. The backbone of our legion is from our non-commissioned ranks. We are the ones who have endured years of training and together have faced combat action around the world. Our officers are often imposed on us from French high command — selected from St Cyr or after they have attended *L'école Superieur de Guerre*. Many have little operational experience and stay with us for only a couple of years. Major Souquet is one of those. I fully support the action you took against him."

I can't help feeling quite emotional about Yves' comments. He is a hardened professional soldier but also a French patriot. His comments make me feel vindicated that I had done the right thing.

About a month after the "prisoner incident", we get fresh orders. It's now July and the decision has been taken to withdraw the Nigerian contingent from the Cameroons as the date of Nigerian independence on 1 October approaches. We are to maintain our base camp in good order and be ready to hand over to a British battalion who will continue to support the French offensive and the local police through to the plebiscite early next year.

I pass on this news to our soldiers and it creates a buzz of excitement. I think we all feel the same. From a military viewpoint, our tour in the Cameroons has been a good experience and we have all learnt from it. But we have been constrained by the roles of our engagement in the police support role. We know that Nigerian independence is nearing and we want to play our part in commemorating it. We look forward to a new chapter in our lives.

Our camp is prepared for handover. Everything is neat and tidy. Our defences have been refreshed and the trip flares have been checked and replaced where necessary. We even smarten up our latrines with fresh disinfectant. On schedule, the advance party of the incoming platoon arrives in a Whirlwind heli but not the same one that has supported us for the past few months. I notice that this one has a British Royal Air Force roundel on its side. We line up ready to greet the incomers. First out of the heli is a young British officer, a second lieutenant like me. Amidst the dust and noise from the heli blades, I step forward to greet him. We shake hands then wait until the heli lifts off when we can hear each other speak. He tells me his name is Martin Bones, and this is his first operational duty since joining his battalion from Sandhurst as a regular officer the previous year. The battalion has come directly from UK. I notice all their skins are lily white and they will need some time to adjust and acclimatise. I feel like a seasoned soldier compared to them!

I show Martin Bones round our camp and explain our defences and our role here. We've made a series of hand-drawn maps of the surrounding mountain and I explain these and leave them with him. CSM Kabala and Sgt Bado are carrying out similar briefings to their British army counter parts. We are told the British heli will be returning in late-morning. It will bring in further soldiers from the British Army battalion and start to ferry our guys back to Ndop.

The hand-over/take-over goes smoothly and by late afternoon, the last of our guys are flown out. I'm on this last flight. I get a good view from the window of the heli and see the base camp that has been our home for over two months gradually disappearing from view. I have mixed emotions about that.

Back at Ndop, I'm at last reunited with my Pawpy dog. She seems pleased enough to be back with me but I see she's getting quite plump. I'm going to have to go for runs with her and put her on a regime to slim her back down.

We're given our movement instructions. We will move out from Ndop and RV with the rest of the battalion in Bamenda. Then we'll leave the British Cameroons and take our own military transport on the long drive back to Kaduna in northern Nigeria. I've been put in charge of an independent convoy of eight Land Rovers. I'd love to be able to have one last visit to Bafali to bid farewell to the FON but that's not possible as we're leaving Cameroons tomorrow. I write him a short note and give it to John to deliver when he can.

Chapter Thirty

When we get back to Kaduna, it feels like returning home. Everything is as it was when we left at the end of March. I've been missing regular training runs while we were up on the Oku mountain and I'm determined to get back into good physical shape as soon as possible. But everything seems such an effort. I don't know why, but I feel lethargic and am struggling on my daily workouts. I keep having the shits and also seem to have a stomach ache I can't get rid of. Even Pawpy is coping better than me when we're jogging. I'm also beginning to get some sort of fever. I wake up sweating in the mornings, though the outside temperature is quite fresh here as it's the middle of July and we're now in Kaduna's rainy season.

Today, I'm due to begin organising a training course for some of our junior non-commissioned officers (JNCOs). We've prepared a series of lectures then a week of practical leadership exercises. I'm looking forward to it especially as I've co-opted CSM Kabala to assist.

As usual, Usman Pele wakes me with a cup of tea. I stagger out of bed and start my ablutions but I can't get going. I'm sweating again and feel bloody awful. I go for a pee and am shocked to see there's blood in my urine. That's not good! Until now, I've been lucky in my life having always managed to stay healthy, except when I had my appendix out as a child. Other than that, I can't even remember ever being ill or missing a day from school or work. I hate to admit I'm not well but I know that today I must report in sick. I've got to get this sorted out.

We have a new medical officer (MO) called Capt Joseph Odabi who's just joined the battalion from medical college in UK. I get dressed, check in with him and tell him my symptoms. He takes my temperature, blood pressure and listens to my heart through his stethoscope. I can tell he doesn't know what's wrong. I tell him I need to get back to work soonest to start our JNCOs' training course. He asks me to wait while he makes some phone calls, then he comes over and says:

"Look Peter, I don't know what you've got but we must play it safe. I've made an appointment for you to see a specialist at Kaduna Hospital this morning. You need to go there right away. Don't worry about your military duties for now. Your health comes first. I'm going to inform Major Sutter that you're sick and will be away from your duties until this problem gets sorted. Our duty Land Rover and driver is outside, briefed to take you to the hospital. I'm also going to jack up one of our medical orderlies to escort you there."

I sit down in the medical centre waiting room. I'm finding it difficult to focus. Capt Odabi is soon back. I hear him saying:

"OK Peter, it's all fixed. I've spoken to Major Sutter and you're off duty till you're better. Oh, and Usman Pele has taken charge of your dog. The Land Rover, driver and escort orderly are waiting outside so off you go now! See you back when you're better."

I get up and stumble outside. The medical orderly takes my arm and guides me to the Land Rover. I remember feeling freezing cold in the fresh morning air as we drive into the centre of Kaduna town. I vaguely remember being escorted down a long corridor and being aware of disinfectant — hospital smells. Then there's a British doctor asking questions that I find difficult to answer. He's pressing me about taking the Paludrine tablets when we were in the Cameroons. I tell him I'm sure I took one every day and still do. I'm then vaguely aware of being undressed, put on a trolley and being wheeled off somewhere. After that, I don't remember anything else anymore.

It's like being in a tunnel but it's neither claustrophobic nor oppressive. I'm weightless, floating on a soft surface but being gently steered towards a light ahead. I have no control but feel relaxed and that I'm being guided by some benign force. It's as if my body and mind have been taken over. The light gets closer and I feel I'm emerging from the tunnel and then I'm now out in the light. I don't know where I've just come from but it's behind me now. I try to orientate and adjust to this new place. I'm aware that I'm lying in a bed. I can tell there's a light over me. Then I feel the soft gentle touch of a hand holding my arm.

Slowly I open my eyes. Above me I see the face of an angel. Perhaps not an actual angel but the face of a beautiful woman. She's wearing a nurse's uniform and I see there's a small watch pinned above her right breast. Her skin is ebony black, her face has soft chiselled features — high forehead, pronounced cheekbones, straight aquiline nose, fine lips that are half parted. She's looking straight at me and she smiles as if she's welcoming me back from a long journey. I know this face. I know this woman. I've thought about her often during our months away in the Cameroons. This is the woman I danced with in the Kaduna High-life club. This is the sister of Lt Mamadu Baldeh. This is Assibi. I struggle to connect, to begin to understand where I am and why this gorgeous woman should be here with me now. My mouth feels dry but I manage to say:

"Assibi, it's you! But I don't —"

Her half smile widens and I glimpse her even white teeth. She puts her hand to my lips and says quietly:

"Shush Peter! There's a lot to tell you but we have time for that later. It's enough for now that you're back with us again."

I'm lying in this hospital bed. I see tubes around me leading from bottles overhead into somewhere in my body. I just stay still and look up into the eyes of this beautiful woman. I know she's Assibi. I remember the delicious feeling of dancing in rhythm with her those months ago and of the touch of her slim sensuous body. I had no idea she was a nurse. I only know that at this moment, she's here with me. Her hand that touches my lips is soft and cool and I see her long slim elegant fingers as she gently pulls away. But she stays close, sitting on the edge on the bed. Our eyes seem to be locked together. She's like a heavenly vision. We stay like this for a while then softly she says:

"Peter, just to tell you I'm the night ward sister at this hospital. You've been very sick but your system is recovering now. It'll still take some time and you need to rest. I'm going to give you a small injection now and soon you'll be sleeping again. Don't worry Peter. You're going to be fine and I'll be coming back regularly to check on you and make sure you're doing as you're told!"

I watch as Assibi prepares a syringe then inserts it into my arm. She then leans over me strokes my arm and gives a light kiss on my forehead. I have a fading picture of her as she draws back. The sight of her smiling face is the last frame in my brain as I slide back into sleep.

The next time I wake, I see sunshine streaming through the window. I recognise the British doctor who had questioned me when I first arrived. I have no idea how long ago that was. He's a tall slim man with an authoritative manner. He's holding a clipboard and is accompanied by a couple of Nigerians, also wearing white lab coats. I suppose they are junior doctors. When he sees that I'm awake, the British doctor comes to the side of my bed and says:

"Lt Peter Chambers. Welcome back to the land of the living! We didn't get introduced properly when you were admitted as you were in a bad state. I'm Dr John Withers, the chief medical officer here at Kaduna Hospital. I have to say that we were very worried about you and it took some time to get a clear diagnosis of the 'lurgy' that had got into your system."

Good point, I'm thinking. What the fucking hell is wrong with me? Dr Withers continues:

"We decided you've been suffering from a variant of a disease locally called bilharzia. Its medical name is Schistosomiasis. The disease is caused by parasitic worms that somehow got into your intestines. How do you think that could that have happened?"

It's easy to answer that one. I tell Dr Withers:

"Yeah, that makes sense. I've just come back from our tour of duty in the Cameroons. On our patrols in the jungle, we often had to wade through stagnant water, sometime it was chest high."

"Well there you go, you must have contracted the bilharzia then. You also had a very high fever when you were admitted. Hence all my early questions about Paludrine tablets. We were concerned you might also have contracted malaria but we've been able to rule that out. We performed a small operation to neutralise the worms and had to pump you full of penicillin and other drugs. Anyway, I'm pleased to tell you that we're now getting the condition under control and your readings are gradually returning back to normal levels. You will have to stay here at least a few days yet then we'll check again to decide when you can be discharged. I can see from your record you're a very active guy but you must be patient. You need to rest and regather your strength."

At least it's good to know what the fucking hell has been wrong with me and that it's being sorted out. But I'm wondering about the rest of my platoon. We were all in the same situation. Are they also sick? I ask the doctor about this. He replies:

"No, we've checked that and it seems to have been just you. I can't give a full medical explanation but African people appear mostly to be immune to the disease. For some reason, it's confined to Caucasian races — Europeans, Americans, possibly Asians — i.e. principally people with white skins like yours Peter."

After being with my platoon of Nigerians and sharing everything together, I had come to forget completely that there were any differences between us. This bilharzia business is a reminder that there are.

I can see that Dr Withers needs to get on with his rounds and I can't think of any more questions for him so I thank him for looking after me. As a parting remark, he says:

"We'll continue to check regularly on your progress. We provide twenty-four-hour cover. At night, Sister Assibi Baldeh is responsible for your ward. I'm sure she'll look after you well!"

This is music to my ears. As I drift back to sleep, I hold an image of Assibi in my mind. I hope she might be here when I wake up again.

The next time I wake it's dark outside. I hear someone approaching and I hope it might be Assibi. It's not. It's another nurse — she's brisk and polite but she's not Assibi. She's carrying a tray, which she puts down on the trolley over the bed and pushes it up towards me. She then comes over and props me up with an extra pillow. She says:

"Good evening, Lt Chambers, sir. My name is Nurse Alice Baffa. It's good to know you're back with us. During the last few days, I've been checking on you but until now, you've always been asleep. Sister Baldeh says it's time for you to start eating. I'll be back shortly to collect the tray — empty I hope!"

On the tray, I find a bowl of soup and a bread roll. The soup is delicious and I find I'm really hungry. Some minutes later, Nurse Baffa is back, collects the tray and settles me back down on the bed. She's about to leave when I ask her:

"Nurse Baffa, that was great soup and thank you for looking after me. Tell me, is Sister Baldeh on duty tonight?"

"Yes sir, she's always on night duty. She will be doing her rounds shortly. My shift is about to finish but I'll see you again tomorrow."

After enjoying the soup, the first food I've had for a long time, I feel that I'm getting better. I'd woken up several times during the day and gradually feel that I'm at last coming out of the zombie state I've been in the past days. The news about Assibi really cheers me up and I'm anxious to see her again.

I'm impatient and it seems an age before I hear footsteps approaching my room. The door opens and there she is. The last time, I was still woozy and only saw her face and hands. Now I watch as she walks over towards my bed. Even covered with her white medical uniform, I can sense the slim lithe figure I had admired as we danced in the High-life club. She's smiling that infectious smile, comes over to the bed and reaches out for my hands. I hold hers and feel the softness of her long fingers. For a few moments, we just stay like that, looking into each other's eyes. I have been waiting all day for this moment. Slowly, Assibi pulls away and tells me:

"Peter, I can tell you're getting better. That's great! Now I have to perform my sister duties to check you over and top up your medication."

Now, Assibi is all professional business. She checks my pulse, takes my temperature and sorts through all the bottles to make sure the levels are correct and all the connections are still in place. She ends with a sigh of satisfaction and clears away a tray with some used medication. She says:

"Everything is going along fine Peter, we'll soon have you back playing soldiers again!"

I'm worried she's going to leave so I say to her: "Thank you for everything Assibi. I'd love it if you could stay a while before you have to get on with your rounds. Is that possible?"

Assibi smiles, puts the tray down on a table, comes back to my bed and sits close to me.

"I'd be pleased to Peter, I arranged to make you my last visit so I'm now free for a while." She pauses then continues: "What would you like to talk about?"

I find it difficult to get into this. I just want to have her here next to me: to talk about anything, nothing special, just to watch her while she's talking. I say:

"Assibi, we first met in the High-life club, now here you are, the night ward sister in this hospital. The first time I'm dancing with you, then the next I'm being administered by you here. I had no idea you were nursing. Tell me a little about yourself."

Assibi lifts her head as she reflects, exposing her long slender neck. She pauses, then begins:

"Peter — well — I'll tell you something about my background if you like. I come from the Fulani tribe. Traditionally we Fulanis have been nomads who live off our livestock, mainly cattle and move from place to place with our animals. Fulanis have rarely settled in one place and we have contacts throughout West Africa. You may have noticed that our physical features are different from those of most Nigerians but throughout our history we have been closest to the Hausa peoples. Concerning my own family, my parents lost four of their children to famine when we were in Niger. My father then decided to settle in northern Nigeria in Katsina province primarily because he wanted to give my brother Mamadu and me a good education and the chance to live more settled lives. As you know, my brother is a lieutenant in the Nigerian Army, as you are, and I studied medicine in Zaria. I am still in training to become a qualified doctor and my work here as ward sister is part of my job experience."

I love listening to her talk. She's very articulate and I love the way she chooses her words. We continue to talk for some time. I tell her some of my background and we both realise just how completely different our upbringings have been. I'd love to continue all evening but I'm conscious that I'm not Assibi's only patient. But when she gets up to leave, we agree we will continue our conversation tomorrow.

After she's gone, it takes a long time before I can go back to sleep. I have so many more questions I would like to ask her. I don't know her age but just from what she has told me about her medical training, I realise she must be several years older than me. I wonder if she has a regular male friend. I suppose she could already be married. I hope I can find out more tomorrow.

Assibi comes again the next evening, and the next and the next. I'm finding that she has a really good sense of humour. Our conversation is becoming more and more informal, even intimate. We relax and love to share our experiences. She tells me she is not married and has recently split from a relationship with a Hausa man. She has no steady partner at present. She asks me about my love life and I tell her about the girlfriends I had in England but confess that I didn't have sex with any of them. I even get encouraged to tell her about my night with the FON of Bafali's two wives. This makes her laugh and she asks:

"Why Peter, that sounds exotic! But tell me what did you actually do with them? Did you have sex, one at a time or what?"

I get quite embarrassed here and don't know how best to answer. This is getting very personal. I tell her:

"To be honest Assibi, I don't really know. I had so many mixed emotions that night as this was the first time anything like this had happened to me. Also, I have to tell you that I was pretty drunk with all the FON's beer I had consumed. I remember I found the experience being very pleasant but I can't really remember what we actually did."

"Oh, come on — you can tell me! Did you have sex with them or not?"

"I think perhaps I did but it all became confused. I loved the idea of spending the night with these two girls but I was worried about — well — amongst other things of catching some sexual disease."

Assibi exclaims: "Peter you really are so naïve! We've just done exhaustive tests on you and you can put your mind at rest about that. You do *not* have any sexually transmitted diseases. I wonder what you did or think you did. Peter, perhaps you need a little help to get you started!"

I don't know whether this is an invitation. Is this fantastic woman making a proposition? Where are we going with this?

The days have gone by and the doctor tells me the tests for bilharzia are now negative; I'm to be discharged from Kaduna hospital. Every day, I've felt fitter and stronger. The doctor reminds me to take it easy for a week then I can steadily get back to training. He thinks that in a month's time I should be fully fit again. I'm ready to go; but I can't leave without a final talk with Assibi.

We've got a date, Assibi and me. We've arranged to meet on Saturday evening three weeks from now in the High-life club. I'd have liked it to be sooner but Assibi says I need time to recuperate and she also has to go on a medical course in Zaria. I accept that I must be patient but it will be worth the wait. We both know what we want and we will also need to be discreet.

Chapter Thirty-one

I've been back in our barracks for a couple of weeks. It's good to be feeling normal again. I did as I was instructed by Dr Withers and took it easy during my first week out of hospital but since then have gradually increased building up my fitness.

Last week I organised the JNCOs' training course that had been deferred while I was in hospital. It's been a pleasure working with these keen young soldiers — the course was a mix of fieldcraft, map reading, tactics, live firing on the range and individual initiative tests. CSM Kabala helped me organise the programme and, when it came to night patrolling, I deferred entirely to Cpl Aiki Riba whose night vision and sense of smell is infinitely greater than mine. During the course, both Major Sutter and Lt Col Johnson visited and watched some of the demonstrations we laid on for them. Their complimentary remarks made us all feel good.

Back in barracks, I've started jogging again and increasing the distance of each run. My little Pawpy dog, of course, comes along with me each time. She's getting fitter. I've also put her on a diet and banned her from hanging around the cookhouse. She's starting to slim down and is looking quite neat and sharp.

We're now into early September and everyone is beginning to get excited about Nigeria's independence — now only five weeks away on Saturday 1 October. Lt Col Johnson has explained to the battalion that there will be two major parades in Nigeria to commemorate the event. One will be in the capital, Lagos, attended by both a representative of Her Majesty, Queen Elizabeth, and by Sir Abubakar Tafawa Belewa, the new prime minister. The second major parade is to take place on the racecourse here at Kaduna. British and Nigerian politicians and other dignitaries will attend this event. The centrepiece will be a parade by our battalion and we will be responsible for all the administration. Our primary focus for the next few weeks will be to prepare and rehearse for this big event.

Today, I'm attending our routine Company morning schedule when Major Sutter tells me that both David Edozi and I are to report immediately to the CO's office. David and I hurry off to Battalion HQ, both wondering what this is about. We report in to the adjutant who tells us the CO is ready to see us. David and I smarten up, march into the CO's office, halt in unison and salute. Lt Col Johnson then says:

"Right, stand at ease and listen in. It's been decided that it would be appropriate for independence to be commemorated at precisely twelve noon on 1 October by a symbolic lowering of the British Union Jack and simultaneous raising of the new green and white Nigerian flag. This flag ceremony will form the centrepiece of the day. Now, David and Peter, this is why I sent for you two today. You both are the same height and approximately the same physique. You will represent the young Nigerian and British participation and be the two flag ensigns in the centre and front of the main parade line up. You, Peter, will lower the Union Jack as David begins to raise the Nigerian flag. The point when the two flags cross, the Union Jack coming down and the Nigerian flag going up, will be at precisely twelve o'clock and mark the moment when Nigeria becomes independent. I've been told that members of the world's press will be present to record the event. I'm relying on you both to put on a good show!"

David and I listen to the CO's remarks, without commenting. He then asks us: "Any questions?"

In unison, we both reply: "No, sir, we'll do our best."

"Splendid! We'll need to have several rehearsals before the big day. I'm confident you'll represent the battalion well. Dismiss!"

David and I snap to attention, salute, turn-about and march out of the CO's office. Outside, David says:

"Phew! I wondered what we were in for there. But I reckon we can hack it. What do you think, Peter?"

I'm actually rather chuffed about this new role. I realise the main reason David and I have been picked is nothing to do with our ability as officers but that, as one black and one white guy, both being the same height, as a pair we should look quite photogenic for the cameras. I reply:

"Yeah! Why not? After all we've been through in the Cameroons, this should be a piece of piss!"

We're nearing the end of the week and I'm getting inwardly excited about my date on Saturday with Assibi Baldeh. No, that's a complete understatement! To be honest, I've been thinking of not much else during the three weeks since I left hospital. I was attracted to Assibi from the first moment I saw her at the High-life club all those months ago. I was struck by her beauty and found her beguiling and fascinating. Several of the rest of the Nigerian girls at the club were attractive and all were good fun but that night I had been mesmerised by Assibi. I thought about her so often during our days on operations in the Cameroons and wondered if I would ever see her again. Then to have found her once more, in the totally different environment of Kaduna Hospital — looking up into her beautiful face as I drifted back from unconsciousness into the real world. It was like a dream come true. It still is.

I know we'll have to be very discreet. I don't know much about the protocol of white/black relationships here in Nigeria but I do know that it could be very hard for Assibi if it were to be known that she is seeing a white guy like me. During our long chats in the hospital, she told me that her father and her Fulani background are very strict. She said that her father had given up much so that her brother Mamadu and she could improve their lives. She's very aware of that and determined not to let him down. Assibi said that her father had disapproved of her relationship with a Hausa man. I dread to think what he might think of her seeing a white guy.

From my side, I haven't got a clue what would happen if it were known that I was dating a black girl. I don't know of any circumstance here. Being on the brink of independence, I think most Brits are playing it safe and trying not to do anything to upset the good relations we currently have with our Nigerian colleagues. I suspect if it were known I was seeing Assibi, it would strain even the stiffest British upper lip and I would likely to be on the next plane home. So, the message is clear: be discreet — very discreet!

Our arrangement is that we'll meet at the High-life club on Saturday evening, that's 10 September. I don't remember that we even agreed a time. I've got myself quite hyped up just thinking about being with her again. Since we've been back in Kaduna, Bill Holding and I have renewed our close personal contact, which had been curtailed in the

Cameroons due to our different roles — me with C Company at Ndop, Bill staying in Bamenda as MTO (Military Transport Officer). Bill has now had his Wolseley car serviced. It acts as our wheels between our barracks and Kaduna town. I'm in luck this Saturday. Bill's going up to Zaria for the weekend in one of our Land Rovers, and he's told me I can use the Wolseley while he's away! My idea is to drive up to the Kaduna club, park there, then show my face at the club, have a drink and do the social rounds. Then I plan to slip away and leg it over to the High-life club to arrive around ten or ten-thirty. Well, that's the plan.

At last it's Saturday, the day of my date with Assibi. I'm free from duties by mid-afternoon. To occupy my time till evening, I take Pawpy for a run; too hot for both of us but we make it. I hose Pawpy with the tepid water from the tap, which she pretends to object to, then towel her down and get her evening meal ready. I tell her she needs to stay and look after our *gida* till I'm back. I don't know how long that might be but, just in case, I know Usman Pele will be coming by early tomorrow morning and will look after her if I'm not there. Pawpy has become a great little actress and looks sad but I know she will cope.

I take a shower and put on my only decent civvy clothes — white shirt, light sand-coloured slacks, new pair of suede desert boots. I'm nervous about the evening. Although I'm now tanned by the African sun, I'm still likely to stand out as the only white guy when later I get to the High-life bar.

I turn up at the British colonial Kaduna club about half-past eight and leave the Wolseley in the members' carpark. Already the club is busy and I hear the orchestra is in full swing. The past two Saturdays, I'd dropped by there with Bill and found that nothing much has changed since we were away in the Cameroons. The only difference I've noticed is that the hibiscus flowers, that line the path up to the entrance, are now in full bloom with their large red bugle like buds. I suppose it's because of the recent rains. They and the other flowers produce a fragment floral aroma to welcome the members. As I walk in, I'm spotted by Major Sedgewick who beckons me over to his table. He says:

"Ah, it's young Peter Chambers! Come and have a drink with us Peter. I want to introduce you to James Chorley — um, and to his charming daughter, Cynthia, who's staying here in Kaduna for a while."

I'd not expected this as I just want to play it low key and slip away as planned. James Chorley seems to be an affable guy in, perhaps, his fifties. His daughter is tall, slender and quite pretty in an "English rose" way. I'd say she's in her early twenties. Mr Chorley gets up, shakes my hand and says:

"Good to meet you Peter. The major here has been telling us about you and your recent exploits in the Cameroons. You seem to have quite a reputation! My daughter was getting restless as she doesn't take to any of the eligible young men here. You're just the guy to cheer her up! You're both excused to join the crowd on the dance floor."

Cynthia is already on her feet and I can see I have no choice. All I can do is go with the flow. I say to Mr Chorley:

"Of course, I'd be delighted, sir." I turn to Cynthia and add. "May I have the pleasure?"

We find ourselves wedged into the small dance area. It's a foxtrot so there's not a lot of complicated steps. In any case, I don't think Cynthia is much of a dancer either so we just shuffle around to the beat of the music. I find Cynthia to be a really nice person. She doesn't push herself and is content to have a low-key relaxed conversation as we move around the dance floor. If this had been some months ago, I think I would have liked to get to know her better. But after Assibi and on this evening of all days. Sorry Cynthia, no contest!

When the music stops, I don't hang around and lead Cynthia back to her father, try to play Mr Gallant and thank her and her dad for "the honour" of the dance. Major Sedgewick plays host and hands me a glass of whisky, which I'm duty bound to accept. I take a sip and settle down in a chair on the opposite side of the bar table to Cynthia. I try to be polite but I don't want to get involved. Major Sedgewick launches into a description of our time in the Cameroons and gives a glowing account, much exaggerated, of our battalion's successful tour there. I sit through this for as long as I find I must to be polite, then make a gesture towards the bar. I say that I need to talk to some of my chums over there, thank the major for the drink and wish Cynthia an enjoyable stay in Kaduna. Before any of them reply, I'm on my feet heading for the bar. I take the glass of whisky with me. It's still nearly full and, when I'm out the

Major's sight, I empty the contents into a flower pot.

I feel a bit sneaky slipping away from the Kaduna club but I'm pleased no one appears to notice. I see the Wolseley is still parked in a row full of other cars so it shouldn't arouse comment if any of my colleagues see it parked there without me being around.

I have to concentrate finding the way in the dark to the High-life club. In hindsight I should have done a recce beforehand. Too late now. When at last I hear the familiar sounds of the music I know I've found the place. At the entrance, the girl in the ticket booth doesn't react to the colour of my skin when I pay my entry fee. Like the last time I was here, the place is full, most people swaying to the haunting rhythm of the music. I see smiling faces everywhere, relaxed and happy in contrast to the stiff formality of the Kaduna club. I need not have worried about being white. No one here cares.

I look around anxiously for Assibi and can't see her. Then I do. She seems to appear out of nowhere, slips her hand in mine and leads me onto the dance floor. It's just as before. We pick up the rhythm and straightaway move together as one. I look down at her beautiful features and marvel at her. I'm swept away by the feeling of joy at being with her again.

When the music pauses between numbers, Assibi leads me away from the dance floor to try to find a quieter spot. She cups her hands and puts them to my ear. Even so, I have to strain to hear her against the chattering buss of the crowds around us. She says:

"Peter, I'm so excited that you're here. Listen, I'm going to leave now and go to my apartment to wait for you there. Don't worry. My brother, Mamadu, is here and is helping us. He's with his girlfriend. When the music starts again, have a dance with her then leave the club. Mamadu will guide you."

With that, she's gone. I turn and find that Mamadu Baldeh is next to me. He smiles, shakes my hand and gives a conspiratorial grin. He gestures to the young woman by his side and that I should take her onto the dance floor. Just then the music starts up again and we're away. Mamadu's girlfriend is charming and it's fun to dance with her. She smiles a lot and I can tell she also understands the situation. The dance finishes and we leave the floor. I smile a thank you to her as we re-join

Mamadu.

Outside the club, Mamadu guides me at first along small unlit passageways. We are in a poor part of Kaduna; then the road widens out and we're passing quite modern apartment blocks with street lighting. Mamadu explains:

"Peter, this area has recently been built to support our hospital — you know the inside of that, of course! Assibi has been allocated one of the nurses' apartments during her time here and that's where we're going now. Assibi has told me about her friendship with you and has sworn me and my girlfriend to secrecy. Peter, I must tell you our father would be very angry if he found out so be careful. OK? I love my sister and will protect her no matter what."

I don't know quite how to take Mamadu's remarks. Perhaps it's partly a threat. But here we are. He's taking me to Assibi. That's all I care about for now. We pass a couple of the apartment blocks, then at the third, Mamadu turns off the main road and leads me along a narrow pathway to the entrance of an apartment. He has a pass key and we go into the entrance lobby, then up a flight of stairs to a row of doors, each of which has a name card. I see the name Sister Assibi Baldeh. Mamadu knocks gently on the door, turns to me, smiles, shakes my hand and walks away. I wait, then the door opens and there she is.

I go inside and Assibi closes the door behind me. Her room is small but freshly painted and cosy. I almost can't believe that at last we are alone together in the privacy of her apartment. When we were in the hospital we had talked so much. Right now, we don't need any more words. I take her in my arms and kiss her, gently at first, learning to adjust to the feel — the touch — of her body. I've never felt like this before.

I'm swept away. It's like being in a different world. New, compelling yet strangely like I'm coming home to a place I've always imagined. Assibi gently leads me to the couch in the corner of the room. I've no recollection of us undressing but now we are naked and together on the couch. I feel a surge within me and we join together in mutual passion. Assibi and me together, I need no instruction manual to follow. This is a natural union of two people, two lovers.

When the first surges of passion begin to subside, Assibi turns to me and quietly whispers:

"My darling Peter, when we talked of this, I knew I didn't have much to teach you!"

Assibi is right. Now I know what it is like to have sex with a woman you care deeply about: mutual, deep and loving sex. And now I know, for certain, I'm no longer a virgin!

Chapter Thirty-two

Assibi and I have been together twice more: each time on a Saturday night and each time in her apartment near Kaduna hospital. The magic stays the same. We lie together, we caress, we tease each other, we make love. Sometimes we are serious, sometimes we are childishly stupid. I never want this deep attraction to end. After the last time, on 24 September, we arrange to meet again the following Saturday but we know there could be a problem as that is Independence Day. I've told Assibi about David Edozi and my flag waving role and warned her that there's a big party after the parade that I have to attend. As that starts soon after midday, I hope we'll all be free for the evening but there's no guarantee. Assibi says she also has to attend the parade in her nurse's function. There are likely to be wild street celebrations to commemorate the day and who knows how things might develop. Assibi has been told that she must be on stand-by and may be called in on Saturday night if people get hurt. That means there's a real question mark for both of us about seeing each other next Saturday. The only way we can contact each other is by using the duty officer telephone in our barracks through both the army and the hospital switchboards. That's tortuous and I'm worried an operator could listen in and report that Assibi and I are an item. Better by far is via her brother, Mamadu.

Then it gets worse for our continuing relationship. In mid-week, Lt Col Johnson informs us that our unit, 2nd Battalion, Queen's Own Nigeria Regiment, has been given a new mission. We are to serve as the Nigerian contribution to the United Nations peacekeeping force in the Congo. Mission details are to follow but our deployment to the Congo will be for a four- to six-month tour of duty commencing in early November.

That's not all. Lt Col Johnson says that our battalion is also due to make a *roulement* changeover with our 3rd Battalion immediately after the Congo tour and we are to move from Kaduna to Abeokuta, a town between Lagos and Ibadan in south-west Nigeria. The move will be initiated by the rear party we leave behind when we deploy to the Congo. It will commence in November.

I try to work out the implications for Assibi and me. It would mean that, if we stick to our Saturday only dates, there might only be about four or five times more that we could be together. Then, after the UN tour in the Congo, my military conscription period will be over and I'll be due to be demobbed back to UK. I need to talk all this through with Assibi and hope we can both make it on Saturday night. At least there's one piece of good news. Assibi's brother, Mamadu Baldah, has been reassigned from his detachment in Zaria to re-join our battalion. He will be coming with us to the Congo. From my personal viewpoint, it also means he will be closer at hand to act as a link between Assibi and me.

There's nothing I can do about these new developments. I tell myself to get on with my job here and hope things work out later on. The first priority now is to concentrate on playing my part in the parade next Saturday.

It's Friday, 30 September 1960, the eve of Nigeria's independence. There's a real buzz as everyone is getting excited about the reality of Nigeria becoming a fully free country. It's one of the largest countries in Africa and has the potential to become a major player not just in the region but in the whole of the continent of Africa. The country has an abundance of natural resources — petroleum products of oil and natural gas and also tin, iron ore and even, I believe, uranium. I've heard the arguments from both sides about whether the British merely exploited the country and its people or whether it helped Nigeria to evolve and mature from groups of disparate tribes to become a modern united country. I don't like to get involved in those discussions but the reality is that Nigeria today, in 1960, has inherited from the British a sound economy and well-developed infrastructure with a civil service, legal system, well-trained police and military, and a network of rail and roads spanning the whole country. From tomorrow, a fully functioning independent Nigerian government will take charge. I hope they will use these assets for the benefit of the Nigerian people regardless of which region or tribe they come from.

We've spent the past couple of weeks preparing for tomorrow's big parade. It's the first time since I joined the battalion that we've had several rehearsals with every element involved — battalion headquarters, the three infantry companies and one administrative company, armoured recce squadron and the band. We're even bringing our crown birds, the regimental mascots, on parade with us. They can be rather noisy at unexpected times but they're very decorative and add colour and atmosphere to the parade.

David and I have done our stuff in rehearsing the flag ceremony and have been given the approval of our CO. By late afternoon, the CO says he's satisfied that the parade will be immaculate tomorrow and there's nothing further to rehearse. We are dismissed ready for an early start tomorrow. Our best uniforms are pressed, boots shone and brasses polished. Now we can relax for the rest of the evening.

Our soldiers take the chance of this free time to get into the festive spirit and the four companies set up stands around our football pitch. The smell of burning wood and the glow of the small fires that have been lit produce a magical atmosphere. It's a beautiful warm starlit night and I can't resist joining in. C Company has produced its own band comprising instrumentalists from our own ranks, which CSM Kabala is organising. The other companies are also competing with their rival bands. I love the sounds they are producing, similar to the rhythms at the High-life club. I've always been attracted to the drumming beats produced by the calabash, a large nut shaped fruit, cut in half and dried. I think it's also called a water drum. I've seen it played in the High-life club usually with the bare hands using the palms or fingers. It's necessary to play the instrument sitting on the ground in order to raise and lower the calabash with bare feet to produce different sounds to accompany the other instruments of the band. CSM Kabala sees me approaching and frees up a place for me in the middle of the group. Everyone is drinking the local beer and I'm kindly given a can. And then another. I'm getting into the party mood. In an abandoned moment, I tell CSM Kabala that I would like to try my hand at playing the calabash. Out of nowhere, one is produced. I take my place next to the other instrumentalists, sit down on the ground, take off my shoes and start drumming. Our soldiers seem to find my new-found hobby amusing and I see smiles of encouragement all around.

I'm getting into the groove and I lose myself in the music. It's hypnotic. I think I'm following the beat pretty well and respond to the support of our smiling soldiers all around. Everyone (except the drum section!) is on their feet and dancing and swaying to the rhythm and beats of our music. Now and again, some kind soldier brings further refreshments of the strong local beer. I never refuse the comforting taste of this fine liquid. I get carried away and lose all sense of time.

I can't remember the end of the evening. Somehow, I've managed to get back to my *gida* and I fall into a deep drink-fuelled sleep.

I'm having a terrible nightmare. I'm dreaming that I've been jolted awake and am looking straight up into the eyes of my CO. Then I realise it's not a dream. This is real. My mosquito net has been wrenched aside and I'm lying naked under a sheet. Towering over me, I see the scowling face of Lt Col Henry Johnson MBE. He's dressed in his starched dress uniform with medals, gleaming Sam Browne belt and bush hat. I force myself to concentrate as he shouts:

"Chambers, get the fuck up! You're holding up the whole battalion. You've got five minutes to get on parade!"

I try to focus and am just about aware of the CO abruptly turning and striding out of my room. I force myself to wake up. He has now left but the adjutant has stayed to ensure I'm properly awake. He tells me:

"Look, Chambers, you've really fucked up! The whole battalion was lined up for twenty minutes, ready to leave for the racecourse. The only person missing was you. They've now gone on ahead. Look, there's a Land Rover and driver right outside. Grab your kit and get in the LR. You need to catch up. You can change on the way to the racecourse. Now get to it!"

I see the adjutant also leave and I'm on my own. I force myself to leap out of bed. Usman Pele has left my complete parade uniform neatly arranged in the room — bush hat with hackle, shirt with black tie, heavily starched khaki shorts and "number one" dress jacket, Sam Browne belt, long woollen socks, puttees, highly polished boots: even the blanco-white leather pouch I'll need to hold the flag during the ceremony. All ready to go.

I rush to the loo and do the essentials, stick my head under the

257

shower to try to get myself fully awake and quickly towel down. I've no time for a shave. I slip on my underpants, grab all my uniform kit and leg it to the door. Outside is a Land Rover, as the adjutant has told me. The driver has the engine running, ready to go. I jump up into the back, clutching all my kit. I manage to tell the driver:

"Kaduna racecourse and step on it!"

He doesn't need any further instruction. He engages gear, presses on the accelerator and we're away. We sway at some speed through the barracks as I'm trying to pull on my trousers without spoiling the immaculately starched and ironed creases. After we get out onto the main Kaduna road, the ride is smoother and item by item I manage to wriggle into my number one dress uniform with all its attachments. Then I notice there's a leather "frog" attached to the Sam Browns belt. This is for holding the sword we carry on formal parades such as today. I was supposed to draw the sword from our company stores this morning but it's too late to turn back now. Not only am I late on parade but I'm also improperly dressed!

Photo: Parade uniform

The Land Rover driver sticks to his task with vigour and I see that, as we reach the racecourse, the CO and adjutant are only just pulling up ahead. The whole battalion is on parade as we'd rehearsed. The morning sun is now rising high in the clear blue sky. Facing us are a series of white marquees that have been erected especially for today's ceremony. Already, I see they are full of spectators and that crowds of Nigerians are spilling out all along the rails of the racecourse. Many are already waving green and white Nigerian flags. The tent marked "Press" is already filled with journalists with their cameras and notebooks. Facing the crowds, our battalion is already lined up. The three ranks of soldiers have been "dressed off" and are standing in the "easy" position but maintaining exactly straight lines. In front of the soldiers, our officers are at present facing in towards the soldiers three ranks. They will turn about and present arms (in their case swords!) as soon as our CO personally marches on parade.

Due to my flag-bearing role, I know my place is right in the middle, facing the centre of the front rank. I jump out of the back of the Land Rover and do a rapid check of my uniform, hoping I've put everything on the right way, bush hat with the hackle on the right side, tie correctly knotted (I hope), socks fully pulled up, jacket down, Sam Browne straight. It seems all OK but there is no mirror to check. I also position the leather flag pouch just up over my crotch. Now I have no option but to march as smartly as I can round the side of the lined-up ranks, then along the front row until I reach my designated position slap bang in the centre of the parade. I see David Edozi and use him as my marker. I march smartly up next to David, halt, turn, adjust my dressing next to him then "stand at ease" and finally "stand easy" matching the position of the rest of the parade. I'm relieved when, in a deliberate manner, CSM Kabala marches up to me and passes me the sword I should have collected earlier. Bless him for rescuing me there! I make a formal movement to place the sword in the "frog" attached to my "Sam Browne". I just hope that my manoeuvre to join the others has been seen by our crowd of spectators as an intended part of the ceremony. Beside me I hear David whisper:

"Heh, Peter, nice of you to show up!" I'm glad he's not lost his sense of humour.

At 11.45 hours precisely, the band strikes up, the CO marches on parade and the ceremony proper begins. We've practised this so many times that all our movements have become automatic. I carry them out like a zombie while my mind is still full of thinking, what a fucking idiot I've been to get so pissed last night. I realise now that Usman Pele had told me he wouldn't be able to wake me this morning as he himself had been ordered to be one of the first to line up on parade. But due to my drunken state last night, I'd completely forgotten. I'm now wondering what's going to happen. What punishment will be meted out? I reckon I might be stripped of my officer's commission and sent straight back to UK. But all that's for later. Now I must concentrate on the rest of the parade.

On the command, we all give a general salute to the VIP dais in the central marquee. I'm not sure who we're actually saluting but I see a mixture of white and black dignitaries standing up. Some are in uniform and are saluting back. At the appropriate order, two soldiers march up and present furled flags to David and me. In unison, we both return our swords into the "frogs" and then take the flags in our right hands and, with the assistance of the two soldiers, adjust them into the pouches. We hold the flagpoles firmly in our right hands. The outer cover of mine, the Union Jack, is removed. As the British National Anthem strikes up, I raise the flag until it is fully vertical. My right hand is held out straight at right angles to the flag, which I see fluttering proudly in the morning breeze. David's Nigerian flag remains furled. I wait until the final bars of "God save the Queen" then slowly begin to lower the Union Jack. Meanwhile, David's flag is unfurled and he begins to raise it from the ground. As the final bars of the British anthem fade, the band changes immediately to play the new Nigerian anthem. At this point, David's flag and mine cross, David's going up, mine going down. This moment represents a monumental point in history. Even while the Nigerian anthem is still playing, we hear a massive cheering from the crowd of spectators. Nigeria is now an independent country!

The parade ends with a formal "march past" and, once clear of the main marquees, we are dismissed. There's still administration to deal with such as securing our weapons and ensuring that transport will be ready to take everyone back to barracks after all ranks have had drinks and refreshments. I see that many of the soldiers' wives with their children have found their way here and it's good for them to be reunited with their husbands while they commemorate this special day together. One of my first jobs is to shake the hand of CSM Kabala and thank him for remembering my sword. At least it meant I was properly dressed on parade. Usman Pele comes up to me and I can tell he's very upset about my being late. I reassure him that it was entirely my own fault and that he did his job to tell me he could not be there to wake me up. He seems relieved but still sad as he knows I'm in trouble. He also tells me that he arranged for Pawpy to be looked after while we're here.

Two large marquees have been allocated for our soldiers and their wives and I know drinks, food and music have been laid on there. Another marquee is for the senior NCOs and warrant officers. The officers have been invited to join the invited guests in the main VIP marquee. After attending to our soldiers, I link up with David and Bill Holding and together we make our way over there.

At the entrance to the VIP marquee, waiters are there serving glasses of champagne, a rare drink here in Nigeria but I suppose appropriate for the occasion. To be frank, I'm really thirsty so I slip round to the bar and get a full mug of cold water which I down in one go. We young officers were told we should circulate among the civilian guests and I find myself talking to several dignitaries, both Nigerian and British. The conversations are interesting but all that's filling my mind is what's going to happen about my "fuck up" this morning. After a few drinks have been dispensed, the waiters come around with trays of hot and cold snacks. Then more drinks. I've been keeping furtive glances at Lt Col Johnson, and see he's in a very good mood as he receives the compliments of several VIPs for the smartness and efficiency of his soldiers. I'm within earshot when a rather well-endowed lady is talking to him. She's wearing a large print floral dress with matching hat. I hear her say gushingly:

"My dear colonel, many congratulations on putting on a wonderful show today. We were all so impressed. And what an inspired idea to have the two flags lowering and raising to mark the point of independence. And those two handsome young officers with the flags. They were both impeccable and so smart. You must be very proud to have them in your battalion!"

I hold my breath, then hear the colonel reply:

"Thank you, Lady Cunningham, for your gracious comments. Yes, they're both fine young men!"

It's good news to hear the colonel's remarks. I'm thinking there will never be a better time to get this sorted. I wait for the large lady to drift off majestically, brace myself, then go directly up to Lt Col Johnson. I'm nervous and fear my stammer will reappear. It does:

"S-sorry to t-t-trouble you c-colonel. I just w-want to ap-pologise for oversl-l-leeping this m-morning. I've n-no excuse. It w-won't happen again, sir".

Lt Col Johnson looks relaxed and I'm hoping I might get off with a reprimand and a light punishment. Calmly, almost pleasantly, he replies:

"Chambers. I'm just going to tell you three things. First: never be late on parade again. Second: buy yourself an alarm clock. And third: take twenty-eight days' continuous extra duty officer, starting today!"

Chapter Thirty-three

I've just cracked half of the twenty-eight days' extra duty officer imposed by the CO and I'm absolutely knackered. I'll never forget that brief, very brief, conversation I had with him at the Independence Day party. Apart from my stupid stammering, I thought it was going to be OK. Lt Col Johnson seemed in a good mood and quite benign towards me. The parade had gone so well for him. Then he started off with "never be late on parade again". Fair enough. Then it was "buy yourself an alarm clock". Good point, I can't always rely either on waking up in good time myself or on Usman Pele to wake me. So far, very fair. I definitely will buy an alarm clock. Then lastly, it was "take twenty-eight days' extra duty officer, starting today." This last point didn't really register until after I had said my "Thank you, sir" bit and gone back to a quiet corner of the room to reflect on what he'd told me.

Then it sunk in. Twenty-eight days' continuous duty officer! The duty entails performing all the out of hours' commitments that take up most of the night — this in addition to everything you have to do during normal working hours. Until then, I'd taken my turn on the duty officer roster — but for only one day/night at a time. I'd always been tired the next day but quickly got over it with an extra sleep the next day. No problem. But twenty-eight continuous days! That's something else! I've counted up the days and reckon that'll take me up to Thursday 27 October. But I'm half way there now and I'm fucking well going to see this through! One positive is that my fellow officers think I'm a great guy because they're all let off the hook for the duty for a month.

Apart from getting virtually no sleep, there's another major issue — Assibi. Of course, there's been no way I can see her while I've got this fucking extra duty still hanging over my head. On the famous Saturday 1 October, I had managed to find Mamadu Baldeh and explained what the CO had said. I impressed on him to tell Assibi that not only would it be impossible for us to meet that day but also for the following three Saturdays until my duties were completed. I got really worried that maybe Assibi might think this was a contrived excuse and perhaps I didn't really want to be with her anymore. Nothing could be further from the truth! Mamadu knows the reality; he's now based here with us in the barracks and can see me manning the duty officer's room every night. I hope he's explained all this to Assibi. Via Mamadu, we've now re-arranged our next meeting for Saturday 29 October. I don't know after that as we're running out of time with the Congo commitment looming up. Fuck it, I'm missing her and yearning to be with her again.

At least all these extra hours awake gives me time to think about where I am in my life.

As far as Assibi is concerned, grudgingly I suppose, it could be a blessing in disguise that we're having this enforced time apart. She's a wonderful person and right now I feel emotionally passionate towards her. But I try to be realistic. We come from totally different backgrounds. I'm still two months short of my twentieth birthday, I have to go to the Congo next month and then I'll be discharged back to UK. Assibi has a good job here in Kaduna as a ward sister in the local hospital. She has a strict Fulani father who is ambitious for her here in Nigeria. So what could be a long-term future for the two of us together? I'm really confused and I know that, in the very short time before the Congo deployment, Assibi and I must talk this through.

There seem to be a lot of changes going on in the battalion, the main one being the CO. At the end of this month, Lt Col Johnson will formally hand over command to Lt Col Abubaker Umara Kagara. I remember meeting Lt Col Kagara once, when we were in the Cameroons. He seems an intelligent and switched-on guy. Apparently, he graduated from the British army staff college at Camberley last year so that's a sign of his calibre. He will lead the battalion during our UN tour in the Congo.

We've also been told that Major Sutter and, I believe, all the other British senior officers in the battalion (majors and captains) will be replaced by Nigerian officers for the Congo tour. It seems there are political reasons for this. I think it's basically that the new Nigerian government has decided that, post-independence, it would not be suitable for its soldiers to be commanded by British officers, particularly in our new role as UN peacekeepers in the Congo. In Major Sutter's case, the new commander of C Company is to be a Major Ngozi Achebe. I've not met him yet. He's an Ibo and I'm getting grumbles about that from some of our Hausa soldiers. I don't want to get involved in any inter-tribal issues: I just hope it won't cause problems in the future.

The good news is that David Edozi is to be promoted captain and will become second in command of our B Company. Another plus is that Bill Holding is leaving his job as Motor Transport Officer and reverting to being a platoon commander. He will be replacing David and joining our company. Bill is due for demob but has been offered a six-month extension. He's become a very keen soldier and has jumped at the chance to stay on so that he can join us in the Congo. I'm not sure how all these changes might affect me as I'm now into my last six month's conscript service. As far as I've been told, the Nigerians are still short of trained young officers so Bill and I will stay until more Nigerian nationals qualify through officer training school.

We've now got a firm date to leave for the Congo: next Thursday 3 November, but we still don't really know what's going on there or the details of what our role as UN peacekeepers will be. Most of what we do know is from newspapers or what we hear on the BBC Overseas Service radio. We know that the Congo gained independence from Belgium this summer. Soon after that, the army mutinied against their Belgian officers, and in response, Belgium sent troops to protect their Belgian nationals there. The whole business then seems to have escalated to the UN Security Council level, which has authorised the sending of UN troops to provide the new Congo government "with necessary assistance until the country's security forces could fully meet their task". Whatever that might mean!

Everything we read and hear about the Congo situation seems very confused. Are we to be Peacekeepers, or Peace Builders or Peace Enforcers? These terms need to be clearly defined and our rules of engagement agreed if we are to do what is required of us to "keep the peace". I hope we'll soon get more clarity about what we will be allowed and not allowed to do.

At last it's Saturday 29 October. I got a message from Assibi, via Mamadu, to come directly to her apartment at about eight p.m. My final extra duty finished yesterday morning, and after struggling through the routine work during the day, I crashed out and must have slept for about eighteen hours. I'd probably have carried on sleeping if Pawpy hadn't woken me up to feed her and take her out. Now I feel refreshed and I'm buoyed up at the prospect of being with Assibi again. Bill has kindly lent me the Wolseley to get into Kaduna town.

She opens the door at my first tap. I enter, close the door behind me and immediately sweep her up into my arms. I'm crying with emotion, I don't care. I just let it out. Then I see that Assibi is crying too. We cling to each other and stay like that for some long time. Finally, I gently put my hands on her shoulders and hold her back so that I can look directly at her. Tears are still rolling down our faces. I take my handkerchief and gently mop the tears from her eyes and cheeks. Then I kiss her lightly on her forehead. We continue still standing like this until eventually I pull her back towards me again and hold her tightly to me. I can't control my male instincts any longer and Assibi is my willing partner as we quickly undress. Making love to her is as deep and meaningful as the first time. After our first passion is spent, we lie entwined together quietly. We both know there is so much we must discuss but first we both want to enjoy these moments in silence. The words will keep till later.

It's a long time till we make a move. Assibi softly tells me she's made us a light supper. We slowly get dressed and I sit on one of the two chairs next to her little dining table. There are plates and cutlery on the table and Assibi brings dishes of salad and fresh fruit. She also brings glasses, water and a couple of bottles of beer. She sits down opposite me. I suggest a beer. She declines but tells me to help myself. I pour the beer in my glass and some water for her. We raise our glasses in a sort of silent toast. We both take salad and start to eat. We know we have to talk but don't know how to begin. I organise my thoughts and am about to speak but Assibi beats me to it. She says:

"Peter, my darling man, our time together has been so precious. I never thought it would be possible to have the feelings that I've had for you. I have to tell you something right away."

I'm not sure what she's leading up to and am about to react but she hand-gestures for me to wait. She almost rushes her words when she continues:

"No Peter, please don't try to interrupt! I need to say this. The first thing is that Dr Withers, my boss at the hospital, has been helping me with my medical studies. This week he told me I have been offered a place at one of the top medical colleges in Lagos. They're associated with training facilities in Accra, Ghana, and also with universities in London and Paris. Dr Withers has confidence in me and feels sure I could become a good doctor. Peter, I've accepted and will go to Lagos next week."

She pauses, waiting I suppose, for my reaction. But I feel she's not yet finished. I try to put my expression into non-committal mode to let her carry on.

"My darling Peter. Going to Lagos next week is the immediate thing but it's not just that. These last few weeks while you had your enforced duties, well — it gave me the chance to think properly about our relationship, you and me. I think we were both swept away by the intense emotional attraction we felt for each other without having any long-term thoughts. It's been wonderful, crazy really, that our two totally different backgrounds, cultures, even skin colour should have attracted each of us to the other the way that it did. But now I've had time to think this through. I know, and I suspect you know too, that all we could ever do was to have a short, an amazing, but short affair. Now I must go on with my career and you must do the same. You have to leave next week to the Congo then you will return to your country, the UK."

I hear her out. It's heart-breaking to have Assibi spell out our future — or lack of it. But I know she's right. I had already reached a similar conclusion but didn't know how to put it into words. Assibi has just done it for both of us. I take a long pause, look across at Assibi, reach for her hand and look directly into her eyes. I tell her:

"You are the most amazing woman I have ever met. I can't argue with you because you're right. I salute you. I know you'll be a wonderful doctor and will repay your training by working with all the people in need here in Nigeria. Assibi, I adore you and always will!"

I finish off my beer and we both quietly enjoy the salad and the fruit. After we've finished, we stand up and I go to the door. I know it's time to leave. No long drawn out goodbyes, no final sexual passion — not now. Just time to go. I hold her to me one last time and kiss her softly.

Then I open the door and leave. That's it.

Our barracks here in Kaduna is no longer a great place to be. Except for Bill Holding and me, the rest of the British officers and their families are now concentrating on clearing up all their personal effects. Already, packing crates have been loaded up for shipment back to the UK. All the rest of our battalion infrastructure is also beginning the process of packing up to leave as the battalion transfers from Kaduna to Abeokuta. For the rest of us, the bulk of the battalion leaves for the Congo next week and all our operational kit is being prepared for our deployment there.

I'm feeling pretty mixed up. In some ways, I'm excited to be about to embark on a new adventure. The details of our role in the Congo are still pretty vague. Now we've been told that our deployment area will be in the eastern province of Kivu. Our battalion headquarters will be based near Bukavu. It seems that we have been given an enormous geographical area to cover. How we will be deployed there will be for our new CO to determine with the UN civilian executives. This will be a new experience for me and I want to make the most of it. As a foretaste, we've just received an airfreighted delivery of pale blue berets. While we're there, we'll leave our bush hats behind and we'll all be wearing the UN "casques bleus".

The downside is that I miss Assibi dreadfully. I know we did the right thing to end on a high before our lives went off in different directions: but it still hurts. I mourn for that wonderful woman.

I have another major problem that I must solve before we leave next week. What will happen to my dear little Pawpy? I can't take her with me to the Congo. Maybe one of the Brits here would have looked after her but they're all leaving — so, too, are all the families of our soldiers as the battalion rear party deploys to Abeokuta. I've asked around and tried my best to find her a new home, but no one has been prepared to have her. I'm stuck. We're here in Africa where hungry local people eat dogs as they do chickens, rabbits etc. I see that in market stalls all around here. I can't bear to think of that being the fate of my darling Pawpy.

I can't sleep well for several nights worrying about Pawpy. Time has now run out before we leave in a few days' time. I have to make a decision. If I really care for that little dog, I think I know what I have to do.

Next free morning, the final Saturday before we leave, I go to our company lines and draw out my Sten gun and charged magazine. I also take a shovel from the QM stores. As normal, Pawpy accompanies me and wags her tail when I tell her we're going out to the bush for a walk. We leave via the back-perimeter gate and walk a mile or so out into the bush. I find a quiet deserted spot. No one is around. I start to dig with the spade. I'm so het up that I work furiously until I've made a large enough trench with the earth arranged on the ground beside it. When I'm ready, I call Pawpy who has been rooting around nearby. She comes at my call and I tell her to sit next to the trench. She does as I tell her and looks up at me with her doting eyes. I charge my Sten gun and brace myself. I manage to control myself just enough to aim and fire. It only takes a single shot. Pawpy jolts and falls at my feet. I force myself to check that she's dead. There's no pulse, no beating heart, her body is now lifeless. I lift her up, place her gently into the trench and cover the earth over her with the spade. I've never taken religion seriously but now I say a prayer for Pawpy — my darling, sweet and loving dog. Slowly, I stumble my way back to the barracks. I try to control my tears before I get back to me *gida*.

Chapter Thirty-four

We were supposed to be leaving Kaduna last Thursday, 3 November and we were all lined up at the airport ready to be airlifted out but then that was delayed — twice. Something to do with availability of aircraft or changed priorities. We weren't told which. Eventually, on Saturday 5 November, we were loaded onto C-130 aircraft flown by the US Air force and, after a cramped, long fight we landed at N'dilli Airport, which, we're told, is about fifteen miles from Leopoldville city centre. Since then, we've been stuck at this airport for four days waiting for the onward move. Such is a soldier's lot!

This is a crazy place. We're packed in around the perimeter of the airport like sardines as we wait for our onward transport. I don't how many UN soldiers are here but it must be into the thousands. Apart from our Nigerian contingent, there's a company of Ethiopians right next to us and we've also identified troops from India, Morocco, Tunisia and Malaysia. The administration here is in the hands of Swedish personnel who are doing their best to create some sort of order out of this chaotic situation. We don't see much of them. We're learning to accept that things here don't operate in the orderly fashion we're used to and we're having to be very flexible. It's the rainy season here and, although we're not getting the torrential downpours with the same intensity as in the Cameroons, the ground has become churned up and we slosh around in the mud underfoot. There's a constant smell of mass humanity which is at its worst around the communal latrines area. The flies have gathered in massed ranks around us.

On our first day here, I was startled when a short plump gentleman in a smart but sweaty suit seemed to single me out and came up directly to me. In good English, he said:

"Look, I'm Belgian. At last, I've got a firm booking to get out of this bloody country. I'll be on that plane, you see with the SABENA sign on it? It leaves for Brussels shortly. I managed to get my family away in July but I had to stay here to clear things in BCB, that's the Banque de

Congo Belge."

He didn't give me time to respond. He thrust a bunch of keys into my hand. He was speaking in a rushed voice and continued:

"Take these keys, I've written the details on the key ring — addresses, everything. See what you can do to look after my house in Leopoldville for me. I can't wait to get out of this madhouse!"

He was about to scuttle off but I called him back and asked him.

"But why me?"

"Isn't it obvious — you're the only white guy in sight!"

I remember looking around and realising to my surprise that this flustered Belgium gentleman was right. I was indeed the only white guy around. After being totally integrated with my Nigerian colleagues, I had forgotten. Skin colour seems so irrelevant. The Belgium had already turned to hurry away towards his plane. I called out to him:

"Sir, I don't think I can help you. Our battalion is due to be deployed to another part of the country shortly. I don't think I can get into Leopoldville city to check for you."

But my words were too late. He was already out of earshot. I looked down at the keys he had thrust into my hand. There were five on the ring plus a card which read:

"Sjouke de Paepe, 16 Ave Wagenia, Leopoldville. In BE, 15^a. De Witte Straat, Brussels."

I had no idea how I might be able to help this gentleman so I stuffed the keys in my ammo pouch and forgot about them. We had more important priorities to attend to.

We have an issue concerning our weapons. The standard rifle for the battalion has been the bolt action Lee Enfield Mark 4, using .303-inch SA ball ammunition with a ten-round magazine. Last week, just before we left for this UN mission, a transport aircraft landed in Kaduna carrying a consignment of FAL rifles with their 7.62 mm ammunition. We were told to issue this weapon for our use in the Congo. The main advantage of the FAL over the Lee Enfield is that its magazine holds twenty rounds and has a much faster rate of fire. I had been trained on the FAL in my UK basic training back in Devizes but it's new to our Nigerian soldiers. We'll need to find time to train our guys. Another problem is that we still have our Bren guns, which fire .303-inch ammo.

Therefore, we'll need to carry supplies of both calibres of rounds. One day we should get the new GPMG machine gun, which also uses the same 7.62 mm round: but, for now, we'll have to make do with this mix. I had decided to leave my trusted Sten gun behind as this uses 9 mm ammunition. Better not to have the problem of three different ammo types.

Bill Holding has been sent into Leopoldville to liaise with the Swedes about flight allocation for our onward move. Lt Col Kagara himself is in contact with the UN authorities and has at last been able to clarify the legal status of our roles and responsibilities. Our instructions are that, as UN soldiers, we may never take the initiative in the use of armed force, but we are entitled to respond with force to any armed attack against us. Lt Col Kagara informs us that the UN has just issued a revised set of rules of engagement. These state that we may use our weapons if attempts are made to:

1. Force us to withdraw from a position already held.
2. Disarm our troops.
3. Prevent our troops from carrying out orders given to them by their commanding officers.
4. Violate UN installations or to arrest or abduct UN personnel.

We're also learning more about the situation here as, last evening, Lt Col Kagara gave a briefing to all our battalion officers based on his own meeting at UN HQ in Leopoldville. The main events are that when the Congo became independent on 30 June 1960, there was a vacuum left due to the lack of trained Congolese personnel. On 5 July, soldiers from the Congolese army mutinied against their Belgian officers and several Belgian nationals were killed. Belgium then sent in troops to protect its people but without the agreement of the now independent Congolese government. Violence ensued and the matter was referred to the UN security council who approved the deployment of an intervention force to restore peace to the country. Politically, there has been a dispute between the Congolese president, Joseph Kasavubu, and the prime minister, Patrice Lumumba. In September, Kasavubu dismissed Lumumba. This caused wide friction among the Congolese people. Other key events occurring just before our arrival here were a coup d'état carried out by Colonel Joseph Mobutu and the establishment of a breakaway state in Katanga by Moïse Tshombe. This state is considered by both the Congolese government and the UN to be illegal. To summarise, the Congo is in a fucking mess!

Lt Col Kagara tells us that our precise role is yet to be finalised but we are to act always in support of the legal Congolese authorities, their military and police and to assist in the maintenance of law and order in our assigned areas. We are always to act within the rules of engagement laid down by the UN. Our CO has had a meeting with General Carl van Horn, the Swedish UN military commander, who has told him that Lumumba's dismissal as prime minister has caused a major split within the Congolese ruling party. Lumumba's main support comes from the Stanleyville area and there have been recent clashes there between rival groups and attacks on government facilities in that area. Consequently, our Nigerian contingent may have to redeploy to that region to reinforce the Ethiopians there if things get really serious. Meanwhile, we are to continue to plan for moving to an area south of Bukavu. Lt Col Kagara tells us he has just been able to fly over to Bukavu for a recce and has provisionally allocated areas of responsibility. He intends to set up our Battalion HQ in Bukavu. Our C Company will be based in Maniema Province, just north of the break-away Katanga Province. If ordered by UN HQ, we may be required to move into Katanga to assist in the restoration of Congolese authority. My first reaction is that, as we are going to be based many miles apart, we will have to be very self-reliant and very flexible in our role. We've brought our Larkspur radios but I'm not confident they will be reliable in this climate and over such long distances.

I listen to Lt Col Kagara's briefing with great interest. It's exciting to be a part of this major international undertaking. We've been hanging around for a long time now. We're all cramped up on the edge of the airport. The sanitation is getting unhygienic and we'll all getting edgy. I hope we can get moving again soon.

Another day at the airport but, unless plans are changed again, this should be our last. We've just been told that some Canadian-manned C-130 Hercules planes have been made available to fly us into Bukavu Airport, in south Kivu this afternoon. We'll bivouac there till we meet up with trucks that have been acquired for the onward move to our operational locations. Detailed movement plans will be made when we are in Bukavu.

We get our gear ready for the move. I sort out my own personal kit and that's when I discover the set of keys the Belgian gentleman had thrust into my hand the first day we flew in here. I had stuffed them in my ammo pouch and forgotten about them till now. I check the details: "Sjouke de Paepe, 16 Ave Wagenia, Leopoldville. In BE, 15ª. De Witte Straat, Brussels." Bill Holding is nearby, getting his own kit sorted. He's often been down to Leopoldville city centre during his transport liaison duties. I call out to him:

"Heah, Bill, any idea where Ave Wagenia is?"

"Sure I do — it's quite a swanky road in downtown Leo. Been there a couple of times looking for travel offices but most of those have closed down now."

I tell Bill the story of the fleeing Belgian gent. Bill replies:

"We could take the duty jeep and go and visit if you like. Better take a few guys with us as protection as there's a lot of civil disruption going on there — at least there was when I was there yesterday. Something about our Ghanaian colleagues being accused of backing the Lumumba side. We'll need to steer clear of that!"

It takes only a few minutes to get the vehicle and Bill is happy to be the driver. The guys I ask to come with us seem delighted to be doing something other than hanging around the airport. The road from the airport is a good quality two-lane highway. Bill tells us it's only about fifteen miles to the downtown area of Leopoldville. When we get there, we find the city centre strangely quiet with many of the businesses and shops shut. Bill gives us a commentary, saying:

"We're now in the main government district of Kalina and we've just turned onto Boulevard Albert 1st. You see that enormous building up ahead — that's the BCB headquarters, standing for Banque de Congo Belge — Peter, I think you said the Belgian guy worked there. Over there is what's called the Interfina building. Right, we'll take a turn here into Place Braconnier and you can see the Belgium embassy building up ahead. Now, we turn into Ave Beernaert, then Ave Basoko — ah yes, and now we come to Ave Wagenia. What number did you say it was,

Peter?"

I check on the key stub and reply:

"Number sixteen. Even numbers seem to be on the right. There's ten, twelve, fourteen, now sixteen. There! That must be it."

We're looking at a very substantial property — a detached house with a large garden, which had been well tended but is now beginning to grow wild. Bill parks up on the road outside. We leave a couple of our guys in the vehicle for safety and the rest of us go the front door. It looks deserted but we knock and wait just to be sure. As expected, there's no answer. I take out the five keys. One is a double throw security key which seems most likely to be for the front door. I put it in the lock and turn it. It works — after the second turn the door opens onto a smart small vestibule area. Ahead is another locked door, which opens with one of the other keys on the ring. We are now in the main part of the house.

We find ourselves in a large living room, fully furnished with comfortable three-piece suites and easy chairs resting on oriental rugs on the fully tiled flooring. It's dark as the deep curtains are all drawn. Bill finds a corner fuse-box, throws the master switch and the lights come on. So everything is still connected to a working system of mains electricity. We walk on through the house and find a large dining room with chairs and place-settings around the table for ten diners. Upstairs, there are four double bedrooms, three of which have en-suite bathrooms attached. The beds are still made up.

Back downstairs, we walk through the well-equipped kitchen and notice it contains ample cooking facilities. In one corner is a modern refrigerator. I've seen one like that advertised in the UK newspapers. Beyond the kitchen is another room - utility room I think it's called — where there's a washing machine, large sink and some garden tools. Then another locked door. Key number three fits this lock and gives us entry to a large garage. It's big enough to hold at least three cars but there are now only two cars parked there. I'm hopeless at identifying cars so I defer to Bill's expertise. He's looking at them in awe then says:

"This is top-of-the range stuff. Look, Peter, this big one is a Mercedes-Benz W111: the 220SE version. Guess it was only manufactured this year and or in 1959 at the latest. The other is a bit older. It's the Merc 220S cabriolet. Made perhaps in '57. Could be the wife's car. Between them, they're worth a bomb. You certainly met up with a rich guy, Peter!"

There are two keys we haven't yet tried but I notice they both have the Mercedes three-point symbol on them. We try the keys in the car locks. As expected, we can open the doors of both cars. We're not quite finished. Bill roots around the garage and finds a switch that automatically raises and lowers the sliding overhead garage door.

The Belgian owner obviously is/or perhaps now was, a very wealthy man. He told me he was working for the Belgium bank but clearly, due to quality of his house and cars, he must have held a very senior job. It seems amazing that, in the few months after Congo's independence, his situation could have become so desperate that he was compelled to leave his beautiful home and cars behind at the mercy of whoever came along. And that he should decide to hand his keys over to a young guy merely because he had a white skin — I find that impossible to comprehend! But here we are. This is the reality of how quickly opulence can turn to destitution in this volatile country. Right now, we could help ourselves to all this — we could pick out the most valuable items in the house, load them into the cars and drive off! Of course, that's not a serious thought — or is it?

I realise it's now time for us to be getting back to the airport and prepare for our airlift this afternoon. We retrace our steps back through the house, locking all the doors behind us. Outside, I look back at the property. So far, nothing appears to have been disturbed. No trace of a break-in, no windows smashed. But this is today. From all we've been told, the situation here remains very unstable. I hope M Sjouke de Paepe, the Belgian guy, will one day be able to return and reclaim his possessions — who knows? I wish we could do something to reinforce the outside of the house, but we have no access to boarding or tools. In any case, we have to leave now and, hopefully, will fly this afternoon to another part of this vast country. I had managed to get an envelope while at the airport. I put the keys into the envelope, write a short note, saying:

"Dear M de Paepe, I have just visited your beautiful house. As at today, 10 November 1960, everything is fine and as you left it. I hope it stays that way, that you get these keys back and can one day return to use them again. Good luck!"

I sign it: Second Lieutenant Peter Chambers, 2nd Battalion, Queen's Own Nigeria Regiment, c/o UN Congo. I write his Belgium address on the outside, ready to give it to one of the Swedish UN administrators before we fly this afternoon. I wonder if I'll ever get a reply.

Chapter Thirty-five

It was good to get away from Leopoldville airport at last. Our flight to Bakavu Airport went fine and we were all delighted to find the air much fresher here than in Leopoldville. We've been told that the town itself is nearly 1500 metres above sea level but there are many surrounding hills much higher than that.

We spend the first weeks here billeted with a detachment of the Congolese Army, which has a base here. Our new CO, Lt Col Kagara, wants to keep the whole battalion together as much as is practical until we disperse to our respective operational areas. We've had all these recent changes from British to Nigerian officers and I think the CO wants to get everything gelling as a unit. He seems a very sound guy. I respect him and am proud to be serving under his command.

General von Horn, the UN Swedish military commander, has reconfirmed to our CO that the battalion is to be deployed to the area south of Bakavu into the province of Maniema. We are to cover as far as the Katangan border but not yet beyond due to the fluid political situation. C Company will be based just to the north of Katanga Province. I have been told my platoon will be centred on the small town of Kasongo and Bill's platoon will be my closest neighbour being in Kibombo.

There're still some essentials to be resolved before we can disperse — the main being transport for all our logistics in this vast country. We understand there's a rail link stretching between Kindu in Maniema and Albertville in Katanga, which should be useable and which passes through Kibombo. Bukavu itself is about 160 miles north of the enormous Lake Tanganyika (that's about 300 kilometres — all the distances here are given in kilometres so we'll have to adjust). From here we could shift our supplies by boat and offload at Fizi then by road up to Kasongo. All these complicated transport options are, happily, not my responsibility. I just hope we will end up in the right place with sufficient supplies to do our job.

One big bonus is that the UN have provided us with a helicopter and crew. This has enabled our CO and his top team to carry out a series of reconnaissance flights to check out the various locations where all our dispersed platoons will be deployed. We've been told the chopper will remain with us for the foreseeable future — a major asset for our logistical movements.

Then there's the local language. The top officials here all speak French but below that level most of the locals speak Swahili, while the Congolese soldiers have been taught to speak a common language between them called Lingala — I suppose that's their version of our Nigerian "barracky" Hausa. It takes some time and hard negotiations but eventually the local Congolese agree to provide us with sufficient English-speaking interpreters for one per platoon to be attached to our battalion for the duration of our tour here. I anticipate that we'll still be using the Hausa language between ourselves so interpreting could be quite a challenge. There's another thing. Our new C Company commander, Major Achebe, who is from the Ibo tribe doesn't speak Hausa. I'm aware that our Hausa soldiers resent this — in fact, I'm hearing very negative remarks from them about Major Achebe.

The Congolese Army have a decent firing range and we've been allowed to use this to familiarise our soldiers in the use of our newly issued FAL 7.62 mm rifles. In the UK, we call these guns SLRs, standing for self-loading rifles. Because Bill and I were trained on these weapons in UK, our CO details us to organise the range training. It takes the best part of two weeks to get all the battalion's soldiers through the training and live firing before we can report to the CO that our soldiers are now proficient in their use.

Our billeting, co-located with Congolese soldiers, is cramped but at least better than sitting on the edge of Leopoldville airport. The military personnel have been quite helpful and friendly to our soldiers but we get the feeling they are on edge after the traumatic events in the Congo during the past few months. Their organisation is somewhat chaotic as all their officers were Belgian nationals until the soldiers mutinied against them in July. These officers have all left. Now, it's difficult to get a firm decision about anything.

The Congolese interpreter allotted to our platoon is called Mweze

Ngongo. I don't know how this was arranged, but about a week before we leave Bukavu, Mweze just turns up, asks for me by name and announces he has been told to stick with our platoon for the rest of our tour. His English is quite good — he was a teacher in a local school but, so he tells me, he also speaks French, Lingala (the lingua franca of the Congolese army), Swahili and other local dialects. I have to take him at his word about that! He's a short skinny guy with thick pebble glasses but he seems fit enough. I guess he's going to be a valuable asset.

Eventually, Lt Col Kagara is satisfied that we are now ready to deploy and get on with our peace-keeping role. He holds a meeting with all of his officers, finalises all the locations we will deploy to and what transport, communications and specialist back-up has been allocated. He ends the meeting by updating us on the local situation. He tells us:

"Gentleman, there have been several developments in the past weeks. I regret to tell you that earlier this month, 8 November to be exact, a squad of Irish UN soldiers were attacked by Baluba tribesmen while engaged peacefully in repairing a road in Niemba, Katanga Province. Nine of the eleven soldiers are known to have been brutally killed. It's too soon to know exact details but be aware that although our role remains essentially peaceful, you should be under no illusion about the dangers our soldiers will be facing once we have deployed to our scattered areas of responsibility. This will involve ingenuity and initiative to be shown by all our officers during our tour of duty here."

"Regarding wider political issues, first: Katanga. I told you earlier that Katanga province has declared itself independent, an act bitterly opposed by the Congolese government. We may later be tasked to intervene there. Second, Patrice Lumumba, the dismissed prime minister, has been enlisting the support of the Soviet Union, thus risking a direct US—Soviet conflict threat. So, you see, the international stakes are now very high. At present, Lumumba is in Leopoldville under UN protection but it's known he plans to go to Stanleyville where many of his supporters are based. If he does, he risks arrest by the Congolese Army. There's even talk that he might be assassinated.

"To conclude, we are involved in a highly charged and volatile situation. Our reputation as a newly independent nation is at stake and I look to you all to do your duty under stressful circumstances. Tomorrow, we commence our deployments. I hope to visit all of your units when possible and wish you all a successful tour here in the Congo."

Map: No 2 Platoon, C Company operational area
just north of Katanga province

We're here at last — Kasongo, home for our platoon for the next few months — unless the UN decide to move us on again. I had sent Sgt Bado on ahead with a small "advance party" to establish a billet for all our platoon's personnel and equipment. When we meet up with him in Kasongo town, I'm chuffed to find he's secured a good collection of buildings large enough for us all and which we can defend against any potential attack. Bill Holding and his platoon are our nearest UN neighbours, about forty kilometres (km) away. He's based in a village called Lulika-Kongolo, which most locals just call Kongolo. I miss

David Edozi as my fellow C Company platoon commander but I'm pleased he's now been promoted. Meanwhile, I've been able to spend many hours with Bill, we've got to know each really well and have become close friends. Bill is a big guy in both personality and physique. He is an excellent mechanic and could well have joined the engineers for his national service but applied instead to be in the infantry. He loves soldiering and it wouldn't surprise me if he applies for a regular commission at the end of this tour. He has an easy, friendly disposition and already I can tell his soldiers have taken to him. Bill and I need to stick by each other as we are the last remaining Brits in the battalion. Bill's tour of duty ends in mid-May while my two years' national service will be up on 30 April. I've not yet had a word about my demob. Meanwhile, there's a lot to keep us busy here. Our supplies of equipment, ammunition, fuel and extra tents and waterproofing have mysteriously arrived and we're delighted when two three-tonne trucks trundle in after a mammoth journey from I'm not sure where. On board are two spare drivers and a medical orderly. They tell us they're here to stay throughout our tour.

Our first job here is to learn all we can about our new area, the local people and to establish our priority tasks in the support role given to us by the UN charter. We learn that there's no permanent military base here but in Kasongo there's a local Gendarmarie station. I send Mweze, our interpreter, on ahead to visit the police here and to explain who we are. I think I'm expecting a hostile response but that is not the case. I'm straightaway invited to a meeting. Through Mweze's interpreting, Sgt Mbuyl Ngangura, the local police chief, gives a short speech of welcome and introduces me to his team of twelve policemen. He seems to have been well briefed about our presence and is very positive that we are here. I stress to him that our role is purely to support the national Congolese government and assist, where necessary, in maintaining stability. He explains how events of the past few months have affected the lives of local people here. He has contacts with the nearest Congolese military base in Kabambare but explains that, since the mutiny last July, discipline within the army's ranks there seems to have broken down. He says that there are rival factions of pro and anti-Lumumba supporters. There have also been some desertions with ex-soldiers involved in looting and even the rape of local girls. In summary, Sgt Ngangua seems delighted that we are here to support him. He readily agrees to attach one of his policemen to be based permanently with us and to help us to orientate to the local geography, to meet village leaders and to understand the main issues affecting the area. "Our" policeman is a delightful character, always smiling and keen to fit in with the routine of our Nigerian soldiers. I can't begin to pronounced his real name but, as a throw-back to our tour in the Cameroons, I call him John. He seems happy with that name.

It's not long before we get our first active task. Sgt Ngangura calls urgently to tell us that the chief of Tongoni, a village some ten kilometres from Kasongo, has reported that a mob of guys has appeared at their local market. There's been looting and intimidation. The chief there is demanding instant police action. Sgt Ngangura requests our assistance and I offer soldiers from our platoon — Cpl Jamil's section — and to transport Ngangura and his eight policemen in one of our three-tonners. I take Mweze with us to explain what the hell is going on.

The road to Tongoni is rough and in a bad state, not made easier by the recent rains. The ten kilometres takes about an hour to cover and I'm wondering if we might arrive too late to offer help. Not so. Sgt Ngangura directs us to the centre of the village. It's in a mess. We find fruit and vegetables lying in heaps on the ground and two of the wooden stalls have been set on fire. A gaggle of young men armed with an assortment of weapons — spears, bows and arrows but also some guns — are threatening the villagers. We also see that some young girls are being held hostage. Sgt Ngangura and his policemen jump down from the truck but I tell our soldiers to stay put for now to see what develops. We watch as an older villager rushes up to Sgt Ngangura and gesticulates towards the mess of the market stalls and towards the threatening young men. Sgt Ngangura marshals his eight police and we watch as they move in line up towards the young men. The police are only lightly armed with batons. There's a stand-off between them. Clearly, the police are telling the young men to back off and release the girls. They're not budging. The youths start sneering at the police. One points his bow at a policeman and, to our horror, we watch as he fires and the policemen falls.

It's now time to for us to act. We jump down from the truck, form an extended line, hold our SLR rifles in the forward-fire position and advance towards the group. I fire one shot, deliberately aiming just over their heads. We continue to advance at a calm but steady pace, our rifles continuing to point directly at them. We watch as they begin to shuffle and we see their arrogant manner begin to deflate. One turns away, which seems to be the signal for the rest. They let go of the girls they were holding, turn on their heels and run. I indicate to Sgt Ngangura to ask whether we should give chase to try to capture them but he signs that we have done enough. Our medic treats the wounded policeman and we're pleased to tell Sgt Ngangara that his man will recover OK. Our first UN support mission has been successful.

We begin to settle into a routine. We continue to patrol actively around our area of responsibility. I vary the composition of our patrols so that all our soldiers get to know the local villages and their inhabitants. Mostly we get a positive reaction when we turn up in the villages and are given offers of fresh fruit and other delicacies. Bill and I liaise closely together to ensure that we coordinate our patrolling programmes. On occasions, Bill comes over to Kasongo and joins one of our patrols and I go over to Kibombo and get to know his area. Once, Bill takes me to a mission hospital based near a village called Loengo. It's run by a Belgian Catholic order comprising nuns who are all either Belgian or Irish. They run a very orderly establishment, caring for a range of sick people from the local area. Bill introduces me to the mother superior, Sister Delphine. She's an impressive lady who, like all her fellow nuns, has dedicated her life to caring for the sick. Sister Delphine seems to have an excellent grasp of how to treat local illnesses. She says that a Belgian doctor used to visit once a week to see seriously ill patients but, after independence, these visits seem to have stopped. They now have to cope on their own. Getting fresh medical supplies is her main problem and Bill has offered to do what he can to get the UN to help.

The weeks pass quickly and suddenly I realise it's 10 December, my twentieth birthday. It seems amazing how much has happened in the past year. I recall that exactly one year ago, we were stomping around the Welsh Brecon Beacons in driving wet snow during the Mons Officer

Cadet School training. Since then, Kaduna, the Cameroons and now here in the Congo.

Twice in the past couple of months, Sgt Ngangura has again enlisted our military assistance in tackling further incidents of looting and threatening activities by gangs of young men. Each time we seem to have dispersed them just by turning up and showing a front of military discipline. Our Nigerian soldiers are mostly tall, intimidating guys, especially the Hausas. We're all armed with our new SLR rifles and wearing the blue UN berets or helmets. This stamp of authority seems to install fear in the minds of these young hooligans. We find that these young men seem to comprise a mix of disillusioned ex-Congolese army individuals and members of the Baluba tribe who are only too keen to exploit the confused political situation in the Congo. Each time they've made trouble in our area, we've managed to drive them off but this is a temporary measure. None or very few have been captured and we're aware that they are still roaming around looking for lucrative targets.

Bill and I have been left pretty much on our own out here. Only once so far have we had a visit by helicopter by Major Achebe, our new C Company commander. He informs us that Patrice Lumumba has been captured by the Congolese Army, sent to Katanga and on 17 January was killed there. This has widened the divisions in the Congolese Army and hardened the Congo government's position against the break-away Katanga. Major Achebe tells Bill and me that we may well now be called to advance into Katanga province to reassert the Congolese government authority there. Sounds like an interesting mission!

We take the opportunity to tell Major Achebe that our radios here are poor. We're still relying on our aging Larkspur sets. We have enough electricity to recharge batteries but, even so, it often takes an age to get through to his HQ, and we've not yet succeeded to communicate with our battalion base back in Bukavu. Every day, we've been sending situation reports (SITREPS) to Major Achebe's HQ but often there's a long delay before we even get a terse acknowledgement. The major has promised to try to get us better radios but still we wait. Meantime, Bill's ingenuity has rustled up a couple of local two-way radio sets, which have enough range for us to communicate together.

As the weeks go by, I start to wonder about my demob. I suppose it might be exciting, before I have to leave, to get orders to cross over into Katanga and get involved with the UN task there. Meanwhile, everything seems to be going fine here in Kasongo. We have good relations with the police and with the local tribal chiefs. Mweze, our interpreter, has integrated well into the life of our platoon — our soldiers are even teaching him some Hausa.

One morning, I'm shaken out of my relaxed state here in Kasongo. There's a call on the two-way radio that Bill set up. I expect it's just for a friendly chat. I'm totally wrong. It's Bill on the line but speaking in a voice like I've never heard before. He's shouting down the phone:

"Peter, thank God I've got you! We're at Loengo Hospital — under heavy fire, taking casualties. Urgently need your help. Come now!"

That's all. He's switched off.

Chapter Thirty-six

It takes a few seconds to comprehend fully what Bill has just said. He's a very level-headed guy and would only have sent such a message if he was in serious trouble. We have no option but to get there ourselves as quickly as we can.

Sgt Bado is nearby. I shout to him and to everyone else within earshot:

"Crash out, crash out!" Then in Hausa;

"Wannan gaggawa ne — gaggawa!"

This is a drill we've practised many times and everyone knows what to do. It includes putting on full combat kit with our UN steel helmets, drawing weapons with spare loaded magazines, forming a protective defence around our camp in case of attack, having our two RL trucks always loaded with spare fuel and with extra ammo, both 7.62 mm and .303 inch, fresh water and rations all ready to on-load. From the "crash out" order this should take no more than five minutes. This morning I reckon we make it in four. While this is ongoing, I check our map to locate Loemgo Hospital and work out its grid reference from our local hand-drawn map. This can only be approximate. I shout to our radio operator.

"Get a report to our company HQ: tell them: 'Contact in Number One Platoon area. Location at Loemgo Hospital, near Kibombo. Casualties. Urgent medical support required.' Keep repeating till you get an acknowledgment!"

By now, our much-practised "crash out" drills are complete. The whole platoon is present, including Mweze, the interpreter, and "John", the policeman. They await my orders. I'm feeling pretty screwed up worrying about Bill and his guys and what the situation might be concerning the nuns and patients at the hospital. But I do know I've got to get a grip and give out clear orders to all our soldiers. Bill and his men are in the shit and the staff and patients of the mission hospital could be in great danger. It's our job to do our best to restore the situation there. I say to our soldiers:

"Our colleagues in Number One Platoon are being attacked. We're going to help them. Cpl Modibbo, your section is to remain here to protect our own basecamp. The rest of you are to get on the trucks. I will take the lead truck with Cpl Aiki Riba's section, plus policeman John, our radio operator with the Larkspur and our medical orderly. Sgt Bado — you will take charge of the rear truck and the rest of our platoon. While we're moving, make sure your weapons are fully charged and ready to fire. Every man should have at least two spare magazines. Questions? *Tambayoyi?*"

There are no questions. I can tell all our soldiers have responded to the emergency and are rearing to go.

We're loaded up and underway. Some months ago, I visited the mission hospital with Bill and met the mother superior. I can remember the route. I reckon it's about 20 kilometres from Kasongo but the road has a rough mud laterite surface and there's been heavy overnight rain. I'm sitting in the front passenger seat of the RL truck. I'm frustrated and want to urge our driver to go quicker. But already we're sliding around on the muddy surface and, if the driver overdoes it, we could well end up in a ditch. At this rate, I reckon it will take about one and a half hours to get there. I just pray we won't be too late to relieve Bill and his guys.

As we slither and slide along the road, I'm trying to work out our best plan of action when we get to the hospital. We have no way of knowing what's happening there now. I've told our radio operator to try constantly to contact both our HQ on the Larkspur and directly to Bill on our "one-to-one" link. If he makes contact, he's to alert me by banging on the interconnecting hatch between the truck cab and the main rear section. So far — nothing. Under these circumstances, it's impossible to make a firm plan. We'll just have to stay flexible and respond to what we find when we're there. I'm glad I'm with such great soldiers. We survived in the Cameroons together. I'm confident I can rely on them fully today. I just pray we'll not be too late!

The time seems to drag by but I know I must try to control my impatience. The driver is doing his best to get us there as quickly as we can without us crashing. I can see in the rear-view mirror that our second truck is also keeping up well and staying in contact. I try to remember, from my one visit, the layout of the hospital and its grounds. It's a quite substantial brick construction, probably built in the last century. I recall that on one side there's a high tower, which is a chapel for worship. There's a larger central part used as the hospital wards, one for men, the other for women. Then there's a third part on the far side which, I presume, is the living quarters for the nuns. I try to remember the layout of the ground around the building but I'm hazy about that. I wasn't thinking in military terms when I visited there with Bill.

At last, I recognise where we are. There's an odd-shaped bend in the road, which I reckon is just under a kilometre from the mission hospital. My watch tells me we're approaching midday. I tell the driver to indicate to the vehicle behind that we're slowing, then to pull up by the side of the road just before the bend. I reckon this is far enough away from the hospital for our vehicles not to have been heard from there but not too far for us to get there quickly on foot. Our driver does a good job of parking up on a firm verge on the edge of the road. Our second truck pulls up behind.

I jump down from the cab of the RL truck and signal for everyone to disembark. I beckon to Sgt Bado and Cpls Aiki Riba and Jamil to come forward. I tell them in a mix of English and Hausa:

"OK, we're less than one kilometre from the hospital. I propose to make our way through the jungle edge to come up to the hospital while still under cover."

"Cpl Aiki Riba. You will lead us in with your section. I will be with your group. When you get the hospital in view, stop and we'll see what's facing us there. I intend that we will clear the hospital of any attackers but we may have to shoot our way in. "John" the policeman is to stay with the lead group as I may need him as a witness to what we might find there. I also want our radio operator to stay close to our group. He is to continue to try to make contact with company HQ."

"Sgt Bado and Cpl Jamil — leave the truck drivers here with two of our men to protect the vehicles. Then follow behind and be prepared to reinforce our advance on my orders."

"Any questions? *Tambayoyi*?" There were no questions.

Cpl Aiki Riba, our tracking specialist, leads us silently through the jungle fringe. We follow in a formation we've practised many times.

There's no track or path here but the undergrowth is quite sparse providing good cover but not greatly impeding our progress. Disturbingly, we can hear sporadic firing up ahead. After about twenty minutes, Cpl Aiki Riba gestures for us all to stop. He beckons for me to come forward. He's just within the tree canopy but from his position, we have a clear view of the hospital and the surrounding grounds.

I move up to the side of Cpl Aiki Riba and, together, we're looking at the scene in front of us. There's the hospital right up ahead, maybe 400 metres from our observation point. We can tell all is not well in there. There's movement. We can see a few young guys appearing from time to time as they move past the upstairs windows that we can see from our side of the building. From there, we hear the odd rough laughter of male voices. What the hell is going on in there?

There's another thing. The last time I was here, the hospital grounds were calm and neat and I remember the sweet smell of fresh shrubs and flowers. Now it's quite different. The air is moist from the recent rain and full of the smell of cordite — even of death.

In front of us, on the open ground between our position and the hospital, we try to make sense of the scene that is playing out before us. We see some ten, twelve, maybe more bodies lying on the ground between the hospital building and our position. To our right we see a few soldiers, some in UN helmets. All are in positions that are in some sort of defensive cover. They are stationary and seem to be unable to move around. These must be guys from Bill's platoon.

On the left, the scene is very different. We see a number of young men, some with guns of some sort, other just with bows and arrows. This group is steadily advancing towards the guys on our right. At first, I'm confused about this. I know that Bill's platoon, as mine, is well trained and well-armed. Why are they in this defensive position? Surely, they should be making mincemeat of these young thugs!

There is still sporadic firing. The thugs are continuing to advance cautiously while they fire at our guys who respond with just the odd shot to slow down the advance. Okay, I think I now understand what's happening. I suspect that Bill got a call for help from the hospital and hurried over with a section of his soldiers. He couldn't have known the size of the gang and that so many were well armed. I'm sure Bill would have seen off the initial gang who were trying to get into the hospital but was then probably faced with a second heavily armed group. This group is still intent in destroying Bill's men and joining their colleagues in rampaging into the hospital. What I think we are now facing are Bill's men being pinned down and running out of ammunition, hence their limited return of fire. At present, the gang clearly has the upper hand.

I tell Sgt Bado and Cpl Jamil to hold their present position but to be ready to move on my order. Then I say to Cpl Aiki Riba:

"We're going in. Get your Bren gun section to move over onto the left flank to provide enfilade covering fire while we advance directly towards these guys with your rifle section. We'll form our usual fire and movement routine. Tell your men. We move in one minute."

I don't have any doubts about our soldiers. I know Cpl Aiki Riba will get his men going. We're all quite hyped up. Our mission is to relieve our colleagues from Number One Platoon.

We're off. Cpl Aki Riba handles his men with skill. He gets them to fix bayonets, then four of his men run at the leading gang of youths firing as they move. After a few metres, this group drops to the ground while the second group of Aiki Riba's section charges forward firing as they move. These men then drop to the ground while the first group are on their feet again charging forward and firing. Concurrently, Aiki's Bren section starts firing, in rapid fire mode, into the rear of the gang. Classic infantry fire and movement drills!

It takes only a few minutes before it's all over. Several of the gang have been killed, others try to escape but are cut down by the Bren gun team. The remaining survivors drop their weapons and hold up their hands in the universally recognised gesture of surrender. I tell Cpl Aiki Riba to clear up, ensure the ground is secure, check there are no more gang members around, and guard our new prisoners.

I call to Sgt Bado to advance with the rest of our platoon. My priority now is to check on Bill and his soldiers. It's bad news. We find six bodies of Bill's platoon. Two of these have wounds but are still alive. The other four appear to be dead. As I'm looking at these poor guys, a tall Nigerian appears. I recognise him as Sgt Musa Maigida, Bill Holding's platoon sergeant. He tells me he'll take me to Bill.

We find Bill lying on a slight ridge facing the hospital. I'm shocked to find that he, too, is badly wounded. But he's conscious — just. I lean down over him as I see he's trying to talk. Even in these terrible circumstances, he can't resist a joke as he whispers:

"Hi Peter, what took the cavalry so long?"

I can see he's now lapsing into unconsciousness. There's a lot of blood. I'm not a doctor but I can see that he's been shot through the middle of his body and his condition must be critical. I turn to our radio operator who I can see is sticking to his task of trying to contact our company HQ. I shout over to him, telling him to keep trying, and to tell any contact that we urgently need a helicopter with a medical team.

Sgt Maigida tells me:

"Sir, our Lt Holding is a very brave man. He was shot quite soon after we arrived here in response to a call for help from the mother superior. She didn't give details or tell us about the armed gang — only that she asked us to come. That's why we brought only a light force. We were about to enter the hospital when we were attacked by a gang from inside. They were well armed and seemed to be highly hyped up with some concoction of beetle nuts and other drugs. When we were dealing with that, a second group arrived and attacked us from the rear. We were caught by firing from both front and rear. This is when the lieutenant was shot. But although he was wounded and couldn't walk, he still organised our defence, contacted you, and continued to hold off the gang until you arrived. Our problem was that we were down to our last few rounds of ammunition and couldn't have held them off much longer."

I tell him:

"OK, we'll take it from here. Your men did a great job. Please look after your wounded men as well as you can. We'll give you all the medical supplies we have but we must have proper medical support. We're still trying to contact company HQ or anyone who can help. Any ideas?"

"Well, sir, I know there's a Congolese doctor in our village of Kibombo. We'll get him up here as soon as possible."

"Good, and also get your own radio op to keep trying to reach our HQ. You might have more success than us. Keep me informed."

I call up Cpl Jamil and tell him to get his section ready to move with me into the hospital. I've no clear idea what we'll find. As we get to the entrance hall, we see a young guy. He's wearing military trousers but on top has a brightly coloured T-shirt. He's smoking some concoction. He's armed with what looks like an AK-47 and when he sees us, he raises his gun to fire. He doesn't get that far as I shoot him dead. We go into the building. I tell Cpl Jamil to leave two men on the ground floor where I believe the main hospital wards are, while the rest of us climb up to the next level.

The scene here is appalling. There are several, maybe ten, hyped up youths who have been indulging in a depraved orgy with the nuns. There's a repugnant stench of sweat, drugs and alcohol. There are a few younger nuns but most are middle-aged ladies. Age obviously didn't deter the gang. They had stripped off the nun's clothing and all are now completely naked. They had clearly been carrying out multiple rapes. As we appear, one is still in the act of penetrating one of the nuns. The gang react slowly to our presence — I suppose they are too full of drugs, booze or whatever and satiated by having had multiple sex with these poor desperate ladies. They have stacked their weapons in a pile in the corner of the room. One of the gang sees us, and makes a dash for his gun. I have no hesitation as I shoot him dead. Cpl Jamil's men point their SLR rifles at the rest of guy who now seem to have woken up to the fact they are surrounded. Sullenly, they raise their hands. I go over to the thug who is still on top of one of the nuns. I put my arm round his neck and forcibly jerk him back away from the nun. For all I know I might have broken his neck. I throw him onto the floor and stamp on his now limp penis. Hell to the civilised UN rules of engagement! I then tell Cpl Jamil to have the young thugs taken down the stairs at gunpoint.

The nuns are still naked and some of them are bleeding. One is still lying on the floor. She might be unconscious or just traumatised. I tell a couple of our guys to go down to the ward below and fetch a pile of bedsheets. When they come back with them, we cover all the nuns with the sheets so as at least they have some degree of dignity. I take a sheet myself to Sister Delphine, the mother superior, and drape it around her. She's a proud lady in her sixties, but even she has been abused and probably raped. But nothing can erase her calm dignity. Her strong belief in her Catholic faith has not failed her during this barbaric ordeal.

We eventually find the nuns' robes, which had been bundled into a heap in one corner of the room. We return these clothes to them then Cpl Jamil's section and I leave the ladies space to adjust and hopefully recover. We go back down to the ground floor and check on the patients in the wards. We find a lot of very frightened people wondering what has been going on. They have been in their beds listening to the fighting outside, the shooting, the reek of cordite and the cries from the nuns upstairs. Fortunately, the gang of thugs seem to have ignored them while they were engaged in their orgy upstairs.

Back outside, we re-join the main force. At last, our radio operator has news. He's managed to get through to HQ, given our location and urgently requested a heli with a medical team. He tells me he's just had an acknowledgement. A helicopter is on its way.

I go back to check on Bill. Our medic has placed bandages around his wound but there's still massive bleeding. Bill is unconscious and I worry greatly for him. Our guys have done a good clearing up operation. Bill's platoon casualties are counted as three dead and five wounded (including Bill). All have been brought together so that the wounded can best be treated and the dead fully documented. I have ordered that all the rebels, dead or alive, are to be concentrated in one area.

Then an amazing thing happens. The nuns come out of the hospital building, led by the indefatigable mother superior, Sister Delphine. All are dressed again in their robes and all seem to have regained their composure. Sister Delphine directs her nuns to assist in attending to the wounded. She makes no distinction between our Nigerian UN soldiers and the gang of thugs who had so recently been abusing them. Their job is to attend to the sick and wounded, not to judge who is good or bad. I've never cared much about religion but now I'm not so sure.

While we wait for the helicopter, I try to recapture the full sequence of events today. I talk it through with "John" who agrees with my interpretation. This is important as I know there will be a major UN enquiry and I need "John's" corroboration.

The doctor referred to by Sgt Maigida arrives and joins with our own medic. The nuns have cleared beds in the hospital for the wounded and are about to move them there when, at long last, we hear the chomping sounds of the blades of the approaching helicopter. I just hope they can casevac our seriously wounded back to the main UN hospital in time to save their lives. I care for them all but, of course, Bill is my particular chum. He did an amazing job today. If he had not got his message through to me and had the courage to continue directing the defence of his men, while he himself was severely wounded, they would surely have been overrun. Both groups of the gang would then have been free to run amok completely in the hospital.

Chapter Thirty-seven

It's not just one helicopter coming, but two. The volume of their chomping revolving blades increases until we see them approaching from the north. As soon as we see they have identified our location, we marshal them down onto the flat space beside the Mission Hospital.

First out of the front heli is Lt Col Kagara, our CO. I go to meet him as we scurry outside the zone of the heli's down-blast. Next is Major Achebe, our new C Company commander. That's not all. Behind the two Nigerian officers, is a very smartly dressed officer who Lt Col Kagara introduces as Brigadier Singh from the Indian Army. He is number two to the UN commanding general. Also, there are three civilians, two ladies and one gentleman who are introduced as members of the UN political directorate. The gentleman is a Mr O'Flynn but I don't catch the ladies' names. I'm realising our operation here has clearly hit the headlines at UN HQ.

Our top priority is the casualty evacuation of our wounded. The second heli to land has a bespoke design for that task. The three dead soldiers from Bill's platoon have been identified (all of us wear dog tags) and are loaded first, then Bill and the other four wounded guys are carefully transferred onto stretchers that are designed to fit into retaining frames inside the heli. The UN medics seem very professional and I'm sure our guys will get the best treatment possible. Without any instruction, our soldiers form up and we all salute our comrades as the heli prepares to take off. We're told it will fly direct to the UN controlled hospital in Leopoldville. I presume there will have to be refuelling stops somewhere en route.

Concerning the Congolese gang, Lt Col Kagara tells me that the Maniema Province police base at Kindu has been informed and is sending a train down from there to Kibombo where the gang members (including their dead and wounded) will be collected and taken back to Kindu prison, which has its own hospital wing. Meanwhile, our own soldiers will continue to guard those gang members who survived.

I'm amazed that, after our fruitless hours today in trying to inform our HQ about the Mission Hospital incident, so much seems to have been organised by Lt Col Kagara and his HQ staff. When I ask him about it, he tells me:

"What you could not have known, Peter, is that our HQ received your emergency call early this morning. We heard the same message repeated over and over again. Then we heard the report of the casualties here at the Mission. Each time, we replied but clearly your radios were malfunctioning; they could send, but not receive. I can understand your frustration when you felt your reports had not reached us. In fact, we quickly calibrated your position, informed UN HQ and organised the casevac-heli. Your reports caused quite a stir in Leopoldville, particularly when we heard that the safety of the Mission nuns and their patients were involved. Hence Brigadier Singh and the civilian team insisting to come and see for themselves."

That explains the mystery! So much for our earlier request to Major Achebe that we need better radios. Lt Col Kagara continues:

"Peter, we arrive here to find major casualties on both sides, ours and from the rebel gang. And we knew that there was trouble here since getting your calls early this morning. But, of course, we had no detail. We need you to tell us what exactly went on. Very sadly, Lt Bill Holding is not able to help so you'll have to talk us through the sequence of events from your perspective."

I was expecting this and I reply:

"Of course, sir, but I'd like Sgt Maigida, who is Lt Holding's platoon sergeant, to attend as he can contribute to your full understanding of what occurred here today. He also speaks good English."

Lt Col Kagara agrees and I ask Sgt Maigida to explain how his platoon was first involved. He reports:

"Lt Holding received a call early this morning from Sister Delphine to say that she had been approached at the Mission in a threatening manner by a group of young thugs. She said they seemed to be on some sort of drugs. She asked Lt Holding to come around as she was concerned for her patients. That was all. We had no idea of numbers or even that they were armed. When we arrived, we immediately found ourselves under armed attack. We countered and killed a couple of their guys.

Some had already entered onto the ground floor of the Mission building and we were concerned not to hit any of the patients or nuns. During this engagement, more of the gang arrived and attacked us from the rear. This was when Lt Holding and a couple of our other soldiers were hit. Our problem was that we were very short of ammunition. We couldn't have held out much longer when Lt Chambers and his platoon arrived."

I then take up the story and explain how we had first neutralised the threat from outside the Mission building and then attended to our wounded. Next, we entered the building, neutralised the thugs inside and ensured the safety of the nuns and their patients. I omit to tell about the rape of the nuns to preserve their dignity. I hope this would be enough to satisfy our visitors.

But no. Mr O'Flynn presses me about our role and responsibilities as UN peacekeepers. He says it was their duty to establish if we had correctly observed the rules that state that weapons may be used only if attempts were made, "to force us to withdraw from a position already held: or to disarm our troops: or prevent our troops from carrying out orders given by our commanding officer: or to violate UN installations or to arrest or abduct UN personnel".

Mr O'Flynn asked how I could justify shooting any of these civilian persons within the rules under which it is my orders to operate.

I suddenly realise that, while I was convinced, I was doing the right thing to come to the assistance of my colleagues, I hadn't complied literally with the rules. I look at the three UN civilian officials. Mr O'Flynn, by his name and accent I think is Irish, is fiftyish and somewhat overweight. I can see that he is repelled by the sight of our dead and wounded soldiers. This suggests that he has never been exposed to danger himself. The two ladies are both fortyish. Only one has so far spoken and that was to challenge my statement that the thugs were high on drugs. I think she's American. She asked me for medical evidence of that. The third lady, who is black skinned, hasn't said a word to me so far but I have the distinct feeling that she is disturbed to find the Nigerian soldiers still have white officers. I feel I'm under the spotlight here and am having to fight to justify the actions we took to restore a crisis situation.

The three civilians get into a private huddle and I can tell they are not satisfied with my explanation. Then Mr O'Flynn turns back to address me and says:

"Lt Chambers, we must impress on you that your role here in the Congo is purely as a peacekeeper in support of the local administration. It is not to act on your own initiative. We need to make a full report and submit it to higher authority."

I can tell I'm under pressure and it's time to defend myself. I know I've got to be careful. I can't afford to antagonise them. I choose my words carefully when I say:

"Ladies and gentlemen. I know the rules and I and my soldiers respect them. About today; my radio operator tried continuously, for many hours, to contact our HQ but we got no acknowledgement. During this time, the nuns here at the mission, their patients and our own soldiers were in great danger. They were attacked by groups armed with lethal weapons. I was faced with the situation I have explained to you. My choices were: either, do nothing and hope to get direction from a higher level: meanwhile, watch the gang abuse or perhaps kill the nuns and the patients. Or: act as I did. You must decide what you would have done in my circumstances. Perhaps it would be helpful to you if you speak to Sister Delphine herself."

In fact, Sister Delphine had come out of the Mission and is standing close by. Lt Col Kagara beckons to her and asks her to join us. He introduces the visitors and asks her if she would like to say anything. She is Belgian but speaks good English. She says:

"I can only say that we at the Mission are sincerely grateful to the lieutenant here and his soldiers for their actions today. We were all in serious danger of being attacked, even of being killed."

One of the ladies asks:

"Sister, were you or your fellow nuns actually attacked?"

Without hesitation, Sister Delphine replies:

"Yes, they seriously abused us all. We were only saved by the brave actions of the soldiers here."

I think to myself: "Good for you Sister Delphine!" I'm wondering what will happen next when Lt Col Kagara intervenes. He says:

"Ladies and gentlemen. I think we've heard enough. You can report what you want but I'm proud of the initiative taken by Lt Chambers and his team today. His men did a wonderful job in protecting the Mission staff and their patients. It's just so regrettable that some died or were seriously wounded as a result. I think we can now leave our brave soldiers to get on with their excellent work."

Phew! I'm relieved that our CO spoke up so well on my/our behalf. He seems to have defused the threat I was under. The last words I hear from him as he escorts the party back to the heli is when he turns to Major Achebe and says:

"For fuck's sake, Ngozi, make sure these guys get new radios soonest!"

I salute the CO and Major Achebe as they escort our UN visitors back to the waiting chopper. I see that Sgt Maigida has got reinforcements from his platoon. They will take over the guard duties of our prisoners until the police party arrives from Kindu. I say goodbye to Sister Delpine as there's nothing left for us to do here at the Mission Hospital. As we make our way back to our parked RL trucks, I'm relieved that our platoon sustained no casualties. Not even a scratch. We experienced a myriad of emotions today: concern for our colleagues, the flow of adrenaline as we went into action against the gang, disgust at seeing how the nuns were abused, sorrow about Bill and his fellow casualties, relief that we had succeeded in our mission, frustration that it should backfire due to the rigid rules of engagement. Still that's behind us now. Let's get back to our base. Tomorrow's another day.

Chapter Thirty-eight

Back at our basecamp in Kasongo, we intend to settle down into our routine of supporting the police as required to help to maintain law and order in this normally hidden part of the Congo. "John" has reported to his fellow Kasongon police about the Mission Hospital operation. I suspect he exaggerated somewhat as we're now all being held in awe by the police chief and his men.

We're surprised when the next day we hear the distinctive sound of a helicopter approaching — perhaps the first ever seen in the village. It circles overhead indicating it wants to land. We marshal it down onto the "H" heli-landing area we have prepared as a Standing Operating Procedure. A Nigerian officer jumps down, followed by a small squad of his soldiers. They lift out some equipment. The officer introduces himself:

"Hi Lt Chambers — Peter isn't it? I'm Capt Christopher Mwapa, the new battalion signals officer. Most people just call me Chris. Glad we could find you! I'm here to bring your new radio equipment. We'll set it up for you, train your radio op and test that we can send and receive to our HQs — both Company and Battalion. Should be no problem. Both Lt Col Kagara and Major Achebe have been stressing the urgency to get this stuff to you and Number One Platoon. So here we are!"

This is great. I call over our radio guy and let them get to work. Inwardly, I'm impressed that our CO is a man of his word.

The next morning, thanks to our now clear radio, we get a message from Battalion HQ telling us to prepare for another heli, which will land at our Kasongo base. The CO himself will be visiting. At 10.30 hours, we hear, then see the heli approaching and marshal it down with the same procedure as yesterday. This time three gentlemen get out — Lt Col Kagara and two civilians, one white and one black.

I lead them to our basecamp next to the heli pad and into the small, rather scruffy, inner room that I grandly call my "office". There's barely room for the three of them plus me and they have to lean down their heads to get in. I have to scramble around to find chairs for us all. I ask Usman Pele to bring us some drinks. When we're all installed, Lt Col Kagara says:

"Peter, first to introduce my colleagues here. This is Mr Charles Morrison from the British embassy in Leopoldville and this is Mr Amadou Umar, from the Nigerian embassy, also in Leopoldville. It's necessary to speak to you on a matter of some sensitivity. I'm just here to make the introductions and ensure fair play."

This sounds ominous. Surely not another witch-hunt about the Mission Hospital operation! At that moment, Usman Pele brings in drinks. He's a dab hand at mixing up a cocktail of our exotic local fruits. We don't have room for a table in here so everyone has to reach out and hold their mug of juice in their hand. When we're sort of settled, Charles Morrison says:

"Peter, yesterday, we learnt from your CO about the attack at the Mission Hospital two days ago. Let me say straight away that we were very saddened to hear about the deaths of your soldiers and of those seriously wounded, including the British officer, Lt Bill Holding. We know Bill was a close friend of yours and regret to have to tell you that he died last evening. The medics in Leopoldville did all they could to save him but his wounds were too severe. We're contacting his parents in UK today to break the tragic news."

I'm stunned by this news. Of course, we knew he was in a very serious condition when he was "medivaced" back to the Leopoldville hospital but we were all hoping he might pull through. He was a great guy and so brave at the Mission. He had volunteered for the Congo and was so nearly at the end of his tour. Truly tragic!

There's a silence in my cramped little office. It suddenly feels very hot. I try to collect my thoughts. It's desperately sad news about Bill but I feel these gentlemen have more yet to say. Surely all three wouldn't have come here to tell me that news.

After a long pause, Charles Morrison continues:

"Peter, the operation at the Mission Hospital has raised a very sensitive political issue, which resulted in a series of high-level despatches between Leopoldville, London and Lagos yesterday. This is the position. The independence of African countries is a very significant development in global politics. When Nigeria became independent on 1 October last year, it was decided that all ranks in the Nigerian Army must be Nigerian nationals. This was particularly important for the Nigerian contingent supporting the UN presence here in the Congo. The Congo crisis arose largely due to the Belgium forces returning to the country after its independence without the agreement of the new government here. The issue is exacerbated by the presence of the largely white mercenary force that is helping to keep Tshombe in power, illegally, in Katanga."

"From our British viewpoint, there is also an issue. Both Bill and you Peter, are (or in Bill's case, were) conscript national service soldiers. It is politically very sensitive for it to be publicised that our conscripts are involved in a conflict situation while employed by an independent, albeit allied, country, i.e. Nigeria. Now that one has been killed in action the whole issue is highlighted."

I can see the logic in what Mr Morrison is saying but what is all this leading up to? Looks like I'm being dragged into some political quagmire just for doing my fucking duty. I'm getting angry when I snap at Mr Morrison:

"All I care about is to grieve for Bill. Why have you come all this way to tell me this political stuff? What the hell has it got to do with me?

Lt Col Kagara intervenes and says:

"Okay Peter, it's totally understandable that you're upset about Bill. We all are. This is absolutely no reflection on you. You know we rate you very highly in the battalion and you handled the situation at the Mission extremely well. Mr Morrison has more to say. Please hear him out."

Morrison continues:

"Peter, when Lt Col Kagara informed his government and mine about the Mission Hospital incident, we realised the political sensitivity that I have described. So far, the UK and Nigerian press do not know that British national service officers were involved and that one has died from his wounds. It is very important to our national interests to keep it that way and out of the newspapers. We would like your word that you will not reveal this to anyone, particularly the press."

I take my time to respond as I need to think through what Mr Morrison has just said. I can understand his point of view. I say:

"Okay, but what are you going to tell Bill's parents? They have the right to know exactly what happened to their son."

"We've thought about that and decided to say he was working for UK special forces, not the Nigerian army, when he was shot. Don't worry, we'll tell them about his brave actions."

I'm still contemplating this. When I get back to UK, I definitely want to go to see his parents myself and to tell them what a great guy their son was. It's the least I can do.

Mr Morrison hasn't finished yet. He continues:

"There's also your own situation to consider, Peter. I was talking to our Ministry of Defence about that last evening. You're already into the final month before your demob is due. The MOD say they've no record of you taking the leave that has been due to you. This amounts to three weeks. It's therefore been decided to replace you with a Nigerian lieutenant who's just been commissioned from Mons OCS. The Nigerians are flying him out from Lagos and he should be here in two to three days."

As I'm taking this in, the Nigerian gentleman, Mr Amadou Umar says:

"Lt Chambers, can I call you Peter? Fine! OK, I just want to add that I support everything Charles Morrison has said. We Nigerians sincerely appreciate the contribution Britain has made to the development of our country. More particularly, Peter, thank you for your personal contribution. When you leave, we'll route you through Lagos and look after you in a good hotel before we fly you (club class at our expense) as a mark of our thanks to you. Oh! and concerning Sister Delphine and the other nuns at the Mission. The Catholic church authorities here have said they also much prefer that we do not publicise what happened there as it might prejudice future recruitment of medically trained nuns volunteering to serve at the Mission. That's a further reason not to tell the press."

I'm thinking: OK, so they want me to leave but all this soft soap is rather over the top. It's hard to believe they've come all this way from Leo to Kasongo just to tell me that. Weakly I reply:

"I understand your points gentlemen. I'll keep quiet about the Mission, as you request, but I do reserve the right to visit Bill's parents. I'll follow your Special Forces line. I'll be pleased to welcome my replacement here and show him the ropes."

That seems to satisfy the gentlemen and we all crouch down again as we scramble out of my little office. Usman Pele appears with fresh drinks but they politely decline. As I'm walking them back to the heli, Lt Col Kagara says:

"Oh by the way Peter, I thought you'd like to know that we're sending CSM Kabala down to take over Number One Platoon. I know you two get on very well."

I watch as the three get back into the heli, its blades begin to spin and then it takes off heading back northwards.

True to his word, Lt Col Kagara has arranged for a heli to come to Kasongo three days later. We know all about it because now our new radio set is working fine and we're in regular contact with both our Company and Battalion HQs. Again, we hear the chopper blades threshing away then we see the heli and marshal it in to land on our improvised helipad.

It's good to see CSM Kabala again. He's become a close friend during the past year that we've been together. I've learnt so much from him, not least how to speak the Hausa language. With him is a young officer. He's tall, slim and very smartly turned-out in a shiny brand-new uniform. He introduces himself as Lt Yul Nduka. He will replace me as platoon commander of Number One Platoon, C Company. I don't know how I'm feeling about that. "My" platoon and I have been through so much together and I feel it's going to be difficult to let go.

The next few days go by quickly. There's a lot to do; introducing Yul Nduka to the platoon, showing him the way we operate, and the drills we use. I take him, with "John" and Mweze, our interpreter, to meet the local police. By now, we've got a great working relationship. The chief of police offers to take Yul on patrol with them to familiarise him with the local geography and personalities. CSM Kabala has decided to stay with us during this handover period to understand how we do things here before going over to Kibombo to take charge over there. We both know that it will be an emotional time, following Bill and the other soldiers' deaths. There'll be a lot of rebuilding to do.

Today, I get a message from our HQ that a heli will be coming tomorrow to pick me up. So that will be that as I'll begin my trip back to UK and demob. But if I think I'm going to slip quietly away, I'm mistaken. Via "John", I learn that the police chief of Kasongo has invited me and the rest of the platoon to a farewell evening. Of course, it would be churlish to refuse.

It's been a firm rule for us not to drink alcohol while on operations but this evening has to be an exception. We leave one section to guard our basecamp and the rest of us pile into the police station as invited. I thought we'd be just with the local police but the chief has brought in police reinforcements from several of the local villages plus the mayors and other local dignitaries from the surrounding area. After getting blotto on the eve of Nigeria's independence last year, and paying a heavy price for it, I'm determined to drink in moderation this time. Also, I really want to remember the evening and make the most of the last chance to talk to as many of the great guys that I've got to know so well during my African tour. I'm so pleased that CSM Kabala is here this evening. We chat for a long time together. He is clearly concerned the way Nigeria is beginning to polarise more and more into the main tribal groups — Hausa, Yoruba and Ibo. He's predicting this polarisation could lead to serious internal trouble in the future, even to violence. I hope he's wrong.

I also spend time with Sgt Bado. Although not perhaps the sharpest of men, he's always been there quietly and efficiently getting things done, organising the platoon's administration in his reliable way. Then there's Cpl Aiki Riba, our tracker specialist and leading section commander. He's a soldier whose fearlessness and drive served us so well both in the Cameroons and here in the Congo. Another star is Cpl Jamil. His self-discipline has been exemplary. And so many of the others, not least Pte Usman Pele, who has faithfully looked after me with conscientious calm throughout my whole tour. CSM Kabala makes a short speech, which is very flattering and I'm pressed to reply. I can't remember what I said but I made a point of saying it in Hausa which I think everyone appreciated — even if the policemen and local dignitaries

306

didn't understand a word.

It's about midnight when we say our goodbyes to the police and sway our way back to our basecamp. My mind is full of mixed emotions as I finally drop off to sleep.

Chapter Thirty-nine

It's a long journey home. In Kasongo, I hand over my SLR rifle, webbing and other serviceable equipment to Lt Uri Nduka. Most of the rest of my kit is in a bad state after months of repeated wear. It's fit only for the bin. I manage to salvage my white shirt, khaki slacks and desert boots, which have been stuffed in a kit bag during our time here. I also dig out the passport and military driving licence that I had obtained while I was in Kaduna, and my pay book, which needs serious updating. I stuff these into a small holdall together with my washbag and a spare pair of shreddies. Ready to go.

When the heli arrives to collect me, I don't want to hang around. We've pretty much said our goodbyes last night at the police party. My soldiers all stand on parade ready to see me off as I get on board. I can't resist one final gesture — hell to military protocol. I go up to Pte Usman Pele and give him a hug. We both get misty eyed. He's given me wonderful and faithful support during my entire time in Africa — tall, strong, quiet, utterly reliable — typical of the Hausa tribe!

The heli takes me to Bukavu where I have a brief final meeting with Lt Col Kagara. He's a very fine officer and I hope he gets the promotion he deserves — maybe even becomes head of the Nigerian Army one day.

A UN aircraft takes me to Leopoldville and we arrive there in the early evening. At the airport, there's a sign with my name on it held up by a soldier in a British Army sergeant's uniform. When I check in with him, he salutes and says:

"Lt Chambers, sir? I'm Sgt Jones, Mr Charles Morrison's driver. He's the first secretary at the British embassy here. I understand he visited your location a few days ago. He detailed me to meet you and drive you to his residence. He'd like you to stay with him tonight before your onward trip back to UK."

I find "the residence" is a large detached house near Place Braconnier in the Kalina district of downtown Leopoldville. It's surprising how little this area seems to have been affected by the internal

Congo crisis. When we arrive at the house, Mr Morrison and his wife are at the door to greet me. I hadn't expected this. Mrs Morrison, who insists I call her Suzanne, is a warm motherly lady who takes charge. She sees my bedraggled clothes and, perhaps sniffs my jungle-absorbed body odours, and tells me she has run a bath for me and that she'll lay out some of her husband's clothes to wear while mine are laundered overnight. I find that Mrs Morrison, I mean Suzanne, is a little like my own mother. I don't dare to decline her kindness.

I see the bath but also there's a sink with a mirror over it. I look in the mirror and see a face that I hardly recognise as my own. My hair is a mess. One of our soldiers used to be a barber so we had put him in charge of giving us all a monthly cropping. I can see my hair is now long and straggly: it must be near the end of the monthly cutting cycle. My face is covered with a thick stubble. In Kasongo, our routine was to shave every few days but we were running short of razor blades so we had to ration them. On the edge of the sink, a new razor and some shaving soap have been laid out, perhaps a hint! I lather up my face and attack it with the razor. Nothing I can do about my hair length except wash it in the bath. At least it will be clean.

I haven't been in a proper bath since being at home in Saltford. And never one like this. The water is warm but not hot and is deep almost to the brim. Suzanne has had some sort of pleasant-smelling salts added to the water and I can't help but lie back and luxuriate in the experience amid all the bubbles. It's quite soporific and I have trouble keeping from nodding off. But that would be "bad form" so I force myself to stay awake. When eventually I drag myself out of the bath, I notice the water is filthy so I do my best to rinse it through. Then I envelop myself in the large white soft towel that's hanging next to the bath. There's a little private changing room connected to the bathroom and there I find underwear, shirt, slacks, socks and a pair of shoes (I think they're called "loafers"). The clothes are a bit too big in the middle but tight on the shoulders and my feet could take a larger size of shoes. But what the heck!

I find my way back through the house to the drawing room where Mr Morrison and Suzanne are waiting for me. Suzanne gushes;

"Ah, here he is and looking a new man after his ablutions! Come over here, Peter, and let's get you a drink. Look Charles, I saw that Peter and you are about the same height but as you see he hasn't got your waistline. I keep telling you you've got to exercise more to get that tummy or yours down!"

She continues:

"Peter, we've decided to have a quiet little supper at home here, just us three. You must be famished and tired after all your recent fun and games. Is that alright with you or would you like to go out and hit the town?"

"Hitting the town" would be the last thing on my mind. I meekly reply:

"That would be perfect. Thank you, Mrs Morrison — err — I mean, Suzanne."

Mr and Mrs Morrison are a very caring host and hostess and I'm flattered that they should be giving me their exclusive attention this evening. Mr Morrison is drinking a gin and tonic so, when he asks me, I tell him I'd like the same. I didn't tell him it's the first time I've ever had that drink. We chat for a while in the drawing room. Mr Morrison explains how the British diplomats and their western colleagues are trying to manage the enormous changes in Africa as so many countries gain independence from their former colonial rulers. Mr Macmillan's famous "wind of change" speech has turned out to be a gale as more and more African countries gain their independence from Britain, France, Portugal, Spain and, of course, from Belgium here in the Congo. He tells me that, next week, he will be flying to Sierra Leone to attend their independence ceremonies on 27 April. He asks me:

"Peter, you've been in Nigeria for the past year or so — in fact, I believe you personally were involved with their independence ceremony on 1 October last year. And I was impressed to hear you speaking to your soldiers in what I presume was Hausa. What's your feeling about the future of that country?"

Pheew! That's a pretty sharp question and I'm thinking it's a bit above my rank level, especially coming from a senior diplomat. Also, I'm feeling that the gin and tonic is beginning to have its effect. That seems to loosen my tongue. I tell him:

"Mr Morrison, my view for what it's worth is" Morrison interrupts with:

"Please Peter, let's make it Charles!"

"Sorry — er — well Charles, I can only speak from the point of view of being totally immersed in the military and having little information or, frankly, interest, in the bigger political picture. Yes, I speak Hausa as most of our infantry soldiers in our battalion are ethnic Hausa men. So perhaps my judgement is biased. But I did get a definite feeling that there could well be future problems between the tribal interests in the country. The Hausas are in the majority, the Yorubas seem well settled in the south west of the country but the Ibos feel disadvantaged, particularly as I understand Nigeria's major oil reserves are in their region. They are an intelligent and ambitious people and I feel they may want to get a larger slice of power positions within the wider Nigerian administration. Perhaps, if I may, I would suggest that the colonial powers should pay more attention to tribal divisions, conflicts and interests when planning for independence."

I think I've said enough — perhaps too much! I blame the gin. To my surprise, I find Morrison has been listening intently to my comments. Perhaps I hit a sensitive nerve.

Just then, an orderly, knocks at the door and says that Sgt Jones, his driver, has returned and wants to speak to Mr Morrison. Suzanne and I wait while Morrison goes out to an adjoining room. Suzanne offers me another gin and tonic. I politely decline. Morrison is soon back. He says to me:

"Peter, this concerns you. Sgt Jones tells me our embassy has produced a discharge document. They say the formal papers will be sent to your parents' home. So, you're now officially free of your military obligations. They gave me an envelope for you. They said it's contains part of the back pay you've earned. They've also sent an open ticket for your train from Paddington station to Bath Spa for your return home — so that's taken care of. But I need your answer to another question. The Nigerians have offered you a night in a hotel and a flight back from Lagos. That will be in a couple of days' time. I have an alternative proposition. There's a US Pan Am flight leaving soon after midnight today flying directly to London Heathrow. That'll get you back to London on Saturday morning. Would that suit you better?"

I can tell Morrison is waiting for an answer. I'm thinking that, frankly my Nigerian days are over. I've already said my goodbyes to all my military friends, I know no one in Lagos. It's time to get home by the quickest route. I tell Mr Morrison.

"Thank you, er, Charles, I'd like to take that Pan Am flight."

Suzanne then interjects:

"Don't worry about your clothes, Peter. We have a wonderful new machine called a "drier". We'll have your stuff dry and pressed before you go!"

I come out of a long sleep, aware of the regular drone of aircraft engines. I slowly open my eyes and, standing in front of me, is a smart air hostess. She's smiling and holding a tray with a full glass on it. She says:

"Good morning, Mr Chambers. I hope you had a good sleep. I thought I'd wake you now as we're about one hour from landing at Heathrow airport in London, England. I've brought you a drink of cold water to help you wake up!"

I look at my watch. Wow! I must have been asleep for more than ten hours. I remember spending a very pleasant evening with Mr and Mrs Morrison; we had a light supper and talked about general subjects, Suzanne forbidding her husband to talk any more politics. One point stands out. They compared my last two years as a national service conscript soldier with their own son, apparently about my age, who is at a London university. They said they were fed up with him always asking for money, which, to their irritation, he seems to be spending at a club called the Blue Lagoon in Carnaby Street, an area of London that is now very trendy with the young set. I wouldn't know. They told me they would have much preferred him to have done his military service as I did, but he'd wriggled out of it with his place at the university. The other thing I remember was that they offered me some wine. I've never drunk that before and, added to the gin, I was feeling decidedly uneven by the time Sgt Jones arrived to take me to the airport. I then remember getting on the plane, a Boeing 707 I was told. Then, I crashed out till now.

I find the water wakes me up but then I have to rush off for a long, satisfying pee. I come back to my seat refreshed having also washed my face with cold water. I look out of the plane window. It's now getting light and we're flying over where I suppose must be France heading back towards England; the country I left some fifteen months ago.

It's just sinking in that I'm no longer a soldier. It's strange how in some ways the two years seem to have shot by. It hardly seems any time since I left my parents' house in Saltford and made my way to Devizes at the beginning of an extraordinary experience. And even before that, when I was discussing with my friends about whether or not to apply for a deferment. If I had done, I could now have a trade or even be well under way to getting a degree. But then I think about what I would have missed — what I have done and learnt during these two years. In basic training in Devizes I learnt to handle rough Portsmouth bullies like Darrel Roberts and Rik Parfitt and I learnt the lesson there that, in that world, nothing is for nothing. In officer training, I learnt about self-sufficiency and that leadership is all about showing not just telling. Then in Africa, I learned to grow up, to experience the dangers of being in combat, of having to face down a mutiny and sometimes of having to kill or be killed.

I learnt more than that. I learnt about falling in love and, for the first time, about having true passionate sex with a woman I adored, and then about the pang of having to let her go. I learnt about the love for a dog, her loyalty and the love she returned, and then the misery of having to end her life. I learnt about speaking a language other than English. I can't think that I will be using Hausa much in the future but at least I learnt the basics of learning a different language.

I learnt the true meaning of comradeship. My comrades were mostly Nigerians. When I was first introduced to them, I had thought that our different cultures and skin colour would inhibit ever forming a close bond with them. I learnt that I was so wrong. Together we worked our way through the challenges of the Cameroons and of the Congo. We learnt to trust and rely totally on each other. We never let anyone down. I learnt to respect other cultures and personalities: notably the patience of CSM Kabala, the wisdom of the FON of Bafali and the intelligence of my Nigerian CO, Lt Col Kagara. I learnt, following my dear friend Bill's death, that life can be short and tragic.

If I had decided for a deferment from national service, I could never have begun to have learnt so much in two short years. So far, I haven't been to an academic university. But I reckon I've graduated from the University of Life!

We land at Heathrow on time on Saturday morning. I'm grateful to Mr Morrison for giving me one of his old anoraks as, although it's late April, it seems freezing cold as we disembark from the aircraft. I've now got money in my pocket — I didn't have the need for any while in the Congo — so I splash out and take a taxi to Paddington station. I change my warrant for a ticket to Bath Spa and give a phone call to home. My mother answers, it's been such a long time since I've heard her voice. She sounds as always. I'm very moved when I hear her again. I love my mother. I tell her the time the train is due in Bath.

As soon as I get off the train, I see my parents waiting for me on the platform. We greet each other and I feel filled up to be back with them again. While I was away, my father has bought an old car so we no longer need to take the number thirty-three bus to get back to Saltford.

It's great to be home again, to be with my parents, to be at the house in Saltford where I was born. But it's rather strange. Both my parents and the house all seem smaller. Or have I got bigger? I can't work it out.

It's Saturday evening and I wonder if I should try to see Linda. By mutual agreement, we didn't write to each other while I was in Africa. But I think I'll take my time to contact her again. Since we were last together, I feel I've changed and grown up — no longer the naïve young virgin! I don't know how I'll feel about her after my passionate time with Assibi. Perhaps Linda has also changed and matured. Perhaps she has another lover. Who knows?

Instead, I tell my parents that I'd like to catch up with my old school friends, or any of my old chums who may still be around. The best place to catch them is the Roundup jazz club in Bath. My parents are fine about this and, when I tell him I've now got a driving licence (of sorts!) my father even lets me borrow his car.

I get to the club about nine o'clock. It's in full swing. As soon as I go in, I see a group of my old chums, some from schooldays, others I got to know at the club. I go over to greet them. I'm thinking they will be really eager to hear about my adventures and war stories while I was

314

away in Africa. But not at all! They accept me as if I'd been there all the time. Their conversation is animated, mostly about recent love conquests and who is hooking up with who. The social life of Bath is the centre of their universe. Then, in recognition that maybe my face hasn't been there every week, one of my chums looks hard at me. He says:

"Heh, Peter, we haven't seen much of you here recently. Have you been away?"